Legend of Apocalyps

of

SISTERHOOD OF LIGHT

1

ARTHUR BARILLAS

Legend of Apocalyps

of

SISTERHOOD OF LIGHT

1

ARTHUR BARILLAS

DMP

ISBN Paperback book 978-1-77400-029-8
ISBN Hardcover book 978-1-77400-030-4
ISBN Electronic book 978-1-77400-028-1

To God above all else and his only son Jesus Christ.

To his Blessed Mother the Virgin Mary.

*To my loving wife Cristina that has guided
and supported me in my craziness.*

*To my daughter Grace Nicole,
May this book show you that nothing is impossible
if you believe in God, family and yourself.*

To my good friend Rebeca for being my number one fan.

*To my editors Sandra and Kaitlyn who provided
help and guidance on this vision.*

"The world doesn't need what women have, it needs what women are."
- St. Teresa Benedicta of the Cross

PROLOGUE

Cliffs of Moher, Ireland; August 5, 10:50 p.m.

THE SOFT CHIRPING OF crickets and low hooting of owls in the nearby woods was the only audible sound on the crisp Irish night. A light fog covered the hallowed green grounds, lightly hiding the stars from the sky. The lonely and haunting ambiance would frighten anyone who dared walk in the night. Dark creatures and monsters roamed the property, searching for human blood and flesh to satisfy their demonic feeding impulses.

The lonely howl of a wolf echoed in the darkness as a small human silhouette of a young girl strolled on the Irish road. Isabella O'Brien Somiere hiked the dirt path slowly. Her worn-out white sneakers grasped the loose gravel, making a strange crunching noise while she admired her surroundings, oblivious to the possible perils a girl her age could encounter. Her mind drifted instead to the sound her feet made as the young fifteen-year-old remembered her many breakfasts during the three-month trip—Captain Crunch and warm milk. She smiled, remembering her entire journey, as well as all the friends she had made across both Western and Eastern Europe. The legendary stories of her mother and father echoed in her mind. To the outside world, the tales sounded like folklore and myth, but to her, it was part of her family's history and dynasty.

The teenage girl climbed what was left of the dirt road. Once she was over the last hill, she looked on and saw the Guardians' castle looming in the darkness as a gray hulk of rock and stone, adorned only by the light fog giving a chilling sensation to mere mortals.

Izzy smiled softly as the dark environment engulfed her being. The sounds coming from the nearby woods were haunting yet peaceful to her. She was still about a mile away from the dark gray stone structure, but she felt safer being so close to home.

She grasped the travel backpack on her shoulders with her right hand while she held her violin case with her left. She continued along the beaten path until she reached the giant oak tree at the edge of the property, planted by her father and herself. She put her large backpack down alongside her violin case, at the base where the thick roots spurted out and sank into the earth. The young girl walked around the tree as she pulled her dark brown hair from over her green eyes and tucked it neatly behind her ears. She searched the tree trunk for carvings and smiled when she found them. It was from her birthday last year, August 23. Above that, her short name, Izzy, and her father's name, Sean, were carved into the trunk. She smiled as memories of previous summers flooded her mind. Picnics with her mom and dad, right at the base of this tree. Quiet times in the summer—simpler times. Family time.

Isabella sat down, leaning her back on the trunk as she took a green apple from her backpack, feeling the light fog surround her body. She was home, and she was grateful for the experience. Izzy pulled out a small knife and sliced the fruit in her hand, putting a piece of it in her mouth, admiring the castle. She had kept her promise and arrived three months later, as her parents had kept theirs by giving her the extraordinary experience of independence. This had given her a chance to see the world and spread her wings, give her a little freedom, and time to figure things out about who and what she truly was. Now it was time to come back and work alongside them, and to fulfill her duties and the role she was born to play. It was time to take her rightful place in her family's tradition.

The young teen pulled out her cell phone and looked for new messages. She saw that her best friend Elsa had not read her texts yet. *That's strange*, the young girl thought to herself. She had spent most of her time abroad with her friend all over Europe. They had agreed to text once they got home. *Must have forgotten to charge her phone*, Izzy thought to herself.

The fifteen-year-old felt the hairs on her back prickle, the familiar rush of adrenaline surging from her gut. Still, her heartbeat did not accelerate; it stayed calm as her senses took over, and she swiftly stabbed above her head with her knife. She brought her hand down to see that she had pierced a large black demon bug with twelve legs and four eyes that was about to attack her. It squeaked in pain as she twisted the knife inside its body until she heard a satisfying crunch. Soon it stopped moving. Isabella pulled her blade out and cleaned it on the side of her dirty jeans. The deep sensation in her gut still lingered, though. Her instincts alerted her to the ever-present danger in the night. She looked behind her and saw a pair of deep yellow eyes staring right back at her in the darkness. The familiar dark aura generated by vampires was unmistakable to the young girl's instincts.

A growl came from the vampire as he revealed his evil presence from the shadows. His facial features were distorted and pale; its fangs were sharp, like razor blades. Drool dripped from the side of its mouth as the aroma of fresh blood plagued its nostrils. The sight of the dark fiend would rend an average human powerless with overwhelming fear. Izzy sighed, however, almost bored as she stood up, giving away her cover from the tree. When she did, the young girl noticed the vampire was not alone. He had two male vampire cronies behind him, both of them with similar features as the first. "This is private property," Izzy said calmly. "You boys are trespassing at this hour."

"No screams of fear?" the vampire said to his companions, before turning back to the girl. "You must know our kind."

Izzy almost laughed out loud at the vampire's futile attempt to seem ancient. By his words, he was trying to sound poetic and mysterious. She did not know what was worse—his stupidity or his ignorance. "You are new around these parts, aren't you?" Isabella asked him in a mocking tone as she took in their physical appearance. "Trying to sound all dark and menacing, while attempting to scare a little girl." As the words left her mouth, she faked trembling as if she were a damsel in distress. The vampires exchanged surprised looks in response to Izzy's mocking attitude and lack of fear. "You came out of your grave about two weeks ago?" Izzy continued while making fun of the undead, stating accurate knowledge of the bloodsucker's age. "If it makes you feel better, I can act the part scared little girl that got lost in the woods." Saying this, she feigned defenselessness as she surreptitiously reached for a wooden stake tucked in the back of her jeans. She pulled it out, and in a flash, she attacked while the vampires tried to read the situation.

Isabella was on the first vampire, straddling him. The wooden weapon found its mark, piercing the demon's chest and penetrating the dead heart, all before the vampire could even scream. The creature exploded in a cloud of ash and dust as Izzy jumped from her crouched position and launched a high kick to the second fiend. Distracted and dumbfounded at the demise of his companion, the girl's sneaker connected hard with the vampire's face.

The third vampire let his demon instincts take over and lunged at what seconds ago seemed to be harmless prey. He tried to grab her arm but got a swift punch in the face for his efforts. The girl was moving at lightning speed, kicking and punching. The vampire swung wildly, but it was all a blur. A vicious uppercut to his chin sent him flying upwards. As he was in the air, he heard the combustion of the second vampire. The surviving bloodsucker fell with a thud on the ground. He tried to get up and looked at the girl; she was twirling her stake in her hand.

"This is my land, and my tree," Izzy said with a confident smile on her face. "Everything in it, including your friends' ashes, belongs to me." She moved forward with death in her eyes. "Leave now, and tell your cronies that no vampire trespasses my property."

"What are you?" the vampire asked, trembling with fear.

"Just a girl who gives the undead nightmares," she said while continuing to give an evil smirk. "Your friends will know… Scram!"

The beast did not need to hear the girl's warning twice as he fled, half tripping, half running into the darkness, taking his cowardice with him. Izzy tucked the stake back to its hiding place and sat back down next to her backpack. The peaceful feeling slowly came back to her heart as she gazed at the castle lights. The young girl picked up her knife, as well as her half-eaten apple. "It's good to be back," she mumbled, and she put another piece of apple in her mouth and munched away.

The soft sound of a rumbling car engine became audible in the distance. Izzy perked up and hid her belongings behind the tree. She followed suit just as a pair of headlights arched their way from the hillside. The young girl watched while a black sedan maneuvered on the dirt road and headed toward the castle and car parked right at the front entrance. She saw a male figure step out from the back seat and walk up the steps inside the castle.

"We have company," Izzy whispered to herself. The young girl picked up her belongings and continued her journey home.

CHAPTER I

The Guardians' Castle, Main Study, Ireland; August 5, 10:50 p.m.

ARTHUR WILLIAMS LOOKED AT the window while he sipped on his hot green tea. The night was dark and menacing as he gazed at the light fog, trying to get a glimpse at the stars that were beyond. The large pane of glass gave him a broad view of the grounds in the center of the castle that looked gloomy and desolated except for two dark silhouettes. He ignored the figures as he pondered on what would have happened if the Guardians of old still existed. Most likely, the luxuries they indulged themselves in would now be a fragment of fiction. He would also be just another Guardian in a sea of men and women in charge of guiding innocent girls in the battle of darkness. He sometimes missed the research and the scent of old books and dry ink on his fingers.

The former Guardian turned his attention back to his desk, then sat down and looked at his computer. I.T. specialists configured the machine so that all he had to do was write. *But write what?* He thought to himself as he looked at the whiteboard in front of him. It was stained entirely with various streaks from whiteboard markers. There was one permanent black line in the upper left corner, where he'd foolishly used a permanent marker. He looked at the written notes, which described the timetable of events leading up to this point. It contained the closing of several demon hot spots, the hell-battles of Cleveland and L.A., and the battle for New York, not to mention other high-profile skirmishes that had caught the Guardians' attention.

The whiteboard also included a list of prophecies and premonitions of high importance. The foresight of the demon champion who would get the reward of becoming human after fighting for the forces of good in the Apocalyptic wars was explicitly underlined. The list of essential fragments from the Guardians' history was the coming of Isabella O'Brien Somiere into this world, as well as the establishment of the New Guardians' headquarters.

But the word that caught his attention was the word 'hunter.' Written in bold black and underlined on the whiteboard. *Hunter*, Williams pondered while he sipped on his tea. The word had a true, strong definition to the outside world. A killer of animals for sport. But in his line of work, hunter referred to the fabled Demon Hunters—the chosen few to battle the forces of darkness. His mind continued to drift as he thought about the origins of the first demon hunter; the myth was as old as time itself. To grasp the concept, one needed to understand the world's origins. As a scholar, he had written his thesis that the world was not a paradise at the beginning of time, but a hell-infested plain where demons, monsters, and creatures of the night ruled the land. His intellectual ego suffered a bruising when the truth revealed itself to him. The world was indeed a bliss before creation came into being. It was only when the seeds of corruption, greed, and unhealthy desire let all types of demonic creatures enter the world as we know it. When humanity first came into this world, they were perfectly good in every way. It was the initial perversion that led to the deviation of humanity's destiny—becoming selfish and unkind—becoming evil.

In this forsaken state, men concluded that creatures of the night did indeed exist. Fear crippled those who were supposed to be brave—not because they feared death, but because they feared to lose control and give power to the abstract and immaterial. Their fear of losing power to the undead was the battle of existence itself. Terror paralyzed those destined to defend the weak as they faced vampires, demons, and all the other creatures only thought to be present in the darkness of the human soul. The foolish men harnessed the power of a dark and powerful demon by trying to wield the forces of darkness. Their triumph in binding the power was equal to their monumental failure in controlling it. It was at that time the primitive man decided to bestow the power of the bound demon unto a young girl, to use the power of darkness against darkness itself—a foolish idea from foolish and frightened minds.

But providence would not leave humanity in such a dire and desperate state; it was providence that came before destiny. And because of this, a group of selected girls was born—young girls with the power to fight and destroy the forces of darkness. Out of a foolish human-made mistake came providence's answer to save the human race from the physical evils the creatures of the night had brought upon the world.

Williams sighed, sipping more tea. The idea of putting history into writing gave him a headache, but it was needed for future generations to learn from their successes and failures. No organization is perfect, and the Guardians were no exception.

Even this new assembly had to learn as time progressed. To become better—to learn from past corruptions of power and self-righteousness. He started typing on the computer.

Providence does not abandon humanity. Out of darkness, a few girls are born and chosen to fight the forces of evil. Chosen to show the light, they alone carry the hopes of the ones in need—a sisterhood born and forged to wield the power of good.

Williams stopped typing as he remembered reading these words a thousand times during his Guardian training years ago. The Guardians of old pounded the idea into his head until nothing else seemed possible. He smiled a little, as the memory of his first and only assignment came. He relived the feeling of the binder in his fingers as he heard the name of the demon hunter he would guide. Elizabeth Somiere. *The name Elizabeth would not inspire fear or terror to the undead,* he recalled thinking to himself. He also remembered that his first impression confirmed his original train of thought. Young sixteen-year-old girl, blonde, green eyes. About five foot one. Not intimidating to anyone or anything. Most likely afraid of bugs and rodents.

Elizabeth Somiere proved him wrong—dead wrong. She was headstrong, independent, and a true demon hunter. She fought for what she believed was right. She fought the forces of darkness while she tried to have a normal life. She fought for her friends and family while facing overwhelming odds at every turn. And she prevailed. After successfully overcoming the numerous obstacles, she fulfilled her goal and was able to have an ordinary life, but not before changing the world they lived in now.

The demon hunter line deviated with Elizabeth Somiere, Williams thought to himself. Elizabeth and her best friend, Kaela Kaplan, unleashed all the demon hunters of that generation.

With powerful dark magic, they extended the hunter line and triggered the hidden power in over ten-thousand young girls around the globe. The same number remained for the Guardians to guide them. The organization grew exponentially with Williams as the chosen leader.

A knock on the door interrupted Williams' thoughts. He looked up and saw Jasmine Taylor come inside, carrying a stack of papers in her arms. She smiled sadly at his dumbfounded face when he saw the pile of documents. Williams took off his glasses and rubbed his eyes as his longtime girlfriend walked up to him.

"More for you to sign," she said in her Northern Welsh accent.

Williams opened his eyes and admired the woman in front of him. He then looked at the papers he needed to sign. Jasmine always dressed casually when there was no official Guardian business, and tonight was one of those nights. She had chosen a long, light green skirt with a white top and a dark jacket; her curly hair neatly braided in a bun. She looked gorgeous in his eyes. The paperwork, on the other hand, looked ugly and stale. And it seemed it would be a while.

"How am I supposed to get work done when I get bothered by every little detail?" he asked rhetorically, as he grabbed the first set of documents and started flipping the pages with his fingers. This ink, he could do without.

"I've told you, Arthur," Jasmine said while she put the paperwork in order. "Delegate."

"This is going to consume the rest of my life," he said, looking at the expense report from California where one Guardian and two demon hunters resided, plus a technician. They were the costliest to maintain.

"If you want, I can handle this for you," Jasmine said, taking the folder from his hand.

"I would not dream of you handling this burden," Williams said, trying not to pass her the large stack of paperwork.

"I won't be," Jasmine said as she gathered most of the documents. "You need to focus on the important. Big week coming up."

Williams sighed, knowing she was right. In two days, the most experienced demon hunters from around the globe would be arriving for the hunter-gathering. It was more of a mission assignment reunion, but Elizabeth had insisted on not calling it that. Being the head of the demon-hunter division, she did have a point. This two-week adventure was Elizabeth's brainchild, and it took a lot of time to prepare for it. Williams shook the ideas from his head and handed the paperwork to Jasmine. "Please handle it," Williams pleaded as he went back to the computer.

"Fine," Jasmine said. She kissed him softly on the lips before she walked out. "Just don't be late for bed." The English woman's cell phone then rang. She answered and looked back at Williams. "Send him in," she said, hanging up after another moment passed. "John Simmons has arrived."

Williams frowned a bit once he turned his attention back to the window. He pulled out a small white container from his breast pocket as he felt his blood pressure starting to rise. His old heart beat faster; the older man could feel it pumping in his ears. He took two pills from the bottle, swallowed them down, and waited for the pain to subdue. The rush of emotions on handling something off the books was palpable. *It starts with this*, he thought to himself. He breathed a bit as he recuperated and drank his tea. He turned around, seeing a handsome, young twenty-year-old in front of his desk.

"John Simmons," Williams said, standing up and shaking the young man's hand. The boy dressed sharply in a nice white button-up shirt, blue slacks, and dark shoes.

"Mr. Williams," John greeted. "Please, call me John. It's an honor to meet you, sir."

"Williams will do," the older Guardian stated, referring to how everyone in the assembly called him. He motioned for the young man to sit on the chair in front of his desk. "How are your parents?"

"Fine, sir," John replied as he explored the office with his curious gaze. His eyes fixated on the whiteboard. The young man then noticed Williams pulling a folder out from his desk.

"Do you know why you are here?" Williams asked, opening the file and examining it.

"My parents filled me in a bit," John responded. "There is a project you need a hand with, and I guess they volunteered me."

"Both your parents are excellent Guardians," Williams said, reading from the file as he glanced at the young man. "They speak highly of you."

"Parents do that," John said, feeling uncomfortable and under the scrutiny of the elder.

"I trust their judgment," Williams said as he continued reading the file. "It says here you have an I.Q. of one-hundred-and-eighty-one. Graduated college at age nine. Finished medical school at sixteen, all while getting a Masters degree in Math and Tech."

John felt squeamish as the older man continued to detail his academic accolades. His palms were sweaty as he tapped the floor with his dark shoes. "After all that, you focused your attention on demonology." Williams continued. "Why the sudden shift?"

"Would blame the parents," John said nervously. "Curiosity about what they worked on, while I studied guided new interests."

"I see," Williams said after he read the file. "Expert in demon anatomy and biology. I guess your knowledge of medicine guided you through that. How did you get the information on those topics?"

"Books," John answered. "Parents provided the information I needed."

"Have you ever met a demon hunter?" Williams asked directly.

"Yes," John said. "When my parents took me on an expedition to Mexico. We met the demon hunter stationed there."

"Yes," Williams said, turning back to the file. "Her replacement will be joining us this weekend." Saying that, Williams closed the file and looked at the young man before him. "I have an overdue project. The history of the new Guardians needs to be documented properly."

"But you have so many Guardians at your disposal," John said, expressing his opinion for the first time. "Not to mention first-hand experience in demon hunters here. Why do you need me?"

Williams sighed and turned his attention back to the window. "We need fresh eyes. Our team has been involved in so many events that I fear sentiment may cloud our judgment while we put everything into formal documents."

John nodded, still not convinced of the reason for being chosen. He looked the older man in his eyes. He saw fatigue as if he carried the weight of the world on his shoulders.

"You're good at what you do, John," Williams continued. "I read your investigation on Apocalyps. Interesting thesis. Not sure if it's valid, though, since we're writing the story as we move along these murky waters."

John felt a chill run down his spine. Apocalyps had become too tangible for him to bear. It was more than a word for him now. It was a small obsession to ponder about. But he was not about to tell that to the head of the organization.

"You're a fast learner, and have great intel on all dark arts," Williams continued. "I need you on this team."

John nodded. "I will do what's needed to help."

"Excellent," Williams said. "It's late, and you've had a long trip. My associate outside will guide you to your room. We will discuss more of this in the morning."

As John left the room, Williams felt his heart settle. John was a good man with a valuable set of skills. The boy was extremely gifted in the dark arts, as well as highly intelligent. A fresh view of the facts would allow him to document the truth appropriately. Williams smiled and nodded as he read the phrase he had typed earlier on his computer. The memories of the past flooded his mind again—the crucial friends who had influenced Elizabeth's life and his own, the companions in battle, the good Guardians and demon hunters they had met— even the vampires and demons searching for redemption. Williams read again what he had written.

Providence does not abandon humanity. Out of darkness, a few girls are born and chosen to fight the forces of evil. Chosen to show the light, they alone carry the hopes of the ones in need—a sisterhood born and forged to wield the power of good.

He pondered a minute before continuing to type.

That changed the moment Elizabeth Somiere was called.

CHAPTER II

Pensacola Air Base–United States; August 5, 3:15 p.m.

NICOLE ROGERS PULLED THE red hair from over her blue eyes and tied it in a neat ponytail, then adjusted her red-framed eyeglasses and looked at the mess of her bed frowning. Her army duffle bag was empty, and her clothes and makeup were all over the place. She had no idea what to pack. Her shoes were a mess, as well as her blouses and dresses. She knew she would take cargo Army pants and jeans, but should she take her Army boots? She shook her head. She then looked at her backpack, where she had tucked away all her spare fifteen pairs of eyeglasses.

"Attention!" she heard a male voice behind her. Nicole stood up straight and faced her father. He had his arms crossed and a grim look on his face, and was wearing his blue Air Force shirt and dress pants. "What's the meaning of this mess, Airman?" he bellowed, pointing at the mess.

"Packing situation, Sir," Nicole responded. "Taking care of it now."

"Are you aware that you're to hitch a ride to Washington at sixteen-hundred hours, and you're not packed?" the man looked down at the young fifteen-year-old. "What's your excuse?"

"Having late lunch with my brother and father, Sir," Nicole answered equally firmly.

The man smiled and hugged his daughter. "Excellent excuse," he said as he kissed his only daughter on the forehead.

"Am I interrupting, Colonel?" Nicole heard her brother's voice ask from the door. She looked at him and saw that Ryan Rogers dressed in a similar uniform as her father. Only that he had his Lieutenant uniform. Nicole knew this would be the last time she would see her family for a long time. She was leaving to fulfill her duties as a demon hunter while both her father and brother were embarking on their first tour of duty together across the Red Sea. Coming from an Air Force family, Nicole knew that honor and duty always came first. She had a different conflict to fight against, and her dad respected her for it.

"Come in," Nicole said, looking at the clutter on her bed. "Sorry for the mess... I just don't know what to pack."

"A teenage girl who doesn't know what to pack?" Ryan asked, teasing slightly. "That's a first."

"I am a demon hunter from an Air Force family," Nicole responded, taking the bait.

"At ease, both of you," the Colonel said, knowing full well the discussion could go on for hours. He turned toward his daughter. "Please behave and make me proud. This Elizabeth Somiere is an acquaintance of General Grant. She runs a pretty tight ship."

Nicole nodded and thought about it for a moment. Her father, Colonel Rogers, had reported back in the day to General Grant and had extracted him from a tight spot. That is where her family first encountered the creatures of the night. That is also the night the Colonel and General Grant became close friends. When the General found out she was a demon hunter, he could hardly contain himself and insisted that this was the way she could best serve her country. The teenager was a soldier who fought against the creatures of the night. And today, she would fly out to meet with the best.

Nicole looked at her dad and nodded. "I will make you proud, Colonel,"

The Colonel smiled and hugged both of his children. "I'm proud of both of you," he said. "Listen up. We may not be together on the front lines. Every time you feel you are getting tired, or feel despair, remember that a Rogers is in the line with you at all times." The Colonel pulled out two small boxes from his dress pants and handed them to his children.

Nicole opened it and saw a small heart-shaped pendant. She opened the jewel and saw a picture of her father and brother on one side, and a photo of her deceased mother on the other.

"A Rogers is never alone," Ryan repeated the sentiment, opening the pocket watch his father had given him.

"Affirmative," the Colonel said as he hugged both of them again. "We are all called for higher things in the missions we are assigned to. Soon we'll be together again."

Nicole smiled to herself. She hoped her family would be safe.

Honolulu, Hawaii, United States; August 5, 10:15 a.m.

Grace Wu breathed hard as she looked at the opponents before her—more than ten grown men, all armed with clubs and knives. They looked like the offensive line of a junior Samoan rugby team. The young teen planted her feet on the wooden floor of her gym. The sixteen-year-old closed her eyes and breathed, feeling every inch of her body tingle with a supernatural force. The air seemed light around her until she felt something approaching her. Like a time bomb, she exploded with intense fury upon all ten men as the raging sea crashed against solid rock. With every punch and kick, she flowed through her opponents like they were made of air. All was silent in her mind while she attacked and moved through the midst of the small group of men. Her brain seemed to be on fire; her rage and energy focused. The central focus in her thoughts was a building set ablaze. She could feel the heat of the flames, as well as a dark, icy coldness in her heart. Both fire and ice fueled every cell in her being. It seemed that no sooner had she started the conflict, she'd stopped. She opened her dark eyes and looked back, only to admire the men groaning in agony on the floor. It had been as if lightning had passed through them. The black-haired girl looked at her Guardian, who was only nodding his head and taking notes. Grace had grown accustomed to his silent demeanor.

"Faster than the last time," he said as he wrote something down on his computer tablet. "What went through your mind?"

"Revenge," Grace replied coolly.

"That will only take you so far," her Guardian responded, as he motioned for her to walk beside him, but not before signaling for the fallen men to gather their things and leave. The young girl walked in silence behind the older man as he exited her private gym and walked out into the garden. The Guardian remained quiet, knowing full well his demon hunter trailed behind him. He slowly breathed the air that surrounded him as he felt impatience consume his young apprentice.

Grace could not take the silence any longer, especially after training. She yearned for feedback on her performance. "What's more powerful than revenge?" the teenager blurted out.

"Love," the Guardian responded, admiring a bright Hawaiian hibiscus.

Grace scoffed at the idea. "Weak emotion," she said.

"You think it's a weak emotion because you're confused. You

get love and fear mixed up. Unfortunately, I've not been able to help you with this. You need other care."

Grace stopped and looked at the older man before her. "You're giving up on me?"

The older man turned back to his demon hunter and looked into her eyes. Behind all that strength, he could detect fear and sadness. He dared not show the paternal emotions he felt, though. This was neither the place nor the time. "I've taught you everything you need to know; your father taught you everything you need to become a perfect demon-killing machine. But pure skill and strength are not enough. You need more."

"The ten men who had difficulty getting up would tell you otherwise," Grace said, pointing at the sad group of men exiting her gym.

The older man smiled. "Your set skills are ready. This gathering will help you, Grace. Once the gathering is over, we will discuss a different training path for you."

Grace felt the rage inside her—it was like a fire boiling over—but she controlled it. She breathed and looked at her Guardian with a steely gaze. "Whatever you say."

Grace's Guardian walked toward the large house that loomed over the garden. "Start packing," he said. "You're taking more than your expensive luggage on your trip."

The Guardians' Castle, Central Garden, Ireland; August 5, 11:15 p.m.

Clara Somiere held the punching bag tight; sweat glistened on her brow as she withstood the force the sack received. *This is a workout in itself,* the brunette thought to herself as she watched her sister beat the boxing equipment down. Right punch and left punch. High kick. Spin kick. The blows of the blonde demon hunter strained the bag to its limits. The one and true demon hunter, whose legend transcended for all, grunted with each attack she fired.

Clara smiled, amazed on how Elizabeth had matured as a warrior over the years and throughout all their adventures. In her late thirties, Elizabeth still had the strength, agility, and speed from when she was eighteen. Her face looked the same as it did when she sealed the gates of hell in New York. Clara looked closely at her sister. Her body seemed the same—a little thinner, maybe. Of course, the black and blue tracksuit did Elizabeth justice as it hugged her figure. At five-feet-one, she looked the same. The difference was in Elizabeth's green eyes. Those truly reflected her age and maturity. Those eyes had looked evil in the eye, and they had suffered for it. But they had also prevailed.

Elizabeth stopped after she noticed her sister staring at her. "What?" Elizabeth asked, feeling a little bit self-conscious. "Do I have something in my teeth?" Elizabeth cleaned her teeth with her grapple-gloved hand. She caught Clara with a devious smile herself. "What?" Elizabeth asked, now getting a little annoyed at her younger sister's antics.

"Nothing," Clara replied, grinning. "I was just pondering that as you age, you don't seem to get older or slower as normal people do."

Elizabeth smiled as she removed her grappling gloves from her hands. "Demon hunter benefits in the long run," the hunter said. "You don't look bad yourself." Clara Somiere was quite different from Elizabeth, indeed. She was three inches taller than her older sister, with long dark brown hair and piercing blue eyes.

"Demon hunter blood benefits," Clara said, admiring her own body. "Almost as strong, twice the hotness." Elizabeth threw Clara her grappling gloves, hoping to smack the grin off her face for the comment. Clara caught them and put them on. *I won that round of playful banter*, she thought to herself. It felt good to train at Elizabeth's side.

Clara adjusted her purple tracksuit and looked at the foggy Irish night sky. A cool breeze of summer brought a peaceful sense to her body as she looked at her surroundings. Elizabeth had certainly thought things through when she decided to put training equipment in the central garden of the castle. Stacked near a brown bench were weights and grappling gloves. Javelins, short swords, knives, and staffs all neatly ordered on a portable brown rack. All the training gear had the moon and stars as a ceiling.

Elizabeth grabbed hold of the punching bag and signaled for Clara to start her routine; Clara threw punches and kicks in the same sequence as her older sister, only with less intensity and speed. Elizabeth could feel the strength of Clara's blows— weaker than her own, but still stronger than eight well-trained men combined. Elizabeth looked at her sister. The hunter blood, mixed with ancient black magic, crafted a different type of warrior, one capable of opening dimensions and rifts. Clara had the strength and the will to contain all the energy. Her hunter blood was powerful— it made her agile and athletic. Not as strong as an original demon hunter, but strong enough to make a vampire or demon regret ever running into her. It seemed as though the hunter blood contributed to the aging process in Clara as well. She looked no older than twenty, yet here she was reaching her thirties now.

Elizabeth turned her attention toward the castle itself. She loved Williams' idea of taking this castle as central operations for the new Guardians. It had fifty well-spaced rooms, seven living rooms, several studies, a large indoor gym, and a vast library. Well-spaced for their needs, the square-shaped building looked right out of a painting of old Ireland. But it was real, and it was theirs.

A few more reps on the punching bag, Elizabeth handed her younger sister a towel. They dried the sweat from their upper bodies when Elizabeth's green eyes lit up, and her face drew a smile. Clara was perplexed by Elizabeth's sudden facial change until she saw what Elizabeth was looking at.

Izzy strolled toward them.

Elizabeth ran toward her daughter and embraced her fully. "My girl is back," Elizabeth exclaimed with watery eyes as she squeezed her tight.

Izzy grunted as the pressure increased on her body, but it felt so good feeling her motherly hug—the only place she felt safe. "Alive and kicking," Izzy said, hugging her mother back. "As I promised I would be."

"Yes," Elizabeth said, with her voice filled with excitement. "Your bag?"

"Left it in the entrance," Izzy said as Clara approached both mother and daughter. "Wanted to see you first."

"My favorite niece," Clara said, embracing the young girl.

"Your only niece," Izzy corrected.

"You've got to tell me everything," Elizabeth said, holding both her daughter's hands as she walked away with her. "The sights, the friends, the romance… everything." Clara took this as a cue to clean up after the workout. *As usual, Elizabeth snaked out of her responsibility.*

"Actually," Izzy dragged on. "I wanted to spend the entire day tomorrow with you and Dad, and tell you about the trip."

"Great," Elizabeth beamed. "We can arrange a day out."

"You sure?" Izzy asked, knowing that in two days, nineteen other demon hunters would be arriving at the castle. It was an event that happened every three years, and it was the busiest time for her parents. It was also the time where her mother transformed into something not-so-motherly, but Izzy was smart enough not to mention that.

"Don't worry," Elizabeth reassured her daughter once they entered one of the main halls of the castle. "Everything is ready; we're just waiting. Besides, it's not every day a daughter wants to spend time with her boring parents."

Izzy smiled at the comment. "My mother, the greatest demon hunter in the world, and my father, a former superhuman demon. My parents are *everything* but boring."

"Pretty cool, right?" Elizabeth chirped.

"Don't push it," Izzy teased, pushing at her mother's shoulder. Elizabeth laughed and hugged her daughter. Their connection was palpable; they were so in tune with each other. And looking at them together, anyone could get confused and think they were looking at twins. "Where's Dad?" Izzy asked, noticing her father's absence since she arrived.

Elizabeth's smile grew wider. "You haven't seen him yet?" Elizabeth asked, half-knowing the answer. Her husband was going to freak. "He's downstairs in his shop, painting. You know how he hates to be disturbed."

Both Elizabeth and Izzy walked toward the end of the hall until they reached a wooden door. They opened it, revealing a concrete staircase leading to the cellars. The only light came from the lightbulbs aligned on the ceiling. Elizabeth descended, followed by her daughter. While they walked, their steps echoed into the bowels of the castle. Elizabeth could not stop grinning. Her spouse hated to be disturbed while he painted, but after hearing a mouthful from his wife, the only people who would be allowed down in his shop were his girls. Their relationship had been put through fire. People had guessed it would be impossible to be together, but both demon hunter and demon had proven the world wrong. They fought and had prevailed, thanks, of course, to their friends who fought beside them.

They walked down a concrete hall which housed empty cell blocks where vampires, monsters, and demons were captured and interrogated. "A pack of vampires was on the grounds tonight," Izzy informed her mother. The moment she opened her mouth, the young teen regretted it.

Elizabeth stopped walking and turned toward her daughter at the news she was hearing. Her face changed from a happy and loving mother to a serious demon hunter. "How many?" Elizabeth asked. The change in Elizabeth's demeanor was something that always bothered Izzy. The icy tone always sliced at her heart, yet she never said a word about it to anyone.

"Three," Izzy said, hating this part of her mother's life. She was different when she was in demon-hunting mode, and news like this always set her off. "I dusted two," Izzy continued. "I let the other one go to inform his nest that no vampire trespasses this property."

"Vampires should not have crossed the property at all," Elizabeth said as they continued walking. The older demon hunter relaxed only a little while she contemplated the variables. There was probably a vampire nest nearby that needed clearing. Her mood started to lighten up, though. The fact that Izzy had taken care of two vampires, without a scratch on her, reassured her of her daughter's skills. *I always knew she could take care of herself,* she thought to herself.

Izzy, on the other hand, took a while to loosen up. Her mother's hunter instinct overshadowed in great lengths her motherly love. Sometimes Izzy felt that hunting came first and motherhood second for Elizabeth. But she was a great mother. The older woman was cool and laid back. She could tell her almost anything, and she knew her mom would have her back always. But no mom was perfect, and Elizabeth's motherly imperfection was apparent.

As they continued walking down the hall, they passed a large, black metal door. On top of the door frame, there was a skull and crossbones with a broad sign reading *Do Not Enter*. Every time Izzy passed that door, a shiver ran down her spine. Both her parents had warned her that only death was behind that door. The single order she never dared disobey was going into that room. She was scared to death of it, and she didn't even know what was in it; she did not dare ask. But the chilling sensation always came. She felt cold and empty inside, just being near it—like happiness was drained from the world through that door and replaced by sorrow and despair.

Izzy shook the dark feeling out and embraced the fact that she was home with her family. Mother and daughter reached the end of the hall and faced another metal door. Elizabeth and Izzy smiled at each other as they saw a handwritten sign hanging on the front of it. It read, *DO NOT DISTURB! DON'T BOTHER ENTERING!*

"I still think he should have written it in crayon," Izzy said. "Would make more of a statement."

Elizabeth held back a laugh. What caused the girls to smile was a smaller sign with Elizabeth's handwriting. *EXCEPT FOR IZZY AND ELIZABETH.* The girls looked at each other and smiled. They both had their man eating out of their hand, and he knew it.

As Elizabeth's hand moved toward the door handle, Izzy's hand stopped her. "What?" Elizabeth asked.

"Did you tell Dad about Aidan?" Izzy asked, with a slightly worried tone to her voice. "I mean… you know how he gets concerning that subject."

Elizabeth nodded as she reassured her daughter. "You told me not to. We will tell him when the time is right. Like when he's drunk."

Izzy exhaled the air she contained in her lungs. It felt so good to have her mother on her side. The Aidan secret she kept from her father would resolve itself in due time. And now it was time for family.

Elizabeth opened the door, and they entered the room. Her husband's studio was a large space, covering one-eighth of the castle cellar itself. The walls were covered in various oil paintings of different styles. Some were portraits, others were of vast landscapes. Elizabeth and Izzy knew Sean poured himself into his art—especially Elizabeth. She smiled to herself as she saw the color in the room. When Sean was a demon, he loved to draw in gray scales. Charcoal paintings. Just as his role in the world, his canvases were gray—almost black. That changed the moment his heart beat again. The color was brought back by the new chance he had on life, and of course, his blonde demon hunter, and Elizabeth knew it. She looked at Izzy, who was always mesmerized by her dad's art. Elizabeth noted that Izzy's presence just added more life and color to Sean, as it did for her. He dedicated most of the time painting from his Irish roots and the life he had lived as a demon. She noticed a painting of the buildings of L.A. in flames. Red and orange and yellow, alongside gray and black structures. Sean remembered those days as if it were yesterday.

Izzy stood in front of one of Sean's new paintings depicting a young girl playing the violin on a hill surrounded by a green field. A lonely oak tree accompanied the girl in the piece of art, on what seemed like a beautiful day. The sky was light blue; the Atlantic Ocean loomed on the horizon. It was gorgeous. Izzy knew the location that painting was based on. It was on the western cliff of the Guardians' property, which had a magnificent view of the vast oceanic landscape. If she knew her father well, that'd be the place they would spend their day together. It was his favorite place. Izzy looked closely at the painting and spotted a dark figure painted right behind the oak tree as if hiding from sight. Izzy looked and saw the girl had blonde hair. Izzy shrugged at the small detail and continued into the room to find her father.

As both moved deeper into the studio, they reached the portraits area. Old friends of both Sean and Elizabeth had had portraits made of them. But here in the studio were located the group portraits, from past and present. The old demon-hunting team, as well as the Delta-Squad from L.A.

Izzy knew most of them from her parent's stories. A solo portrait of the red-headed Wiccan made Izzy smile. *That was Aunt Kaela*, she thought to herself. The memory that was forever present in both her parent's minds was now captured in an oil painting. She was glad because of this.

Elizabeth and Izzy finally reached Sean, way in the back. He had a large square canvas, six feet in height and length in front of him. Probably a new landscape. *It must be the woods,* Izzy thought to herself as she noticed a dark green and brown on her father's paint pallet. She recognized it as the woods about two hundred yards from the castle.

Sean used charcoal to draw freehand before adding color. His hand moved across the canvas, desperate to transfer the image in his mind onto the new piece of art. His mind focused on his task and the music blasting on his headphones.

Must be classical music, Izzy thought to herself. Her old man was old-fashioned—Centuries old-fashioned.

Elizabeth crept up to him, knowing full well that he was oblivious to his girls' presence. She stood behind him and hugged his waist from behind.

Sean stopped moving, feeling the warm embrace of his wife. He put his brush down and turned, kissing his wife passionately.

The dark-haired man then looked up and saw his daughter in front of him. He almost tripped over Elizabeth as he launched himself toward his little girl and hugged her. "Thank heavens you're back," he said as he squeezed hard.

"Getting hard to breathe," Izzy wheezed out, resting her head on her father's chest. She looked up to see her six-foot-two dad.

His warm brown eyes looked at her adoringly. He kissed her forehead and smiled.

"When did you get in?" he asked.

"About fifteen minutes ago," Izzy replied after Elizabeth positioned herself by Sean's side.

"You should've called," Sean scolded softly. "I would've made dinner."

"I know," Izzy said, fully aware of her father's cooking skills. But frankly, she was just too tired from the trip. "I didn't want to bother you. Maybe you can make it up for me tomorrow when we go out with Mom."

"We're going out?" Sean asked, looking down at his wife. Being part of a couple, he felt it was easier for Elizabeth to coordinate social events. "We have a lot of prep to do for the gathering. Is there space for an outing in our schedule?"

"Well," Elizabeth stretched her arms out. "We can go out tomorrow, into the field, and have a family day out. No demons or vampires. No darkness. Just us."

"We have the girls coming in two days," Sean pointed out. "Are you okay with us going out?" Sean knew his wife well. She knew how in-control she wanted to be of everything, especially anything related to the gathering that was at hand.

"Williams and Lewis are on it," Elizabeth said, dragging her husband out of his cave. Sean almost tripped over his feet. Izzy caught up to them, and Sean had both of them on his arms.

"Besides," Elizabeth continued. "What's more important than spending time with our little girl?"

"Besides battling demons and the undead?" Izzy asked, playfully taking a slight jab at her mother's uptightness.

Sean's heart melted as he felt both his girls tug him from side to side. He pulled his arms together, bringing Elizabeth and Izzy closer. He hugged both of them. "Okay," he said, looking at Izzy. "Let me hear a preview of your stories while I help you unpack."

CHAPTER III

Underground, Town of York, Ireland; August 5, 11:15 p.m.

DROZ RAN HARD AND fast through the tunnels of the underground ghost town. Muddy water splashed as his combat boots landed in dirty puddles. If he were alive and had functioning lungs, he would be exhausted. But the undead don't care about such trivial things as air. He ran down the stairs and looked down upon the gathering that had already begun. Gathered in the central square plaza of the cursed town were about two dozen vampires. Few living human beings knew the place existed; even fewer had explored it. A cataclysm centuries ago had trapped the cursed town underground. The walls of the buildings were green with mold and dampness.

The center square was the gathering point for Dante's assembly. Droz jumped the final steps and threaded his way among the vampires moving to be the first in line. Many vampires had come for this request. For far too long, the oppression caused by the Guardians and their demon hunters fueled the undead's hatred. The purpose of the meeting was to discuss a plan to strike back.

Droz noticed a tall, six-foot-five blond-haired vampire dressed in a black suit, with a black silk shirt and red tie, stand up. His long, blond hair was tied in a ponytail. *This is a leader I can follow*, Droz thought to himself. Following the blond vampire was his second-in-command, a dark-haired vampire with a black trench coat. Siegfried was his name. Dante's strong enforcer and bodyguard was a legend among the vampire community—a creature of the night whom few dared to challenge.

"The time is now!" Dante exclaimed to the small crowd of vampires. "For too long, we have let the Guardians and their wretched group of demon hunters dictate our way of life. They are everywhere, not allowing us to feed or reproduce. Our numbers are diminishing. Their time is coming to a bloody end. As vampires, we must rise. We will take the battle to them, and claim this cursed continent that rightfully belongs to us."

The crowd bellowed a cry of war. Dante calmed the pack, lowering his hands slowly. "Send the word out," he said. "All across Europe. All vampires must come and aid our moment of triumph. We will break the Guardians at the head, and their army will crumble. The time of the vampires will endure!"

The vampires cheered as the words of their leader reached their ears.

"Dante!" Droz stepped up, showing initiative. "My friends and I investigated their castle and their property. They have vampire detectors on the perimeter. But there is a blind spot on the south of the property. We attack that side, and they will never know what hit them."

Dante turned toward Droz. His yellow eyes pierced right through the pitiful creature. "Who authorized you to access those grounds?"

The vampire horde stood silent.

"It was by my initiative," Droz replied, proud of the call he had made.

Dante lowered himself down toward Droz, frowning at naivete. "And where are the rest of your friends?"

Droz gulped. "They were destroyed."

"By a demon hunter?" Dante asked.

"Yes," Droz replied. "A young brown-haired demon hunter."

Dante smiled and put a hand on Droz's shoulder. "A bold sacrifice! A bold sacrifice indeed for the information you provided. You must be rewarded."

"Thank you, sir," Droz said gratefully. As the words left his lips, Siegfried jumped upon him in a flash and stuck two daggers into his eye sockets. Droz screamed in excruciating pain as the metal burned past his eyeballs. He tried desperately to fight, but his arms dangled helplessly as the stronger vampire tortured his undead body.

Dante turned toward his horde of vampires as he walked among them. "Never take a shot on your own." he lectured calmly while Droz screamed in agony in the background. "You have no idea how you can bring disarray to a carefully layered plan."

"The demon hunters know we're nearby," a vampire said beside him. He tried not to show fear, but he failed miserably. "They could come and kill us."

"I am well aware," Dante replied as he heard combustion behind him. "Do not fear, my family," the vampire said, turning back to where he came from, trying to calm and comfort his vampires. "We have aerial support now." The vampires turned around and saw three giant, muscular, winged seven-foot gray-skinned demons come out. The ground shook as they stomped into the main square.

"We are changing the rules of the game," Dante said as he

walked away and patted one of his gargoyles on the arm. "Stay low," he called to his vampires. "Feed in the darkness. We must keep our presence a secret."

Siegfried followed his blond friend into a half-destroyed building as the vampires behind him scattered. *The message was clear,* Siegfried thought to himself as he walked down the dark corridor. *We must be patient; soon, our time will come.* Siegfried continued walking, only to find himself inside a medium-sized room with a round wooden table, around which four vampire masters were already seated. Each master had a second-in-command assigned. Siegfried's task was to care for Dante. So he stood slightly behind him as the blond vampire spoke.

"My kin," Dante said, gesturing to the other four vampires, "I appreciate you making the trip to the old continent."

"We couldn't resist," a female vampire said as she looked at the other vampires. She had long, dark, silky black hair that reached her waist. Her pale features contrasted with her ruby red lips. An oversized leather trench coat protected her body from the damp environment of the underground city. "Any initiative to restore balance to our world is worthy of our physical presence."

"Dante," a second fiend stated. His facial features seemed younger than the female vampire, but his lifeless eyes and determination showed he was the eldest of them all. He wore an elegant, gray three-piece suit. "Your invitation was very persuasive. I have battled countless demon hunters in my time, but their increased numbers have become a tiresome nuisance—like a small, boring itch at my side that doesn't leave me alone."

"I understand you, Neil," Dante said, walking around the table. "For over a decade, the Guardians and their cursed demon hunter army have beaten us to the core. Never in the history of demon hunters and vampires have our numbers been stretched so thin."

"We know this!" the large vampire at the end of the table exclaimed, smashing his fist on the flat wooden surface. Fat and disgusting-looking, he looked like he was part of an old motorcycle gang with sleeve tattoos on his arms and covered in leather garments. "Give us a solution to this hell, Dante!"

"Patience, Dragnor," Dante said with a soothing voice. "If history has taught us something, it is that we must use our immortality to our advantage. We have nothing but time. Strong as the demon hunters are, they are mortal."

"What's your plan, Dante?" the female asked. "My family is standing by and ready."

Dante smiled at his friends and signaled for Siegfried. The brown-haired vampire smiled and disappeared to a nearby door. He came back out, rolling out a six-foot-long brown wooden crate with chains surrounding it. It looked like a coffin, holding something dark inside. The vampires stood up to get a better look, as Siegfried removed the metal chains from the crate and opened the front lid. The vampires gasped, seeing a young blonde-haired girl in a straitjacket, with heavy chains around her body. A stream of blood flowed down the side of her face. The girl seemed unconscious but very much alive. The vampires could hear a faint beating of the girl's heart; the smell of her blood was intoxicating. It was demon hunter blood.

"I give you," Dante said, pointing at the girl, "Demon Hunter Elsa from Austria."

"You captured a demon hunter," Neil said once he sat down, clearly feeling bored. Seeing a lesser warrior did not impress him. "Excuse me if I contain my excitement."

"Neil," Dante said in a condescending voice as he walked behind his vampire comrade, "You are one of the most powerful vampires to walk this cursed earth. Yet you are incapable of having a vision of the future."

Neil smiled. "To have a vision of the future, you must know the past, child. I am the past. But seeing children trying to wield the destiny of our kind, and attempt to drive it forward, has always amused me. You're not the first and will hardly be the last."

Dante smiled, knowing full well he had pushed the right buttons. "The demon hunter line has been put in disarray for more than a decade. It's time we vampires caught up." As the words left his lips, the seven-foot winged demons stomped inside, carrying a smaller yet more vicious beast. It was bound tightly in chains as it struggled to get free, growling with each attempt.

The female vampire looked horrified, seeing the beast that needed no introduction. It was the Uroks-Nah demon—a vicious creature, more demon than vampire, extremely strong and agile, all accompanied by a brutal killer instinct. It was five-foot-one, gray-skinned with sharp fangs and claws. It was a strong and ferocious animal that gave average demons nightmares. "What madness drives you?" she asked Dante, as she stood up and stepped back, in fear of the vicious demon. "You bring forth this beast?"

"Our race drives me, Lucinda," Dante replied, caressing Elsa's cheek. "And of course, blind hatred toward the Guardians and their cursed demon hunters."

"Well," Neil said, standing up and buttoning up his suit. "This has all been very amusing. I am anxious to see how it all turns out. I assume my room is ready."

Dante smiled, pointing to Siegfried to guide Neil out. Neil started walking out but stopped suddenly. "A word of caution from one of the ancient ones, Dante."

"Please," Dante urged, sitting down and motioning for Neil to continue.

"Don't put all your eggs in one basket," Neil stated. "When you have an uncontrollable beast at your side, it could break you and leave you with nothing." The ancient vampire then walked out with Siegfried at his side.

"You don't have to control a beast," Dante said, turning around and facing the group. "You just have to unleash it."

The Guardians' Castle, Main Control Room, Ireland; August 5, 11:30 p.m.

Alex Cooper took off his reading glasses and rubbed his eyes, lowering his head. There were so many small details that still needed to be handled, and he did not have the time to do so. Alex put his glasses back on and ran his fingers through his black hair, turning his attention back to the nine forty-two-inch LED screens arranged in front of him. In the center screen, he had the list of demon hunters who would be arriving in two days. He looked at file after file, trying to determine the correct demon-hell-spot assignation based on their skills. This was his job. In the top corner screen, he could see their light-haired technician, Andy Richardson, arranging cameras down in the hell-spot of California. According to the books, that would open in two days as well. Good thing, the Guardians' Alpha Team was on the scene.

Clara Somiere entered the room, carrying two cups of coffee. She looked at Alex's back, frowning at all nine screens—and at Alex's determination to keep on watching while his eyeballs rotted away. The displays were lined up in three-by-three formation. One showed HQ's security system; another screen showed the outside perimeter cameras. She shook her head as she walked up to Alex. She placed the coffee cup on the desk and planted a kiss on Alex's lips. "Brought you some coffee goodness," she said, smiling at him.

Alex smiled at his girl and turned his eyes to her, refreshed by the sight. They had been together for a while now, but he just could not get used to the idea that this girl was actually his girlfriend—she was gorgeous in his eyes. The dark-haired man took a break from his work and sipped a bit of coffee, savoring the bittersweet beverage. Just as he liked it.

"Izzy just arrived," Clara said, staring at Andy on the screen. He seemed oblivious to the fact that he was being watched.

Alex's eyes lit up at the news. "That's great. Elizabeth and Sean should be ecstatic."

"Yeah," Clara said, turning toward him. "I heard that they planned to spend the entire day together. So tomorrow we should not count them into any plans."

Alex sighed and shook his head. The gathering of the demon hunters was their biggest two weeks that did not involve an end-of-the-world scenario. Elizabeth always played a significant role during those weeks, providing lessons and speeches. She and Sean also participated in the prep work. Not having them around just made the jobs a lot harder. But it was Izzy. She had been gone for a couple of months. "We'll manage," Alex reassured Clara as he squeezed her hand and turned his attention back to the screens. He closed the files on the demon hunters and pulled out the schedule for the next two weeks.

Clara looked at it as she took a sip from her mug. She could see by the program on the screen, she was on crossbow detail this year. She smiled, thinking about her previous experience. New crossbow models had arrived just the day before. It was a gift for all the girls, but Clara had to test them first in the range. She also noticed Latin 101 provided by Lewis. She grimaced at the idea.

"Is anyone there?" Andy's voice echoed through the room. His squeaky voice made both of them jump. The couple turned their attention to the corner screen, and Andy's freckled face was all over the camera. "Hello," Andy called, opening his big mouth.

"I think the entire island heard you," Alex said into his in-ear microphone while pressing a few keys on his keyboard. Andy's image expanded onto all nine screens, now showing a broad picture of him. "You don't have to yell," Alex said, rubbing one of his ears.

"Sorry," Andy said as he adjusted the camera.

Clara paid close attention to the screen. She was partially responsible for discovering what was going on. The screen showed Andy moving cables out of the way. Clara could see a small power generator feeding electricity to five heavy-duty work lights. They all pointed to a round black rock with strange symbols engraved on it. The main stone was not what caught Clara's attention—it was the two circular stepping stones on the side of the rock that made her uncomfortable. Andy was inside an old cave in the outskirts of St. Helena, California, the heart of Napa Valley. Who would figure a hell spot was right under the old wine country? Clara remembered the notes she had taken on this particular cave. In two days, those gates would open, and all hell would break loose.

"Where's Joy?" Clara asked Andy, referring to the Guardian helping out on this incursion.

"She's resting," Andy said, moving the camera to the entrance of the cave. Clara could see a body all cuddled up inside a sleeping bag.

"Point that camera elsewhere, nerd!" Joy exclaimed without lifting her head.

"She needs to reserve her strength," Andy said as he placed the camera back in its place.

"Teresa and Anna?" Alex asked, referring to the blonde twin demon hunters assigned to that hell spot.

"At home," Andy said. "They'll patrol the perimeter tonight and tomorrow."

Clara did not look convinced, but she had to trust the team; this new assembly was based on that. Trust the elements. Trust that they would do their job. Her mind wandered to three years ago, the day she met the Smith twins. Teresa and Anna were two of a kind indeed. Elizabeth had assigned them exclusively to Clara.

The two California girls had a way of linking to each other, in mind and soul. *A twin thing,* Clara had figured. They were both straight-A Catholic students. They fed off each other, pushing themselves to exceed their own limits. Clara recalled her parents' decision—a family of five, where the eldest brother had studied to become a Catholic priest. They felt good about having their children fight the battle against darkness on every front. They felt chosen as a whole family, but the girls were extremely good. She had been their first Guardian. The twins were exceptionally responsible, efficiently completing all tasks at hand. They were also her first line of defense as far as demon hunters went. They were to patrol St. Helena's hell spot for three years, and this would be their fifth heavy-duty confrontation. These girls were the only thing stopping them, but the forces of darkness would die in their attempt to open the gates of hell. That is why Clara had done her homework on this one. If the seal was opened, there was no telling how much time the world would have.

Alex's voice brought back Clara to reality. "Okay," Alex said. "We'll be on watch. Williams and Lewis will be overviewing the op monitors in two days."

Andy frowned. He knew well Clara referred to the senior Guardians and leaders of the organization. Even though they were wise, the older men found technology somewhat overwhelming. "What about you and Clara?" he asked over the camera microphone.

Alex was well aware of Andy's fears. "I am on the transport commission," Alex replied. "Have to pick up twenty teenage girls from the airport. But Clara will be here with the books and the intel. Don't worry." Andy looked a bit relieved. Having either Clara or Alex in these crucial moments was always good news. "Good luck," Alex said, as the color in Andy's face returned. "GAHQ out." The monitors turned off, and Alex turned toward Clara, who had a worried look on her face. "What is it?"

"I don't know," she replied, looking at the blank monitors. "Just anxious, I guess. Another attempt to open that hell spot."

Alex smiled. "Everything will be fine. We did our homework. Teresa and Anna are two of the best demon hunters on the planet, and they're in good hands; Joy is down there. It's just like you or Elizabeth being down there. They'll take care of things."

Clara sank her head onto Alex's chest when he hugged her, and she tried to push the bad sensations from her mind. The thought of Joy being down there helped her to be a little bit more at ease. She was a retired demon hunter, as badass as could be. Some argued that she was the mirror-opposite of Elizabeth. Even though she seemed like a loose cannon, she was a valuable asset.

Clara looked at Alex warmly, trying to put aside her anxiety. That feeling would return in two days. Hopefully, another mission would be completed.

St. Helena, California, U.S.: August 5, 3:30 p.m.

Daniel Anderson adjusted his eyeglasses and expensive dark suit as he got out of the luxury sedan the firm had arranged for his travels. He looked at the driver and signaled him to wait as he entered the run-down diner at the side of the road. The man opened the door and entered, then walked down to the back of the building and sat down in a booth. A waitress approached him and lazily offered a cup of coffee, which he accepted gladly. He inspected the deteriorated diner. It seemed that maybe thirty years ago, the place must have been a sweet family gathering spot. Today, not even the scum of the earth would enter it. The waitress brought him his cup of coffee when the door of the diner opened again, and a large man came in. He seemed six-foot-ten and looked like a linebacker from a football team. Behind him, a woman in her thirties entered the place and walked toward the booth where Daniel was.

"You're early," the woman said, as the big brute sat next to her and opposite to Daniel.

"Anticipating your move, my dear Athena," Daniel said in a bored tone. "Your client awaits news from you."

"My client can rest assured," Athena said, as her hand became a translucent shadow. It went right through the white cup of coffee. "The hell spot will be open like clockwork. And the information he is requesting will be delivered as arranged."

"He does not share your confidence," Daniel said while he drank his coffee, oblivious to the magic trick Athena created with her body. "The Guardians are all over the gate. Two demon hunters are guarding it."

"Is it he who doesn't trust what I can do," Athena asked playfully, "Or you?"

Daniel drank a bit of coffee, ignoring the question.

"You are worried only about your commission. Unlike you, I have skin in this game. The team guarding the hell spot will be no match for my vampires," Athena said. She then turned toward the large man at her side. "Draco will be there, leading the offensive while I open the gate. Just have my client ready."

Daniel Anderson sighed as he adjusted his glasses and his suit. "I know I am not intimidating, Athena. But your client is. And when he hears of your failure, he will hunt you down."

"I will not fail," Athena said as her hand again became translucent, only this time in the form of a dark shadow. It was as if she were made of smoke.

"Good," Daniel said, standing up and looking at Draco. "Don't send Draco in. Give him the day off. I will provide two elements for you to bash your way through."

"Why?" Athena asked.

"Just covering all the bases," Daniel said as he paid for his coffee and walked out. "Just covering all the bases."

CHAPTER IV

The Guardians' Castle, Ireland; August 5, 12:05 a.m.

IZZY OPENED THE DOOR of her bedroom and smiled as she took in the old familiarity of her room. It had been three months since she had been inside, but it looked as though she had never left. The bed was neatly made, with a stuffed blue teddy bear guarding her pillows. A small dresser with her makeup and other accessories was neat and tidy right next to her white closet door. The teen girl looked at her guitar and keyboard, both spotless against the wall where she had left them. She was home. On top of her bed lay her big backpack and her violin case. She sat on the bed while both her parents entered the room behind her.

"I've been cleaning your room every day," Elizabeth said, admiring her work. "Just reminded me of you. Dust fills the rooms here in no time."

"You cleaned my room?" Izzy asked incredulously while looking at her father, who leaned on the frame of the door. "The only moment you picked up a broom was to make a stake out of it," Izzy said while she unzipped her bag.

Elizabeth scoffed and looked to Sean for support. His devilish smile let her know she had none. "Well, I had it cleaned every day. Okay?"

"I've never seen you with a broom or a mop," Sean said, pretending to ponder looking at the ceiling. He loved pressing his wife's buttons.

"Too busy fighting the undead," Elizabeth retorted, punching him in the arm.

He blocked the punch and pulled her close to kiss her lips.

"Chill, parental units," Izzy said as she pulled out a small leather book and handed it to Sean. "I found this in Amsterdam. It has drawings similar to yours."

Sean opened the leather book, and his eyes widened. "These are my drawings. Where did you get this?"

"Found it in a demon's lair," Izzy said, remembering. "I heard a brothel demon was working its way through the red-light district, taking women as slaves. Put an end to that."

"You were in the red-light district?" Sean asked, not taking into consideration that his fifteen-year-old had been demon-hunting while doing so. His overprotective parental instinct turned on in a flash.

"Not in it, per se," Izzy dragged out. "More like in the vicinity of it."

"Young lady…" Sean was about to start a lecture when he felt Elizabeth's hand squeeze his arm.

"What your father is trying to say is that we'd hoped you wouldn't get into trouble while you were vacationing. After all, you were supposed to be relaxing," Elizabeth said.

"I'm a demon hunter," Izzy said, defending herself. "You would have done the same thing. It's part of who I am."

Sean was about to protest, but Elizabeth interrupted him. "Yes. We just want you to be extra careful. We all know what goes bump in the night, and we don't want you taking unnecessary risks."

Izzy shrugged and continued looking inside her bag, pulling out a necklace. "I was trained by the best. This is for you, Mom."

Elizabeth took it in her hands and examined. "Izzy... It's gorgeous. Unlike the mystical necklaces your father gives me, I have outfits that go with this."

"Hey," Sean protested. "Your wedding ring and earrings went well together with the white dress."

Elizabeth smiled and looked at her love while she set the necklace around her neck. Sean gave her a soft smile, acknowledging he loved it. They were really in tune with each other, knowing what the other was thinking.

"The other trinkets for Alex and the rest, I'll hand out tomorrow," Izzy said, setting the bag on the floor. "I think I'll go to bed now. I saw a car come in just as I approached the castle. Are demon hunters arriving already?"

"Not that we know of," Elizabeth said, looking at Sean for confirmation. "I think this is the new Guardian Lewis told us about."

Sean nodded his head in agreement as he heard a soft wolf howl pierce the calm night. Sean's eyes lit up when he heard the sound. The brown-haired man turned toward Elizabeth, then Izzy, and then to the open window. He walked toward it and stuck his head out. The wolf howl continued from a distance. "Sounds like a werewolf."

"Or it could be a normal wolf," Elizabeth replied, rolling her eyes. She could not take the hunt from her man. You can take him out of the vampire world, but you couldn't take the demon instincts out of him.

"We should go out," Sean said, turning toward Elizabeth. "Make sure the grounds are secure."

Elizabeth looked at Izzy, who was playing with her cell phone. She seemed really interested in what she was doing, too much so to pay attention to what was happening. It was not fair for her daughter to hunt today. She would have her entire life for that. She had already killed two vampires anyway. "All right," Elizabeth said. "This is not what I look forward to when you say date night. Let's go."

Sean smiled and went to walk out the door when Izzy's voice pulled him back in. "Dad," he heard.

That word melted him since the day she uttered it for the first time. He looked back and saw his daughter still looking at her phone. That was one way he knew Izzy was okay while she was gone—the cell phone bill remained high.

"Check this picture out," she said, handing him the phone. "Saw that demon in Rome. Locals told me he was an old enemy of yours."

Elizabeth's body tensed. The idea of her daughter being near one of Sean's enemies sent a chill down her spine. She walked toward Sean and looked at the picture. It was a muscular, six-foot-five vampire dressed in a leather jacket. "He seems familiar," Elizabeth whispered, trying to remember the numerous foes she and her friends had encountered in the past.

Sean just stayed quiet, with a grim look at his face. "Could you send me this picture to my phone? Doesn't ring a bell to me."

Izzy looked at Elizabeth, and they both knew Sean was lying. He didn't want to worry them. But he would involve them eventually. "Okay," she said, sending the picture over the phone to her father and flopping on the bed. "Happy hunting." She then focused on her device while plugging in some headphones, and within seconds, music came on.

Sean walked out, with Elizabeth following, closing the door behind her. She caught up to Sean, ignoring the fact that Izzy had turned down the music as soon as they left, and opened the door just a bit so that her demon-hunter hearing could pick up the conversation. "You know you're a bad liar?" Elizabeth asked softly. "And you shared that body with a master of lies. Could any of those skills rub off on you?"

"I am not lying," Sean defended himself. His voice made Izzy smile. He was a lousy liar. Surprisingly, since the demon Ankrnot, who resided in Sean's body, was the lord of cheat and deceit. But her father was different. He was a man under the spell of his wife and only daughter.

"Out with it," Elizabeth demanded, crossing her arms.

"It's Nemo the destroyer," Sean said flatly, with a grim tone.

"P. Sherman, forty-two Wallaby Way, Sydney?" Elizabeth asked, smiling at the silly name of the villain, but the look on Sean's face meant *don't play dumb*, so she composed herself. She knew he'd gotten the reference. The movie *Finding Nemo* played all the time when Izzy was little. In fact, she had a clownfish but wanted to free it, so she flushed it down the toilet and then cried about it. Good times. "Yes, I've read about him," Elizabeth said. "He rides with the motorcycle vampire clan."

"He is the right hand of Dragnor," Sean said, turning toward Elizabeth. "I knew we should have taken care of them before. This is a problem of the past and is not supposed to be happening now. Nemo being in Europe can only mean that clan is in Europe. And where they ride, there is always trouble."

"And we'll deal with it," Elizabeth said, holding his hand. "Like all the other times that trouble has reared its ugly head. We have been there to decapitate it."

Sean looked at the ceiling, trying to hide what he felt. All he wanted was to protect his family. Being human had its downside; he did not have his full demon powers. The man was still strong but mortal. Nemo was vicious and insane—a dangerous combination. He had seen first-hand what he was capable of. But that information was not shareable, not to his wife. "Okay. Let's go hunt."

Izzy watched her parents walk away. The young demon hunter slowly closed the door and looked at her phone. Elsa still had not viewed her messages. An icy cold feeling in her stomach made her shiver. She dialed her friend's number, only to go right to voicemail. It seemed that the cell was turned off. She then tried calling her home. No answer. Izzy tried to calm down. She just got home, and maybe Elsa was busy with her parents. She would call when she had a chance.

Izzy headed toward her violin case opening it, revealing a gorgeous brown violin. The brown-haired girl grabbed the instrument and tuned it while she looked outside the window. Both her parents jogged out into the night hunting for the undead. The teenager smiled as she saw them; they looked awesome going on patrol together. She fumbled with the strings a bit more before stepping out through the window and standing on the ledge. Izzy jumped up hard, grabbing the edge of the roof with her free hand. She flipped over and landed on the top of the castle, right over her room. The girl sat on the ledge as she watched her parents runoff in the distance. Placing the violin under her chin, the teen played a soft tune to calm herself down. The young girl closed her eyes, and the memories of her entire vacation flooded back to her mind: the newfound friends and the new demons she had identified, the fights and adventures she and Elsa had endured. A small smile crossed her face, thinking of her parents' reactions if they knew what the two young girls had been up to.

Izzy breathed slowly while the music played. The image of a black and white solitary wolf centered in her mind as the tune of her violin intensified. She played the instrument with passion as the wolf strolled alongside in her mind. She opened her eyes and looked down, then smiled as she saw the same black and white wolf wandering right below her. She signaled with her head, and the wolf ran around the castle. Izzy played the instrument again. This time, a softer tune flowed through the air. As she played, she felt a warm breath at the side of her ear. She stopped playing and turned around, seeing the black and white wolf right there with her. She knelt and hugged him, rubbing the soft and black and white fur. "What took you so long?" she asked.

The wolf yawned lazily, sticking out its tongue and licking its lips.

"You hungry?" Izzy asked.

The wolf walked around her, rubbing its nose around her jeans.

"Hold on," she said, pulling a plastic bag out of her pocket. She had raided the fridge before going to her room so she would be ready; inside was a piece of raw meat. Extending her hand, she put it in the wolf's mouth.

The wild animal ate it rapidly.

"I'm here for you, Aidan," she said as she rubbed the animal's head. "I will protect you as you protect me."

The wolf sat down and started howling as Izzy sat back on the ledge and focused on her music. The howling and the violin soon became one sound in the night.

Izzy breathed hard in the thick air. The sun was out, and no clouds were in sight in the middle of the clear blue sky. She looked around the central garden and saw around fifteen girls wearing all white, training in all different sorts of disciplines.

A group of girls was staking wooden dummies on her left, while another group was decapitating them on her right. Their minds screamed at her, all sorts of emotions being flung at her from every angle. The girls appeared to be from every corner of the planet representing different nationalities. Some seemed to be talking to each other, but the sea of emotion drowned out any logical thought. "This is pointless," she said out loud.

A soft voice echoed in the wind. It was sweet but urgent; it sounded like a plea, but Izzy could not make out what the voice said. She could barely make out her name. The young demon hunter kept on walking, noticing her aunt Clara, sitting on a bench while she read out loud to Alex, who was sitting cross-legged at her feet.

"... The wolf ate the grandmother... and waited for Little Red Riding Hood to arrive..." Clara looked up from reading.

"Don't stop now," Alex protested, not noticing Izzy behind him.

"I love that story," Izzy said, somewhat confused. "My version has a happier ending, though."

Alex laughed. "There's no happy version," he said. "It's all about loss and despair, and kids not doing what they're told."

Izzy was surprised at Alex's reaction. Clara shrugged and continued reading, in a distorted and muffled voice drowned out by the harsh wind that blew from the side. Izzy knew well that this was not Clara. In her heart, she knew it was only a projection of her aunt.

Izzy continued to walk through the gardens and saw two older girls with light blonde hair and bright blue eyes. They were twins, sparring with each other.

"Just a few more days," one said to the other while she dodged a blow. The first girl wore a gray Notre Dame sweatshirt while her sister wore a simple white top and black sweatpants.

"How do you think it will be?" the one with the white top asked.

"Don't know," her sister replied. "And I don't care. All I heard is that it's a beautiful thing."

"Elizabeth knows," replied the girl with the white top.

"*Elizabeth knows what?*" *Izzy interrupted. The conversation was so out of place, but she needed to understand.*

"*It's Elizabeth's daughter,*" *said the girl wearing the Notre Dame sweatshirt, feeling Izzy's presence but unable to see her.* "*She's trying to understand.*"

"*Too young to understand?*" *her twin said, ignoring Izzy completely.* "*Elizabeth understood at her age.*"

"*She should read about her mother,*" *the first twin said.* "*The answers are always in books.*"

Izzy shook her head and continued walking. She saw two girls dressed in red. They're demon hunters, *Izzy thought to herself.* They're my age.

"*Izzy,*" *one red-headed girl called out. There seemed to be two memories that swirled around the young girl. One was made of light, the other of pure darkness.*

"*Why are we here?*" *the second one asked. Her voice was drowned out by flames that overwhelmed her body. The girl seemed to be immune to the fire, though, as if she controlled it.*

Izzy was about to respond when she saw a large shadow looming behind the two demon hunters. The shadows seemed to be hugging them from behind, almost choking them. "*Look out!*" *Izzy exclaimed, pointing at the danger.*

Both demon hunters returned the stare and pointed at something behind Isabella. "*Elsa needs us!*" *they exclaimed.*

Izzy turned around and saw Elsa's pale body floating in the air. A dark shadow engulfed the young demon hunter. "*Elsa!*" *Izzy screamed.*

"*Help me, Izzy,*" *Elsa said weakly.* "*I need you!*"

"*Something is coming for us,*" *the redhead said as she ran toward the other group of demon hunters. She was trying to warn them, but the sea of emotions and ideas was too much. It was like screaming amongst a crowd.*

Izzy turned around and felt a black shadow running after her in the opposite direction. The girl ran out of the castle, into the green parries outside of it. The teen looked back and saw the shadow gaining on her, so she turned toward her oak tree. I'll be safe there, she thought to herself.

When she got to the oak tree, the shadow was gone. She turned to her front and saw both of her parents—her mother was in tears, and her father's face was pale. They were looking at a curly, golden-haired girl in front of them. The back of the girl was facing Izzy.

"I didn't know!" Elizabeth sobbed, pleading, not noticing Izzy. Her attention was focused entirely on the curly-haired girl in front of her.

"We wouldn't have let this happen," Sean said, his voice almost breaking.

The blonde girl pulled out two swords, one in each hand. She stabbed both Elizabeth and Sean in the chest to Izzy's horror.

"Noooooo!" Izzy screamed, trying to move, but paralysis held her body captive. She looked at the girl who had murdered her parents with pure hatred and rage. Tears streamed down her face.

The killer turned around, and Izzy gasped. She was staring back at a reflection of herself. The differences lay in the killer's long, curly, dirty blonde hair and her eyes—bloodshot red. The savage ghost girl bled from her eyes as she slowly walked up to Izzy.

Izzy felt a shadow grab her from behind and choke her. She tried to struggle, but her strength was gone.

"You are responsible for this," the blonde Izzy said, pointing at Elizabeth's and Sean's dead bodies. Her voice was distorted, almost lost, and foreign. "You have everything I ever wanted. And now I take what you value most. Feel what I feel. Destroy your heart. Destroy your spirit. You're nothing…" She caressed Izzy's cheek. "You're air… Like me." The other Izzy plunged the cold steel into Izzy's chest. Instead of blood, energy flowed from the wound.

Izzy screamed as she woke up. She grabbed the golden cross

that hung from her neck and looked around. She was in her room—it had been a terrible nightmare. She put her face in her hands and whispered a prayer in Latin. *"Áve María, grátia pléna, Dóminus técum. Benedícta tū in muliéribus, et benedíctus frúctus véntris túi, Iésus. Sáncta María, Máter Déi, óra pro nóbis peccatóribus, nunc et in hóra mórtis nóstrae. Ámen."* She could feel sweat covering her body and she could not stop trembling.

Izzy got up and changed her clothes, feeling spaced out; she barely said hello to anybody who greeted her in the hall. Their voices sounded with echoes. She seemed to be in a state between the real world and the dream world. The echoes of the other demon hunters still lingered in her mind as she acknowledged the older guardians in the castle. She simply nodded at her parents as they instructed her to go to the Jeep outside since they were going out. Without a word, she walked to the entrance and climbed into the Jeep. Her mind drifted from the physical world to the abstract, only feeling her parents board the vehicle joining her. Izzy's eyes soon closed.

Izzy stood up and walked down the long hall of the castle. Her parents' room was just a few doors down. She felt like a little girl now, but she just needed to hug her parents. She opened their door and peeked in. "Mom? Dad?" When she was younger, she remembered crawling in their bed and feeling protected. She walked toward their bed and got under the covers between her mother and father. She heard her dad grunt as he moved to the side, making room for Izzy. "I had a bad dream," Izzy said, almost in tears.

"What was the dream?" Izzy heard her mom ask from above.

"I dreamt I killed you," Izzy said, hugging her mom.

"That's some dream," she heard her mom say. "Don't you think so, honey?"

"Yeah," Sean said, turning toward her daughter. "What would be worse? What you dreamt of, or what you are feeling right now?"

The question confused Izzy as she looked up and saw her parent's faces for the first time. Both Elizabeth and Sean had demonic features; they both had fangs drenched in blood and drool. Izzy screamed as both her parents bit her from either side. Izzy screamed, loud and hard as the sound of her flesh being torn apart reached her ears.

Sean hit the brakes, hearing his daughter's screams. He got out of the Jeep and opened the back door of the vehicle, where Izzy had been sleeping. The brown haired-man hugged his daughter tight. "Izzy!" he called, trying to wake her up. "It's a bad dream!"

Izzy woke up and smelled her father's cologne. She could feel his heartbeat as she pressed her ears into his chest. He was alive. Izzy sobbed, hugging her father tightly, fully awake now and comforted by her dad

Sean pulled Izzy from the car and stood her up. "You fell asleep." Sean looked desperate, looking for answers. He looked at his wife, who also shared a worried look from the passenger seat.

Elizabeth handed Sean a bottle of water and watched helplessly as Sean tried to console Izzy. Elizabeth remembered having those nightmares when she was Izzy's age—they'd felt vividly real. She also remembered keeping her mouth shut when her mother asked what they were about. Izzy did not have to go through this process alone. Her parents were trained to help her. Still, it felt terrible not being able to help when her child needed it the most. *This is Parenting for Demon-Hunters one-oh-one*, Elizabeth thought to herself.

CHAPTER V

The Guardians' Castle, Ireland; August 6, 7:30 a.m.

JOHN SIMMONS LOOKED AT himself in the mirror. His brown hair was still wet from the cold shower he had taken. His eyes looked tired. The jet lag was killing him, but he couldn't sleep all night. He hadn't been able to sleep well for the past three years, but he knew how to hide that fact well. His parents were none the wiser, nor was the rest of the Guardians' council.

He got out of the bathroom and opened his suitcase, which he hadn't opened since he arrived. A small black and white picture was the first thing he looked at. He grabbed the portrait and admired the dark-haired girl with glasses on it. His heart wept at the memory as he closed his eyes, knowing full well his soul was trapped in the past. He could still hear her last words in his mind.

"You have to let me go, John," the voice echoed. *"There's no other way."*

He stored the picture and took out some dry clothes. The weather was perfect for a day out on the field, but he was here to work, and the confinements of a library and old books would be his sanctuary.

The young man dressed and reflected on the knowledge that he stored in his mind. A knock on the door brought him back to reality. He opened the door to his room and saw an older, beautiful, black-haired woman.

"Good morning, John," the woman said while extending her hand. "Clara Somiere. I will be your guide during these two weeks."

"Nice to meet you," John said.

"Ready to start your day?" Clara asked.

"Yes," John said. "Let's go."

As both walked down the halls of the castle, Clara broke the ice. "You have no idea what you're doing here, do you?"

John gave a sheepish smile. "Is it that obvious? One moment I am in Canada, finishing up on some documentation, and all of a sudden, I get a call to fly here to Ireland."

"Happens to all of us," Clara said. "It's the nature of the demon-hunter business."

"You'll enlighten me, then?" John asked. "Why am I here?"

"For some time," Clara started, "Williams has been tasked in writing the last twenty years concerning the Guardians' historical records, as well as the tales of the Demon Hunters."

"Why would he do that?" John asked. "Each Guardian keeps records of demon hunter activity. Isn't that enough?"

Clara smiled softly. "The records are all documented from the perspective of the Guardian and his or her respective demon hunter. The bond between them is much too great. Sometimes lines are blurred between facts and feelings."

"The Guardians get emotionally involved with the demon hunter," he concluded.

"Sometimes in something innocent, such as in a maternal or paternal way," Clara said. "Other times, it gets much murkier than that."

"So Williams wants me to go through all the records of the last twenty years and help draw an objective picture of what's happened?" John asked.

"He said you were smart," she said with a smile as they headed toward the main library. "There is also another thing."

John stopped and looked at her. "Apocalyps?"

Clara looked at John and shrugged. "You are the expert on the matter," she said. "No other Guardian has compiled all the knowledge there is to that. And Apocalyps is part of this assembly's history."

John sighed and continued to walk beside Clara. His purpose was becoming more evident. It was the knowledge he possessed the assembly craved.

Both Guardians continued to walk until they reached the library. John gasped when he saw the number of books inside the large two-story room. It was shelf upon shelf of literature on everything.

"This is unreal," John said.

"The Gathering starts tomorrow," Clara said. "All the staff will be focused on that exclusively."

"Including me?" he asked.

"You are part of the team now, John," she said. "You wouldn't be here if you weren't."

"How many demon hunters are coming for the gathering?" John asked.

"Twenty confirmed," Clara said, guiding John to a corner of the library. "This will be your workstation. I've gathered the first two years in all of these records."

John nodded as someone entered the library. He saw a tall, well built, dark-skinned man, most likely in his early thirties.

"That's Thomas Brent," Clara said as the older man approached both of them. "He's a weapons expert, and a Guardian as well." As the man came closer, Clara noticed he had a few folders in his hands. "Hey, Brent. This is John Simmons, our new Guardian."

"Nice to meet you," Brent said, shaking John's hand. "Heard you're quite the prodigy."

"That's highly exaggerated," John said. "I just read a lot."

Brent smiled as he showed the folders to Clara. "Thought you might want to read these."

"Excellent," Clara said as she took the folders from Brent's hand.

"We have twenty girls coming soon," Brent explained to John. "We arrange groups based on their files. These two files were missing from the list."

"They were not missing," Clara clarified. "The Senior Guardians were updating them."

"Yes," Brent said, smiling. "Williams gave them to me a few minutes ago. He said that they were ready."

Clara frowned and opened the file. She and Alex were in charge of logistics and accommodations, and they needed all twenty dossiers. For months now, Alex had been working with eighteen records only. Clara sat down on one of the library chairs as she read the first file. It belonged to Grace Wu, the demon hunter coming from Hawaii. "Have you read these?" Clara asked Brent.

"Had to," Brent replied. "Needed to arrange weapons accordingly."

Clara shook her head as she noticed the first file was not like the others. Grace Wu was of Chinese descent, living in Hawaii. Her Guardian took care of her. Her parents knew of her demon hunter lineage; they had taken extreme measures in Grace's training to make her a perfect demon-hunting machine. Then Clara saw why Williams had kept the file. "Williams knows the Guardian. Mashahiro Nagayama. They went to school together."

Clara wondered a bit about the old times when Williams meddled with the black arts. From the looks of it, Grace's Guardian had trained his demon hunter in that area. The girl was gifted with knowledge in certain magic spells and potions; it was rare to see that in a demon hunter at that age. Grace Wu was exceptionally gifted.

"This one is Nicole Rogers," Brent said, giving out the second dossier. "Likes to be called Nikki for short. An army brat, from the looks of it. Father is a colonel in the United States Air force. Her brother is in the Air Force as well. Their connection to the Guardians is General Grant."

"Let me see that," Clara said as she took the folder from Brent's hand. The name Derek Grant struck a chord with Clara. He was one of the good guys. This demon hunter was one to keep an eye on. Grant's recommendations were always diamonds in the rough, and there were few the General would stick his neck out for.

"Satisfied?" Brent asked, requesting the files back.

"Yes," Clara replied, standing up. "Have the rooms prepared accordingly. Let's regroup after breakfast."

The Guardians Castle Main Grounds, Ireland; August 6, 8:00 a.m.

The Guardians' main property was vast, about fifteen square miles, with the castle in the middle of the property. Sean loved every part of it—it had several hills and a small dark forest; it also had a cliff that had a spectacular view of the enormous Atlantic Ocean. That is where the ex-demon had taken his family. With Izzy, he had planted several trees around the property. One was near the Atlantic cliff, as he liked to refer to the place. A lonely tree just fifty feet away from a one-hundred-foot drop into the rocky and icy Atlantic water.

He looked at the scene and sucked it all in. He loved the fresh air. He loved that today was a rare sunny day in the usually cloudy Ireland. Looking at the blank canvas in front of him, he drew the scene with his charcoal. Sean looked near the tree behind him and saw his wife laying out a large sheet at the base of the tree.

The blonde demon hunter extended it, neatly covering the short grass. She then walked over to the Jeep and picked up two heavy picnic baskets. She set them on the white sheet and pulled out fruit and bread, then pulled out a bottle of wine and two wine glasses. Elizabeth walked over to Sean as she handed him the bottle.

Sean smiled and looked into her deep green eyes as he opened the bottle. Fate had been kind to him. He had married the love of his life, and they had a wonderful daughter. Sean poured wine into the glasses Elizabeth held and looked over to his daughter, who had her earphones on and was tuning her violin. She seemed submerged in her world. Sean took a sip of his wine, while Elizabeth turned her eyes toward Izzy.

"Do you think she's all right?" Elizabeth asked. "That dream really shook her up."

Sean smiled and looked at Elizabeth. "It was just a bad dream. We've had bad dreams often enough, remember?"

Izzy removed the earphones from her ears and played a soft tune on her violin.

Elizabeth and Sean looked at each other as they heard the sad notes coming from the instrument. They knew that sound well—they were the notes from an old opera. It was a love theme, slow at first, high pitched but gentle. Sean and Elizabeth were very in tune with the musical composition. It was the music Izzy played when she needed comfort in times of trial and sorrow. Elizabeth walked up to her daughter while Sean began drawing. Listening carefully to his girls talk, amazed at how much they looked like each other.

"Hey," Elizabeth said, sitting next to her daughter and softly rubbing her daughter's shoulder. "Want to talk about it?"

Izzy stopped playing and looked at her mother. Her eyes were red from crying.

Elizabeth knew well that the nightmare had shaken her to the core. The fear in her daughter's face brought so many memories.

"It was so real," Izzy said, trying as hard as she could not let her voice break, but it did anyway.

Elizabeth nodded and hugged her daughter. "It was just a dream," she lied.

Izzy looked at her mom, incredulously. "Really? You know exactly how demon-hunter dreaming works."

"Point taken," Elizabeth admitted. "Please tell me what you dreamt about. I wasn't there."

Izzy looked at her father, who was painting. The moment their eyes met, Sean hid behind his canvas, pretending to draw. "It was the hunter-gathering," Izzy started. "All the girls who are coming were linked. Some knew each other; four of them talked with me. Elsa spoke to me—she was in some sort of trouble. Then I saw you and Dad crying, pleading with a reflection of me. You died at my hand. Then I was with you in bed, and both of you turned to vampires and sucked me dry."

Elizabeth nodded as Izzy tried to describe the dream's details. Hunter nightmares were always vague; she remembered that. But some ideas were concrete. Whatever was happening involved other demon hunters, especially the twenty who would start arriving tomorrow.

"Nightmares are usually composed of our worst fears," Elizabeth said, channeling Williams the best possible way she could.

"Elsa is in trouble," Izzy said as she looked at the grass. "I haven't been able to contact her or her parents. Something terrible has happened. She's calling for me."

Elizabeth tried to keep her composure at the news. She looked back at Sean, who pulled out his cell phone and started dialing. She then turned back toward Izzy, who was looking at her.

"Mom," Izzys said, her voice cracking. "I am scared."

"Scared of what?" her mother asked, concerned. She was one-hundred percent sure she already knew the answer, but she needed for Izzy to say it out loud—get it out in the open.

"Everything," Izzy said. "Elsa is in trouble, and I can't do anything but tell you. Something big is coming our way, and I don't know what it is. What if I crumble just when things go from bad to worse? I feel that I can't deal. I feel like the whole world is on my shoulders."

Elizabeth looked at her daughter and hugged her, conscious of the burden she carried. Elizabeth had experienced that long and knew this issue would come up. It couldn't be easy, being the daughter of the demon hunter everyone looks up to, especially if you look like her. Questions would arise. *Is she as strong? Can she live up to the legend?*

"You're strong," Elizabeth reassured her. "You have the heart and will to carry the responsibility that comes with the calling."

"I just feel paralyzed. I feel this overwhelming sensation. I feel that I need to be somebody else," Izzy said, wiping the tears from her eyes.

"You'll be Izzy," Elizabeth said as she rested her back along the tree. "A demon hunter that is part of something greater. You will find the strength to do what is needed. Play something for me?"

Izzy smiled as she looked at her mother. She placed the violin under her chin and played again.

Elizabeth looked at Sean, who returned a worrying look as he shook his head. She then turned her eyes toward the tree above her, deducing what Sean knew. Elsa and her parents were missing.

A small gust of wind moved the branches to the side. Her daughter's music brought a strange sense of calm, causing her mind to wander to that fateful day.

Elizabeth stood up on wobbly knees, bent inward, trying to sustain the weight of her body. She cradled her broken left arm with her right hand. The unstoppable weapon, Apocalyps, which had ended the fight, lay at her feet. She felt the warm crimson liquid as it streamed down the side of her face and watched as it stained her white blouse. Her body could not take any more punishment. She looked to her side and saw Sean groan, straining to get back up. His body had also been badly battered. They hoped it would not come to this, but it did.

Elizabeth looked at her best friend, Kaela Kaplan. Her red hair was gone, and her skin had turned pale, black veins snaking down her face. Her body glowed with a red light, displaying the evil power she channelized—the forbidden power she had sworn not to use.

Before Kaela stood Daristos, Hell's most powerful general. His broken gray muscular body gashed from head to toe from the damage Apocalyps had caused. Dark black liquid streamed from every open wound. "You will not send me back to hell, witch!" the red-eyed demon screamed, trying to move. But the dark magic held him in place, and his weakened body could not muster the power needed. "You will condemn yourself with me."

"So be it!" Kaela shouted back, her voice deep and distorted, as blue light mixed with red hit Daristos in the chest.

The demon screamed in pain while Elizabeth watched,

paralyzed at the power. Sean and Elizabeth had battled Daristos to the last drop of blood, but Kaela's powerful magic was the only thing that could send him and his minions back to hell. And the witch was succeeding.

A red-and-blue portal opened behind Daristos. He screamed as his body tore apart, and the hellish dimension sucked him back in, disintegrating as he plunged into oblivion. The portal closed, and only ash remained where the powerful monster had stood.

Elizabeth looked at Kaela.

Her best friend fell to her knees, struggling to control the dark magic inside.

Elizabeth hobbled toward her and squeaked, "Kae. Kae, you gotta fight this."

"I can't," Kaela responded as she grunted in pain. "The magic is too powerful. Darkness is overwhelming."

Elizabeth closed in and tried to hug her with her good arm, but Kaela pushed her away.

"Don't touch me," Kaela said, as her voice distorted again, a mixture of darkness and light, unrecognizable. "The evil power might spread."

A blue light appeared before them, and a humanoid, blue-skinned white-eyed being appeared before them.

Elizabeth recognized him immediately as someone representing The Higher Power, the mighty and all-knowing beings who forged time and life, those who were there in the beginning.

The creature looked at her and said. "Thank you, champion. You have defeated Daristos." The messenger walked across the observation deck of the Empire State Building and surveyed the devastation Daristos had caused to the city, taking in the pain, death, and suffering. "Terrible loss."

The way he said it made Elizabeth's blood boil. It is as if mere insects had died in the demon's rampage across the city, *she* thought. "Sounds great, when you're comfortable looking down from whatever nest you come from."

The messenger glared at her and extended his hand. A blinding pain surged through Elizabeth's gut, making her scream and crumple down to her knees.

"Elizabeth!" she heard Sean scream as he stood up.

The blue-skinned humanoid used his other hand to grab Sean with an invisible force. Sean screamed in agony as his beaten body was being manipulated. The messenger put Elizabeth and Sean together, then looked at them with disgust. "Lesser beings," he said with contempt. "You dare question fate?"

Elizabeth looked up, in pain. "Just when you stand around doing nothing, while your peons do their dirty work." She smiled as she said this, knowing she would regret it. Pain surged through her body, making her gasp in agony.

The messenger looked at Kaela, who was trying to focus her dark magic; sending Daristos to hell had drained her. "The demon hunter and the demon," the blue-skinned humanoid said as he walked toward Kaela while leaving Elizabeth and Sean in destructive anguish. "A tale of legend in this world." The messenger knelt, looking at Kaela's face. "But you, my dear… You are what we need in higher plains."

"What do you want?" Kaela asked weakly.

The messenger stood up and looked at all three mortals. "The natural balance is in disarray. You have access to power beyond this world. You do not belong here."

"You can't take her from us!" Elizabeth wheezed out, finding strength from nothing, as she battled the invisible force and prepared her body for another major battle.

The messenger looked at Elizabeth, somewhat marveled. "You are a persistent champion. But this is not your concern. The witch knew the consequences if she tapped into this power."

Elizabeth tried to move, but an invisible force did not allow her to.

The white-eyed humanoid looked at her. "Still, we cannot take someone from this plane without altering the balance." It walked up to Sean and lifted him. "There is no action without reaction."

Elizabeth struggled, to no avail. "What are you talking about?"

"You refused to tell the love of your life of that day?" the being asked. "Must have been a burden."

"Sean," Elizabeth asked. "What is he talking about?"

"We could only remove that fateful day," it said, lowering Sean. "But balance dictated that we needed to take care of the consequences of that day. Now we must bring balance again."

The being walked up to Kaela, who was standing up. Her red hair was back.

"Elizabeth," Kaela said sadly, "It's okay. I knew this would happen. It was my choice."

"Kae... " Elizabeth started.

A blue light emerged, sucking both Kaela and the messenger back—then they were gone.

Elizabeth looked at the empty space that now reflected the state of her heart. She turned toward Sean, who was standing up and looked at him. A mixture of rage and sadness overcame her entire being as the blonde looked at her beaten lover. "Do you know something I don't?" she asked through her clenched teeth.

"I can explain," Sean started as he stood up.

A sweet, young voice broke their conversation. "Mommy?"

CHAPTER VI

Ennis Cathedral, Ireland; August 7, 7:15 a.m.

IZZY KNEELED, LOOKING AT the wooden floor of the Ennis Parish Confessional. She could hear Father Gabriel's steady breath on the other side. "Bless me, Father, for I've sinned. It's been three months since my last confession."

Father Gabriel listened carefully as the young girl opened her heart to him.

"I'm lying to my mother. Well... not lying. More like hiding the truth from her."

"A truth by omission is still a lie," Father Gabriel said. "Go on, my child."

"I can't seem to speak the truth around her," she continued. "She wants the best for me, but as I get more into her line of work, the less I seem to trust her with my personal feelings about it, the less I trust the Guardians."

"Go on," Father Gabriel said, as he continued to pass the prayer rope through his hands.

"I feel this immense pressure," Izzy said, getting a little anxious as she spoke. "It's like I have to be as good as, or better than she is, yet I can't open my mouth and tell her how I feel. I just feel emotionally stomped. Then again, it doesn't help that she becomes this entirely different person when she is in her demon-hunter zone."

"As the gathering approaches, you've realized more of the truth," Father Gabriel said. "Don't fight the reality that surrounds you. Embrace it. Cherish it. Your mother is a great warrior for good. You can't run from it. You tried, and it didn't work. The time has come for you to face this. Don't be afraid to do so."

"What if I don't live up to the expectations?" she asked. "What if I fail? What if I am not strong enough?"

"The only person putting up expectations is yourself," Father Gabriel said, smiling a little. "No one else has expectations of you. Not your parents, not your friends, not even God. If you fail, you will learn to get back up again and move forward. Life works like this. We stumble and fall. But we learn, and we get back up. And those who love us will be there in the thick and thin."

"What about what I feel toward my mom? I feel I can get along with her so well when she's just my mom."

"Be free with her. People tend to surprise us in more ways than one can imagine. Learn to trust her. She's gone through this path already."

Izzy nodded as she bowed her head and listened to the priest's prayer in Latin, receiving the absolution. She then stepped out of the confessional, seeing the tall priest stare down on her.

He was six-foot-two, with dark black hair and intense brown eyes. He didn't look over thirty years old, but his eyes screamed *ancient* to her. "Good to have you back, child," the priest said, handing Izzy a leather bag. "How was the trip?"

"It was fun," she said, opening the leather bag. It was full of stakes and bottles of Holy Water, all freshly blessed.

"Glad to hear that. Did you find what you were looking for?"

"More or less," Izzy replied, as the priest escorted her toward the entrance of the parish. "Battling the undead cramped my style of sightseeing."

"It happens when we have a calling to greatness," Gabriel said with a laugh.

"Thanks again for the goods," Izzy said, referring to the bag as she walked out of the parish toward the large bus waiting outside.

"Isabella," Father Gabriel called out. "Learn from your mom. Learn to trust her. She knows exactly what you're going through."

Izzy nodded back at the priest as she boarded the parked bus. She saw Alex had dozed off over the driver's wheel. "Vampires! Vampires!"

Alex jumped from his seat and looked around, startled. Then he saw Izzy's mischievous grin. He was not impressed. "One day, a horde will come and kidnap you for an unholy sacrifice."

Alex closed the bus door as she sat down and said, "Been there and done that."

Minutes later, Alex steered the large black bus through the M18 motorway toward Shannon Airport. He loved driving the massive vehicle—one of many things he had learned while being part of the new assembly. He looked in the rearview mirror and only saw Izzy with her headphones plugged into her ears, in the seat right behind him.

The girl seemed lost in her thoughts and music.

"You know," Alex started, "I remember a long time ago, in a world without technology, we had these things called conversations. It was where two people opened their mouths, and sound came out of them."

Izzy turned toward the older guardian and smiled when she got up and stood behind him. They were reaching Shannon Airport. "This is going to be a long two weeks."

"Excited?" Alex asked, searching for a parking spot for the large vehicle.

"Eh," Izzy scoffed and grabbed her backpack and violin case, leaving the priest's leather bag of goodies under the chair. This morning before they left the castle, she had cleaned her bag and filled it with fresh clothes. She wanted to appear as one of the girls as much as possible.

The doors of the bus opened, and they both left. Alex opened the belly of the bus and pulled out two large signs. They both read "GA Convention" in bold black letters. Flights would be arriving soon, so Alex placed one of the signs against a stone pillar while he walked toward the arrivals gate and stood there with the second one.

Izzy smiled at the productivity of the man. He was there to perform a task, and he was going to carry it out. Izzy grasped the backpack and walked into the arrivals area, toward one of the seats, and sat down. She looked at the people coming and going. Most were flight attendants and airport personnel, but soon it would be filled with tourists. Izzy pulled out her cell phone. She frowned, as there had been no activity from Elsa or her family. She was now officially worried. It had been more than forty-eight hours with no contact.

She pulled out her violin and played a soft melodic song. She would never admit it, but playing the violin was her self-defense mechanism. It brought down the angst. Her father joked that she started playing before she could walk. She was born with her mother's strength, but her father's artistic sensibility—it was in her genes. As the bow made its way across the strings, Izzy's senses awoke. She had her eyes closed, but was well aware of her surroundings. She could feel the energy of all that moved, even the strength of the demon hunters that were arriving. They were close now.

The Guardians' Castle Main Control Room, Ireland; August 7, 8:00 a.m.

Elizabeth held her warm cup of tea, looking at the nine forty-two-inch screens in front of her. Sean was at her side, with a grim look on his face. Full focus was now on the St. Helena hell spot.

It was 1:00 am right now in California; soon it would begin.

Elizabeth looked closely at the drone camera that moved around the cave.

Joy was right at the stone gate, crossbow and sword ready. The camera then pointed at Andy, who was on his tablet computer, making sure communications stayed online. The camera finally focused at the entrance of the cave. It took time for it to adjust, with the industrial lights installed.

Elizabeth noted that Anna Smith stood right beside the entrance. She looked gorgeous in her black leather jacket and jeans with a white blouse. She stood armed with a longsword and a few wooden stakes wrapped around her waist with her blonde hair tied in a ponytail. *One of the best*, Elizabeth thought to herself, confident about sending the right girls to this mission. Still, she couldn't shake the emptiness present in the bottom of her stomach.

Elizabeth looked at the control helm at her side and saw Clara on the keyboard, with Williams at her side, books open and ready. Next to Williams was the fifty-year-old senior Guardian Lewis. Dressed in black slacks and a light brown turtleneck sweater, he had not stopped monitoring his cell phone since he entered the control room. Elizabeth and Lewis rarely saw eye to eye in guiding and nurturing the demon hunters. While Elizabeth saw them as innocent girls with a gift, Lewis saw them as weapons against the undead. Him being a close friend to Sean and Williams was the only reason Elizabeth had relented in giving the man a position in the current leadership structure of the Guardians.

Elizabeth shook those thoughts away and tried to focus on the current operation in California. Alex and Izzy were off at the airport, picking up the demon hunters who would be arriving that very day. Brent was setting up the classes and leading the security of the perimeter. These operations were when Elizabeth felt the loss of her best friend the most. The absence of Kaela Kaplan was ever-present on her team and in her heart. She knew she was here in spirit, but sometimes she just missed speaking to her best friend. The memory of her sacrifice was a wound that would never heal.

Lewis' voice brought Elizabeth's attention back to reality. "Something's wrong."

"What is it?" Elizabeth asked.

"We've lost contact with both our Guardian and the demon hunter in Austria."

Williams frowned at the news. The current system obligated Guardians to report periodically, every forty-eight hours. When one failed to do so, Lewis got a notification. A Guardian not contacting the headquarters meant the line was silent.

Sean opened his phone and called his friend's number. "Izzy mentioned it to us yesterday. Their phone has been disconnected."

Anna's voice brought the team back to their current situation. "No activity in the front," Anna said through the intercom in her ear while looking at the camera knowing full well, the Guardians were on the other side. "Teresa, any visual contact?"

"Negative," Teresa replied through the radio. Her voice sounded distorted by static from the frequency. "I'm about one hundred yards from the entrance. No contact."

Anna turned her attention back to the woods outside and waited. *It would be a long morning,* she thought to herself, hearing Joy's zippo lighter behind her. She turned her head, seeing her black-haired Guardian light up a cigarette. The seasoned demon hunter and Guardian looked battle prepared and badass, with her crossbow and a short sword on the side. Her pale skin only had a dash of red on her lips. Other than that, the brunette wore all black for the battle. Her crossbow was a custom fabrication, air-pressure-based one of a kind, and designed specifically for these types of incursions.

"Contact! Contact! Contact!" Anna heard her sister's voice through her ear. Her sister's presence in her mind activated her hunter reflexes. She turned her attention back to the entrance as her body pumped adrenaline to her muscles. She felt her sister's adrenaline, as well as Teresa's accelerated heartbeat; she was running back toward the cave. Anna glimpsed back at Andy, who hid behind two large yellow crates. Joy loaded her crossbow and aimed at the entrance.

Teresa ran through the cave and stood next to her sister. Her blonde hair streamed down her face. She used her hands to move it away from her eyes as she caught her breath and pulled out her longsword from her back. "Twenty vampires and demons are heading this way," she informed the group and HQ back in Ireland, looking at the camera. "They are heading right toward the cave. They also have some large demon with wings—almost seven feet high."

"Sounds like a hell gargoyle," Clara said through the intercom. "It preys on fear. Don't fear it, and you can defeat it."

Anna looked at Joy. "Ready that crossbow!"

Joy took a step forward toward the entrance of the cave. "Time to get dirty." She saw the line of vampires start running up the cave. Her team had the high ground.

"Fire at will!" Anna ordered.

Joy pressed the trigger, and arrows spurted out of the contraption. The projectiles hit their marks, and vampires started turning to dust, but they still kept coming up. Ana and Teresa stepped outside, with swords in hand on each side. They twirled the deadly blades, hitting the soft spot between the head and torso. Dust and heads fell at their sides, while Joy covered them with arrows from behind. Vampires were falling, and the demon hunters were winning. Teresa and Anna looked at each other and smiled.

"Another day at the park," Anna said, punching a vampire back to strike him with her sword a second later.

"Looking slow, Sis," she said as she flipped to the side, kicking a vampire down.

The number of vampires was diminishing when a loud growl echoed in the night. The twin demon hunters saw a seven-foot beast stand up and extend its wings. It jumped from the ground and flew above them.

"Incoming from above!" Anna screamed at Joy. The senior demon hunter reloaded her crossbow and fired at the flying demon. The arrows stuck in its body, but it did not stop.

The creature growled and flew down at breakneck speed.

Joy readied herself as the demon's body smashed across her torso, pushing her inside the cave. Joy and the beast flew to the back of the wall, cracking the rock. She grunted in pain as she hit the demon across its backside, trying to pry him off.

The beast shook the blows off, countering with a vicious headbutt to the demon hunter. The attack only served to enrage the black-haired Guardian further as she started to wrestle the beast.

Elizabeth and Sean tensed when they saw the hell gargoyle in the cave. The defense was cracking. They had to take out the demons before they activated the door, yet none said anything.

Elizabeth grasped her cup of tea. Any more pressure and she would break it. *They will pull it off,* the blonde thought to herself as the blonde saw the gargoyle manhandle Joy like she was a ragdoll. Being almost as old as her, she continued putting her body on the line. Even though Joy was reaching forty, she was one of the strongest demon hunters on the planet, and it showed, as Elizabeth watched through the monitor the black-haired guardian push back the gargoyle.

"She's got this," Sean mumbled under his breath.

Elizabeth tried to smile but couldn't. She looked at Clara, who remained focused on the screen. It took all the discipline in the world not to speak and only watch. One wrong command and it could distract the team in action. They had to wait and observe.

Back in California, Anna and Teresa finished off the rest of the vampires when they heard a massive growl from the front. They saw a giant, brown-skinned muscular troll running toward them. They tried to move out of its path, but the six-foot-nine beast smacked the twins to the side barging right into the cave just as Joy floored the gargoyle. She caught the troll's tackle by full force.

"Defense has fallen," Andy whispered through his intercom. "Two large demons have breached the perimeter."

"Brute force is the only way for those two," Clara said as she read a note from Williams. "Soft spots are the neck and heart area."

"Easier said than done, squirt," Joy heaved, slashing at the troll's chest with her sword. The beast screamed in pain and slashed back at Joy, with his claws across her belly. Blood erupted from the wound, but it only angered the woman even more than she already was. She fought the animal back, screaming loud and hard to try and intimidate it.

Teresa and Anna shook off the cobwebs from the troll's attack, both standing up and running back into the cave. They turned around and saw two bald red-skinned demons run inside with them, swords in hand. Teresa and Anna, now weaponless, battled them back. A dark shadow passed right through them.

Anna noted it and pushed back the demon she was fighting. "Dark Shadow has entered the perimeter. Going for the portal." She tried to reach the shadow, but out of nowhere, a fist from the darkness smashed into her jaw. Grunting in pain, she staggered back, immediately feeling dizzy. This demon hit hard. She felt another punch hit her in the chest, and a third in her lower back. She screamed in agony.

Teresa grabbed the sword from the demon she fought, swiftly decapitating it. She then flung the blade toward the second demon; it struck in the center of its chest. The creature fell to the ground. Teresa then saw fists pummeling her sister from a dark mist that surrounded her. She could see Anna throwing punches but hitting nothing but air. "Dark Shadow has Anna!" she screamed through her intercom. Her guts twisted in pain, seeing her twin sister helpless in a fight.

"Luminescent spell!" Clara barked back.

Teresa's magical training took the wheel now as she pulled ingredients from her jacket pocket. "*Luceat lux vestra,*" she said in Latin, throwing the elements on the ground. A blinding light formed, temporarily rendering her sightless. When she opened her eyes, she saw Anna fall to her knees in pain, holding her side as the dark shadow materialized in the corporeal form of a young black-haired woman dressed in purple.

The dark demon screamed as a result of the spell.

Teresa jumped and kicked the demon back, then lifted the woman and smashed her fist with all her might.

Joy grunted as the troll sunk his fist in her belly. The older demon hunter spat out blood due to the blow. The metallic taste in her mouth gave her an adrenaline boost; she smiled and battled through the agony, then jumped and grabbed the troll by the head, snapping its neck. She then proceeded to walk toward the gargoyle, who was getting up. She kicked at its back, but the demon seemed made of stone. It briefly reminded her of fighting her strongest foes.

The demon stood tall and extended its wings, looking massive grabbing Joy by the throat.

She gasped at the pressure, and an ounce of fear grew in the bottom of her heart. It was all the gargoyle needed, as the beast lifted the demon hunter over its head and smashed her hard against the floor of the cave. Joy screamed in pain as the creature lifted her back up and flung her across the cavern. Joy's head smashed against the stone wall and fell unconscious.

The beast then proceeded toward Teresa. She was busy beating Dark Shadow to a pulp when she felt a dark claw grabbed her from the scruff of her neck. The beast hit Teresa's face with its knee, causing her nose to bleed immediately. Her world spun from the savage blow; for a split second, she lost track of where she was. She saw her sisters and her big brother from when she was young—it was a single moment that her mind wandered. A stabbing sensation in her stomach brought her back to the present. The demon had pierced her with its claws, right in the center of her stomach. Blood poured from her mouth. She could feel her demon-hunter healing power feebly attempting to heal the damage, but the wound was too much.

Elizabeth's world seemed to move in slow motion as she watched on the screen. She did not feel the cup of tea slip from her hand and smash on to the floor. She did not hear Clara's scream in horror at the scene. She did not even hear Anna's cry as she saw her sister being stabbed right in the middle of her stomach. Time seemed to stop at that precise moment.

Anna screamed, pulling one of the large swords from the crates and slicing the beast's hand off. The monster bellowed in pain. Tears streamed down Anna's cheeks as she swung the deadly blade. The blade found its mark, right in the soft spot on the gargoyle's neck, slicing its head clean off. Anna dropped herself at Teresa's side, cradling her sister's limb body. "Titi, talk to me." The young eighteen-year-old grimaced at the wound, trying to keep the blood in, but there was no hope in her mind or her heart.

A dark red light emerged from the portal. Dark Shadow laughed maniacally as the door to hell opened. The demon turned her face toward the camera, as black shadows emerged from the open mystical gateway and exited the cave. "You've failed!"

Anna slowly dropped Teresa's body on the ground and flung her sword at the shadowy demon that had opened the hell spot. The energy from the portal blended with the blade.

Dark Shadow screamed in pain as the power and steel pierced its chest and blended her with the doorway itself, bringing her to her knees. Blood came from its eyes and nose. "I'm not going alone!" Dark Shadow said through the torturous pain, pointing at Anna, who was back cradling Teresa in her arms. She fired a purple bolt of lightning; the energy, combined with the doorway light, struck Anna and Teresa.

Anna screamed as the energy hit her. She grabbed her sister, trying to protect her from the blast. The purple light flashed, popping the emergency lights inside the cave, bringing total darkness. Then the noise stopped.

"Anna!" Clara screamed through the intercom. The images she had seen would be burned in her brain until the grave took her. "Anna! Teresa!"

Only silence.

Everyone held their breath, waiting. A soft humming of the emergency generator echoed in the darkness... followed by a soft groan. A flashlight turned on.

"Clara," Andy called weakly. "Can you read me?"

"Andy!" Clara exclaimed, her face stained with tears. "Turn the lights back on!"

Andy obeyed as he tried to make some connections. Three industrial lamps came back to life, illuminating the cave. The hell spot was sealed and intact, the doorway blocked by solid rock. Andy strolled to where he had last seen Teresa and Anna.

"My God!" Lewis whispered at the horrific scene.

The twins were petrified in stone, as a beautiful, large gray statue of Anna hugging her sister—their last pose together.

"Noooo!" Clara screamed, falling off her chair. Her demon hunters were gone.

Williams hugged her on the floor as Lewis looked on, speechless at the horrific scene. He turned toward Elizabeth, who was also on the floor weeping, Sean hugging her.

CHAPTER VII

Shannon Airport, Ireland; August 7, 9:30 a.m.

IZZY HAD BEEN PLAYING for a few hours now, softly and to herself. But her instincts were alert. She had seen several demon hunters walk around the terminal; they had arrived as soon as the first flight touched down, and she had noticed they were from all over the world. They represented countries like Russia, Romania, Nigeria, Brazil, and Argentina. All were fifteen or sixteen years old. Some came alone, like the demon hunters from Mexico, Australia, and China. Others seemed to know each other, like the trio that came from Russia. After picking up their luggage, they walked directly to where Alex waited. They all seemed like regular girls, full of joy and excitement because of their trip. They all shared a common bond, though—all of them had the gift to fight the forces of darkness.

Izzy stood and packed up her violin when a commotion caught her attention.

She saw a young red-headed girl picking herself up after crashing into a pilot and a copilot. "I'm so sorry," the girl stammered as she tried to help the pilots up from the floor.

When she did, she miscalculated her strength and the weight of the pilot. Next thing she knew, the pilot stood up, and she lost her balance, tripping over her military duffle bag, which was on the floor behind her. A small scream escaped her lips as she fell flat on her back, bringing the pilot on top of her. "Sorry," she apologized again.

The pilot just grumbled while he stood up and tipped his hat, walking away from the human accident.

Izzy took note as the girl stood up and removed her broken glasses, frowning at them as she inspected the damage. She wore green cargo pants, large black boots, and a white sweatshirt. The redhead then turned toward Izzy, and their eyes met. The redhead had deep blue eyes.

Izzy smiled and walked up to her, extending her hand. "Hi. I am Izzy O'Brien. Are you here for the Guardians' gathering?"

The redhead smiled warmly, shaking Izzy's hand. "Nikki Rogers. You're a demon hunter, too, I suppose."

"We stick out like a sore thumb," Izzy said, shrugging with a friendly smile

"Do you know where we're supposed to go?" Nikki asked.

"Yes," Izzy replied, pointing to the exit. "Our ride is over there."

Nikki walked with Izzy at her side. "So. Are you from around here?"

"Yes," Izzy replied. "I live here with my parents. Is it obvious?"

"Just a feeling," Nikki replied. "You have a big Claddagh ring and Celtic cross sticker on your violin case."

"Oh," Izzy said, smiling a little. "Yeah. I've lived in Ireland for almost all my life. I'm American, as well as my mom. My dad is Irish, though. We've traveled around the world, but we have a permanent residence here. What about you? What's your story?"

"My mom died a long time ago," Nikki said once they reached the exit. "It's just my dad and my brother and me. They're both in the Air Force, so I've been forced to move around a lot."

Both girls reached the bus and saw Alex putting bags in the belly of the bus while other demon hunters climbed in. It looked almost like a school trip for junior high.

"No more bags, please," Alex pleaded. "No more bags."

"Sorry," Nikki said as she placed her bag with the rest. "Nikki Rogers and Izzy O'Brien reporting."

Izzy smiled at Nikki's Air Force talk. She was indeed a military brat.

"Get on the bus," Alex playfully scolded as he marked his checklist and continued packing the bags.

When both Nikki and Izzy entered the bus, they saw about a dozen demon hunters already inside, talking among themselves about vampires, demons, school, and relationships. Izzy and Nikki headed toward the back of the bus.

"How long have you been playing the violin?" Nikki asked Izzy.

Izzy looked at her case and realized she was still attached to it. "Oh. Ever since I was little. My dad says I was born with a musical instinct."

"Cool," Nikki said. "Have you ever needed to smash it and pull a stake to dust a vamp?"

Izzy turned the instrument around, revealing a stakeholder with a wooden stake attached. "Never needed to."

"Like your style," Nikki said, leaning back in her seat and looking at all the girls. "Always wanted to meet another demon hunter. Have you met others?"

"Yes," Izzy replied carefully, not wanting to give away that she knew both Joy and Elizabeth. "My best friend, Elsa, is from Austria. Her parents knew mine from a long time ago, and we just kind of grew up together. We're like sisters."

"That's awesome," Nikki said, pulling a picture from her back pocket and showed it to Izzy. "This's my family."

Izzy looked closely at the picture. They were two men with Nikki, clowning around near her. The resemblance was uncanny. It was funny how many parents were so supportive of their daughters in their calling to fight the forces of darkness. At least that is what her mother used to say. How different things would have been if her mother wasn't involved since the beginning.

Things have changed for the better with the new Guardians in charge, Izzy thought to herself as Nikki rambled on about her brother and father, the Air Force, and demon hunting.

The Guardians' Castle, Ireland; August 7, 10:30 a.m.

Elizabeth, Sean, Clara, Lewis, Williams, and Brent were all standing up around a circular table in the main conference room. Voices were raised—especially Williams, Lewis, and Sean.

Elizabeth heard a cross of ideas from all the men in the room while she looked at Clara, who looked glassy-eyed. The loss of both Anna and Teresa took an emotional toll on her. There were no words to describe the pain inside.

"We need to get our people down there!" Lewis exclaimed. "There is no word on how many demons escaped the hell spot before it was closed."

"I need people in Austria," Sean said. "We need to check on the Weissers."

"We cannot jump to conclusions," Williams said, trying to bring calmness to the conversation. When things went wrong in an operation, tempers flared, and the chances of making more mistakes were always there. They needed to calm down. Two demon hunters were dead, and a third was missing. But jumping into action did not help anyone now, especially with the best demon hunters heading toward them as they spoke.

"Millions are at stake if the hell spot is open!" Lewis exclaimed.

"You don't know that!" Sean retorted.

"Enough!" Elizabeth exclaimed. She needed to put order to this. "Anna and Teresa gave their lives to guard the hell spot. The hell spot is closed. Whatever came out will not hurt us immediately. It still needs to get its bearings. That gives us time."

Lewis shut up the moment Elizabeth spoke; she was the leader in this crusade. She and Sean knew very well how the forces of darkness operated. He was not going to contradict her. Not now. Not today.

"I want Joy back here as soon as possible," Elizabeth ordered. She saw Williams trying to protest, but she signaled for him to stop talking. "She's been through enough, seeing two demon hunters go down." She then looked at Sean. "Have your people in Europe check on the Weissers. But you stay here. I can't afford to lose you at this time for an investigation outside of the country. Not now."

Sean nodded, understanding what his wife meant. He dialed a number on his cell phone and stepped out of the meeting. He had a call to make.

Elizabeth then turned toward Clara, who was trying hard to keep it together. *She needed to,* Elizabeth thought to herself. "Clara, I need you to make the call."

Clara looked at her sister and nodded. She understood what the call was about. Still, Elizabeth felt the need to explain it to her.

"I need you to contact the Smiths and break the news to them about their daughters. I know you have the urge to go to St. Helena, but I need you here as well."

Clara nodded. She had recruited the Smith twins; the Smiths had entrusted their daughters to her. She had to be the one to break the news to them. "I'll contact their brother," Clara said, trying to hold back the tears. "He'll help me with the news."

Elizabeth walked over to her sister and hugged her.

Clara wiped the tears from her eyes and walked away.

Elizabeth turned toward the older Guardians. "We receive the girls today. We cancel the evening activities and start fresh in the morning. I want you to rank them all as soon as possible. Have Joy use one of the travel portals. I want her in the castle tonight."

With those words, she walked out onto the balcony before any of the Guardians had anything to retort. She looked at the sky; the gray clouds that covered Ireland were emerging. It promised to be a gloomy day. Tears ran down her cheeks. It was always a cloudy day when death visited her.

Shannon Airport, Ireland; August 7, 11:00 a.m.

Grace Wu turned down the volume of her iPhone as the heavy metal rock music blasted through. She slipped her pink Dolce and Gabbana polarized sunglasses over her forehead and watched as the other passengers of the first-class section left the plane. Her silky black hair streamed a little over her shoulders as the girl adjusted her pink designer scarf. She looked out her window and frowned at the weather. It was cloudy. She hated this weather, very different from her warm island of Hawaii. She sighed in boredom as she placed her phone in her purse and stood up.

One of the flight attendants awaited orders with her pink carry-on suitcase in hand. Grace indicated for him to follow her outside the aircraft, so she walked comfortably in her designer four-inch-heeled pink shoes through the Irish airport hall, with the flight attendant right behind her.

A throng of passengers walked and ran past her. The world around her seemed to move at twice the speed she was moving.

She smiled, knowing full well she was in control at the moment. She was in no rush. She made it to baggage claim, sitting down in one of the waiting-area chairs while she signaled the flight attendant to the rotating baggage carousel.

"If it is pink and expensive…" Grace said without looking at him, pulling out a compact mirror from her designer bag, "…then it's mine." The girl looked at her features and tried to smile at her reflection. Her dark eyes told a story that would be unbelievable to many.

She was a demon hunter, born and bred since birth. *"Trained to perfection,"* she recalled her father saying. Her parents took her calling as a matter of honor. Both her parents were immigrants from the Republic of China. Grace pondered at that memory for a moment, recalling old Chinese traditions her parents taught her. Her mother was a little more open-minded about her upbringing, but her father was all about eastern discipline. It was her destiny to walk that path for the honor of her family. Being an only child, Grace followed the rules to the fullest, and she was pampered exclusively as a reward. She smiled, knowing full well she was spoiled.

As a demon hunter, she had helped drive the forces of darkness away from Hawaii, all while being the proper lady she was supposed to be in the eyes of society. Her parents were pioneers in a software development company and had more money than they knew what to do with. That left lots of time to train and study. Her father always told her that if she was to do something, she had to be the best at it. If not, there was no point in it. Her Guardian followed her father's instructions to the fullest, pushing her body to its limits until she reached her full potential. She was perfect in every way, and Grace knew it.

"Miss Wu," the flight attendant called, breaking Grace's train of thought.

She looked up and saw that he had her three pink suitcases on a luggage trolley.

"Your luggage is ready," he said as he wiped the sweat from his forehead.

Grace smiled and pulled a five-hundred-euro bill from her purse. The flight attendant extended his hand to receive the tip when she pulled her hand away. "Where are my wooden chests?"

The flight attendant looked confused at the question. Grace stood up, bored by his incompetence. She pointed at the baggage carousel, where two wooden chests were the only pieces of luggage rotating. The flight attendant ran toward the wooden trunks and tried to lift one.

Grace smiled at the strain he put into raising the large box. It was heavy; it had special equipment her Guardian had sent back to Arthur Williams.

The flight attendant, who was assigned by the airline to help her, clumsily walked back with one of the large brown chests. He placed it near her luggage and went back for the second one.

Grace looked at the crate at her feet, and the thought of her parents crossed her mind; the chests were a gift from them. She remembered the day they gave them to her—she remembered it well because that was also the day her parents died. The image of that master vampire killing them was burned in her mind. The scene she recalled was always the same—a dark shadow biting her mother's neck while her father begged for mercy.

In Grace's imagination, she tackled the vampire and killed him. The reality of the matter was that she froze on the spot. The vampire escaped, leaving her alone with only the bodies of her parents at her feet. That was two years ago. From then on, Mai, her Guardian, had been her family, friend, and trainer. She never saw the vampire again. The memory of the perfect demon hunter, standing frozen in fear, haunted her dreams.

The voice of the flight attendant brought her back to reality.

"Is this all, Miss Wu?" he asked politely. He had stacked the crates under her pink luggage on the trolley. She was so immersed in her thoughts, she hadn't noticed.

"Yes, that's it," Grace said as she gave him the bill from her purse.

She saw, near the main exit, a tall man with a dark leather jacket and a light blue shirt. He had eyeglasses and had a sign in his hands which read, "*GA Convention.*"

"My ride is outside," Grace said, giving her best smile to the flight attendant and pulling another fifty. "Please help me with the bags."

"Yes, miss," the young flight attendant responded as he pushed the trolley.

Grace walked up to the man, who seemed in his late thirties. He looked as though he did not want to be there. She walked up to him and extended her hand. "Hi," she said. "I am Grace Wu."

"Alex Cooper," Alex replied, shaking the girl's hand and looking at her luggage. "I see you come prepared."

"Yes," Grace replied. "The crates have some things addressed to Mr. Williams, from my Guardian."

Alex nodded and guided the hunter outside the busy airport. Taxicabs and other vehicles were parked at the edge of the roadway.

Grace noticed, at the end of the line, a large blue bus. As she neared the large vehicle, she noticed several other demon hunters were already inside. Some were talking to each other. *Trying to make friends*, she thought to herself.

"I'll take care of the bags," Alex said as he put the luggage in the bottom compartment of the bus.

Grace got on the bus, and all the girls stopped talking, turning their eyes toward her. Grace was not intimidated by being the focus of attention; she was used to it. She looked at all of them, staring intensely. The dark-eyed girl could see most of them were her age. *Nothing out of the ordinary,* she thought to herself.

She then met two piercing green eyes at the end of the bus of a brown-haired girl wearing gray and white track pants and a gray hoodie. Her eyes were what caught Grace's attention. *This one has seen battle,* Grace thought to herself. *She has faced death.*

Grace walked through the bus, not paying attention to the other demon hunters, knowing full well all eyes were on her. The girl in the back returned the stare. As she approached, Grace noticed she was beautiful; her tracksuit hugged her figure well. Without saying anything, Grace sat down opposite the girl and put on her headphones, then looked at the window and pondered for a moment. *This is the demon hunter to beat,* Grace thought to herself.

Outside Town of St. Helena California, U.S.; August 7, 8:00 a.m.

Daniel Anderson looked at the cross-country road in front of him. He loved to ride along the back roads instead of the concrete freeway. It gave a sense of normalcy to his demon-infested life—the trees to the side, the clear sky above. The day was perfect.

"Is it day outside?" a demon sitting across from him in the limousine asked, with a deep scruffy voice.

Daniel looked at the demon. He was rugged and ancient; his hair was long and white, matching his mustache and beard. He had hooves for hands, and his medieval armor reflected damage by fire, spears, and blades. "Indeed it is," Daniel replied.

"Why is the sunlight not piercing through?" the demons asked while tapping on the glass.

"Special glass," Daniel said. "A lot has happened since your time."

"Is this the twenty-first century?" the demon asked. "Does not seem so different from my time."

Daniel smiled a little condescendingly. "I am sure you will spot certain differences."

"Are you responsible for bringing me back?" the demon asked, looking carefully at the human in front of him.

"In part, yes," Daniel said, playing it aloof. "But it's really a team effort."

The demon looked around the limo, disoriented and confused. "My weapons. My sword and shield. Where are they?"

"Your sword is in the back," Daniel calmly stated as he poured himself a glass of scotch. "Your shield is being recovered. It will soon join you. You need to trust us. Drink?"

The demon nodded and took the glass from the human's hand. Daniel poured another drink and toasted with it. "Welcome to a new world," he said, as the limo moved away from the hell spot.

CHAPTER VIII

Guardians Castle, Ireland; August 7, 3:00 p.m.

THE RIDE TO THE castle was a calm one. The demon hunters were talking, getting to know each other. Izzy found that it was easy to speak with Nicole; she seemed so relaxed and open-minded. Her dad seemed like a great guy, as well as her brother.

Out of the corner of her eye, Izzy caught a glimpse of Grace, the demon hunter from Hawaii. She had designer clothes and expensive accessories. The only thing they had shared during their trip were their names and where they came from. She kept very much to herself, almost snobby. She just focused on her cell and headphones.

Izzy continued her conversation as she noticed the Guardians' castle looming on the horizon. Some of the demon hunters stopped talking the moment the giant structure came to view. The fortress was magnificent in its grandeur. The gray and white stone made it seem as if it had come out from ancient medieval history. As the bus crossed the outer perimeter wall and headed toward the center building, all the girls noticed several men dressed in black and white waiting outside the front door. They were the different servants who worked in the building.

"How do the Guardians pay for all this?" Nikki wondered out loud.

Izzy shrugged as she felt the bus come to a full stop. She knew very well where the Guardians' income came from: hidden and forbidden treasure taken from vampires and demons around the world, gold and silver from the underworld—coveted treasures from the undead put to good use. The bus came to a stop, and Izzy recognized Lewis among the butlers.

His expression looked grim and tired. Beside him was Brent.

Where's Clara? Izzy thought to herself. It was the first time she would miss the arrival of the demon hunters. The bus came to a stop and all the girls disembarked. A small gust of wind caught them off guard as they jumped into the gravel driveway.

"Welcome to your Guardians' Castle," Lewis started. "My name is Lewis Powell. I am head Guardian, and it is an honor to meet you all. Please follow my associate Thomas Brent to the main conference room so we can begin."

Izzy felt something tug in her insides as she saw a confused look on Alex's face. Clara always welcomed the demon hunters and said the opening words. *Why was she not here to greet us?* Izzy thought to herself as Alex pulled Lewis away to talk with him. Alex knew enough to lure him away to a safe distance. Away from demon hunters' range of hearing.

Brent, in the meantime, guided the girls into the castle. The demon hunters were in awe as they walked through the halls of the Guardian stronghold. Weapons were mounted on the side walls, next to old oil paintings, portraits of past demon hunters and Guardians. Most of the art came with the castle, but some, Izzy knew, was her father's. Thomas Brent turned right and opened a wooden door, signaling for the girls to go inside. The conference room was large; brown wooden finishing adorned the cold stone walls. A large window gave a perfect view of the central garden of the castle. The wood and gray stone created a gorgeous contrast. Shields from ancient times adorned the upper walls. A name was under each shield. Several comfortable chairs were set around the room, all facing a small wooden stage where a table and a group of chairs were located. Behind those, a white screen was projecting.

"Welcome to Warrior Hall," Brent said with a smile, as the girls marveled at their surroundings.

Izzy frowned when she saw the back door of the room open.

Williams, Lewis, and her parents came in; their faces were grim. *Something is wrong*, Izzy thought to herself. *Clara not being present right now meant she is taking care of more important matters, and few things were more important than this.*

Izzy tried to focus on something else. She looked around her and took note of the demon hunters who were joining them. There were nineteen other girls, with her meeting most of them on the bus. The group consisted of the best demon hunters in the world. The appearances of each of the young women could have fooled anyone.

From the U.S., there were Nicole and Grace.

Mexico had sent their newest demon hunter, Anna Rodriguez, from what she had described on the ride over. Anna was the shortest of them all, very pretty with long brown hair and dark eyes, and seemed to be the youngest, just turning fifteen.

After Anna, Izzy had met Sofia Razuvaeva from Sweden, Louise DuMaine from France, and Andreia Popa from Transylvania. Izzy thought of them as the European girls. During her European tour with Elsa, she had heard about these girls, but she'd never had a chance to meet them.

Izzy turned behind her to see the Russian demon hunters. They were Arinka Anfalova from Moscow, Kristina Novtskaya from St. Petersburg, and Angelina Burmistrova from Yakutsk—two blondes and one brunette, all of them sixteen years old.

Then came the demon hunters from Africa. Eisha Aina from the Congo, Katia Daia Nour from Algeria, and Tansey Keswar from South Africa. The three got along very well. Both Eisha and Katia had dark skin and dark eyes; Eisha had short, curly hair, while Katia had long, silky black hair. Tansey was fair-skinned with light brown hair; she had a huge smile on her face that just charmed everyone she talked to.

Izzy turned her attention to her right and saw the demon hunters from Asia and Australia. There was the black-haired girl from Sydney, named Sophia Rose. She was very animated and perky. Then came Fei Luo from China, Chhavi Powel from India, and Ammarra Yanin from Indonesia. Ammarra was the oldest of them all, being seventeen years old. Izzy had heard from her mother that Ammarra had prevented a cataclysmic event the previous year in the South Pacific.

On the bus, Anna had sat alongside the demon hunters from South America: Almeida Sousa from Brazil, Selene Rossi from Argentina, and Valerie Dominguez from Colombia. All three girls were sixteen but very different. Almeida had dark curly hair and dark brown skin while Selene had long, curly black hair, and fair skin with freckles. Valerie was the tallest of the entire group, at five feet nine inches. She had long brown hair and fair skin with beautiful green eyes.

Izzy picked a chair in the middle of the large conference room and sat down; soon, most of the girls followed her example. She was surprised to see that Nicole sat right next to her, and gave her a friendly smile. Her red hair was now tied in a neat ponytail. Because her hair was pulled back, a small bruise was visible on the side of her face. Izzy could see it was healing quickly. Nicole grabbed her backpack and pulled out another pair of eyeglasses, purple-colored. Izzy noted that she must have a whole warehouse full of them, being a klutz and all. Nicole had been in Ireland for just half a day, and she had already broken her first pair. Izzy smiled back and curled back into her gray hoodie, hoping Nicole did not match her face with her mother's, who was now standing in the front of the room, along with Williams and Lewis.

The muffled whispers of the Guardians were not audible to the rest of the hunters, who were now filling up the empty seats.

Izzy took note as Grace sitting in front of all of them, right in the middle of the first row. Her dark eyes surveyed the girls behind her. Izzy had to give it to her—Grace was measuring them up.

Grace's black eyes met Izzy's green ones. Both girls remained focused, trying to read each other's intentions. Grace smiled as she turned back to the front of the class, looking at Elizabeth, Williams, and Lewis.

Izzy frowned. Grace knew. With one look, Grace knew Izzy was Elizabeth's daughter.

Lewis and Elizabeth sat down behind the long brown table, while Williams looked at all twenty demon hunters in the room. Izzy could see the older Guardian was beaming with pride, but his eyes held a hint of sadness that was not present a few hours ago. Something was definitely up.

"Welcome to the Guardians' headquarters," Williams said to the group of girls, snapping Izzy's mind back to reality. "As your respective Guardians may have informed you, you are the chosen few who will receive special training for your next assignments."

The girls paid close attention to the older man's words, but their focus was on Elizabeth. Until now, Elizabeth had existed only in books and in what the Guardians told them. For most of them, it was the first time they'd seen the demon hunter of legend.

Guardians scattered around the globe explained the gathering's purpose to their demon hunters, but Williams was responsible for going into details. Izzy had the privilege of having her parents be her Guardians. She wondered who else had that privilege.

"My name is Arthur Williams," Williams continued. "I am a senior Guardian, and head of the Guardians' Assembly. I have been working for the organization for twenty-five years." Williams then turned toward Lewis and Elizabeth. "Behind me is Lewis Powell. He is second-in-command of the assembly. He has been with us for almost eighteen years."

Williams beamed with pride as he looked at Elizabeth, who smiled back at him with a hint of sadness. He was proud as a father would be.

Izzy could not help but smile behind her gray hood, as Williams and Elizabeth looked at each other.

"Next to him is Elizabeth Somiere O'Brien, Senior Demon Hunter and head of the Demon Hunters Division."

The girls looked at Elizabeth in awe as she stood up, and Williams sat down.

Elizabeth walked among the girls and smiled at them, careful to stay clear of Izzy. As a mother and a demon hunter, she knew what her daughter was going through. But it was a necessary step. "When Williams says 'Senior Demon Hunter,' it makes me feel so old," Elizabeth joked, drawing a few smiles and giggles from the girls.

Izzy noted that Grace looked at Elizabeth with the same intensity as she did with her. *Is she measuring my mother?* Izzy thought to herself.

"Across the globe, there are ten highly active hell spots," Elizabeth continued, as Alex started a projection in front of her.

Brent turned off the lights and pulled the curtains of the large window. The projection showed one located in North America, one in Central America, one in South America, one in Europe, two in Africa, and the rest in Russia, Asia, and Australia. They were all well-distributed around the globe.

"The old assembly considered that just a few demon hunters were enough to battle the forces of darkness," Elizabeth continued. "Many lives were lost as a result. Today, over ten thousand young women walk the earth. We have a well-organized network of Guardians monitoring and training our girls, preparing them to fight the dark elements in their respective areas." Elizabeth walked to the front of the room and looked at all the girls. "Except you twenty. You've been chosen because you're above all of them. In training and demon hunting, all pale in comparison to you. You are the top two-tenths of a percent—the elite, the best of the best." Elizabeth paused as she let the idea sink in. "We'll make you even better. For the next two weeks, our team of Guardians and demon hunters will push you to your limits," Elizabeth warned as she turned toward Sean, Alex, Lewis, and Brent. "You will study hard, learning about new types of demons. And you will face your most profound fear."

Grace turned her attention toward Izzy with her dark eyes penetrating her green ones.

Is she daring me? Izzy thought to herself.

"Some of you..." Elizabeth continued, turning her attention toward Grace, "are asking yourself if you're the best in this room," Elizabeth stood before Grace. "Do you think you're the best in this room?"

"Yes," Grace said, without missing a beat.

Nicole giggled at the answer, which brought a smile to Izzy's face.

"That's tough talk, considering the company you're in,"

Elizabeth said with a sly smile, as she crouched and looked directly into Grace's dark eyes. "I love seeing that in a demon hunter."

Izzy noticed her mother was also measuring Grace. Sher had not missed a beat on her younger counterpart.

Elizabeth stood up and walked to the front of the room while Brent turned the lights back on. "Most of you have traveled a long way to be here. Get some rest and try to get used to the time difference. We'll start bright and early tomorrow. For now, Guardian Thomas Brent will guide you to your room. Dinner is in four hours. Hope to see you all there."

Elizabeth walked back to Williams and Lewis, while Thomas Brent took the helm.

"Okay, girls," the Guardian started. "Your bags are already in your rooms. If you have problems in your rooms, like hot water or doors not working, you come to me. If you have issues you think I can't deal with, then you talk to Clara Somiere. She's a great demon hunter."

"Where is this, Clara?" Angelina asked in her deep Russian accent.

"She's handling a small errand," Brent said. "I'm sure you'll see her later today. You can't miss her—a tall, black-haired woman with steely blue eyes."

Izzy lagged back, wanting to talk to her mom or someone about why Clara was not there, but Nikki pulled her arm, dragging her with the rest of the group.

"Come on, Izzy," Nikki said, pulling her new friend. "Want to find out if we have to bunk with the Hawaiian princess."

"I heard that," Grace replied, turning back toward both Nikki and Izzy.

"Well, I said it out loud," Nikki replied, playfully trying to get on Grace's nerves. The other girl was not biting, though. She had been cold and unresponsive ever since she got on the bus.

Izzy sighed and followed the group.

Brent distributed the demon hunters according to their arrival order.

Since Nikki and Izzy registered together, they bunked together. As they entered their room, Izzy noticed when Grace took note of where she and Nikki were staying.

"Inside your rooms, there is a map of the grounds and the castle," Brent said to the group. "You'll find our spacious gym and training area in the center garden. There are only three areas you can't access, and they're blocked for your protection. Those are the eastern forest, the castle cellar, and the west wing of the castle."

"What's in the west wing?" Nikki asked, smiling. "A giant furry beast guarding a rose?"

Some girls giggled at the comment, but Brent took a long pause and had a stern look on his face that made the young demon hunters tense up. "Those are our quarters," Brent said after a brief silence. He could have sworn they all let out a sigh of relief.

Izzy and Nikki entered their room. It was quite beautiful, just like everything else in the castle, with two beds, two closets, and one bathroom. The bathroom had a sweet floral scent. Izzy loved what the butlers had done with their accommodations; they were always neatly prepared. The wooden finishes of the walls matched what the castle already offered. The room was larger than her own, which was on the other side of the building.

"Do you mind if I take this one?" Nikki asked, pointing to the right-side bed.

Izzy shook her head as she set her backpack on her assigned bed. Her mind was only half there, wandering to what had happened in the morning operation. Something must have gone wrong. Things were out of place. Nikki's voice brought Izzy back to reality.

"So?" Nikki sat on the bed with her legs crossed. "What does it feel to be the daughter of the famous Elizabeth Somiere?"

Izzy twirled, looking at Nikki. She shouldn't have been shocked, but she was. The question was so blunt and out of thin air.

"Sorry," Nikki apologized. "I figured we should just acknowledge the elephant in the room."

"Acknowledge it, or kill it?" Izzy asked nervously while she unpacked her bag.

"It's okay if you don't want to talk about it," Nikki said, lying down on the comfortable bed. "I just think it's great for your mother to be a demon hunter. *The Demon Hunter*. She basically wrote the Demon Hunting manual. She knows exactly how you must feel in those tight situations. I find that cool."

"I get that a lot," Izzy said, softly returning her attention to her luggage. Father Gabriel's words from her earlier confession echoed in her mind.

"I wish my mom were still alive," Nikki said, pulling a stake from her bag. She twirled her weapon as she lay back down. "I could have someone to share with about all this vampire and demon killing."

Izzy turned around and looked at Nikki. "What happened to your mom?"

"Cancer," Nikki said, looking at the ceiling. "I was five."

"Sorry," Izzy said, feeling quite awkward. At first, she thought the idea of being Elizabeth's daughter would cause problems. But Nikki's story just made her feel a bit more grateful.

"It's okay," Nikki said, standing up. "Has your mom told you all those great apocalyptic stories?"

Izzy smiled, sensing some normalcy in the odd question.

"More than I can remember."

"Do tell," Nikki said, paying close attention.

"Why don't we head to the kitchen?" Izzy proposed. "Let's get something to eat, and I'll tell you all about it."

"Awesome," Nikki said, smiling at the idea of food and a story.

Both girls walked out of their room and started walking down the red-carpeted hall. "The first one she told me about was the battle with this Master Demon and her meeting my dad."

"Oh yeah," Nikki recollected from her readings. "She had moved recently to the California hell spot."

Izzy told the story, guiding her friend through the halls of the castle.

Nikki was so immersed in the story that she did not notice they were heading into the west wing of the castle.

Izzy lowered her voice as they neared Williams's study. Behind the closed wooden door, muffled voices came through. Izzy noticed the window above the door frame. It was open.

"Nikki," Izzy said, interrupting the story. "Something is happening right now. I need to find out what it is."

Nikki looked up at the window and shrugged. "Sure. Why not?" The response of the redhead surprised Izzy. Nikki giggled. "I'm an army brat. If I am not getting in trouble, there's something wrong with me."

Izzy smiled as Nikki stood to the side of the door. She climbed onto her friend's shoulders, and her demon-hunter hearing did the rest.

Still, Nikki moved right in front of the door while balancing Izzy on her shoulders.

Izzy could see her parents, Williams, Lewis, and Jasmine talking. The news she heard brought a shiver down her spine.

"Joy is at the portal," Sean said, referring to the dimensional gateway located in the northern parts of the woods. "She'll arrive this afternoon as planned."

"Good," Elizabeth said upon hearing the news. "Have Andy support Clara from our safe house. Also, have John and Jasmine provide support on this. I want daily reports on any activity down St. Helena. I don't want engagement. Just report back. Did you tell Alex about Teresa and Anna?"

"Yes," Lewis replied.

"How did he take it?" Elizabeth asked.

"Like any other Guardian getting news that his demon hunters got killed in action," Lewis replied with a little snark.

Elizabeth winced at the response, but that was it. Teresa and Anna weren't only Clara's hunters but Alex's, too. She turned toward Sean. "Any news from Austria?"

Sean shook his head. "They found the Weissers. They're dead."

Izzy let out a soft gasp hearing the news about Elsa's parents' as the memories from the past three months filled her mind. All the late-night hunting parties and dinners. All the ancient stories and folklore.

Elizabeth nodded, strolling toward the door while she listened to Williams. "Can we trust the information from Austria? What else do we know?"

"Vampires were responsible," Sean said, looking at Elizabeth, who stood next to the door. "Blood was drained dry—visible signs of a struggle. Elsa was taken and moved somewhere else. Our trackers are on it."

"Demon Hunter kidnapping," Elizabeth pondered a moment, looking at the Guardians and her husband. "Ideas?"

"A lot comes to mind," Lewis said, looking at the ceiling. "Human sacrifice, an act of revenge, blood alliances, etcetera."

"Demon Hunter blood is powerful," Sean said, trying to think like a master demon. "A demon hunter can be harvested to feed vampires on a nightly basis."

"Great theories," Elizabeth said and turned to Sean. "Some ideas are really dark and spooky. Harming a demon hunter is the fastest way to get the attention of the Guardians. Double the trackers and find where they could have taken Elsa. If she's still alive, her clock is ticking."

She then opened the door and saw Nikki, with Izzy standing on top of her shoulders. "How're you, girls?"

Nikki smiled nervously as her cheeks turned bright red, while Izzy came down, looking rather sheepish. The eyes of her parents and the Guardians focused on both teenagers.

Izzy opened her mouth, but Elizabeth was already shaking her head.

"Nikki, right?" Elizabeth asked politely.

"Yes, ma'am," Nikki said, composing herself and extending her hand. "It is an honor to meet you."

"May I ask what you're doing on this side of the castle?" Elizabeth asked, ignoring the younger hunter's futile attempt at flattery.

"We were looking for the kitchen," Nikki replied truthfully. "I needed a snack, and it's a long time before dinnertime, and..."

"The kitchen is beside the gym, on the other side of the castle," Elizabeth interrupted. Her commanding voice made Nikki shut her mouth immediately. "Go get the snack. My daughter will join you shortly." Elizabeth made sure the word daughter sounded louder than it should.

It got the job done, as Nikki looked apologetically at Izzy before walking back the direction Elizabeth pointed.

Izzy stepped into the room just as Williams, Lewis, and Jasmine exited by the side door. All who remained were Sean, Elizabeth, and Izzy. Izzy bit her lip nervously. It was not that she was never in trouble, but she knew her parents well. Trust was a big deal in the family. Breaking that bond brought a heavy burden on the person who broke it.

"What were you doing?" Elizabeth asked with a stern voice. She already knew the answer, but she wanted to give Izzy the chance to explain.

"I was worried," Izzy replied, as truthfully as possible. "I didn't see Clara at her usual position when we arrived. Something happened, right?"

"What happened does not concern you," Sean said, pausing a moment. "Not yet, anyway."

"I'm a demon hunter," Izzy protested. "I should always be in the loop."

"You're in no position to ask for anything," Elizabeth said while crossing her arms. "You are on a need-to-know basis. This is not your business to deal with. Do you understand?"

"Yes," Izzy whispered in a low voice while looking at the floor. Her mom's words stung her heart.

Sean looked at Elizabeth and just gave her a soft look.

Elizabeth took a deep breath before approaching her daughter. "Izzy."

Izzy turned toward her mother. Her eyes were red.

With all that was going on, Elizabeth had failed to realize that the news that Elsa's parents were dead was hitting hard on her daughter. "I'm sorry," Elizabeth said. Izzy remained silent as she looked into her mom's green eyes. "Have I ever lied to you?" Elizabeth asked softly. "Have I ever kept anything from you? Have I ever kept you in the dark?"

Izzy looked down at the floor again, knowing her mother was right. She was blunt and honest about everything.

Elizabeth walked closer toward her daughter and put her hand on her shoulder. "Elsa is missing. Her parents are dead, and we are doing what we can to find her. Let us handle it. If we need you, I will not think twice about calling you, okay?"

Izzy nodded as she tried to calm herself and wiped her eyes. "What about Clara?"

"An unknown demon killed Anna and Teresa in today's raid," Sean said.

Izzy's expression turned to horror. Two dead hunters and one missing were too much to handle.

"Clara is informing the parents and heading research operations on everything that is going on."

Izzy felt as if her heart was getting smashed with a hammer. She had asked to know what was going on and her parents had obliged, blunt and straightforward.

"We will inform the other demon hunters early in the morning tomorrow," Elizabeth said, adding more to the story. "Please let us handle this."

"Okay," Izzy said as she walked away.

"Izzy," Sean called. "Do you trust us?"

Izzy smiled sadly. "With my life." She stepped out of the room, swallowing hard as the memories of Elsa and her parents started to flood her mind again. Tears streamed down her eyes as she walked back to join the others.

Nikki entered the kitchen and looked around in awe. It was a marvelous stainless steel kitchen; several cooks moved inside like a synchronized swim team.

A waiter came up to her with a tray of peanut-butter-and-jelly sandwiches. They were neatly made and with the crust removed. "Sandwich, miss?" he asked in a very proper manner.

"Don't mind if I do," she replied, a broad smile on her face as she took a piece.

The waiter held up a tray of cold energy drinks in his other hand.

Nikki grabbed one and marveled at how coordinated the cooks and waiters were.

"They're not human," a British female voice said behind her.

Nikki turned around and saw a tall, dark-skinned woman with a clipboard in her hand. "Jasmine Taylor. Senior Guardian."

"Nikki Rogers," Nikki said, shaking the woman's hand. "What are they?"

"Servant Spirits," Jasmine said. "Servants, forever linked to the castle's service."

"They're ghosts?" Nikki asked as she touched one of the waiters. "I thought ghosts couldn't be physically touched."

Jasmine smiled. "These are a different type. They are here only to serve the needs of the castle. Cooking and cleaning for the guests."

"They're not dangerous?" Nikki asked.

Jasmine smiled. "They can't be. As long as there are guests in the castle, they will be here to serve."

Nikki smiled as Jasmine returned to her clipboard and walked toward the back of the kitchen. Nikki went in the opposite direction, stepping out from the kitchen and heading toward the indoor gym. She munched down her snack as she entered the large room. There was a lot of training equipment: blue mats, mounting horses, punching dummies, and a rack filled with all assortment of weapons. Nikki could see half a dozen demon hunters had found their way to the gym. They were in groups, trying out the equipment.

At the end of the room, a waiter stood still beside a table. Sandwiches and energy drinks were available to everyone.

Nikki walked toward the weapon racks and sifted through them. Long and short swords. Daggers and throwing knives. Battle-axes and broadswords. If you could imagine it, it was there. She then turned toward the center of the room and caught a glimpse of Grace sitting with her legs crossed on the floor. She was meditating. Nikki took the last bite of her sandwich and approached the Hawaiian demon hunter.

As Nikki grew closer, she felt a shiver down her spine. Not of fear, but of power—power to be reckoned with. She looked down at Grace, who still had her eyes closed.

The girl had changed out of her fashion designer clothes and was now in a gray Adidas tracksuit and Adidas trainers. "I can see you," Grace said, without opening her eyes. Her voice was calm and soothing. "You're a powerful demon hunter. At least more powerful than most here."

"Is it always about who is the strongest?" Nikki asked. She crossed her legs, sitting down across from her counterpart.

"Power is everything," Grace replied, again keeping her eyes closed. "Power over the forces of darkness. Having the strength to bind the darkness and keep it sealed."

"So, is that why you're here?" Nikki asked, tapping Grace's buttons. "To prove who's the best? To prove you are the most powerful?"

"Not to prove," Grace said, finally opening her dark eyes. "It has already been proven. I've come for my next assignment, and I plan to carry it out to perfection."

"Wow," Nikki said with a smile. "You truly believe there is no one better than you here?"

"The truth is a heavy burden," Grace said as she stood up. "I am better than Elizabeth herself, from what I've measured."

"What are we talking about?" Izzy asked, interrupting the conversation. Her voice was a little loud and got the attention of all the demon hunters in the room. The moment Izzy entered the room, she could feel the power between Grace and Nikki. They were two of a kind. But it was Grace's perfectionist attitude that got to her.

"Ah, yes," Grace said, referring to Izzy looking at her from head to toe, measuring her again. "Izzy O'Brien. The famous daughter of Elizabeth and Sean. Your reputation is well known. I've always wanted to know if I could take you. I'm confident I can."

"We're not here to fight each other," Izzy said nervously, noting that the other demon hunters were surrounding her. She could hear their whispers close to her ear.

Grace giggled. "Do you really believe that? We're here to see who's truly the best of all of us."

"That's not true," Izzy said. She not only tried to convince the other demon hunters but herself as well. "We're here to get hell spot assignments."

"Really?" Grace asked incredulously. "We travel all this way to Ireland for something that an email can solve? What do you think is the first thing we'll do tomorrow? Or haven't you read the program?"

Izzy frowned. She had gone over the program of the gathering with her mother. Tomorrow was the day that their skills were balanced out. The Guardians arranged a small sparring tournament to measure each hunter's ability. She had seen it for a couple of gatherings now. Still, Izzy remained silent.

Grace smiled with satisfaction. "Tomorrow, we'll confirm what everyone in this castle knows already. That I'm the best demon hunter here."

"That's great," Nikki said, trying to break the tense setting. "But will we have cupcakes? The Guardians' cupcakes are said to be legendary."

Izzy smiled at her redheaded friend only to walk out of the room with Nikki following. Izzy's mind spun with ideas. Did Grace know more than her about this gathering? *It's going to be a long two weeks,* she thought to herself.

CHAPTER IX

Underground, Town of York, Ireland; August 8, 3:00 a.m.

DANTE STOOD STILL, LOOKING at the underground town from his balcony home. His long, blond hair streamed down to just below his shoulders. His fierce blue eyes watched as several more vampires entered his domain; they all looked weary and beaten, most likely from the distance traveled. Most of them seemed to have not fed for some time. Others looked gaunt and weak, as though they'd fed off the blood of vermin and scum. The six-foot vampire felt a presence behind him. "Lucinda," he purred with a soft voice. "It has been a long time."

"Too long," the female vampire said. Her black heeled boots clicked on the marble floor. She stood next to Dante and looked out at the dark town.

Besides the murmuring of vampires, dripping moisture from the damp green walls echoed in the underground cave. Rats and other foul rodents were the only companions the vampires had with them in the vast underground tomb.

"More come every day," Lucinda said. "You've given them something they had long lost."

"What is that?" Dante asked.

"Hope," Lucinda said.

"A dead human word," Dante spat out as he walked back into his room.

"You deny the little ounces of humanity in you," Lucinda said. "But you don't realize that your quest to extend the vampire lineage is pushing you to the brink of love and care. Qualities that I had not seen in you before."

"I only care for what is rightfully ours," he said, looking at the ceiling. "The human race is not supposed to exist. This world should have been ruled by darkness long ago." Dante then turned toward Lucinda. "That is all that matters. Vampires and demons are meant to walk this land. And I intend to see this through."

"There is truth behind your words," Lucinda said. "But you still hide something from me. Why?"

"You know me too well," Dante said, turning back toward the balcony.

"You crave power. A hidden power that is known by a chosen few. Your mind is an open book to me, and you know it."

"Apocalyps," Dante whispered. Certain circles considered the mention of the forbidden weapon an act of heresy.

"Few know the true meaning of that word," Lucinda said.

"And the number will not grow," Dante said, turning back toward her.

"I see," Lucinda said, walking toward Dante's bed. "The quest is more important than any earthly and human pleasures." She slowly climbed onto the bed. Her leather clothing hugged her figure tightly.

Dante smiled at the black-haired beauty. "You entice me with the pleasures of the flesh."

There was a knock on the door and both vampires growled at the interruption.

The dark-haired Siegfried entered, noticing neither Lucinda's presence nor her anger. "The hell spot of St. Helena opened briefly," the vampire informed.

Dante smiled and forgot momentarily about the female vampire sprawled on his bed. "How long?"

"Long enough," Siegfried replied. "Our guest escaped, as well as a few Hillions."

"And the shield?" Dante asked anxiously at the response. "Did the shield get out?"

"It did," Siegfried said. "We expect our agents to make contact with us and request transport."

"Excellent," Dante said, looking at Lucinda again with lust in his eyes.

"Athena perished in the incursion," Siegfried continued. "She took two demon hunters with her."

Dante stopped approaching the bed and looked at Siegfried. "Did she now? St. Helena's demon hunters are dead?"

"Yes," Siegfried said, smiling himself.

Dante walked back toward the balcony. "St. Helena is your territory, Lucinda."

"Indeed," Lucinda said, smiling.

"Right now, the Guardians are scrambling like clockwork," Dante said, looking at the ceiling of the cave. "They will refresh the watch, relieving the current Guardian. With the gathering this week, they will wait before sending a new demon hunter to the scene."

"What do you need from me?" Lucinda asked.

"Right now, send messengers to your clan. Keep the Guardians' sight on that side of the globe. Keep them guessing."

"Unleash hell?" Lucinda asked with a devilish smile.

"Feed," Dante ordered. "With caution, but feed."

Lucinda pulled a cell phone out from her leather pants while Dante walked back to Siegfried. "If that is all, I wish not to be disturbed."

Siegfried took his first look at Lucinda since he entered the room and smiled. "More vampires are flocking toward here. But not all know the entrance."

Dante's smile grew wider. "Serve them to the demon hunters in the castle. After all… this is all a game for them, isn't it?"

Siegfried walked out of the room, closing the wooden door behind him. All he could hear was growling and scratching behind him. He walked toward the plaza and found fifty weakling vampires. "Spread out and feed. Exit through the cliff entrance. Feed on the village. Dusted before capture."

"Dusted before capture," they replied together.

"Go!" Siegfried ordered.

Guardians' Castle Main Headquarters, Ireland; August 8, 4:00 a.m.

Elizabeth woke up breathing hard; she felt her entire body covered in sweat. She looked to her side and saw Sean sleeping peacefully. Elizabeth stood up and looked at the bedroom clock on her night table. It was four a.m. The memory of the dream she had was vanishing fast. She grabbed a notepad and pen and wrote what she remembered before the thought disappeared entirely from her mind. Vampires… demons… Elsa… gargoyles. The memory was gone. Elizabeth shook her head and headed toward the bathroom, where she splashed water on her face and looked in the mirror. She did not look a day older than her early twenties, but she did not kid herself. She was older—much older. It was all in her eyes.

She slipped into a pair of gray pants, then put on a white t-shirt and track shoes. She walked out of her room, carefully closing the door behind her. As she strolled through the halls of the castle, she could feel the demon hunters and their energy. They were all resting. She could also feel one strong force coming from the gym. Elizabeth loved the secret mystical powers the demon hunters hid—the instant connection to others of her kind. The strongest emotions from love, hate, and anger were ever-present in her mind. As long as the demon hunter line stood, she would feel them.

A memory flashed in Elizabeth's mind. She stood still as she leaned for support on the side wall. She registered pain to her side as Elsa's memory pounded in her head. It stopped as soon as it started. Elizabeth frowned. Elsa was alive; she could feel her energy. She could also feel her fear, anguish, and helplessness. They needed to find Elsa, fast.

Elizabeth kept walking toward the gym, cursing herself for not having a better idea on how to find the girl. Williams and Lewis had tried asking for information on old contacts. They even recruited John to help with the investigation. No luck. Wherever Elsa was captive, a barrier was not allowing them to penetrate with their magics. Jasmine and Clara were going through the internet, trying to dig out information; Brent and Sean were bashing their Europe contacts. No sign of the missing hunter.

As Elizabeth entered the gym, she could feel the anger and hatred that provoked the energy she felt. It was Joy beating the living daylights out of a large punching bag. Her body glistened in sweat as she punched and kicked the defenseless sandbag. Elizabeth could feel Joy's powerful strikes almost rip the bag apart. "Mind if I join you?" Elizabeth asked.

Joy punched hard one last time and turned toward her sister. She nodded and continued hitting the bag, harder than before. "It's not my fault, you know," she said as she delivered a devastating punch to the bag.

"No one is saying it is," Elizabeth said, walking toward her, as Joy continued to bash the sack. Joy was obviously talking about Anna and Teresa. Death took a toll on any Guardian.

"We were there," Joy said, punching hard. "We knew what we knew. We had your support from here and kept the gate closed. We had all the information and were on the spot. Dead on target."

"I know," Elizabeth said as she reached the bag.

"The girls died in battle," Joy said, kicking hard. "There's not a more glorious way to go."

"Yes," Elizabeth said sadly.

"I taught them everything they needed for this," Joy said. "They were ready. They had this in the bag." Elizabeth nodded as she listened to Joy's voice. The blonde looked at the bag, and she knew it was about to give. Joy gave one final punch, her fist smashing into the bag. The impact tore the leather fabric, spilling the bag's contents all over the floor. "I did everything that I was supposed to do. We followed the rules in every way. The way we had done it every single time."

"Yes," Elizabeth said, almost tearing up.

"I know it is not my fault," Joy said as she ripped her grappling gloves from her hands while she looked at the ceiling. She then turned toward Elizabeth. Joy's eyes were red from the tears she had shed. "Then why do I feel like I am dead inside?" As the words left her mouth, her voice cracked.

Elizabeth stood next to Joy and hugged her demon hunter sister. Ever since they met, their relationship was that of rival siblings. Both had faced overwhelming odds, but Joy was the one who had tasted the dark side and returned.

Joy sobbed on Elizabeth's shoulder. There were no words to say. Ever since closing the California hell spot long ago, Joy had become a pivotal part of the new Guardians. She had provided more on-hand training than any other demon hunter/Guardian. She had trained more than two dozen demon hunters. Over the past years, hunters and Guardians had come and gone, but Joy would have never admitted that both Teresa and Anna were her favorites. And Elizabeth knew this. Now, the twins were gone, and only their memory remained, along with the pain.

After a few minutes, Joy got a hold of herself and cleaned the mess she made. "I haven't even buried two girls, and you've already got me here, convincing me to train some more."

Elizabeth caught the ironic tone and resentment in Joy's comment. "I can't do this without you."

"I've heard that one before, Liz," Joy said as she picked up the destroyed bag and put it to the side.

"We're legends to these girls," Elizabeth said. "They look up to us. We've gone through things that they're going through right now, maybe far worse. They need our help."

Joy sighed. "I know. I'm staying. I just wanted to give you a hard time about it." With those words, she walked away.

Guardians' Castle Main Headquarters, Ireland; August 8, 6:30 a.m.

The morning started with a sad note for the gathering. As soon as the girls were up in their training attire, the Guardians gathered them for an announcement. Williams delivered the somber news concerning the death of the two demon hunters who guarded the St. Helena hell spot—devastating news to the group of teenagers since they were supposed to relieve Anna and Teresa from their duties in the fall. Three years was the standard length of time a demon hunter served on an active hell spot. Anna and Teresa's service was over, ready to go to college when tragedy struck.

Izzy observed the Guardians and the demon hunters closely.

Alex looked somber as Williams delivered the news to the new group. Since he was responsible for the California incursion, he was fighting not to show his anger and resentment in all of this. He should've been there. But the hunter-gathering got in the way.

Elizabeth's daughter then turned toward Joy, who now joined the instructor team working with them. Her eyes were bloodshot from lack of sleep, but she was standing like a true warrior, waiting for the next challenge.

Izzy turned her attention towards Williams. His words were short and straightforward—no emotion, no anger, or sadness—just words. Izzy looked down and shook her head disapprovingly. For far too long, she had heard about the detachment the old Guardians had with the demon hunters back in the day. And here, the new Guardians were committing the same mistakes. She had opened her mouth about this to her mom and dad, but they brushed her off, saying she was too young to understand certain things.

Finally, Izzy looked at the new Guardian, John. There hadn't been time to be adequately introduced last night over dinner. He'd just shown up next to Clara and Brent. She'd heard a comment from her father that it was the new guy who had come to help Williams. The news of two demon hunters dying in the line of battle didn't seem to rattle the young man, Izzy noticed. But he wasn't indifferent, either. From a distance, Izzy could see in his eyes. The young Guardian had looked death in the eye.

After delivering the tragic news, the Guardians held a small symbolic ceremony to honor the fallen sisters. Brent had brought in a ladder and started placing two new shields on the upper wall of the hall, with Teresa's and Anna's names engraved on them. Williams later offered a moment of silence like he did every time a demon hunter perished in battle.

Just a name on a plaque hanging from a wall. Was this how the Guardians looked at the demon hunters? Izzy thought to herself.

She shook the thought away, knowing things were different now. Two decades earlier, the Guardians wouldn't even do this, let alone make proper arrangements with the families of the fallen.

After the small meeting in the main hall, breakfast was served. Izzy walked to the line and nodded to one of the waiters helping out. The waiter nodded back and handed Izzy an egg sandwich and a small paper bag.

"What you got there?" Nikki asked from behind, making her jump.

"My breakfast," Izzy replied, faking a smile.

"Cool," Nikki said as she grabbed an egg sandwich and some bacon. "Where shall we sit?"

Izzy smiled sadly. "I can't. Mom is on my case for my little stunt last night. She's come up with chores for me before I start the day. I can join you for lunch, though."

"Okay," Nikki chirped. "You will find me at the table, poking fun at Grace."

Izzy smiled while she grabbed her things and walked out the door. She sprinted through the halls, empty as always during chow time. The green-eyed girl headed toward the side entrance of the castle and walked outside the grounds where she found the side stairs to the cellar making her way down. Izzy opened the door slowly and peered into the small storage room. The gardening equipment for the castle gardens was stored there.

As soon as she closed the door, her wolf came out from the shadows. Her scent was a dead giveaway. The wolf licked its lips as Izzy pulled bacon strips from her bag. "You need to hunt, Aidan. You can't be a lazy wolf. Need you in top form."

The beast ignored the girl's comments as it fed.

Izzy looked around the dark storage room and thought about all she was about to endure for the next two weeks. "Frankly, I would wish to trade positions with you right now."

Elizabeth stood next to a punching dummy as she looked at all twenty girls stretching and shadowboxing. The demon hunters seemed focused and ready—all except Nikki Rogers. The girl had already had a full breakfast, and she still was eating a peanut butter sandwich. She appeared to have no cares in the world. Elizabeth looked at the table where Alex, Lewis, and Williams sat. They all had clipboards in front of them, ready to write what they saw.

Joy entered the room with an energy drink and stood on the other side of the dummy. "What do you think?" Joy asked Elizabeth.

"All have great technique," Elizabeth said. "Nothing to be surprised about."

Joy nodded and looked at the big whiteboard on the side. Alex has taken his time in writing the girls' names in bracket fashion, facing off against each other. Some matches were in threes. In the end, there would only be two left. She then turned her attention toward Izzy, who was quietly stretching on the side of the gym, trying not to call attention to herself. Joy smiled, knowing the task was impossible. The only difference between her and her mother was the hair color. And soon, she would be in the center of the spotlight. A sound from where the weapons hung caught Joy's attention. She noticed Nikki Rogers had finished eating and was now trying to pull a short sword from the weapons rack, only she was having problems detaching it. Joy looked at Elizabeth, who was now frowning at Nikki. The girl was pulling hard, but the sword was not budging.

"Rogers," Joy called out at the struggling redhead. "You have to unlock it from the top."

The veteran's advice was too late for the rookie. She pulled hard, forcefully unlatching the sword from the rack, but because of her momentum, she fell back, releasing the deadly blade from her slippery hands. The sword flew past the other hunters, nearly missing them, instead hitting the dummy that was between Joy and Elizabeth right on the head.

Elizabeth and Joy took one look at the sword sticking out between them, and then they turned toward Nikki.

"Sorry," the redhead whispered, her cheeks turning bright red as the color of her hair.

"Are you sure she's part of this group?" Joy asked Elizabeth, who pulled the blade from the dummy.

"We'll see," Elizabeth replied.

Joy nodded as she saw Sean come into the gym. She smiled a bit as some of the younger demon hunters took notice of the former demon making his presence known.

He was an older man, yet he still made some school girls' hearts flutter a bit. He walked toward the coffee machine installed next to the Guardians' table. A butler prepared for him a gourmet beverage. With cup in hand, he sat on the side bleachers and watched the action.

Some of the girls marveled at the newcomer. After all, he was a legend in his own right, walking the line that divided the darkness and the light.

Izzy was among the exceptions. After all, he was her dad. She proceeded to stretch as she looked at the board with her name on it. Following the bracket, she realized that she would face Grace near the end. Izzy turned her attention toward Grace, who sat with her legs crossed and eyes closed as if she were in another world.

"All right, girls," Elizabeth called as she walked toward the Guardians table. "We begin. I want a clean match based on what we've written on the board. I want to see the best of all of you. The exercise continues until one is left standing, or I say it ends."

Joy looked at the board to see the first two names. "Aina and Rogers! You're up!"

The rest of the girls walked toward the bleachers and sat down. Izzy watched as Nikki stretched with a plastic stake in her hand. On the other side, Eisha Aina from the Congo twirled her own weapon, measuring Nikki. Both plastic stakes were custom made to light up and beep as soon as they hit the target. The technician Andy designed the weapons for demon hunter training.

Eisha lunged at Nikki, who just twirled in her spot, avoiding her.

"Too eager," Izzy murmured to herself as she saw the girl from Africa attack Nikki. Her moves were fast but predictable. Eisha's technique was basic, nothing Izzy had not seen before.

Nikki moved like a robot—not attacking, but waiting for the opening.

Eisha punched and kicked, only for Nikki to dodge and avoid. Nikki's style was programmed, almost soldier-like. Her background proved that. When Eisha plunged the stake, Nikki moved to the right, and there was the opening Izzy would have used, only Nikki didn't. Instead, she rolled out of the way and created distance between herself and the other demon hunter.

Izzy looked at her mom, who was frowning.

Izzy wondered for a second what her mom was thinking. She turned her attention back to Nikki, who was still waiting for Eisha.

Eisha changed tactics and started kicking, hard, and fast.

Nikki blocked, taking the full impact on her forearms and shins.

Eisha staked low, forcing Nikki to block low. She moved fast, jumping and hitting Nikki with her knee just below her chin.

Nikki staggered, leaving herself completely vulnerable for the next attack, and indeed it came.

Eisha jumped and twirled in midair, connecting a powerful kick to Nikki's chest.

Nikki fell on her back, stunned.

Eisha jumped, aiming her stake toward Nikki's unprotected chest.

Then Izzy saw something unbelievable. It was so fast she rubbed her eyes to make sure of what had happened.

Nikki rolled out of the way while Eisha was in midair. The red-headed hunter flipped back on her feet and waited for Eisha to land, stake ready. As Eisha landed, Nikki staked her sister hunter in the back, then twirled and staked her in the front. The stake buzzed and lit up twice.

"Rogers advances!" Joy announced.

Izzy looked at Williams, Lewis, and back to Williams. If their jaws could fall to the floor, this would be the moment. Nikki moved lightning-fast. No sign of being hit on her body. Izzy wondered whether they caught everything, then she remembered the gym security cameras. The fight was worth a second review.

Nikki smiled at Eisha, shaking her hand. "You land pretty hard hits. Some of the hardest I've taken."

Eisha smiled softly, trying to hide her disappointment. "Not strong enough to keep you down." Her accent was heavy as the words came out of her mouth.

"Sit down," Elizabeth instructed.

Both hunters sat down as Elizabeth took the floor.

"We're here to learn," Elizabeth continued. "Can someone tell me what you saw that was completely wrong with their exercise?"

Izzy had an idea of what she saw. But she was not going to open her mouth. She saw Grace's hand shoot up, not surprising Izzy at all.

"Eisha was too eager to confront Nikki," Grace answered.

"Very good," Elizabeth replied, looking at Eisha. "You come in too strong. Without measuring the vampire or demon you're facing, he has the opportunity to pull an ace up his sleeve—something you're not prepared for."

Eisha nodded and drank in the new information.

"Anyone else?"Elizabeth asked.

None raised their hands. Elizabeth noted that Grace had something else to say. "Grace?"

"I think that Nikki took too much time in taking Eisha out," Grace replied. "As if she was doing it on purpose."

"Wasn't she measuring Eisha?" Ammarra asked.

Izzy looked closely at the hunter from Indonesia. Being the oldest of the group meant she had more experience in the field, and her brown eyes showed it.

"She calculated Eisha's moves and waited for an opening."

Elizabeth smiled, looking at Joy, who smiled back. Then both looked at Nikki, who was looking at the floor. Elizabeth then turned her attention to the rest of the hunters. "Demon hunting is not a sport for showing off your skills. That behavior could violate rule number one of demon hunting."

"Don't die," the girls said at the same time.

"We don't need an entire engagement with a vampire to figure out their weakness," Joy said. "Take a few seconds to analyze the enemy, then engage. Take longer just to beat a vampire to a pulp, and you might end up as the vampire's dinner."

"Is that clear, Nikki?" Elizabeth asked.

Nikki looked up with a serious face. "Crystal."

"Okay," Joy said, looking at the board. "Wu, Powel, you're up."

Grace and the demon hunter from India stood up, ready to engage.

Izzy took particular notice of Grace's moves. The moment she stood up, she realized Grace measured everything with her mind. The Hawaiian girl considered everything—the air she breathed and the floor she stood on. Out of the corner of her eye, she saw Joy lift her hand, signaling for the fight to begin.

Grace launched her attack. Quick and decisive, with a calculated and precise move set. It was a mixture of *kung fu* and *jeet kun do*—very fast and very deadly. Powel blocked the first attack, but the rest hit their mark with unparalleled skill.

Chhavi staggered in response to the multiple hits her body took. Every time she tried to mount an offense, Grace responded with a block and a blow to retort.

This is no contest, Izzy thought to herself. Grace had this in the bag. Izzy looked at her watch and saw that only twenty seconds had passed. She heard a grunt and a beeping sound.

"Wu advances!" Joy announced.

Izzy tried to hide her amazement. Grace had taken care of her opponent in less than thirty seconds.

"Did you all get that?" Grace asked the Guardians and the hunters.

Joy and Elizabeth looked unimpressed, sitting with their arms crossed.

The Guardians had a different expression.

"Perfect," Elizabeth said. Her voice lacked emotion. "Movements were precise and to the point. Your opponent was studied."

"Well done," Joy said as she looked at the board.

"Any pointers?" Grace asked.

Izzy tried to figure out whether this was just the black-haired girl trying to show a little humility.

Both Elizabeth and Joy looked at each other and smiled.

"One of your sisters will show you your weakness," Joy said. "But not now. O'Brien and Sousa. You're up."

Izzy gulped as she stood up. All eyes were upon her now, the demon hunters as well as the Guardians. She just hoped that her dad would not do anything embarrassing right now, like cheer for her. She looked at him out of the corner of her eye and caught a glimpse of him smiling.

Her mother, on the other hand, just had her arms crossed.

She shook the jitters off and focused on the Brazilian demon hunter in front of her.

Almeida Sousa did some style of Capoeira moving her legs back and forth, from side to side. Her upper body remained low.

Izzy had dealt with a demon in Ibiza who had moved like that. She readied herself.

Joy's order came for them to begin, and everything moved in slow motion. The whispers faded, and she felt the familiar stinging sensation on her spine.

Almeida flipped to the side, then diagonally, sending a kick to Izzy's head.

Izzy moved to the side, smacking the kick away.

Almeida recovered her posture and lunged the stake at Izzy's chest.

Izzy moved her body to the side, and her fist hit Almeida's outstretched arm.

Almeida yelped in pain, dropping her stake.

Izzy caught it and did a foot sweep, trying to knock Almeida off her feet.

The Brazilian hunter flipped away.

Izzy breathed hard, twirling both stakes in her hands. She ran toward Almeida, throwing one of the stakes and aiming for the heart.

Instinctively Almeida grabbed the stake in the air.

Izzy increased her speed, moving Almeida's arm out of the way with the other stake while punching her in the side.

Almeida staggered, leaving herself completely open for Izzy to stake her. The satisfying beeping sound echoed in the room.

"O'Brien advances!" Joy exclaimed.

Izzy shook Almeida's hand and turned toward her mother, waiting for her critique.

"Not bad," Elizabeth said dryly. "Almeida. You never lose your only weapon. In real life, you find another. You do not try to take back the one you lost."

"Speed is dead-on, though," Joy said, looking at Almeida. "Need to focus those attacks better. Make sure you connect."

"Take a seat," Elizabeth ordered, looking at Sean.

Sean just nodded and smiled softly.

She knew what he saw. Izzy had her style down to the letter, and it showed.

"Okay," Elizabeth said, turning back to the girls. "Who is next?"

CHAPTER X

Guardians Castle Main Headquarters, Ireland; August 8, 11:00 a.m.

CLARA SOMIERE LOOKED BLEAK as she stared at her tablet, emotionally exhausted by what she had just gone through. Transmitting on the nine screens in front of her, was the video feed of the same dark cave entrance where her girls had perished, but she could not let go of the tablet. She had to go over the evidence of the previous night's battle, as well as their battered gear. The words Father Michael Smith, the girls' oldest brother, had uttered minutes earlier echoed in Clara's ears and heart. They still felt empty, though. She closed her eyes and pictured the holy man in her mind. He was a little bit older than her, with dark black hair and a chiseled chin.

Clara pondered the uncomfortable moment she'd just experienced, delivering bad news over a video feed instead of doing it in person. The visions in her mind meandered through the events as she contacted the Smith family, with Father Mike and Andy, in video conference mode. There was a lot of weeping. Tempers flared. Still, Father Mike had guided the difficult conversation—talking about the greater good, the glorious death in battle, fighting for those who could not fight for themselves. All were hollow words that could never erase the pain of losing your loved ones. But the priest did his best to ease the family's burden and pain of losing his younger sisters.

Frank Smith, the patriarch of the family, calmed down after hearing his eldest son's words. He grabbed hold of his weeping wife and his remaining children, praying for his dead daughters, as the spirit of death floated in the conversation. Michael prayed with them while Clara and Andy looked awkwardly through the web camera.

The next part was even trickier and just as morbid as the first. The Smiths wanted their daughters to have a Catholic burial. Tempers flared again the moment Andy spoke. It was not only what he said but the way he said it, so stoic and monotonous, like nothing had happened. The geek explained, rather bluntly, that a mystical petrification trapped the twins creating a cork with their corpses. Their statues were now the doorway to hell. It all went downhill from there. Even though Michael tried to explain the supernatural, the Smiths cursed the "evil organization" that had led their daughters to their demise.

Now Clara was watching another cursed feed, where a few hours earlier, she had seen the girls get killed. There was a knock on the door that broke Clara's thoughts. She looked up and saw Jasmine enter the room, with John at her side. Clara wiped her eyes and motioned for the two Guardians to come in as she placed the tablet down and focused on the images on the nine screens. "Any news from Austria?"

"We may have something," Jasmine replied, pulling a chair and connecting her tablet into the system. She did not even ask how it had gone with the Smiths. There was no need. "I was trying to find information on anything unusual in the transportation system."

Clara looked at Jasmine curiously.

"It was John's idea," Jasmine responded, looking at the young man.

"I figured after kidnapping a demon hunter, they would need some sort of transportation," John said. "It would be a good place to start."

"We know Elsa was wanted alive," Jasmine said. "So whoever kidnapped her needed to move her without attracting suspicion."

"We cross-referenced stolen vehicles with suspicious deaths surrounding them," John said.

"It seems someone stole a truck near the Weisser residence," Jasmine said. "That same truck was spotted near the coast of Italy, where a boat was stolen. I contacted Interpol, and they said they would call back if they had information on the boat."

John looked at Clara, not sure how to tell her the next piece of information. "Interpol stated they caught a group wearing black on the coast security feed. They carried a large wooden box with them."

Clara crumpled down in her chair. Things looked bleak as she pondered everything that was going on. She nodded and looked at John apologetically. "I'm sorry, John. I should've been more focused on bringing you up to speed on all this to help us out."

"It's okay," John said, looking at the camera feed transmitted on the monitors. "I know it's not the best time to bring a new guy in."

"It's not okay," Clara grumbled as she opened a drawer and pulled out a cell phone, a computer tablet, and a clipboard. "This is your gear. Andy connected the tablet and cell phone to our mainframe. He set up the username, and the password's ready to go."

"Guess I'm hired," John quipped as he turned on his gear.

"You're part of the team," Clara said, turning back to the monitors. "We're doing multitasking on this one. Andy is the only POC in St. Helena, and with Elsa's kidnapping, we're all hands on deck."

"Got it," John answered as he logged into the system.

Clara focused on the images Andy was transmitting. She tried not to look at the statues of her friends, but she was unable to look away. Clara closed her eyes and waited a few seconds while the camera focused on the sculptures themselves. The twin demon hunters had been transformed into beautiful marble figures, while the demon who killed them was turned to one made of black stone.

"That's weird," Andy said out loud through the feed.

"What is it?" John asked as he looked over the statues on his monitor.

"The demon hunters got hit with the same hell-spot energy," Andy said. "As well as the demon. Why are they white marble, while the demon is charcoal stone?" He pulled out a notebook and wrote.

John frowned as he saw something else in the feed. "Andy, there is a symbol at the base of the demon. Can you focus on that?"

Andy adjusted the camera and focused on the base of the black statue. Burned on the bottom of the petrified demon was the symbol of a half-moon with five nails. "That wasn't there before. You recognize it?"

Clara opened her eyes and looked at the symbol closely. It did seem familiar, but she couldn't put her finger on it.

"St. Grievous," John said as he turned his tablet around, showing the picture on his device. "That's the symbol of the Grievous clan."

Clara could not hide her amazement on how quickly he'd found that. "Grievous? As in the feast of Grievous?"

"Its one-thousandth anniversary is this year," John said.

"But the feast is in October," Andy said as he widened the angle of the camera.

"The hell spot seems closed to me," John said. "But something related to Grievous came out."

"I am sorry," Jasmine interrupted. "Who is this Grievous, and why is there a feast to him?"

"He's a vampire from the early tenth century," John replied, looking at the older Guardian. "He was a mutated form of a vampire with hooves for hands. He is considered a legend in the vampire community for his immense power. He raised an army and devastated North Africa and part of Eastern Europe until a small army of demon hunters banished him to hell."

"Vampires adore him as a god," Andy continued. "They commemorate his legacy in October when their vampire strength is enhanced."

Clara sighed as she leaned back in her chair. "Andy, cross-reference vampire activity on all active hell spots. Also, look up St. Grievous and get back to us when you get to the safe house. Make sure the cave is sealed. The last thing I want is civilians entering the cave by mistake."

"Will do," Andy answered as he closed the feed and logged out.

Clara looked at the screens and tried to focus on Elsa now. She was about to ask a question when Jasmine's phone rang.

"Hello?" Jasmine asked. "Yes. Let me transfer you." Jasmine looked at Clara and handed her the phone. "I left your name as a point of contact."

"This is Clara Somiere," Clara said over the phone.

"Hello," a voice on the other line said. "Sorry for taking this long to contact you, Miss Somiere."

"No problem," Clara said. "Did you find anything?"

"We have a report of a ship leaving the docks," the man

spoke with an Italian accent. "They left at two a.m., without authorization."

"Did you try and pursue them?" Clara asked.

"Yes, ma'am," the man said. "But that night, we were covered by a dense fog—it covered almost the entire Mediterranean. We couldn't see anything. We pursued using only GPS."

"Where did you find the ship?" Clara asked frantically.

"Off the west coast of Ireland," the man said.

"Thank you. Can you give me the name of the ship?"

"The Minx," was the dry reply.

"Thank you," Clara said, hanging up.

"The information matches?" Jasmine asked.

"Yes," Clara said, scribbling the last piece of information on a sheet of paper: *"Here's what we know. Three days ago, a truck was stolen in the vicinity of the Weisser's residence. That truck was later spotted near the Italian coast of the Mediterranean. Security footage shows dark figures carrying a box with them to a ship that was taken that very night. That same ship has been spotted abandoned off the west coast of Ireland."*

"Vampires bringing a kidnapped demon hunter to the Guardians' territory?" Jasmine asked. "Something doesn't add up."

"There are few demons and vampires who follow this M.O.," John said. "I can do some cross-reference."

"I know it's not much," Clara said, closing the folder. "But it's all we have. Should we send Sean to check it out?"

"Might as well," Jasmine said, returning to her tablet. "It's better than waiting for something to happen."

Clara walked swiftly out of the HQ room and headed toward the gym. She could hear the groans and cheers of the twenty girls inside. Sudden screams of excitement made Clara jump. As she entered the door, she saw Nikki Rogers, somewhat bruised up, standing over Ammarra Yanin.

"Rogers is in the final," Joy announced. The other demon hunters clapped, especially Izzy, with a huge smile on her face.

"Found something?" Brent asked from the side. His voice made her jump.

"Yes," Clara replied, composing herself. "A lead off the Irish coast."

Brent signaled for Sean to join him while Joy announced the next pair. "Wu and O'Brien," the older hunter called. "You're up."

The hunters cheered as Izzy stood up. Mostly because of her good nature and her sportsmanship during their morning exercise. She had won the affection and respect of most of the girls assembled. Nikki pulled Izzy close.

"You got this," Nikki said. "She's not invincible."

Izzy walked toward the center stage, finding Grace ready for her. She then took a moment to look at Sean and Brent, talking to Clara. *Something is up*, the girl thought to herself. She cleared her mind and focused on Grace, who had her eyes closed. Izzy gripped her stake tightly. Grace was dangerous. Her movements were fluid and extremely powerful; it was like fighting moving water. While Nikki fought like a brawler from what she had seen, Grace fought like a skilled dancer.

"Begin!" Joy barked.

Izzy's mind froze, sensing all eyes on her. Her mom and dad were evaluating her every move. She sidestepped Grace's initial attack, then shook her head, trying to focus more on the fight. She wanted to call for a timeout, but in demon hunting, there was no such thing. Izzy dodged a one-two combination from Grace, and ducked under a fast roundhouse kick, then scurried away.

Grace had missed all her attacks.

Izzy watched as she took a deep breath, trying to regroup. This gave Izzy time to refocus.

Grace attacked, while Izzy blocked the blows; she dared not

strike back. She knew that when she attacked, her defense was wide open—and a hit from Grace would put an end to the exercise. Grace's onslaught pushed Izzy back toward Elizabeth and Joy, who simply stepped out of the way.

Izzy's back was to the wooden dummy; she ducked when Grace threw a hard punch.

Grace's fist smashed through the wood where Izzy's face would have been.

Then, Izzy saw her chance. She fired a roundhouse kick of her own, but Grace ducked out of the way. Izzy's leg cut the dummy in two, sending splinters of wood flying everywhere. Izzy did a backflip, trying to put some distance between herself and Grace.

Grace was having none of that. She jumped, kicking Izzy in the chest while she was still in the air. The impact was blunt and powerful, causing some of the demon hunters to gasp.

Izzy ricocheted off to the side and landed right on the Guardians' table, crashing it to the floor. Alex, Lewis, and Williams got out of the way just as Grace jumped, ready to land on top of the dazed Izzy, but Izzy moved just before Grace's leg hit the broken table. Izzy fired off a kick, but Grace grabbed Izzy's ankle and punched her thigh. Izzy yelped in pain and tried to stand, but the pain in her leg caused her to crumble down.

Grace fired a roundhouse kick, connecting with Izzy's face.

Izzy spun in the air because of the blow, then fell awkwardly, knowing full well it was over.

Grace strolled toward her defeated opponent and tagged her in the chest with her electronic stake. The beeping sound echoed in the silent gym.

"Wu advances to the finals," Joy said in a monotonous tone as she looked at Elizabeth.

Elizabeth had her arms crossed with an expressionless face. She was in full General mode, and nothing would get her out of the zone. There were a few claps in the room, but the murmuring was louder than anything else.

Grace extended Izzy her hand, to help her up. It was the first time Grace had shown an opponent that sportsmanship courtesy. Izzy stood up, but her leg ached, and she could not stand straight.

"Ow," Izzy said. "I can't..." Izzy crumpled back down, but Grace held her by the arm, not allowing her to fall back down.

"I pinched your ankle nerve," Grace explained as she helped Izzy back to her seat.

Nikki helped Grace sit Izzy down.

"It disables the limb for five minutes. It feels like your leg fell asleep, right?"

Izzy nodded as she rubbed the sore spot.

"You will be good as new in about five minutes," Grace continued.

"Does the move work on vampires?" Izzy asked, still rubbing her leg.

"Indeed it does," Grace said. "All creatures with a nervous system can have a weak spot. Vampires share the same conditions as humans."

"Are we done, girls?" Joy asked, her temper flaring. "Can we continue?"

"What did we observe?" Elizabeth asked the group. She noticed Sean waiting for her at the entrance of the gym, holding a folder.

"Grace's technique is perfect," Izzy said, being the first to recognize it. She winced because of the pain. "There's no opening for an attack. And her counter-attack is simply demolishing."

"It would appear so," Elizabeth said, smiling softly. "Anybody else?"

"Izzy has a good technique as well," Ammarra said. "She was resourceful, finding new moves. Even if she faced a superior opponent, she still didn't back down."

"We all have been there," Joy said. "Facing an opponent that is far stronger and faster."

Joy's words stung Izzy. She looked at Williams, Lewis, and Alex. They all had this puppy-dog look of sympathy. Izzy looked at her mother and tried to read her; it was impossible while being in hunter mode. She then looked at her dad, who was distracted, trying to catch Elizabeth's attention.

"In those cases," Joy continued, "The only reason you don't leave the engagement is that the world is at stake. But most of the time, I suggest you run and fight another day."

"Still," Elizabeth said. "We're almost finished with the exercise, and no one has noticed Grace's weakness."

"What weakness?" Grace asked. She almost felt insulted as she measured Elizabeth once again.

"If Nikki doesn't discover it," Elizabeth replied with a steady tone, "I will personally show it to you myself."

The other demon hunters fell silent at the interchange. One could drop a pin in the room and hear it.

"We'll take a few minutes," Joy said, breaking the tension. "Then Rogers and Wu are up."

Joy and Elizabeth walked to the entrance where the other Guardians waited, while the demon hunters gathered in small groups.

"You were kind of hard on Grace," Sean said to Elizabeth as soon as they were within each other's earshot.

"She's getting too cocky," Elizabeth said, her temper flaring a little bit. "That attitude will definitely get her killed."

"Got news on the missing demon hunter from Austria," Brent said. "Seems a ship suspected of carrying her arrived near the Irish coast."

"To Guardian grounds?" Joy asked Clara as Elizabeth took the folder from Sean and inspected it.

"It seems to fit," Clara said. "The info matches the dates the kidnapping took place. There's also security footage."

"I'll go check it out?" Sean asked, looking at Izzy, who was still rubbing her leg.

"Go," Elizabeth said. "Take John Simmons with you. Teach him stuff you don't learn from books."

"Can get bloody out there," Clara said. "He's not a field Guardian."

"We all get a taste of the field someday," Elizabeth said. "Might as well get him out there now. He'll have Sean to watch his back."

"That will be fun," Brent said with a smile.

"One more thing," Clara said, remembering something. "There was an attack yesterday, in the villages surrounding the property. Social media is calling it gang-related. Eight bodies have been found—completely drained."

There was a grim silence for a moment.

"Thanks for the intel, Clara," Elizabeth said, trying to process the information. "Hand over the information to the other Guardians before lunch. Get John up to speed on all this, and send him out. I want all available hands on it. I also want to see what this boy is made of." Elizabeth then turned toward Brent. "Patrol the area. We may need to make a night excursion—tonight."

Clara and Brent nodded and walked away.

Elizabeth was about to walk back with Joy when Sean pulled her aside. "You okay?"

"Well," Elizabeth started. "There are the recent dead bodies near our castle, two demon hunters dead, one demon hunter missing, and seeing my daughter's ass get kicked, I think I've got a lot on my shoulders."

"I can help with the burden," Sean said, rubbing his wife's arm softly. "You know I'm here, right?"

"Thank you," Elizabeth said, standing on her tiptoes and kissing him on the lips. She then turned and saw some of the girls staring back at her with amused looks on their faces, except for Izzy, whose face registered disgust.

The older Guardians were cleaning their glasses, pretending nothing had happened, and Alex was just trying to ignore everything.

Elizabeth felt her cheeks warm up, being the focus of attention. "Ummm…"

"Come on!" Joy barked at the girls. "We're not watching romantic movies here! We're fighting the undead! Wu… Rogers… Front and center, now!"

Both Nikki and Grace jumped up, ready to engage.

"All right," Joy said, looking at both demon hunters. "One stake to take it all. Begin!"

Grace ran toward Nikki, who was jumping from side to side, attempting to avoid taking a hit. Grace fired a hard kick, hitting Nikki right in the chest.

Nikki grunted, taking a step back to recover from the impact.

Grace fired two swift jabs, this time hitting Nikki's face. The red-headed demon hunter just took in the blows. Grace tried a stake to the heart, but Nikki darted away just in time.

"Wow," Nikki said, shaking off the cobwebs, "that really hurt, kitten."

Grace growled in anger as she launched herself for another attack; the speed and the strength behind her punches and kicks were considerable. Some hits made it past Nikki's defenses, catching her in the chest and face, but Nikki was not going down. Grace tried to stake again, but Nikki evaded it and measured up her opponent again.

"Fast and strong," Nikki said out loud, as she wiped the blood from the side of her mouth. "Just how I like it."

Grace screamed and fired her punches faster and stronger. The sound of flesh pounding flesh echoed throughout the room.

The other hunters winced and moaned at what they were seeing.

Nikki took the punishment, but as soon as Grace went for her staking move, Nikki moved out of the way.

Grace was breathing hard now.

"You're not tired, are you?" Nikki asked, a little shaky. There was a large purple bruise on the side of her head; her arms were also reflecting damage from blocking Grace's attacks.

Grace recomposed herself and slowed her breathing, then closed her eyes and rubbed her hands together.

Izzy noticed her posture—it was the same posture from before Grace had crippled Izzy's leg. *Pressure points*, she thought.

Grace moved slower this time, trying to reach Nikki on specific parts of her body.

Nikki dodged, ducked, and cartwheeled out of the way, until a kick caught her in the chest. The air left her lungs as a double-fisted hit got her in the back, followed by a touch on her left arm and right shoulder. Nikki jumped away from Grace, grunting in pain. The pain in her limbs was excruciating. Izzy could tell in Nikki's eyes; it would soon be over.

Grace readied herself, holding her stake high, and attacked; her movements were calculated and precise.

Nikki saw the attack coming as if in slow motion; she raised her weakened left arm and blocked the attack. With her right arm, Nikki fired a punch, connecting with Grace's unprotected midsection.

Grace's eyes opened wide as the pain registered. It was now her turn to have the wind knocked out of her. The pain was unbearable; she stepped back and dropped her stake as she fell to the ground, holding her stomach.

The moment Grace got hit, all eighteen hunters gasped in awe. It was the first time they had seen her take a blow all morning.

Izzy couldn't hide her amazement at what she had just witnessed.

Nikki weakly walked toward the dropped stake and picked it up, then twirled it in her hand and strolled toward Grace, who was not getting up. Nikki kneeled and tapped Grace's chest with the stake. The red light turned on.

"Rogers wins," Joy flatly stated.

Elizabeth walked toward Grace as the other demon hunters rushed their fallen sister. She was not getting up. She held her stomach, trying to fight the pain—and the pain was winning. "Can you get up?" Elizabeth asked.

Grace squinted her eyes and shook her head, trying to control her body as small tears built up in her closed eyes. Elizabeth kneeled and put her hand on top of Grace's hand.

"Relax," Elizabeth said soothingly. "Relax. Take it in. Feel the pain. Embrace it."

"Can someone now tell me Grace's weakness?" Joy asked the hunters.

Only Izzy raised her hand.

"O'Brien?"

"She had never experienced physical pain," Izzy said. "So, she didn't know how to react to it."

"Very good," Joy said to the group. "No matter how perfect your technique is, it doesn't matter if you cannot process the pain that goes with it."

Elizabeth looked at Grace, who tried to wipe the tears from her eyes now. "It's okay," Elizabeth said, reassuring the young girl.

Her demeanor made Izzy's heart melt. This was the mother she loved and adored, the one who would pick her up after she

148

had fallen and scraped her knee. It was rare to see that when she was in demon-hunter General mode.

"It's after we fall that we realize how strong we are when we get back up." With that, the older hunter extended her hand. Grace took it and stood up. "You are good, Grace Wu, but you have much to learn."

CHAPTER XI

Irish Road, Ireland; August 8, 1:30 p.m.

SEAN DROVE THE JEEP toward the Irish coast, with the young Guardian riding shotgun. The ride had been silent all the way through; John hadn't stopped looking at his tablet, going over and processing all the information he'd absorbed in the past two days. Few people truly understood what his brain was going through. It was as if his mind was on fire, trying to piece everything together as he moved from screen to screen.

Sean looked at the silent young man beside him. It was just as well that the junior Guardian hadn't said a word since they'd left the castle. The older Guardian was in no mood to talk, either. Seeing two young girls die was taxing on his soul. It was not easy being part of this organization. So many lives were juggled in the eternal fight against the forces of darkness. For more than a quarter of a century, the older man had been active in this war. Even though he won the right to return to human form, his mind and soul remained scarred by his past atrocities. Sean tried to shake the feeling away.

"You don't say much, do you?" Sean asked the young Guardian, trying to break the ice.

John turned away from the tablet and looked at Sean. His brown eyes hid a secret sadness. "I try only to speak when I'm needed. I have no additional information to add."

"Any theories on what is happening?" Sean asked.

"None that I would put money on," John replied.

Sean turned his attention back to the road as he maneuvered the car to the next exit giving them a clear view of the Atlantic Ocean. The beach was calm and deserted, except for the Interpol official vehicles and the local police. Sean brought the car to a stop and got out. Both he and John headed toward the area that had been sealed off by the authorities. The police barricade blocked them from reaching the marooned boat on the beach.

"Is Briggs here?" Sean asked one of the officers. The police officer measured up both Sean and John, then whistled to the detectives over at the scene. A man in a gray suit motioned them to enter the crime scene. Sean and the younger man sidestepped the barricade, merely acknowledging the officer who had signaled the chief detective.

"O'Brien," Briggs said, shaking Sean's hand. "Why am I not surprised?"

"Briggs," Sean responded, signaling to John, who was looking at the area as he pulled out his cell phone. "New colleague. His name is John."

"Yes," Briggs said as he looked at his men in the boat. "There are two men dead inside. The type of deaths that always catch your attention."

"Two small holes in the neck?" Sean asked.

"Same MO," Briggs replied. "The chief is on my ass because of these weird unsolved cases. Now I get a boat from Italy on my shore, with two corpses drained of their blood."

Sean looked at Briggs. "Anything recent besides this?"

Briggs looked at Sean, somewhat surprised. "Yes," Briggs replied. "About ten kilometers east of your place. Two bodies in the last couple of weeks. I thought we notified you."

Sean frowned at the new information as he turned his attention to John. The young Guardian was looking at the sand closely.

"There were five of them," John said. "Four walked straight, while they dragged the fifth body." John looked at the road. "Car was waiting for them."

"You know who's missing?" Briggs asked. "I need to be involved."

"Do you really want to know what's going on?" Sean asked, already knowing the answer to the question.

Briggs paused for a moment. He then nodded and barked orders to his forensic guys. "There are car tracks on the road. Find me that car."

Sean walked toward John, who was looking up toward the sun. "So?"

"Vampires," John said. "There are ashes on the entrance of the boat. Our demon hunter dusted one before the rest overpowered her."

"Was she trying to escape?" Sean asked doubtfully as he looked at the ashes.

"Not with those odds," John replied. "The girl was trying to get killed."

Sean nodded, realizing the truth. "They want Elsa alive."

"It would seem so," John said. "If vampires brought her to this country, there must be a place they would take her. A shelter of some sort, perhaps an abandoned building to keep her in."

"I have a contact on the other side of the island," Sean said. "If there is vampire activity, he may know something."

"That would be a good place to start," John said.

"Let's go," Sean said, pulling out his cell phone. "We got a lead," he said over the line. "Vampires have Elsa, and they want her kept alive."

Guardians' Castle Main Headquarters, Ireland; August 8, 8:30 p.m.

Izzy read her Latin textbook, while her headphones played instrumental violin music in her ears. The music helped clear her head. Immersed in her world, she tried to push out all the ideas that pounded at her brain. Her nightmares—Elsa's disappearance—a sense of imminent doom. Her troubled heart would not give her rest. Even though her mom was a demon hunter, she dared not bother her with teenage angst. Elizabeth had no time for that.

Izzy shook her head, with the violins playing a little softer now, as she tried to focus on the textbook. After lunch, Williams had put all the girls through an intense Latin class. He explained the need for demon hunters to read and understand the ancient language. Split-second decisions would have to be made in case an ancient spell was needed.

Izzy turned her attention to the book and bit her lip as she grasped the crucifix that hung from her neck. The memories of her father taking her to mass and Sunday school filled her mind with peace. The storm of thoughts ceased for a moment as she remembered those peaceful times. Her Catholic faith, which her father had encouraged, brought the sense of tranquility that was always needed. The image of her friend came back. Izzy closed her eyes and whispered in Latin. "Deus, dirige viam tuam."

"Still reading?" Nikki yelled.

Izzy put her book down and saw the redhead standing in the door frame with a smile on her face. Izzy pulled the earplugs from her ears.

"You may be used to seeing this place," Nikki said, "but it's my first time in a castle."

"Enjoy it," Izzy said, getting back to her book. Izzy hoped Nikki would leave her alone, but the military brat was having none of that. Izzy felt the mattress shift as Nikki sat on the foot of her bed. "You're not going to leave me alone, are you?" Izzy asked.

"Unless you tell me I am a terrible pain," Nikki said, smiling. "Want to talk about it?"

"About what?" Izzy asked, trying to focus on her book.

"About why you feel like crap," Nikki pressed a bit.

Izzy buried her face in her book.

"Elsa is a great demon hunter," Nikki started. "My Guardian told me she stopped a legion of hellhounds with only a butter knife."

"It was a bit larger than a butter knife," Izzy said, remembering that fateful night in Amsterdam. "And yes, she's awesome."

"You know," Nikki said, trying to find a crack in Izzy's emotional armor, "I come from a military household. When my dad receives an order, he does it. And when he gives an order, he knows his men will do it."

"So?" Izzy asked. "What's your point?"

"Well," Nikki said, "If your mom says she'll do something, and she says she's working on it, I am sure she is doing exactly that. If your mom is on it, everything will be okay."

Izzy pondered a moment. Nikki had a point. Since the new Guardians were in charge, humanity was a big thing, something the old Guardians lacked.

"Come on," Nikki pulled on her new friend's leg. "They are serving dinner, and I don't want to eat alone."

Izzy sighed as she relented and put the book down. She walked out into the hall with Nikki, who was busy adjusting her glasses.

The redhead did not notice the shiny silver suit of armor located on the hall's side until she bumped into it. The armor crashed to the floor with a loud clatter. "Oops," Nikki said as she finished adjusting her glasses.

"I don't get it," Izzy said as Nikki struggled to pick up the metal parts. Izzy giggled at Nikki's futile attempt to put the contraption back together again. "You're this walking klutz demon hunter. How the hell did you win over Grace?"

"Sea turtles," Nikki said.

"Ha ha," Izzy said, catching the stupid reference. "Very funny."

Nikki struggled a bit more with the armor. After she finished putting it together, the redhead took a step back and admired her work. She frowned. It didn't look right. "Do you think anyone will notice?"

Izzy shook her head. "I am sure it's fine," Izzy said as both demon hunters walked to the dining room. The room was empty, except for just a few waiters on the side, watching over the beverage area. "I thought you said it was dinner time?"

"It was," Nikki replied. "I left the girls here a minute ago."

"The girls are out on patrol," Brent said as he walked in with a medieval battle-ax in his hands. "Vampires have been infesting the property and the neighboring towns."

Izzy and Nikki looked at each other and ran toward the back door of the castle. Nikki caught a glimpse of Izzy stopping by a waiter and receiving a paper bag. She wondered for a moment about the bag but then forgot about it as she reached the outside castle walls.

The sky was cloudy, and the sun was setting. The only demon hunter visible was Ammarra, who had an anxious look on her face.

"Where is everybody?" Nikki asked as Izzy joined her.

Ammarra looked disappointed. "Mr. Williams and Mr. Powell took all the girls, along with Joy. They told me I should stay here and wait for instructions."

"They left without us?" Izzy asked. She looked around and saw Grace running out of the castle.

Ammarra nodded. She seemed to feel a little better that she was not the only one left out. "Hey," she greeted Grace as she joined the small group.

"Where is everybody?" Grace asked.

"They went patrolling," Nikki said, looking disappointed.

Grace looked at her sister demon hunters, looking for confirmation. "You're kidding, right? Did they leave without us? Come on. We're the final four."

Izzy was about to say something when she noticed what Grace said. "Something is not right."

"What do you mean?" Grace looked at her, inquiring.

"I…" Izzy started. She was trying to figure out what to say, but her mouth suddenly stopped cooperating. "I…"

"Spit it out," Nikki ordered.

"I've spied on the gatherings in the years before," Izzy said, looking embarrassed. "My parents always lead this event, so I know when and what happens in the program."

"You mean the one that is handed out?" Ammarra said, pulling out a small pamphlet from the back pocket of her jeans.

"Yeah," Izzy said. "But it's more than that. There are few changes every year. But there has never been a vampire patrol with the demon hunters on the first day."

"Game's changed," Brent said, coming out with a large wooden chest.

"Who changed the program?" Grace asked in a demanding tone. Izzy noticed that the spoiled hunter hated when things didn't go as planned. Maybe she has OCD, Izzy thought to herself.

"I did," Elizabeth said, coming out of the castle. Izzy immediately looked down at the ground. "Good evening, girls."

Ammarra and Nikki looked at Elizabeth in awe. Grace looked embarrassed; her attitude had gotten the better of her again. Izzy was embarrassed for another set of reasons.

"New rules on this gathering, girls," Elizabeth continued as she rubbed Grace's and Izzy's shoulders. "You four are patrolling with me tonight."

Brent smiled at Nikki's and Ammarra's reactions. They were true fangirls. Grace still looked embarrassed.

Elizabeth opened the wooden chest, revealing a set of medieval weapons: small swords and knives, stakes of all sizes, and containers that had crucifixes and holy water in them. "In demon hunting, we all make mistakes," Elizabeth said, pulling out two stakes. She handed one to Grace and one to Izzy. "The important thing is to walk out alive and learn from them."

Grace and Izzy lightened up a bit as they twirled their stakes and looked at each other. For the first time, both Izzy and Grace genuinely smiled at each other. Elizabeth smiled and handed stakes to Ammarra and Nikki.

"We're all here to learn," Elizabeth continued her lecture. "We're here to be better at what we do. And after that… possible long-term retirement."

The girls giggled a bit as Elizabeth turned toward Brent. "You got our back?"

"Are you kidding?" Brent asked, twirling his battle-ax and pointing at the four girls. "With this kind of firepower at your disposal, I'll most likely be playing the role of damsel in distress."

The girls giggled as Elizabeth put an earpiece in her ear. "Do you read me?"

"Loud and clear from central," Clara's voice came through the communicator. "Patching you with Alpha Team."

"Moving to the northeastern side," Joy's voice crackled. "Williams and Lewis have taken the northwestern side. The rest is up to Delta Team."

Elizabeth looked at the girls. "What I would've done with all this tech at your age. Delta team moving toward the southeast. Woods are ours."

"Good luck, girls," Joy said. "Alpha out."

"Let's go," Elizabeth said to her small team as they walked toward the woods. "The Guardian grounds are vast—vampire detectors have been active in the woods. The vampires are aware of our presence, so we find out why they're testing us."

"Is this related to the Austrian incident?" Nikki asked.

"It might be," Elizabeth replied. "The Guardians believe that if vampires wanted our attention, all they needed was to hurt one of our demon hunters... but..."

"But what?" Izzy said softly.

Elizabeth looked at her daughter, grimly. "The villages near our property were attacked early in the morning. Vampire sightings before the sun was up. That's not regular vampire activity."

"So this is not a regular patrol," Izzy concluded.

Elizabeth smiled softly at her daughter. "Remember the first rule of demon hunting?"

"Don't die," the four hunters said at the same time.

CHAPTER XII

Kenmare, Ireland; August 8, 8:30 p.m.

SEAN SMASHED A DEMON against the sidewall of the bar in the dark alley. Night had fallen upon them near the beaten-down Irish tavern. Several sailors and fishermen walked on the street, oblivious to what was going on in the darkness. John stood on the lookout while Sean did his business.

"Talk!" Sean growled. "New vampires are in town, and they kidnapped a girl."

"I know nothing," the yellow demon insisted, as the tentacles coming from his ears wriggled in the midst of his thrashing. The beast trembled as Sean smashed him over a wooden crate. "I swear!"

"You hear that?" Sean asked John, faking amusement. "He swears… guess he's telling the truth." Sean punched the demon hard. Purple blood spurted out its mouth.

John looked at the back entrance of the demon bar nervously. It was the last one in their demon-spots tour. All the others had turned out to be dead ends. Only one, far up north, was left beside this one.

Sean had figured that if vampires were transporting a demon hunter, they must be in the vicinity; they would not risk moving her too far up North. John hoped he was right. He had seen demons and vampires before, except that they were always secure and locked up.

The young Guardian heard Sean smash the skull of the demon against the asphalt. The sounds of bone and flesh cracking made John a bit ill. He dared not look at the damage Sean had caused.

"He had nothing to say," Sean said, joining his young companion.

"I guess you can tell that by his brains splattered on the side of your boot," John said as he looked at the side of the ex-demon's boot.

"Hey," Sean said as he cleaned the side of his boot. "We're at war against the undead. We do what is necessary. If you are going to do the job, you've got to get your hands dirty."

"That's why I'm here. Sometimes we take the bullet so that the demon hunter doesn't have to," John said, opening up a bit.

Sean looked for a moment at the young boy's eyes. There was a hidden sadness behind them. As soon as he noticed this, John turned away and walked towards the bar. "Hey," Sean called out, grabbing John's attention.

The young man looked back.

"Yes," Sean said. "Sometimes we do the dirty work so that a young girl doesn't have to. The demon hunters have a greater burden to bear."

"We should be able to help with that burden," John stated as Sean passed him and walked toward the bar.

Sean searched for an answer deep inside him. The three-year service term was a good idea, but in that period of time, a lot could happen. He had nightmares about it—not being there for his daughter—seeing her take the bigger risk because it was her duty. Sean looked at John. He tried to read him.

"We do what we can," Sean said as he opened the bar door and entered. His imposing height and presence made the scum of the underworld turn back to their drinks, not wanting to mess with the male Guardian. Most of the demons that still lingered in Ireland knew of the New Guardians. If they lived, it was because the Guardians were allowing them to live. If they stepped over the line, there would be hell to pay. Others, though… did not follow the rules.

Sean walked toward the bar as John entered. The young Guardian felt unsettled, seeing the undead drinking casually in the dive. There were all kinds of demons present, but the Guardians did not see any vampires.

John walked carefully toward the bar and took a seat on a stool.

The barkeep looked at him, and then at Sean while cleaning a glass mug.

"Have you seen any bloodsuckers around these parts?" Sean asked.

The barkeep just shook his head.

Sean looked at him carefully; the demon's eyes pointed to the far side of the run-down joint. He patted John on the back as he walked to the corner of the bar. He saw three vampires, all dressed in black leather. They seemed to belong to a vampire motorcycle gang. They were a new lot compared to the other patrons.

"You are not from around here," Sean said, pulling up a chair and sitting at their table, interrupting their hushed mumbling.

"Why do you care?" the head vampire growled back.

The moment the vampire spoke back at Sean, the seats cleared around them.

John saw the demons back up and he followed suit, trying to avoid the monsters and the commotion that was about to take place.

"This is my town," Sean growled back. "You don't enter without my permission."

The vampire smiled smugly and leaned forward, toward Sean. "Haven't you heard? New management is taking over."

Sean had had enough. He fired his right fist, breaking the vampire's face. As Sean sprang into action, John heard a growl from his side.

A demon jumped into the fray, smashing the whiskey bottle into a vampire's face while kicking another one.

The vampire backed into another demon, and all hell broke loose. Chairs and tables started flying, as well as bodies.

Sean was quick and resourceful in dodging incoming attacks. He pulled one vampire from his chair and kicked him below the knee. A loud crack was heard. He did the same to the vampire's other leg. Sean dropped him and started flinging demons from side to side.

John's face was white. His heart pumped harder as he tried to make it to the exit. Fists and furniture were flying in the brawl. The young human felt a hand on his shoulder, turning him around.

A demon with horns on his chin looked at him. "Where are you going?" the beast growled.

John ducked as the beast fired a punch at his face. He crawled out of the way and looked back, only to see a stronger demon grab hold of his assailant. The larger monster snapped the smaller one in half and continued plowing through the bar.

An hour later, both John and Sean walked out of the pub. Sean's clothes were ragged and dirty, while John's white shirt had a big red stain on it. Thankfully, it wasn't his blood. Sean dragged the vampire with the broken legs with him.

The demon growled and struggled, but he was not going anywhere.

"Is this your normal method of getting information?" John asked, pulling out a handkerchief and cleaning his glasses.

Sean ignored the question and pulled the vampire into a standing position. "What are you doing here?"

The vampire just laughed at Sean, ignoring the pain. "You truly have no idea, do you? The Guardians are lost. You lack direction."

Sean smashed him against the wall, pulling out a small crucifix with a chain. "We can continue doing this the hard way.". He then stuck the holy object into the vampire's eye.

The demon screamed in pain as the searing metal perforated his eye socket.

"I guess there is only the easy way."

"You don't get it!" the vampire said, ignoring the pain. "You're dead! You're all dead! And it all starts with your wife!"

That did it for Sean. John saw the shift in emotion in the tall, brooding man. He grabbed the vampire and smashed him hard onto nearby wooden crates. The vampire just laughed as Sean punched him hard in the chest.

"Did you kiss them goodbye?" the vampire asked. "Because after tonight, you'll never have a chance."

John heard that and pulled out his phone. He could listen to his own heart beating as he dialed Clara's cell.

Sean continued punching the vampire down.

"No signal," John said to himself after he heard the tedious voicemail. He dialed HQ as fast as he could.

"John," Clara answered immediately.

"Where are the girls?" John asked urgently.

"Joy and Elizabeth took them patrolling," Clara said, becoming alarmed by John's voice.

"Get them back to the castle!" John said. "Something is going down tonight!"

"What is?" Clara asked, getting scared.

Just then, John heard the radio transmission of the patrol over the phone. The voice of Joy was recognizable from all these miles away.

"Contact! Contact!" Joy exclaimed over the radio. "Hillion spotted!"

Eastern Woods, Ireland; August 8, 9:30 p.m.

Joy's voice sounded serious to the other demon hunters, but Elizabeth knew best just how serious it was. What Joy had seen put the older hunter on edge. A Hillion in Ireland meant a dangerous demon was loose, and she knew it. Only Elizabeth and Sean could have noticed the hint of fear in the voice over the radio.

"Give me a location, Clara!" Elizabeth exclaimed, looking at her girls.

"Half a mile north of your position," Clara replied.

"Move!" Elizabeth said to her team as she started sprinting north, hearing Izzy, Grace, Nikki, and Ammarra trail right behind her. Poor Brent was left trying to catch up. Delta team moved quickly through the woods, with their instinct guiding them in the darkness. All the while, Joy's voice echoed in the night, barking out orders.

"Flank to the right!" Joy exclaimed. "Fire!... He still moves!... Need something sharper!... Go!... In the chest!... Excellent!... Step back!... Step back!... A dozen vampires have appeared!... Liz! Where the hell are you?"

"Inbound!" Elizabeth exclaimed while running as fast as she could. "Give me two minutes!"

"Bullshit!" Joy hollered out. "This will be over in a minute... Hurry!"

"Spread out!" Elizabeth ordered her team running alongside her. "Take the vampires first! Leave the Hillion for last!"

"Hurry, Liz!" Joy yelled over the radio. "The girls are okay!… The Hillion is not going down!… More vampires!"

Elizabeth's senses picked up the dark energy close by. They were close. "Dust them all!" Elizabeth ordered as they cleared the woods and found themselves in an open field. The battle was just up ahead, on top of the hill.

Grace and Nikki pulled ahead, running faster. They reached the fray and saw two dozen vampires fending off the best demon hunters on the planet. The hunters moved with precision and agility. Grace and Nikki zigzagged through the fray, staking the vampires with their wooden weapons in the heart.

Izzy and Ammarra joined the battle just as another dozen vampires appeared from the right side; Izzy noticed they were wearing motorcycle gear. They looked intimidating, growling at the girls. Izzy and Ammarra engaged the last batch of vampires to show up with two stakes in each hand. Before they could growl a second time, the vampires got put down. Izzy and Ammarra switched positions, using their backs, thereby gaining more room to maneuver. Izzy watched as a vampire threw a sister demon hunter away and then launched itself at Grace, who did not notice the move.

"Cover me!" she exclaimed at Ammarra, who just nodded while plunging a stake into a tall, bearded vampire.

Izzy covered the distance and jumped, tackling the vampire in midair. Both demon hunter and vampire went down. As Izzy recovered, Grace was on top of her opponent. Vampire combustion soon covered the field as the hunters did quick work of the vampires.

All that remained was the Hillion that had fought both Elizabeth and Joy; they had outmaneuvered him in every way. The Hillion growled, knives and arrows sticking out of its flesh. The creature had slowed as both Elizabeth and Joy ran toward him, each with a sword in hand.

The beast launched itself.

Elizabeth slid down in the grass while Joy jumped up. Elizabeth skewered the demon's torso, while Joy stuck her blade in the demon's skull.

The beast screamed in agony, then fell lifeless.

The young demon hunters cheered as Elizabeth and Joy smiled at each other.

Williams and Lewis just nodded in approval.

"That was intense," Elizabeth said. Suddenly a purple mist started surrounding the group.

"Regroup!" Williams ordered.

All the demon hunters surrounded both Lewis and Williams, forming a protective barrier around the humans.

"Dark Shadow," Lewis muttered under his breath, as the mist moved against the soft summer wind.

Joy and Elizabeth pulled their blades from the dead Hillion and prepared for battle. The dark purple mist moved away from the demon hunters and formed a beautiful, black-haired woman in a dark purple suit.

"So... these are the best demon hunters on the planet," Dark Shadow purred. "Not as tough as I imagined."

"You were destroyed," Elizabeth mused, remembering the demon blocking St. Helena's hell spot upon its demise.

"And yet here I am," Dark Shadow said, pulling out a small red blade. The woman became mist again and quickly plunged itself toward the group of hunters.

Izzy moved Williams out of the way as Nikki pushed Lewis.

A metal blade stuck out of the shadow.

The girls dodged and moved, but it was like running through water.

Izzy stood up as the shadowy mist surrounded her.

"Izzy!" Elizabeth screamed as Dark Shadow materialized in front of the young demon hunter.

"Now you see me," the shadow said to Izzy, brandishing the blade in her face.

Izzy froze for a second, and then the shadow disappeared from her sight. She turned toward her mother, seeing the black-haired woman was now behind her.

"Now you don't," Dark Shadow said, piercing Elizabeth in her lower back with the red blade.

Elizabeth grunted in pain.

"Mom!" Izzy screamed.

Joy made a grab for Dark Shadow, but the demon was too fast.

It removed the blade from Elizabeth's back and stuck it into Joy's gut.

Joy felt the metallic taste of blood in her mouth as the metal pierced her skin, then fell to her knees, clutching her wound. She saw Dark Shadow smile at both fallen demon hunters.

"Your girls will be mine," the female demon announced, putting away the blood-stained knife. "Enjoy the precious time you've got left." She then turned to mist again and moved quickly through the woods.

Izzy ran up to the fallen demon hunters. Her heart skipped a beat the moment Elizabeth fell; now, it would not stop pounding. She reached her mother's side just as Joy laid on the ground next to her "Mom!" Izzy exclaimed, cradling Elizabeth's head and torso.

"Not so hard," Elizabeth whispered in a strained voice, as her body jolted in pain.

"You're okay!" Izzy cried, hugging her mom. Just then, all the hunters and Guardians reached Elizabeth and Joy.

Lewis was beside the brunette and started tending to her wound.

"Seen worse," Elizabeth said, wincing a bit without releasing pressure to her wound. "How are you doing, Joy?"

Joy was trying to keep it together. "I am okay," Joy said as she spat out more blood.

Lewis shook his head as he looked over the wound. "One-inch puncture. It's superficial, but it damaged something inside. You are bleeding internally. Your hunter body is trying to repair the damage, but it's taking time."

"I feel it working," Joy said, looking at the sky, trying to relax. She then winced as a surge of pain ran through her body.

Elizabeth's body arched in pain as well.

"What's happening to them?" Grace asked. Her voice seemed frightened for the first time.

Lewis's face was grim. "Coloration around the wound. The blade was poisoned. We need to move back to the castle now."

"Can you walk?" Williams asked Elizabeth.

Elizabeth shook her head in pain, and Izzy's heart raced again. Questions flooded her mind right there in the grassy prairie near the Guardians' Castle.

CHAPTER XIII

Guardians' Castle, Ireland; August 8, 10:30 p.m.

SEAN RAN UP THE stairs, not caring about the looks he was getting from the younger demon hunters. He had a bigger priority on his mind. Sean ran past the hall and saw three young girls sitting on the floor right beside his bedroom. He opened the door, not bothering to knock. His heart fell as he saw Williams at the side of the bed; on the other side was Izzy. Lying on the bed was his wife, Elizabeth. The scene haunted his nightmares. He closed the door behind him and walked toward the love of his life. "Elizabeth," he whispered, almost like a prayer.

"Hey," Elizabeth replied weakly. "I am okay. Just hazards of the job."

"What happened?" Sean asked Williams.

Izzy had her face buried in her hands. She was still trying to process the situation. It had all happened too fast.

"Dark Shadow ambushed the patrol," Williams explained. "She must have stood hidden until Elizabeth and Joy were least prepared, then she struck."

"Demon Hunter healing powers?" Sean asked. "Elizabeth will be alright?"

"Our enemy used a poisoned blade," Williams said, looking defeated. "Clara, Andy, and Jasmine are looking into it."

"That's not good enough!" Sean exclaimed.

"We are doing what we can with what we have!" Williams shouted back.

"Quiet," Elizabeth said weakly. She closed her eyes tightly as the pain surged through her body again.

Williams and Sean looked at Elizabeth. She was strong, and her body was fighting. "The body of the demon hunter," Williams stated. "Their healing power is the only thing fighting the poison now. The wounds are sealed, but poison is circulating throughout the nervous system, causing intense pain. Until Andy generates a cure, we have to trust the healing power will be enough."

"And if it isn't?" Izzy asked, looking up at the adults.

Elizabeth weakly turned toward her daughter. Her face was as pale as a sheet of paper. "Don't be afraid. You're a demon hunter. You'll pull through this."

Izzy grabbed Elizabeth's hand while looking at Williams' and Sean's terrified faces. Izzy kissed her mother on the forehead and walked out of the room. Grace, Nikki, and Ammarra stood up as Izzy walked out. "I need to stab something," Izzy said, gritting her teeth in rage. She knew her anger was flaring now. She needed to channel it.

"Lead the way," Nikki said, turning back to look at Grace and Ammarra. "We got your back on this."

Izzy nodded and led the way down the hall. "Grace?" she asked as she opened the door to the Guardians HQ. "We need to find this Dark Shadow demon. Any ideas on how to trace her?"

"I could try a locator spell," Grace answered, looking at the tech.

Izzy turned on the computers, knowing exactly how everything worked. The nine monitors came to life. "I could add some ingredients from Hawaii that can pump the intensity up."

"Okay," Izzy said as she dialed St. Helena from the primary control system.

Andy's voice and face jumped onto the screen."Hey, Izzy," Andy said, recognizing her. "Sorry about your mom."

"She'll pull through," Izzy said matter-of-factly. "Tell me what happened in St. Helena."

"What do you mean?" Andy asked.

"The same demon that stabbed Mom and Joy was present in St. Helena," Izzy said. "The demon moved from California to Ireland in a matter of hours."

"There's a video," Andy said while typing some commands.

"Can you show it to us?" Izzy asked.

Andy sat on the desk as he continued typing. Soon the video feed popped up. The four demon hunters watched in silence as they saw the twins valiantly put up a fight and prevent the hell spot from opening. Just as expected after their fall, darkness flooded the feed. It took a moment for the four to react to the feed.

"The Dark Shadow we saw tonight was faster," Ammarra pointed out. "Could be a different demon altogether, and not the same one."

"True," Nikki said. "It's vulnerable to magic. But you have to be fast for the spells to work."

"Simple spells," Grace said. "But effective."

"All good," Izzy said. "But there must be a link. Why is this demon in both locations, separated by so many miles?"

"Because it's two different demons, controlled by one entity," Brent interrupted.

The girls turned their attention to the dark-skinned warrior who had entered the room.

"What are you doing here?" Brent asked knowingly. "This area is off-limits."

"We're taking over," Izzy said as she searched for the Dark Shadow on the Guardians' Encyclopedia online.

"Your dad's going to be pissed," Brent said as he walked toward the desk.

"It won't be the first time," Izzy said as she pulled a picture of Dark Shadow. "The article in the encyclopedia is incomplete."

Brent frowned and gave Izzy the folder he was holding. "We thought she was a myth. We were dead wrong."

Izzy opened the file and started reading through it quickly. "The Order of Karratt?" She then passed the folder to Grace for her to read.

Brent nodded as he looked at Andy.

Andy nodded back as he listened to the conversation.

"The ancient assassin order," Brent explained. "The organization has existed since the early eighth century—an order of demons tasked with killing high-profile targets. Contract killers. Your mom had a contract on her head a few years back."

"What happened?" Izzy asked.

"Elizabeth did what she did best," Brent replied with a smile.

"Kicked their asses," Nikki guessed.

"The order terminated the contract after that," Brent concluded as he pointed to the image. "This new demon, Dark Shadow, is the head of the order now. Our contacts have a lot to say about her, including most of her aliases. The most recent one is Athena, which is how clients can get in touch with her. One of her major gifts is that she can turn into a dark purple mist and become solid at will. It is this ability that allows her to replicate herself and be in two places at the same time. We believe the one that Anna and Teresa fought was just a replica. She also has necromancer abilities."

172

"Necromancer?" Nikki asked.

"Yeah," Brent continued. "She raises zombies to do her bidding. There is a theory that she can assume the identity of a corpse; only we've yet to confirm this. She's one of the most powerful demons we've come into contact with."

"Powerful, maybe, but she's a hired gun," Grace said. "She doesn't have a motive to open a hell spot. Nor kill two high-ranking demon hunters."

"Somebody must be pulling her strings from the shadows," Ammarra said.

"And the demon hunters are not dead," Izzy corrected. "They'll get through this."

"I was talking about Anna and Teresa," Grace said, pointing at the paused video.

"Oh," Izzy said while minimizing the window.

"Wait," Nikki said aloud. "Did Dark Shadow miss her targets? Or did she do what she was supposed to do?"

"What do you mean?" Brent asked.

"I mean," Nikki said, "she had Izzy. She could've killed her. She had Elizabeth and Joy. But she just wounded them."

"With poison," Ammarra said.

"A poison that a hunter's body has a chance to process?" Nikki said. "An assassin goes for the kill. Quick and effective. The demon is not going to wait to see whether the poison works. The demon kills. End of story."

Izzy thought about what Nikki was saying. "What's the protocol if the head demon hunters are taken out of action?"

Brent thought for a moment. "Sean and I patrol the area. While the Guardians choose substitutes for the head of operations."

Izzy nodded and thought for a moment. She tried to piece the puzzle of information together. "They don't want to kill the demon hunters. They want to weaken the Guardians. They want you and my dad to go out and so they can take you out."

"Taking out the Guardians' strongest warriors," Nikki said.

"And then the assembly is ripe for the picking," Grace concluded.

The girls looked at each other and then at Brent, searching for approval of their farfetched theory.

"Why?" Brent asked. "For the past decade, this has been a stronghold. What's their purpose?"

"That theory is a bit thin," Ammarra said. "And the demon hunter missing from Austria doesn't fit in…"

"Not to mention St. Grievous," Andy piped in. "Whatever is happening involves him in some way."

Izzy's mind was spinning with all the information when Williams, Lewis, and Sean came in. They all froze, including Izzy. Izzy's heart raced a bit, but the look on her father's face helped her calm down. It was going to be okay. The Guardians entered the room and looked at the screen. Andy simply waved from where he was.

"Elizabeth and Joy are pulling through," Lewis said. "It is unbearably painful, but they're strong."

"Their supernatural healing is focusing on getting the poison out of their system," Williams said. "While they're like this, they are extremely vulnerable."

"The poison has no antidote," Lewis said. "At this rate, it will take three days before Elizabeth and Joy will be up."

"We stick to protocol," Sean said. "Brent and I cover the woods. The Guardians mind the Hunter Gathering. No girls leave the castle."

"Okay," Izzy said as she stood up. "This is your show. We start tomorrow early at eight a.m., right?"

"Right," Williams said, adjusting his glasses, seeming a bit surprised at Izzy's reaction.

"Come on, girls," Izzy motioned to her group. "The Guardians have this."

They followed her out the door.

"I'll say goodnight to my mom and go to bed."

When the girls left, Sean looked at Brent, at Lewis, then at Williams, and then at Andy on the screen. Sean nodded a bit for a few seconds before walking out the door after his daughter. As he stepped into the hallway, he saw Izzy's companions run into the kitchen while Izzy entered his room. Sean followed Izzy inside and saw her daughter at the head of the bed, kissing her mom goodnight.

"You're going to disobey me, aren't you?" Sean asked.

"Wouldn't be your daughter if I didn't," Izzy replied. She was as short as her mother, and she had his temper. It was on days like this that Sean truly felt powerless. But he was going to put up a fight.

"You're not leaving this castle," Sean ordered. "We're on lockdown."

"You're wrong, Dad," Izzy said as she stood up. "This is not me being rebellious. This is a demon hunter telling her Guardian that he's wrong." Sean was about to say something when Izzy put her finger on his lips. When she opened her mouth, she spoke softly, not losing her cool. "The bad guys know us. They know our every move. For too long, we have worked on a specific pattern—and the bad guys know this. They know our patrol routes. They know our demon hunters and our Guardians. Everything is set right up to the steps we take. They knew we would be out there. They sent a horde of vampires to attack us. They knew we would be vulnerable, and they sent their most skilled assassin to weaken us. And they've succeeded."

"You're still not going," Sean said firmly. Deep down, Sean knew Izzy had a point, but he needed more. And he was not about to sacrifice his only daughter to the unknown.

"If you go out there," Izzy said. "They'll kill you. They've got something prepared just for you and Brent. You've got to stay here and guard this front. They're not expecting a small squad of demon hunters."

As Sean looked into his daughter's eyes, he could see Elizabeth speaking to him. He remembered all those times Elizabeth took higher risks while he stood back and waited. But still, Sean would not budge. "You're not your mother. You don't have to prove anything."

"It's not about that," Izzy said, wincing at the hurtful comment. The dark shadow of her mother was ever-present. But she would not submit to it. "It's about doing what's right. This is my path. I choose when and how I walk it."

Sean's heart sank. Those were the words he dreaded hearing.

"She's all grown up," Elizabeth whispered. "It's time."

Sean sighed and looked at his daughter, adoringly. "Okay," he said as he walked to the dresser. He pulled out a wooden box and showed it to his daughter. "This is your birthday gift. Your mother and I have been holding onto these. They belonged to us; now, they belong to you."

Izzy remembered—her birthday was a couple of weeks away. Sweet sixteen. She took the wooden box from his father's hands and opened it. It revealed two leather bracelets with stakes attached to each one. Izzy's mouth dropped as she lifted them out of the box, revealing a long wooden stake underneath. "This is your gear," Izzy whispered as he looked at Sean, and then at her mother, who was smiling.

"Happy Birthday," Elizabeth said weakly.

Izzy twirled the stake in her hand. It felt right at home. Then she realized something. "Wait a minute. I am still getting my sweet sixteen party, right?"

Sean smiled and hugged his daughter. "When you're done. You have to catch up on all the classes that you miss from The Gathering. Talk to Clara on your way out so that she can give you a tracker and some cash. You'll have forty-eight hours."

"Okay," Izzy said, holding the wooden box firmly. "All I heard was a lot of mumbo-jumbo. But no answer to my party question."

"Don't forget to charge your phone," Sean said with a sly smile. "I want constant reports."

"I get it, Dad," Izzy said. "Gear and cash with Clara. Constant reporting. What about my party?"

"We'll talk when you get back," he said as he opened the door and closed it.

There was a moment of silence as he walked back toward Elizabeth.

"That's not a *no*!" Izzy said through the door. "Okay... we'll discuss it later."

Sean walked toward Elizabeth and lay down next to her.

"You took that rather well," Elizabeth said weakly.

"I've been dreading that moment since she came to us," Sean said.

Elizabeth hugged Sean while she closed her eyes. Her body felt limp and weak, but she felt her demon hunter power working to fend off the poison. While she tried to fall asleep by matching her breathing with Sean's, a clear image popped into her mind. It was a large, beautiful medieval sword. She remembered the power it emanated at the mere touch of the weapon. But as soon as she realized what she was thinking, her mind started to drift. She was falling asleep. "Apocalyps," Elizabeth whispered as the memory faded.

Izzy ran back toward her room, carrying her precious gifts, when she noted the hall seemed crooked somehow. Izzy stopped and braced herself against the wooden wall. Her surroundings were spinning, and she felt nauseated. Izzy closed her eyes for a moment, waiting for the queasy sensations to stop.

"O'Brien," Nikki called from her room. "You okay?"

Nikki's words snapped Izzy back to life. The room stopped spinning, and the sickening feeling was gone. "Yeah," Izzy said, finishing her way back to her room. "Just a little head rush." When Izzy reached the bedroom, she saw Grace and Ammarra sitting on her bed, dressed for battle. Izzy smiled. "We have forty-eight hours."

"Yay!" Nikki said. "Never before seen in a demon-hunter gathering."

"What's the plan?" Grace asked, pulling out a bag of magical ingredients.

"We find Dark Shadow," Izzy said, putting on her dad's bracelets. "We find her and find out who hired her for the job. Then we move up the chain."

"We kill Dark Shadow," Ammarra said in a severe tone. "That demon killed two demon hunters yesterday."

Izzy nodded as she slipped on a dark jacket while she looked at Grace. "Do we have all the ingredients for the locator spell?"

Grace looked at her bag. "We need something that belongs to the demon we're looking for."

"Maybe we can find something out in the field," Nikki said.

"It is a great place to start," Izzy said, looking at Grace, who was using the dresser to keep herself up straight. "You okay?"

"Yeah," Grace said. "We gear up?"

"Gear up, and let's meet at the Eastern entrance in ten minutes," Izzy said. "We've got forty-eight hours. After that, the Guardians take over."

The night was well upon them now, as the small group of girls walked the border of the eastern woods.

Nikki felt something tug at her insides just as they had reached the one-mile checkpoint. "Girls? Do you feel that?"

The other three turned in the same direction, sensing dark energy coming from the inside of the woods. All but Izzy pulled out their respective stakes, just as Izzy took a small step forward. The girls heard a soft growl coming from the darkness. Two light blue eyes shone out at them. Izzy crouched and looked at the creature.

"Aidan," Izzy called.

The black-and-white wolf appeared and walked lazily toward her.

"It's okay," Izzy said as she rubbed the black-and-white fur. "Aidan is a friend of mine."

"You have a pet wolf?" Ammarra asked, bewildered.

"Yeah," Izzy said while pulling a bag of meat from her pocket.

"Do your parents know?" Grace asked, making a face while the wolf ate the raw meat.

"Mom does," Izzy said. "And besides, it's just like having a dog."

The wolf growled as he heard the comparison to an ordinary dog.

"Kidding," Izzy said as she rubbed the beast while he ate. "He's a vicious man-eater."

Ammarra and Grace smiled at Izzy's interaction with the animal. They turned toward Nikki, whose face was white as a sheet of paper. She held on to her stake as if her life depended on it.

"You okay, Nikki?" Grace asked with a sly smile on her face.

"Yeah," Ammarra said, catching on. "It seems like you've seen a ghost."

"Me?" Nikki asked, coming out of her trance and shakily putting the stake away. "I'm fine. Just not too hot on wolves or dogs or any canine creature, that's all."

Izzy giggled a bit. "Aidan doesn't bite. He can help us."

"You're afraid of dogs?" Grace asked, laughing. "I feel so happy now, and I don't know why. Maybe because it's the best thing I've heard since I arrived."

Ammarra giggled a bit now, and Nikki was turning red from anger and embarrassment.

"Will you quit it!" Nikki said as she started walking toward their destination. "We're wasting time."

Izzy stood up and whistled, sending the wolf to where the battle had taken place.

Nikki jumped as Aidan ran past her. Her reaction prompted Ammarra and Grace to burst out laughing.

"It's okay," Izzy said, giving Nikki a friendly punch in the arm. "I'll not let the big bad wolf hurt you."

"I'm going to kill you!" Nikki hissed at her friend, prompting more laughter and giggling from the demon hunters.

CHAPTER XIV

Underground Town of York, Ireland; August 8, 10:45 p.m.

LUCINDA GROANED AS SHE stretched her slender body. The black-haired vampire looked to her side, seeing the cold, naked body of Dante. He slept peacefully, with a smile on his face. *He is probably dreaming of blood, death, and devastation.* She stood up, completely naked, and walked toward the balcony. The cold and damp environment of the underground city did not affect her; her dead body embraced the cold.

She looked at the rock ceiling. Her dark black eyes pierced through the granite, earth, and sand to peek at the stars that adorned the heavens. While the stars whispered to her mind, she pondered on the vampire friends she had lost in this endless war. Her friends and family had perished—all because humans did not know their place. Only the stars remained as her friends.

Lucinda paid attention to the stars and their whispers. Her sire had a gift that passed on to her when she was turned. But the devil woman had lacked the good sense to teach her how to use it. Instead, she abandoned her right after her birth into darkness. Her sire's insanity had caught the Guardian's attention, and ultimately to her end at the point of a stake. She abandoned Lucinda to deal with the voices in her head alone. That is when Richaldone came into her life.

She recalled the vampire from California who had moved from the tropical islands of Fiji—a wanderer who traveled to the best beaches in the world. He fed in the night, leaving human bodies sprawled in the sand while he enjoyed the waves. Rick was the name he used among intimate circles. Lucinda recalled his short, dirty-blond hair and his steely blue eyes. He only cared about the night and the surf. The female vampire smiled at the memory of him. He once had compared her to a great white shark, with her black, dead eyes. They only transformed when the blood-sucking demon was out. Rick loved her black eyes because it reminded him of the gorgeous night sky. He was the one who taught her to control her gift of sight. He taught her to listen, decide, and not give in to the insanity. Now, she was one of the most powerful and feared vampires on the planet—all thanks to Rick.

The dirty demon-hunter twins had extinguished Richaldone's immortal life—her friend, her brother, her lover. He died protecting her from the rampage of the demon hunters when they tracked down their nest and dusted her family right before her eyes. She alone had escaped. Rage boiled inside her when Siegfried delivered the news that the twins were dead. It was her destiny to end the lives of the pesky California girls. It was she who wanted to play with their insides and drink their demon-hunter blood for all the pain they had caused. She'd felt cheated out of her destiny, betrayed by fate.

Her rage died down once Dante took her into his clan. The master vampire confided in her his need to listen to the stars. The plan of taking down the Guardians and their demon hunters was in motion, and there was nothing that would stop things from coming to pass. The idea of escalating the human vs. vampire conflict into a full-time war made her mouth water. The taste of human blood empowered her. *Soon,* she thought to herself.

Lucinda felt Dante's arms wrap around her. The master vampire had awakened and snuck behind Lucinda's naked body.

"Have the stars spoken?" asked Dante.

"Indeed they have," Lucinda responded, letting the tall vampire caress her body.

"And?" Dante inquired.

"You were wrong," Lucinda said with a smile. "Assembly is on lockdown for forty-eight hours."

Dante stopped and processed the information for a minute. "That's impossible." For the first time, Lucinda detected a crack of fear in his voice.

"Is it?" Lucinda asked, turning around and looking up at him. "That's what's happening. Dark Shadow got to both Elizabeth and Joy, but did not kill them. Now the Guardians are on full lockdown, and they haven't sent out Sean or Brent as you foresaw."

Dante released Lucinda and walked toward the window. He grasped the balcony hard. "Unexpected. What are they doing?"

"Four demon hunters are tracking down Athena," Lucinda said as she grabbed her clothes and dressed. "They will track her down and most likely get the information from her."

"She knows nothing," Dante said.

"She knows where we are, silly," Lucinda said with a smile. "All your work from the shadows could crumble down if the assassin does not keep her mouth shut."

Dante stretched as the pieces of the puzzle rearranged in his head. "You said that Dark Shadow succeeded?" asked Dante, turning around.

"She got to both Elizabeth and Joy. They were wounded, but she did not kill them," Lucinda said. "Just as you ordered."

"Excellent," Dante said, smiling evilly. "Hunters are ripe for the taking."

Lucinda looked at Dante, puzzled. "You're hiding things from me," she whispered, detecting something sinister behind the crooked smile on the vampire's face. "Tell me."

"Surprise, baby," Dante responded, walking back to his closet. "All I can say is that I miss the old-fashioned Guardians and how they treated their demon hunters. I miss their old traditions. I miss their archaic exercises in cruelty."

"That's a bit vague."

"Answers are coming," Dante said. "When the demon hunters do arrive, please prepare a warm welcome."

Lucinda smiled as she relished the idea of killing a demon hunter. "It will be so, lover."

Dante finished dressing just as his brother-in-arms, Siegfried, entered the room. "We lost many in yesterday's battle."

"Nobody important, I hope," said Dante as he buttoned up his shirt.

Siegfried smiled. "None important," Siegfried said coolly. "Grievous is on his way. He seems a lot angrier than the books picture him."

"Not afraid, are you, brother?" Dante said as he put on his black suit jacket.

"I just had other ideas about the guy," Siegfried said. "Anything else you need?"

"Yes. Lucinda will take care of the inner security of the town."

"That's good," Siegfried said. "Meaning you want me outside?"

"Yes. We're going to Dark Shadow is going to leak some information. Well... at least one of them will. A squad of demon hunters is going to intercept her. Please make sure to treat the girls in accordance with our highest standards."

"Did Dark Shadow succeed?" Siegfried asked.

"Yes," Dante replied, almost bursting into laughter.

"Then I will take only two of my boys," Siegfried said, smiling back. "The hunters will be no trouble. The gargoyles will stay here."

"Very good," Dante said, all ready to go. "Did you get take-out?"

Siegfried snapped his fingers, and two vampires dragged a young couple into the master's bedroom. "Always spoiling me," he said, getting his vampire mode on. His fangs protruded from beyond his lips, sharp as knives. "I have always liked European."

Siegfried closed the door as the humans screamed in agony, while Dante pierced their flesh with his fangs.

Northern Woods, Ireland; August 8, 11:00 p.m.

Izzy watched as the wolf, Aidan, sniffed out the battle area. For far too long, she had depended on the wild animal to help her in situations such as this. The brown-haired girl remembered the wolf helping her out in Amsterdam alongside Elsa. Things could have ended up differently if it weren't for her pet. Izzy turned her attention toward Grace, who was sitting crossed-legged on the grass while she prepared the ingredients for the location spell. "How long will it take for it to work?"

"Just a few minutes," Grace replied. "Less if your wolf can find us something tangible."

Izzy turned toward the wolf, who was now returning with something in its mouth. Izzy took it and threw it at Grace. "Dark Shadow's?"

"Looks like it," Grace said as she placed the small piece of cloth in the batch of ingredients. Grace chanted something when Ammarra and Nikki appeared.

185

"Nothing on the perimeter," Nikki said. Her voice was a little tense, still a bit uncomfortable with Aidan being around.

Ammarra looked at Grace, who was now in a full trance. "I assume you found something," Ammarra said.

"We did," Izzy answered, looking out at the black night. "We wait now."

There was a moment of silence as they waited for Grace to come out of her trance.

"So," Nikki started, trying to break the ice. "You had a small Armageddon last year." She turned to Ammarra, who jolted as she heard the words. "Can you talk about it?"

"Nothing to tell," Ammarra said, shutting down, trying to avoid the conversation. "Spirit demon opened a gate to hell. I killed the demon. I stopped the end of the world."

Nikki nodded and looked at Izzy for support.

Izzy just shrugged.

"Come on," Nikki pressed. "No juicy details?"

"We all face life-and-death decisions." Ammarra was becoming visibly upset. "I faced mine a year ago."

Izzy could hear Ammarra's voice breaking. "Are you sure you don't want to talk about it?"

Ammarra looked away for a moment. The older hunter closed her eyes as the memories invaded her mind. "My Guardian died that night."

Nikki let a small gasp escape her lips as she heard the news.

"The assembly has been sending temporary Guardians or trainees until I get assigned a new one."

"You've had a rough year," Izzy said, knowing it was a challenging subject.

Ammarra wiped her eyes and turned toward her new friends. "Haven't spoken to anyone about it until now," she said, wincing a bit. "Time helps. But the emptiness of losing

186

someone who cares for you will never disappear."

"You will get a new Guardian," Nikki said, trying to lighten the mood. "Who knows. Maybe you met him or her already."

"What about you girls?" Ammarra asked Nikki and Izzy. "What stories do you have?"

"My demon-hunting life is pretty boring," Nikki said. She then turned her attention toward Izzy. "But Izzy's life—that must be exciting."

"No excitement here," Izzy said, surprised that the focus of the attention was on her now.

"Really?" Ammarra said. "No offense, but your parents are Elizabeth and Sean. There is nothing more exciting than that."

"How does that work, anyway?" Nikki asked. "After all, this isn't a crappy teen demon movie."

"What do you mean?" Izzy asked, knowing full well where the question was going.

"Ohhhh," Ammarra said, realizing where the conversation should go. "You mean how demons cannot procreate sexually with humans."

"Yup," Nikki agreed. "We follow the rules established in demonology. Vampires don't twinkle with sunlight, demons walk in the night, and humans don't have sexual encounters with the undead."

"Sean was a demon before Izzy was born?" Ammarra continued, trying to piece the history together.

"There you go!" Nikki said as she turned toward Izzy, whose face was turning red with embarrassment.

Izzy looked at both Nikki and Ammarra, and then toward Grace, who was in her meditation trance to get the tracking spell to work. "I was conceived naturally."

"B.S.!" Nikki exclaimed. "Your birthday is in two weeks. Your mother was probably eighteen or nineteen…"

"Enough!" Izzy exclaimed, stopping Nikki from going any further with her assumptions and the math. She walked away from Grace, with Ammarra and Nikki trailing her. "I was conceived naturally. I was born naturally. And I was raised naturally."

"But that's impossible," Ammarra said, doing the math in her head. "There's no record of Elizabeth ever being pregnant."

"There is," Izzy said, treading carefully. "There are pictures, and there is a birth certificate, and there was even a Catholic baptism. Brent and Lewis are my godparents, which I find ridiculous since they have no idea what the Catholic faith implies."

Nikki and Ammarra looked at each other, somewhat confused.

Izzy smiled sadly and tapped the side of her head. "Memories implanted in my mind. Well, those are the memories my parents implanted until I could do the math and figure out it wasn't possible."

"So, what's the true story?" Nikki asked.

Izzy turned back and started petting Aidan, who had strolled toward her side. "Because of a Gradius Demon, my dad had a small window of time to contemplate his humanity. For twenty-four hours, my dad became a heart-thumping, breathing, fully functional man. That day was the happiest day of my mom and dad's life. Their physical love no longer had a boundary. Unfortunately, in human form, my dad could not fulfill his duties as a champion in fighting the undead for the Guardians. So he killed the Gradius Demon that turned him human and erased the day from existence."

"Ultimate sacrifice," Ammarra noted.

"What my dad didn't know," Izzy continued with a frown forming on her face, "was that despite taking the day away, the consequences of that day still had to be taken care of. Hence me."

"Okay," Nikki said. "So where were you and how did you come to be with your parents?"

"Almost eleven years ago to the date," Izzy said out loud. "It was my birthday."

"The hell spot of New York," Ammarra concluded, recollecting the history of the demon hunters and the Guardians.

"On the day that my parents saved the world again," Izzy said, "They also destroyed the balance of power. My Aunt Kaela, who was a mighty Wiccan, needed to leave this world since her magic could not be contained in human form. For her to leave, someone from the higher plane needed to come back. Balance everything out."

"You were born on a higher plane," Nikki said. "That is the place where you were nursed and raised until you met your parents."

"They wiped my memory from that place," Izzy said, referencing the first five years. "New memories filled the gap. The higher powers added memories about my parents as well. Nobody else. But sometimes, my memory clears up, and fragments of the Limbo flood my mind."

"What was that like?" Nikki asked carefully.

"It was blank," Izzy said. "Lonely. No walls, no windows. Just a bed and a small library filled with books."

"Books?" Ammarra asked.

"Yep," Izzy said. "History books, and ancient folklore in Greek and Latin and other dead languages."

"Languages?" Nikki asked, amazed.

"Yeah," Izzy said, shrugging while tapping the side of her head. "Human dictionary. The higher powers made sure I knew at least a dozen languages."

"Wow," Ammarra said. "Now I know who to ask when I need the answers for my literature test."

"What are we talking about?" Grace asked, joining the group and interrupting the conversation.

"Izzy's capacity to understand literature in multiple languages," Nikki teased.

"We got a location?" Izzy asked Grace, ignoring the redhead.

"We got her," she replied.

"Lead the way, then!" Ammarra said.

CHAPTER XV

Guardians' Castle, Ireland; August 8, 11:55 p.m.

CLARA RUBBED HER STINGING eyes, feeling overwhelmed with everything that was going on. She wiped the sweat from her forehead, sensing she was coming down with something. The young woman couldn't stop, though—not now. She looked at her watch and frowned at the harsh reality that it was almost midnight. She took a breath and continued to look through the microscope. She had never figured that after all her adventures, she would be stuck in a room analyzing dark poisons from blood samples. It had been difficult training for this task, but Andy had given her pointers, and the internet was a wealth of information. Now she was the Guardians' lab specialist, but the real expert was Andy. There were very few things that the nerd did not know.

"You okay?" John asked, looking at the young woman, who seemed a bit pale.

"I'm okay," Clara said, typing some data into her tablet. "This is so tedious."

"I know," John said, closing the book he was reading. He closed his eyes and tried to process every piece of data that he had dug up. The only clue to go on was St. Grievous from the California hell spot. John had theories and conjunctures, but nothing substantial to put his money into. What he did find out was that Grievous was indeed a powerful vampire—a force beyond comparison in that time and place. The books painted him as a legend of folklore, too great and terrible to confirm whether he actually had existed. Legend had it that this great beast had led an army of demons and vampires across old eastern Europe. When warriors battled the monster, Grievous could take up to one hundred well-trained fighters with one blow. The task seemed exaggerated, as folklore often was, but that didn't bring any calm to John's mind. The fact that a monster filled with so much power existed, bringing pain and suffering everywhere he went, could make anyone tremble. The female demon hunters were the most reliable weapons the Guardians had—and their formidable power seemed to pale in comparison to this beast.

Clara completed the procedure and scanned the results just as Brent and Sean walked into the small lab.

"Any news?" Sean asked.

"Not before Andy looks at the results," Clara said, sending an email and printing out a document. Once the report was printed, Clara grabbed the piece of paper and handed it to John. "Want a crack at it?"

John looked at the piece of paper and took a glance at the components. "Seems familiar."

"We should head to the control room," Brent said. "Lewis and Williams may have new information on this Dark Shadow or Athena."

The foursome walked back toward the main HQ room. The mood was somber. A lot of clues, but no concrete leads to anything—just more questions. None of them pointed them in a specific direction.

Brent turned his attention toward Clara, who seemed to be tumbling as she walked the hall. "Are you okay?"

"I'm fine," she said, shaking the cobwebs. "Just fatigue setting in. Haven't been sleeping well."

"You can sit this one out," Sean said, noticing Clara's pale face.

"Seriously," Clara insisted. "I'm fine. Let's process the information."

As they entered the HQ room, they noticed Williams, Jasmine, and Lewis going over a few books while Alex handled the computer. On the screen, Andy poured out information as fast as his fingers could type.

"Where are we?" Sean asked the group. He was in charge of operations while Elizabeth was down.

"The poison is tricky," Andy said as he reviewed Clara's information. "It doesn't match perfectly to any of the patterns on our database. It does fit several assassinations in the past five years, though—all linked to the order of Karratt."

"We know it's the order of Karratt," Sean said. The information seemed pointless.

"Yes," Andy said. "But we're figuring out the culprit and motive. The poison works on other demons and humans. Not our demon hunters."

Sean paced around the room. This was not his strong suit, being patient. The information was there; it was just not at his grasp to put it all together.

"Funny," John commented as he read the components of the poison used.

"What is?" Williams asked his new Guardian.

"The poison contains a mixture of several powerful sedatives," John said. "All components strong enough to put down a horse. Other ingredients include troll bone for the pain effect and Obsidian."

"Obsidian?" Sean asked Williams and Lewis.

"It's an element rarely used in potions," Lewis said, looking at Williams for confirmation. "It's used for replication."

"Like dominoes falling in line," Williams concluded, looking at Lewis. "It's used to replicate the effect of the potion itself. In poison, the element could replicate on the hunter's organs."

"Or after they get it out of their system, it replicates internally, to hit them again," Lewis said. "Like an eternal cycle of pain going through their bodies."

"That could mean recycling the poison in their system," Sean said. "The magic could keep them in this state for life."

"Obsidian is a chain reaction element," Andy said to the team over the screens. "It would be the first time I would see a potion being used to link itself inside the same person."

"These guys are clever," Brent murmured. "Permanently incapacitating the main demon hunters."

"But it doesn't make sense," John interrupted. All eyes turned toward the newcomer to the team. "A well-known assassin uses debilitating poison instead of a deadly one to take out two high-profile targets? Why not use a deadly one? Why use a replicating poison that recirculates the curse of pain?"

There was a knock on the door. Sean turned and saw young sixteen-year-old demon hunter Andreia Popa looking pale and weak.

"Sorry to interrupt," the girl said in a heavy European accent. "Louise and I are not feeling too good; I think there was something wrong with the food."

Jasmine stood up and tended to Andreia while Sean looked in fear at Williams, Lewis, and Andy.

"The demon-hunter line," Sean said gloomily. He reached

for his cell phone, noticing that his hand was shaking as he dialed his daughter's number. The man only heard a busy tone on the other end. His heart was pounding as he realized the awful truth.

Alex, Williams, and Lewis came to the same realization.

"Andy," Williams said. He tried to remain calm. "You reversed engineered this poison to its basic ingredients. We need an antidote."

"On it," Andy said.

They all heard a loud thud behind the team. "Clara!" Alex screamed. "Clara!"

Sean looked in horror and saw that Clara had fainted right behind where Alex was sitting. His daughter's phone kept giving him a busy signal. "John!" Sean exclaimed. "Track Izzy and the rest of the girls, now!" The dead line at the end of the phone kept destroying Sean's life each time he heard it.

Five miles Northeast of Guardians' Castle, Ireland; August 9, 12:15 a.m.

"Dad is going to kill me," Izzy whispered, looking at her phone. No signal. She then looked at the cave entrance, where Grace's spell had led them. Dark Shadow was inside. "Are we ready?"

Grace and Ammarra nodded.

Izzy looked at Nikki, who was a little pale. "You okay?" she asked, seeing a small drop of sweat on Nikki's forehead.

"Just excited," Nikki said, trying to calm the girls down and get her composure. "Let's do this."

The four demon hunters walked up to the cave when Grace stumbled a bit.

"You okay?" Izzy asked.

"I don't know," Grace said. "Feeling nauseous."

"Feeling under the weather, girls?" the purple female demon appeared in the entrance of the cave. The woman had long black hair tied neatly in a ponytail that reached down to her waist. A dark purple leather jumpsuit covered her slender body. She stood on higher ground, which was a disadvantage for the girls.

The demon hunters pulled out their weapons and waited as Aidan growled at the demon.

"Four against one?" Dark Shadow pondered. "Doesn't seem fair."

"When you stabbed a demon hunter in the back, fairness went out the window," Nikki retorted.

"Who sent you?" Izzy asked.

"You're going to make me talk?" Dark Shadow purred. "You spoiled brat. You have no idea whom you're dealing with."

Izzy had had enough. She ran to the side while the other demon hunters covered her.

Dark Shadow just stood her ground.

Izzy fired a right haymaker to where Dark Shadow's face was. She only hit mist. Izzy fired a kick to the side and backhanded a punch behind her, but the purple haze surrounded her. A purple hand shot out and grabbed her throat. Athena lifted Izzy off the ground, her black Converse shoes dangling a foot above the earth.

"You brat!" Dark Shadow said as her face materialized in front of Izzy. "How dare you come and bark orders at me? You would have never existed if my order had completed the job years ago."

"*Solidum!*" Grace exclaimed as she threw something at the base of the mist. Dark Shadow gasped as her body solidified.

Izzy kicked her opponent hard, causing her grip to loosen. She could feel she had not kicked her opponent hard enough; she looked up and saw Dark Shadow beginning to recover.

Nikki came out of nowhere, kicking Dark Shadow in the lower back.

The demon screamed in pain, then backhanded Nikki across

the face, sending the red-headed girl flying toward the entrance of the cave.

Grace covered the distance and fired a kick, connecting with the demon's face.

Then Ammarra did a one-two combination on her chest.

Dark Shadow flew several feet away from the force.

Izzy jumped up and plunged her short sword through Dark Shadow's leg. The demon screamed in pain, to Izzy's satisfaction. All of a sudden, a wave of dizziness hit her.

Dark Shadow saw the opening and punched Izzy in her jaw.

Izzy grunted in pain at the blow; her surroundings spun even more.

She looked up and saw Nikki deliver punch after punch, connecting with Dark Shadow's face and body. But the hunter's attacks did not seem to do the damage they were supposed to do. Dark Shadow fired a right at Nikki's midsection. Nikki gasped and went down, only to receive a knee to the face.

Grace kicked hard at the demon's chest.

The demon simply took one step back, wiping the dust from her chest. "Is this the best the demon hunters have to offer?"

Ammarra jumped from out of nowhere and punched Dark Shadow, sending the demon flying. The demon did not have time to react before the girl picked her up by the arms. Ammarra jerked upward on the demon's extremities, hearing an audible crack, followed by a scream of agony.

Dark Shadow kicked her in the mid-section, pushing her away.

Athena reevaluated the situation. The demon hunters were tired, but not out. They seemed weak and stumbling on their feet. Dark Shadow screamed, and a dark purple liquid poured from her fingers, reaching the ground.

The girls froze for a moment, not sure what was happening. Suddenly, dead arms sprouted from the ground. Zombies.

"Necromancer," Izzy noted as Athena raised the undead from their tombs. They seemed so different—they seemed to be alive. A mark on each forehead revealed they were fallen Karratt operatives.

"Nothing escapes your sight, does it?" Dark Shadow said, wincing from the pain in her disabled arms as she took a step back.

The Karratt zombies attacked precisely and quickly. The hunters staggered as the expert undead warriors fought with all their might.

Izzy fell due to the punishment. She looked in horror as the zombie twirled its sword, ready to take the plunge. A growl distracted the zombie as Aidan jumped and sunk his fangs into the creature's arm.

The zombie dropped the sword as it wrestled with the wolf.

Izzy grabbed the blade and swung horizontally, decapitating the undead creature. In one swift motion, she threw the sword, connecting with the head of Grace's opponent. The beast fell dead.

Grace fell to her knees. The pain of the blows was unbearable. She thought air would never reach her lungs. Her surroundings would not stop spinning.

Izzy reached her friend.

"I'm fine," Grace lied before Izzy could ask the question. She closed her eyes, hoping the pain would stop.

Izzy looked up and watched Ammarra fend off the last zombie while Nikki looked on from the ground. She looked bruised and beaten.

Ammarra turned her attention toward Dark Shadow, who took a step back in fear. She threw her blade at Dark Shadow's good leg, piercing her flesh, causing the demon to fall and scream. Ammarra reached the beast and pulled the sword out, spurting purple blood all over. She then sliced an arm off. "Talk, and I will kill you quickly."

Athena crumpled like a house of cards. "Dante! He put out the contract!"

"Human, demon, or vampire?" Ammarra asked, cleaning the blade.

"Vampire," Dark Shadow said. "Old one. He's here in Ireland. Underground Town of York."

Ammarra swung the sword, removing Dark Shadow's head. "Was that what you needed?" Ammarra asked Izzy, who was helping Grace stand up.

Izzy nodded and helped Grace, but her knees buckled. Both Grace and Izzy knelt on the disturbed soil. "Feel weak." She saw Ammarra help Nikki, who was out cold.

Ammarra laid Nikki down next to Grace and Izzy. "Must be the poison. When your mom and Joy got hit, the poison must have contaminated the hunter line."

Izzy nodded at the information. It made sense.

Aidan walked up to them, growling softly.

"Why are you still okay?" Izzy asked, trying to keep herself straight up.

Grace crumpled, unconscious, next to Nikki.

Ammarra slowly sat in front of Izzy, who was now powerless. "Well, maybe because I am not a demon hunter."

Aidan growled and lunged at Ammarra, who simply smacked him out of the way like a fly. The wolf flew out of control, hitting the side of the cave. Izzy tried to punch Ammarra, but the demon hunter from Indonesia simply deflected the blow. "You're about to pass out, you little brat," Ammarra said. Her voice turned deeper—more menacing, yet familiar. "Do you want me to tell you?"

Izzy tried to move, but her body was not cooperating.

Ammarra looked at Izzy with an evil smile.

All Izzy could see in front of her was Dark Shadow Athena.

Izzy looked behind the purple figure and saw Ammarra's dead body flop behind her. The carcass of the demon hunter quickly decomposed.

"Ammarra succeeded in not letting me open the hell spot in Indonesia," Athena said. "It cost only her Guardian's and her own life. As an assassin, I could not think of a better way to infiltrate the organization that had the only open contract of the order."

Izzy's stomach lurched. "Everything is fake. All this to take out my mom."

"At first it was, silly," Athena said playfully, as she took control of Ammarra's dead body again.

Izzy was now seemingly facing the demon hunter from Indonesia. She seemed so alive.

"Then, Dante approached me with a better contract—and a vision."

Izzy questioned Dark Shadow with a look. She saw three dark figures approach the demon from behind.

"Siegfried," Athena called out to the dark vampire behind her. "Come to make sure I was okay?"

Izzy tried to process all the information, but it was too much. She was slowly passing out. The girl tried to battle the unconsciousness that was taking over her, wobbling in the position she was in. The vampire smacked Izzy across the face; her cheek stung as she clung to consciousness, but she was losing. It was like sinking into a dark pool.

CHAPTER XVI

Guardians' Castle, Ireland; August 9–1:00 a.m.

ELIZABETH SCREAMED AS SHE woke up, feeling sweat dripping from her forehead. Something was wrong. Something was deadly wrong.

Williams opened the door a few seconds later. "Elizabeth?" His tone, as always, was comforting. A father figure to the end.

"Izzy?" Elizabeth asked with a panicked voice.

Williams shook his head sadly. "No word yet. Sean went after her."

Elizabeth tried to stand up, but a wave of dizziness hit her, followed by a dull pain in her chest.

Williams came to her aid and steadied her.

"I don't remember my eighteenth birthday being this painful," she said half-jokingly.

"You should rest," Williams said, trying to gulp down her comment.

Elizabeth's eighteenth birthday was a bittersweet memory for him. It was the day he betrayed his hunter's trust. Her green eyes looked pained and broken when she found out he was responsible for her agony and suffering. The memory was burned into his mind, and he vowed to himself to be there forever for his demon hunter. The memory was bittersweet because, on that day, he came in terms with the fact that he loved Elizabeth like his own daughter. For too long, the old Guardians had stripped the humanity in his task. Now he was here, as always, supporting his demon hunter as he vowed he would.

Elizabeth noted Williams' silence as he tried to steady her while she tried to stand up. His scent of vintage scotch and old books always brought comfort to her heart, but she needed more today. She needed her daughter safe. "Izzy's in danger."

"We know," Williams said as he helped her. "We're taking care of it. You need to rest. You can't help Izzy now—not in this state."

But Elizabeth was having none of it as she struggled to stand up straight and grab her robe. "Izzy needs me," she declared as she put on a robe and walked out groaning. The pain was excruciating as the blonde woman exited, using the wall for support while slowly walking toward her office. She gasped as a surge of pain passed through her entire being.

"Elizabeth," Williams said as she held her. "Moving is only making the poison spread faster."

"But moving is the only way I can get the poison out of me," she answered, pain evident in her voice as she entered the office.

Her office was small compared to Williams'. Neither books nor fancy paintings adorned her wall—just a small wooden desk with folders and papers on top, and case files of the army of demon hunters around the world. But that was not what she sought; that was not what she longed for. She reached the back of the office and opened the small wooden cabinet. Her hands shook as she turned the key. The whispers of the night spoke to her heart, telling her the danger her daughter was in. She opened the cabinet and revealed a red leatherbound book—her demon hunter journal. Her own hand had written the document, of all her past dealings with evil and the undead. It called to her. The last page lingered in her mind, as it also contained the only thing not written by her—a colored drawing.

"Apocalyps," she whispered.

Williams removed his glasses and looked at Elizabeth as she stared at the last page of her journal.

"It calls out to me," Elizabeth said. "For some time it has been calling to me."

"It was that fateful day that you chose everyone," Williams said, knowing full well what she talked about. That day, she called unto that dangerous weapon. That day, she used it to channel the power to all the girls around the world who shared her same gift. But the sword was too mighty to be controlled. Not even Elizabeth, being the strongest of all demon hunters, could master its power.

"You infused all the girls who had the gift with the power to fight demons," Williams said as she sat across from her. "No longer would they fight alone."

"The key to our cure is here," Elizabeth said, looking at the drawing of the sword and showing it to him. "We're forever linked. And today it may be the key to helping the girls who have a target on their back."

Williams cleaned his glasses while he looked at the drawing. It was a long, medieval battle sword. The blade was of a soft, blue heavenly metal. Where the hilt and the blade met at the silver plate, a silver heart merged with a cross, both made of solid gold. The drawing did not do justice to what the sword looked like in reality. That weapon was what caused the demon hunter lineage to extend beyond what it was meant to.

Williams put back his glasses on and held Elizabeth's hand in comfort, as any father would for his daughter. "There are no books about what you want. Nothing has been written because there is no precedent. We write the story of Apocalyps as we move along."

"The girls need this," Elizabeth said, her eyes welling up. It needed to be done. "Izzy needs this."

Williams smiled softly as his heart melted r. "Izzy needs you. You and Joy are the eldest of all. The girls look up to you two. You need to be strong." He took one more look at Elizabeth's drawing as he stood up. "I will work with Lewis and see what we can do."

Underground, Town of York, Ireland; August 9, 2:30 AM

Dante smiled as he saw his brother guide three demon hunters down to his city, their hands chained in front of them. His vampire army cheered and hollered, then growled as the demon hunters were paraded in front of them, right in the central plaza of the cursed underground lair. At least fifty vampires surrounded them; the girls could feel their cold breath down their necks as they were exhibited and humiliated in front of the vampire army. The vampires wanted but a whiff of their precious demon-hunter blood. They looked and laughed, but they did not touch them—they would not dare, not with Dante overlooking the spectacle.

Lucinda purred as Siegfried brought the demon hunters down to their knees right in front of Dante. The dark-haired vampire then stood behind them. The two vampires who had accompanied him held the girls' weapons.

Athena, still in possession of Ammarra's dead body, walked toward Dante and Lucinda. "They are powerful."

"Indeed," Lucinda said as she caressed Nikki's cheek. "I can feel it."

"Where are our manners?" Dante asked Siegfried. "Please,

my friend. Stand them up." Siegfried signaled for his vampire entourage to stand the girls up forcefully. Dante walked up to Izzy and looked at her from top to bottom. "Sweet girl. You are a mirror image of your mother."

"You're behind this, I assume," Izzy said with a calm tone. She felt her body numb, but at least the dizziness had stopped.

"Indeed," the vampire said, taking a small bow. "Dante, at your service. Welcome to my home. Glad to see you've met my extensive family."

"Where's Elsa?" Izzy demanded. "We know you're behind her kidnapping."

"You know nothing," Dante said as he took Izzy's bracelets and inspected them. A stake popped up due to a mechanism he activated unknowingly. The vampire smiled evilly. "Cute toy," he said as he slipped the bracelets on his arms. Seeing her weapons on her enemy's hands made Izzy's blood boil. "The Guardians and the demon hunters are blind now. You are here because I allow you to be here."

"What do you want?" Nikki asked.

Dante turned his attention to the redhead. He could see right through her—she was trying to reason with him. He tried out the bracelets on his wrists, making a stake pop up.

The vampires cheered at his actions.

"I want balance," Dante said, looking over his army of vampires, who quieted down as he spoke. "We all want balance. The demon hunters have been given too much power. It is time to take some of it back."

"So, you kidnap a few demon hunters to prove your power to the Guardians?" Izzy asked, looking at Grace, who only stared at the ground. *She is too quiet. Is she scared?*

"My plan is much bigger than you can possibly fathom," Dante said, turning around and watching a large vampire emerge. He seemed to be a warrior from ancient times; metal-plated armor covered his body. A strange cross was encrusted in the metal. The demon had long red hair and a beard; fangs emerged from his hairy face. Two vampires walked behind him, dragging two large coffins. The first coffin was opened, revealing a beaten and chained blonde demon hunter.

"Elsa!" Izzy exclaimed, trying to move toward her friend.

Siegfried pulled Izzy by her dark hair, causing the heroine to scream in pain as she crumpled down.

"Friend of yours?" Dante asked with a smile as he walked toward the beaten demon hunter from Austria. "Relax. She's almost dead." He caressed the young blonde, while the other vampire opened the second crate and revealed the Uroks-Nah demon. His appearance brought shock to the girls. The monster was one of the deadliest beasts that walked the world of darkness—any demon hunter who fought an Uroks-Nah vampire most likely perished by its hands. The recommendation from the Guardians was to run from them if they ever faced one.

"Are we ready?" the large vampire in armor asked Dante. "The hour is upon us."

"We are indeed," Dante said, motioning his vampires to move the crates.

A third vampire appeared behind them, carrying a large circular shield. "I will need to feed after my power is restored."

"Yes," Dante said, walking back toward the massive beast. "Vampires obtaining power need to feed." He then turned toward the demon hunters and winked. "And demon hunter blood will be the perfect dish."

Izzy noticed Dante's eyes. Was the vampire winking at her? She did not have time to process the information. Siegfried pulled her harshly back to her feet and pushed her back up the stairs. Vampires cleared the space, while the demon hunters were guided toward the top stairs. They had a perfect view of the plaza below. Izzy wondered why they were being moved; then, she realized that they had been given front seats to whatever ritual Dante was preparing. The vampire wanted them to witness it all from above. Izzy turned toward Nikki, who made eye contact with her.

Nikki motioned what she already knew—the exit was just a few feet away.

Izzy then turned her attention toward Grace, whose head was still down. A small puddle had formed at her feet. Izzy could not believe it—the perfect demon hunter seemed to be scared to death.

Ten vampires formed a line behind them while Siegfried and his lackey bodyguards kept them in place. The rest of the vampire horde made a circle around Dante and the giant hairy demon.

"Where do I stand for this ritual?" the large vampire asked. "In the middle?"

"No," Dante said calmly. "You stand at the head of the triangle. Top of the food chain. The energy will canalize from the demon hunter and the Uroks-Nah to bring you new and untapped power."

"Excellent!" the demon said. "My weapons?"

"You don't need them right now," said Dante as he instructed his vampires to place the Uroks-Nah and Elsa at the base of the triangle formation. Dante guided the giant demon to where he was supposed to stand.

Two vampires appeared and chained the demon to the ground.

"Why the chains?" the demon asked.

"Control, Grievous," Dante replied dryly. "The surge of power will be strong. You have to remain in place, or the ritual will not work."

Izzy shuddered as she looked at Elsa from above. She looked dead. The only sign of life was her chest slightly moving with each breath the blonde girl took. Her attention moved towards Dante, who grabbed the shield and sword, placing them on a table in the center of the square. Vampires surrounded him while Grievous, Elsa, and the Uroks-Nah demon made a triangle around the offering.

"Years ago," Dante exclaimed as he walked around, "the Guardians tipped the balance of power, along with the demon hunters. Tonight, we vampires take back what is ours!"

The vampires cheered, and Izzy felt a cold shiver run down her spine.

"St. Grievous—" Dante said, pointing at the large vampire. "He showed us the way centuries ago. Tonight he does it again!"

The vampires cheered as Grievous looked at the demon hunters above him. He already imagined feeding on their flesh.

Dante chanted a dark and evil language in the center square. The vampires looked at the offerings before them as a dark essence surrounded them

Elsa screamed in pain.

Izzy struggled in her chains as she watched helplessly the dark magic torture her best friend. Izzy saw Elsa's chained body shake violently inside her coffin, her screams deafening. She smashed her head against the walls of the coffin; blood spurted out of the wounds she caused herself.

Dante walked up to the defenseless girl and looked at her, then pulled out a stake from one of Izzy›s bracelets and stabbed Elsa in the heart.

"NOOOO!" Izzy screamed helplessly as she watched her best friend die at Dante's hands. Memories of her past adventures with her sister flashed before her eyes.

A dark mist spurted out of Elsa's mouth, nose, and eyes.

Izzy watched in horror as Elsa's body slowly disintegrated into nothingness, tears streaming down her face as she saw the essence of her best friend's life fade away.

Dante used his hand to move the dark essence he had extracted from Elsa's body toward the shield and the sword. He then lifted his hand, and the Uroks-Nah vampire started to twitch violently in agony. The beast roared and tried to free itself from the chains that had it trapped. A dark essence emerged from the undead creature, turning the vampire it left behind into dust. Dante guided the power toward the shield, joining it with Elsa's power.

"Yes!" Grievous exclaimed, craving the dark energy. "I can feel the power! Feed it to me!"

Dante turned his attention toward Grievous and grinned. "Who said it would be for you?"

Grievous watched in fear as he realized the truth. He roared in pain as something inside him snapped at a single movement of Dante's hands. "No!" He tried to free himself, but the chains kept him in place. The demon knelt as the power abandoned him.

"Yes!" Dante exclaimed, as the power left Grievous and turned the vampire into ash. Grievous' essence reached the center of the square and merged with those of Elsa and the Uroks-Nah. The energies combined into a reddish glow of power above the shield and sword. "The evolution of the vampire is in the palm of my hand!" He said as he brought the energy down onto the shield and sword. The power merged with the weapons, creating a blinding glow. The ground trembled softly as black magic affected the surroundings. The red glow expanded slowly through the cavern. As the light reached Dante, he felt a power surge through his body. "It's working!"

Izzy turned away, only to see the vampire behind her join in the trance Dante was in; his yellow eyes glowed a dark blood-red. She could see his fangs start to grow, ever so slightly. She then turned toward Nikki, who was pale in fear upon realizing the truth.

Suddenly, Grace released herself from her chains. Izzy saw it all in slow motion as the chains that trapped the black-haired girl were now around the palms of her hands. Izzy and Nikki ducked as Grace swung the chains in deadly arcs; the chains smashed against two vampires.

They screamed in pain as smoke spurted out of their open wounds.

Siegfried tried to react, but because of the magical trance he was in, his movements were slower than usual.

Grace took full advantage as she swung the chain and wrapped it around the vampire's neck.

Smoke and the smell of burned flesh came from the vampire as he grunted in pain and tried to remove the metal from his throat.

Grace pulled hard with what little demon hunter power she had left.

Nikki and Izzy extended their legs, making Siegfried trip over Grace, who smoothly flipped him over her back.

The vampire screamed as he fell thirty feet onto a concrete column, back first.

Izzy grimaced as she saw the awkward position the vampire had landed in.

Nikki's voice snapped her back to reality. The redhead shoved Izzy hard and pointed toward Grace, who was swinging her chains that somehow burned the vampires as the metal touched their skin. The vampires, in their magical trance, were unable to defend themselves. Grace cleared the path toward the exit the hunters had spotted earlier.

"We are leaving!" Nikki exclaimed, pulling Izzy by her chains—half-stumbling, half-running toward freedom. Both girls followed her toward the exit. As soon as they exited, they felt a warm red glow behind them. The red light seemed to pursue them inside the cave and flooded the dark passageway.

Grace's heart pounded hard, keeping her adrenaline going while the ground rumbled inside the cave. She needed to focus and get them out of the caves. A vampire jumped from an opening, which made Grace jump back in surprise. The vampire screamed in pain as red light filled his body. Grace jumped over the demon and continued forward; she felt Izzy and Nikki right behind her. Another vampire popped out. This time, Grace pressed the blessed chains over the vampire's throat. The vampire burned as the energy engulfed him. Grace pressed harder, grunting with force as the metal links passed through the vampire and decapitated the demon. Dust filled the cave.

"Wait!" Izzy begged. "We need to stop!"

Grace turned toward Nikki and Izzy just as the brown-eyed girl crumpled down.

She was on top of her and started picking the locks on her chains. "How?" Izzy asked as her shackles fell to the ground.

"Magic," Grace said, smiling as she proceeded with Nikki's chains.

Izzy stood up and looked back, hearing screams from the vampires they were leaving behind. The memory of Elsa's death tore her up inside, but there was no time to mourn. "I thought you were scared to death."

"I am scared to death," Grace said as she guided the trio out of the cave. "But I have a strong will to control the fear." Grace dropped empty bottles of holy water on the ground.

Izzy looked at Nikki, who was shaken as well.

"Have we lost our powers?" Nikki asked.

Izzy shook her head. "It has to be temporary," she replied, walking and looking back behind her. "But in these conditions, we're sitting ducks."

"This way," Grace interrupted them. "I remember we came through here."

A vampire jumped out of nowhere, prompting the three hunters to jump and scream in fear. Red energy poured from his eyes, nose, and mouth. His vampire fangs seemed to be growing and looking sharper. The vampire pushed hard on Grace, making the girl crash against the cave wall hard and making her crumple down. Nikki jumped in front of the vampire and tried to punch it, but her strikes were way off. She swung weakly, while the vampire dodged and moved from side to side. It was still under the effect of what Dante had been doing. It moved and fired a knee that connected with Nikki's midsection. The redhead gasped for air as she felt two fists strike down on her back, putting her down.

Izzy watched in fear as her friends groaned in pain. She grabbed Grace's blessed chains and flung them at the vampire catching the vampire with a metal ring on the face. The impact was not hard, but the searing, burning pain was all it took. The vampire staggered back, grabbing its face in agony. Izzy pressed on, hanging the chain around the beast's neck. The creature flung its arms and screamed while energy kept pouring from the orifices of its face. Izzy pulled hard until she heard the bone snap. The chains burned through the dead flesh, decapitating the demon. Izzy walked weakly toward her friends and helped them up. "We must hurry," she urged.

Underground, Town of York, Ireland; August 9, 3:00 a.m.

The dark power inside Dante grew, increasing his vampire strength and agility as the changes in his body took effect. The energy of the demon hunter, mixed with the ancient demon and the hellish creature, was fueling his essence. "More power!" Soon the rumbling and the noise died down. Dante flexed his hand and arms. The transformation was now complete feeling his senses enhanced. The desire for blood hurt his throat. He needed to feed. He looked at his brothers and sisters and saw the hunger in their eyes. They looked stronger. Their eyes were no longer yellow like they had been before, but were now bloodshot red. The vampires were not looking back at him, though.

He turned and saw Lucinda weeping by Siegfried's broken body. Dante ran up to his friend and confidant kneeling beside him, seeing that the transformation on both Lucinda and Siegfried had worked. They were more powerful than ever, but additional power did not restore broken bones. And Siegfried was broken. "Brother," Dante softly said as rage boiled over him. He looked up and saw several vampires burned and beaten.

"They did this," Lucinda hissed. "They hurt him. They flung him down here while we were all in a trance. He was defenseless." Lucinda grabbed Dante's arms. "Make them pay!"

Dante stood up and looked at his hoard of vampires. He needed to recompose himself—no rash decisions. Without his right-hand friend, the blond demon felt crippled. He then looked at Siegfried's two large enforcers vampires who seemed bloodthirsty, ready to feed and kill.

"Our boys are inside the caves," he said, looking at his large minions. "Take a dozen and find the hunters. Break their bodies, but bring them to me alive." Both muscular vampires ran up the stairs at Dante's command. The master vampire turned toward his entire clan, ready to make war. "GO! Feed and get strong. All who join us will be part of our glory. Witness the end of the demon-hunter line. The time of the vampire is upon us."

The vampires roared in approval and made a run toward the different exits of the underground city. Dante strolled toward his friend. He was alive but broken and unconscious. "They will pay for this. They will pay." The master vampire then turned toward Athena, who was there waiting for orders. "You're in charge of my security now, Athena. Congratulations on your promotion."

Underground Cave Network, Ireland; August 9, 3:15 a.m.

Izzy, Nikki, and Grace ran through the caves. The air was heavy, stale, and humid. They could hear the growls and screams of the vampires behind them. Grace turned right and then left, always going up, trying to lead her newfound sisters to safety. She could hear the beating of her heart pounding in her ears, almost shutting out the howls and roars from the demons behind them. The demonic sounds that echoed in the dark cave came from everywhere and seemed to engulf them. They were gaining on them, getting louder and louder. Grace could feel a little adrenaline rush—it was not her demon hunter powers, but her survival instincts. The only time she remembered feeling like this was when she saw her parents die. The adrenaline had petrified her to the floor, helpless and scared. The feelings washed over her as she shook her head and took another left. She needed to get out. Those feelings would not overpower her. Not again.

Nikki was hyperventilating. She was also scared, but for another reason that she had not shared with her friends—she was claustrophobic. And the confined space of the cave tunnels was getting to her. She had managed to control her fear of small spaces, but without her demon hunter powers and the echoes of the vampires coming closer, she was losing it. Only Izzy's strength was keeping her moving.

Izzy felt the vampires get closer, but she could smell fresh air nearby. A light breeze caught a piece of her brown hair. "Hurry!" she urged, pushing Nikki.

Grace led them out of the cave, finding themselves in the middle of a dark forest. Nikki fell to her knees, breathing hard; her heart felt as though it was going to burst out of her chest. She heard a low growl in front of her; a bead of sweat streamed down the side of her face. Nikki slowly looked up and saw a black-and-white furred wolf in front of her. She could have sworn that her heart skipped a beat as the growl grew more menacing. The wolf launched itself, and Nikki emitted a soft gasp, but the wolf did not attack her—it hurled itself at the first vampire that followed the girls out of the cave.

Izzy grabbed Nikki and stood her up as the wolf started tearing the vampire apart. Nikki squeezed Izzy's arm as Grace stood beside them. The wolf stopped and left the vampire's mangled body at the entrance of the cave, growling as it guarded the girls while three more vampires emerged. Their demon features altered, no longer resembling regular vampires. The larger fangs made them more vicious and menacing as they growled at the girls. Izzy thought quickly—Aidan could not take all three at once. The girl clenched her fist hard, trying to find her strength. It was not there.

The vampires smiled through their hideous features staring the girls down with their fiery red eyes. They were about to attack when a whizzing sound cracked the air. The girls gasped when they saw an arrow pierce one vampire in the eye and go right through its skull. The vampire screeched as smoke poured out from the wound. The girls turned around, seeing Sean reloading his crossbow as Brent fired another arrow. It hit a vampire in the chest, where the heart was supposed to be. Smoke poured from the wound, but the vampire did not combust.

"That's a first," Brent said, feeling a bit surprised. The Guardian reloaded, while the girls ran up to stand behind Sean. Sean fired his arrow, hitting the third vampire in the chest.

Again, no combustion—just smoke and burning undead flesh.

Aidan viciously attacked the biggest vampire, while the other two removed the arrows from their bodies. "Get to the Jeep!" Sean ordered the girls as he fired a second arrow, hitting a skull again. The girls needed no other instruction. They ran up to the hill and saw the Guardian's Jeep parked up the grassy heel. They stumbled up to it and jumped in the back seat. Izzy looked back and saw Sean and Brent run-up. Aidan was busy mangling the third vampire when a dozen vampires poured out of the cave.

"Aidan!" Izzy screamed. The wolf noted the new danger and fled into the woods, where darkness engulfed it. The vampires cared little for the wolf or their fallen companions. They wanted the demon hunters, and they ran for them. Sean's Jeep roared to life and darted out, searching for an exit through the woods.

Brent looked behind them and saw the vampires running after the Jeep. "What are these vampires?" he asked as he stood up on his seat and fired. A vampire went down, but the others came faster.

Izzy looked frantically under her seat and pulled out two small crossbows. She gave them to Nikki and Grace. "We get in this, now!"

"My aim sucks without my powers," Nikki said, half-joking feeling scared to death, but standing up and looking at the small horde of vampires running after them.

"Is it too much to ask to keep the Jeep steady?" Grace asked as Sean swerved around the beaten road of the forest. The girls fired their arrows, missing badly. The girls shrieked as a vampire jumped up toward the Jeep. Brent fired, and an arrow went into the skull of the vampire, bringing it down. The Jeep swerved right and jumped a road bump making the girls hang on to the metal structure of the Jeep. The vampires disappeared on the turn.

"Did we lose them?" Sean asked. A growl from the side made him swerve hard to the right. A vampire clung to the jeep side door for dear life. Izzy looked at him in fear but punched him hard in the face. She felt as if her fist had shattered, even though the vampire released the vehicle because of the strike. Izzy blinked and looked at her hand. She felt an ounce of strength returning—which she was missing a few seconds ago. The green-eyed girl looked at her sister hunters. "I'm getting my powers back," she said.

Grace and Nikki nodded and pulled their crossbows. They fired at the vampires that kept on coming. They made more shots than they missed, as vampires were going down. They were missing the heart, though. A vampire jumped from above and landed on the Jeep. He kicked Brent hard, knocking him out cold. Grace and Nikki gasped as the vampire grabbed them both by their hair and smashed their heads together. Izzy fired a hard punch hurting her fist and only slightly disturbing the fiend. He smiled sadistically and fired his back at the teenager connecting hard with the side of her face, making her sit down next to her fellow demon hunters.

Sean saw the action, rage engulfing his being as he hit the brakes hard. The vampire flew forward from the momentum, landing a few feet in front of the Jeep. Sean pressed on the gas and smashed the bumper of the Jeep against the vampire's skull as he was getting up. The dark-haired man heard the sound of satisfying combustion.

Sean pressed the gas even harder while he looked at the rearview mirror. He could see that his daughter's eyes were a bit glazed while she rubbed her face. She was hurt, but she was going to live.

Izzy turned her attention toward Nikki, who was shaking the cobwebs. "Ow," she said, and looked at Grace, who had tears in her eyes. "You okay?" Nikki asked.

Grace shook her head in pain, closing her eyes, trying to process the painful sensation in her skull.

"I think we lost them," Izzy said, turning towards her father.

"The vampires did not die when the arrows hit their chests," Sean said, steering the Jeep to the outside of the woods. "Do you know why?"

"A ritual," Izzy said. "It involved two vampires, and…." Izzy trailed off as reminders of Elsa reached her mind. Sean looked at the rearview mirror, and the look on Izzy's face was enough to conclude the obvious. Elsa was gone.

CHAPTER XVII

Guardians' Castle, Ireland; August 9, 4:45 a.m.

"OW," NIKKI GROANED AS Jasmine applied some ice to the side of her head. Jasmine smiled sadly at the redhead as she checked her scars. They were mostly scratches that seemed to be healing. She was not sure if it was because of her natural human condition, or the demon hunter blood kicking in.

Jasmine turned toward Grace, who was shaking in her seat. This was a close call. The adrenaline had kept her alive, but now, inside the castle's infirmary, she wanted to collapse and fall apart. She felt so helpless, not being able to deal with the pain—not being able to deal with adversity. She had come to the castle to prove she was the best of the best, but right now she felt like a joke. And she had no idea how to overcome the complex negative thoughts in her head.

Izzy looked blankly at the door of the infirmary. She could hear the voices of the Guardians discussing the situation with Sean. It was pretty heated. They wanted to debrief what had gone down in the cursed underground city. But Sean was having none of it. *Where's Mom?* Izzy thought to herself. Her demon-hunter powers should have worked by now, getting rid of the poison. She would put order to the pointless discussion. Izzy's mind drifted while she contemplated her sore body. The moment they entered the castle a few minutes earlier, the word *defeated* pounded on her mind like a sledgehammer. She saw fear and hopelessness on the faces of her sister demon hunters as they walked back in. If the best had been beaten, what would happen to the rest?

Izzy closed her eyes, trying to forget the fear in her sisters' eyes. *Were they no match to this new breed of vampires? Even with demon-hunter power, what would happen? Why didn't the vampires combust when they got hit with arrows in the heart? Had the demon-hunter power been corrupted?* Her history lessons from Williams and Lewis had taught her many things about the origins of the demon hunters. *Had the vampires caught up to them after all this time?* And adding to everything, the death of her friend lingered in her heart and mind. The young girl wiped her eyes. She had sobbed a few minutes earlier, alone in a closet. She was right there—and unable to save her best friend. Tears started streaming again down her cheeks as the memory of Elsa disintegrating replayed in her mind.

Izzy's thoughts were interrupted as the door opened and revealed a pale-looking Elizabeth walking in. Izzy ran up to her mother and hugged her tightly. She wanted to cry on her shoulder, but couldn't do it there. Elizabeth lightly rubbed her daughter's head and smiled sadly at her. The older demon hunter turned her attention toward Nikki and Grace. They were looking at her with a combination of sadness and shame. "Well," Elizabeth said weakly, "You didn't break rule one of demon hunting."

Nikki and Grace looked down in shame. Even though they survived, they had witnessed the death of a fellow demon hunter. Elizabeth sat down just as Sean walked back in. The hall outside went quiet as he entered. The tall, brooding man stood next to his wife and looked at the young demon hunters in front of them.

"Okay," Elizabeth said, wincing a bit as a surge of pain ran through her body. "Let's start from the beginning."

All three girls spoke at the same time, trying to explain the enormous predicament they were all in—explaining the perils and their slim chances for survival. All of the girls speaking in their high voices just intensified Elizabeth's headache as she grasped Sean's arm.

"Hush," Sean said, calming the girls down. His height towered over all the girls in the room. "One at a time."

The girls looked at each other and slowly retold their unsuccessful journey. Elizabeth listened carefully, trying to piece all the information together. She winced as she heard about Ammarra's death and the infiltration of Athena within her ranks. That was on her watch, and she had not bothered to follow up on it. That was the probable leak of information regarding everything related to the Guardians and the demon hunters. One year of information was enough to put the crippled assembly to rest. Still, above all else, she felt a little hope, knowing the girls had made it out of that hell hole she had sent them into. Any other warrior would have perished, but the girls made it out. They lived to tell the tale.

"Okay," Elizabeth said when the girls finished telling the story. "Have Lewis and Williams contact the rest of the Guardians," Elizabeth ordered Sean. "Have our demon hunters pull out and lay low. I don't want them exposed another minute. Not until we figure out this spell they have put the line in."

Sean nodded and walked out of the room. Elizabeth then turned her attention toward the three young girls in front of her. "It's okay to be scared," Elizabeth said, smiling sadly. "Fear will keep us alive."

"What do we do now?" Izzy asked nervously.

"Dante wanted to destroy us," Nikki said. "All of this is not to bring balance. It's to exterminate."

Elizabeth nodded as she looked at Grace. "You think it's our strength and our ability to fight that makes us what we are? We are more than what we appear to be. Much more. Our essence may be bound by darkness, but our heart is what grounds us, what makes us better than we can ever imagine. We have a calling. We have a gift." The girls took in Elizabeth's words. "Our power is in us. We are powerful because of our calling. We are demon hunters. And that title can't be taken from us. This vampire has replicated a spell the Guardians used years ago. He has used the essence of darkness to create an artificial balance. He thinks he's in our playing field. But he'll never win. Darkness hasn't taken over this world, and it will not begin now."

"They don't die," Nikki protested. "How do we handle vampires that don't dust?"

"They dust," Elizabeth assured them, remembering her personal encounter with the Uroks-Nah vampires she faced long ago. "What doesn't put down a demon hunter only makes us stronger. Remember my words. We'll pull through this. You'll pull through this. Our common bond is something that can't be matched, no matter how much dark magic our enemies use against us. We used to fight alone. We're not alone anymore. We'll win, as we have done before."

Izzy was having a hard time keeping it together. Her mother was striving to keep them motivated against overwhelming odds. Her body was battling a poison that could kill her, yet the older demon hunter only thought about keeping her girls on the right path and helping them not to give in to despair.

"Go and rest," Elizabeth ordered. "We'll figure this out." The girls stood up and walked out the door, but not before Izzy hugged her mother one last time. As soon as the demon hunters left, Elizabeth grimaced with pain. She braced herself as the surges ran through her body. She needed to keep on fighting—for her demon hunters—for her daughter.

Guardians' Castle Cellar, Ireland; August 9, 7:00 a.m.

Williams pondered a moment while Lewis explained the gravity of what was going on. The younger Guardian laid out flatly what was already known to them. All the knowledge, contained in every single piece of written evidence they had researched and investigated, presented itself in black and white right then and there. Williams felt sick inside as Lewis rambled on about the only solution to this mess. Both Guardians had played this out too close to the chest, and now it would pierce one of them through the heart. It could open emotional wounds that were never fully healed. Images from his previous life flooded into his mind as Lewis continued to speak. His voice seemed distant and echoed in his subconscious. Williams sank deep in his chair, replaying the scenario over and over his head. The hurtful memories could not be forgotten. The voices echoed in his mind.

"Damn it, man," Williams hissed. "There must be another way. We always find another way."

"Not on this, and you know it," Lewis said. "John has been on the books all this time and he concurs it's the best solution. The past decade proves that there is no other choice."

"We can't do this to Elizabeth," Williams said, defeated. "I can't do this to her. Not again."

"How do you think I feel?" Lewis asked. "I may not have been her Guardian, but I have been her friend. Hers and Sean's.

We must bring them into the loop now."

Williams removed his glasses and placed his head in his hands. The more significant wound was that of treason. He had looked at his demon hunter in the face, begging for her trust. And he now felt like he'd betrayed her. It was happening all over again in his mind.

Williams looked up at Lewis and realized the truth. They were in charge of the assembly now. They needed to involve Elizabeth on this—sooner, not later. Williams stood up and looked at his friend sadly. "Have Elizabeth and Sean meet me downstairs. And talk with John."

Guardians' Castle Gym, Ireland; August 9, 7:00 a.m.

Izzy played her violin on the floor with her legs crossed, inside the Guardians' gym. Her sad notes echoed in the empty room, while Grace punched a sandbag with all her might. Nikki laid beside Izzy, looking blankly at the ceiling. A melancholic sense of dread and doom filled the demon hunters.

Izzy's heart was broken. In her mind, she replayed the scene where Dante took Elsa's life over and over again. Never had she experienced death so close to her. So intimate. It was like ripping her heart out. Her eyes were tired of shedding tears. Her body simply felt numb to the weight of everything that was happening. For the first time in her life, she felt utterly helpless. She hated the feeling.

Grace dealt with her emotions differently. She was trying to hit a punching bag with all the strength her body could muster. Izzy could see that even though Grace had technique, the punches were feeble. The bag barely strained at Grace's attacks. Grace screamed in frustration as she landed two final punches. Izzy stopped playing and noticed Grace's fist dripping with blood.

Both Nikki and Izzy stood up and walked over to Grace, who just held onto the bag as the pain registered in her arms and hands. "Don't," Grace said to her sisters, noticing their intention to help. "Just don't." The sensation of powerlessness felt like ice picks in her stomach. She felt sick inside.

"We're in this together," Izzy said, trying to calm her down. "We don't have to deal with everything alone."

"I'm not strong enough," Grace whispered, more to herself than anybody else. "I can't face this."

"What do you mean?" Nikki asked. "You led us out of that cave. If it weren't for you, we would surely be dead."

Grace laughed at the comment. "If I had a dime..." she started, then trailed off. The memories pierced her mind. "We got lucky. One wrong turn..." She couldn't continue. She winced as she grabbed a towel and wiped the blood from her hands.

"But we didn't," Izzy said. "We're still here. That means we still have a purpose in all this. Because of you, we're alive."

Grace laughed. It was a sad and ironic laugh. "Silly girl. You still believe in a fictitious, divine Providence. It was all meant to happen, and that makes it good."

"I didn't..." Izzy started, but Nicole stopped her. Grace needed to vent.

"Bad things happen, and it sucks," Grace said. "And you can't do anything about it. You can't control it. You can't move. You can't even breathe."

"This isn't about what we went through?" Nikki asked, realizing part of the truth. "It's about something you went through."

Grace's head jerked up. Izzy could see an unhinged rage in her dark eyes accompanied by profound hatred. It was a terrifying look that brought chills down Izzy's spine. "An ancient one rules my nightmares," Grace said flatly. "Have you ever faced an ancient one?"

Both Izzy and Nikki shook their heads. In the back of her mind, Izzy remembered her dad mentioning an old enemy. *Was it the same one?*

"These… things," Grace started. "They're powerful vampires. More powerful than any master vampire. Old as time. My father was the last of a special order of the old Guardians dedicated to gathering information on these demons."

"I've never heard of them," Nikki said.

"That's their purpose," Grace said. "They're vampires of old. They hide in the shadows, and they work hard to keep themselves hidden. He who sees an ancient one is bound by death. They leave nothing but suffering."

"The ancient ones found out about your father?" Izzy asked.

"Only one," Grace said, remembering that night. "He burnt down my home. That was three years ago."

"Did you get a good look at him?" Nikki asked.

Grace's eyes glazed, as the memory that had been scorched in her mind passed before her eyes. "It was dark. And it was raining."

Thirteen-year-old Grace looked helplessly as her mother lay dead on the ground. She looked up and saw a dark silhouette holding her father while her home burned in the background. The blaze and the heat did nothing to melt the icy emptiness in her stomach. She could fight, killing over two dozen vampires already at her young age. She had faced countless creatures of the night. Why was this night different? Why was she petrified when those evil yellow eyes pierced her soul?

"Are you afraid, child?" the vampire hissed. His voice was calm and collected, almost sweet and hypnotizing. Why was she trembling?

"Don't be afraid," her father whispered.

"She's past that moment," the vampire said as he continued to stare at Grace. "You should be afraid. Fear will now be your master, and you forever will be its slave."

Grace winced as the vampire snapped her father's neck right in front of her. Grace could feel a warm liquid stream down her legs as the vampire approached her. The tall vampire knelt before her and gazed with his yellow eyes. "You belong to me now," he said with a cruel grin on his demonic face. "Every time you feel scared and helpless, this is the memory that will haunt you. Every time fear grips your heart, this is what you'll remember. I've no idea what will become of you, and I don't care. You could kill yourself if you want to end this misery. What I do know is that if you decide to carry on with this pathetic and meaningless life, you must get something very clear in that young mind of yours."

Grace's heart seemed to stop as he whispered the words in her face. "I own you now. I own your bloody heart. I own your bloody mind and your bloody soul. You belong to me. Every time you're transported to this moment, you will remember me as the vampire who took everything from you. This moment where you questioned the very essence of your being and wondered whether your pathetic existence is worth a damn."

Tears started to stream down the young child's face. The vampire dried the tears from her cheeks as he stood up. "I've met demon hunters with more grit in my day. But you have heart, child—I'll give you that. A weakling heart, but a heart at the end."

The vampire started walking away, leaving the young girl alone with the corpses of her parents. The blaze continued as the storm failed to let up in the cold dark night.

Nikki and Izzy looked at each other with gloom in their eyes. Grace took a deep breath as she finished cleaning her hands and started walking out of the gym. "Storytime is over, girls," the black-haired girl said, walking out on her friends. As she stepped out of the room, Grace felt an icy pit in her stomach; she wanted to throw up. She ran up to her room, collapsed on her bed, and sobbed bitterly on her pillow. The emptiness of her room reflected the void in her heart. Grace screamed as she cried. She felt useless and weak. Suddenly the girl felt an intense energy inside the room. She stopped and turned around to see Joy standing by the door.

"Feel better?" Joy asked Grace as the older demon hunter slowly walked in and sat on what used to be Ammarra's bed. "I heard your conversation with the other girls. Sorry for eavesdropping."

Grace remained silent as she looked out the window.

"I was never good at this," Joy said, "Giving the motivational speeches and the inspiring crap Lizz is known for. I am more of a kick-ass first and talk later kind of girl."

Grace listened on to the older demon hunter.

"I never knew my dad," Joy said. "And my mom was a drunk that spent most of the time passed out. I didn't know what it was like to have a family until I met my Guardian." Grace looked up at Joy, who was staring at the ceiling. "She was great. Provided this warmth I didn't know existed. She pointed me in the right direction and always knew what to say."

Grace knew where this was going, but she did not dare interrupt.

"An ancient vampire named Garnel took her from me," Joy said, looking at the young girl. "You and I are worlds-apart different, Wu. But we share a common suck in our lives. Something that no one else can ever understand."

"How do you deal?" Grace asked.

Joy smiled a bit. "You deal. Lizz has had my back. Reluctantly, but she's been there when the chips were down. And now you have friends that have your back. You have these sisters that you didn't know could be there for you. All you have to do is let them in." Joy stood up, a little wobbly, and started to walk out of the room. "It has been forever that demon hunters were told that they stood alone in the middle of all this darkness. It still takes a while for us to understand that's a lot of bullshit."

Joy walked out and ran into Nikki and Izzy. "Your friend is waiting for you," Joy said as she started walking away, in the direction of her room. She smiled a little as she heard Grace start sobbing again—only this time, she wasn't alone. She had her sisters by her side.

CHAPTER XVIII

Underground, Town of York, Ireland; August 9, 7:00 a.m.

NEIL LOOKED OVER THE balcony of his room. He frowned as he watched fellow vampires dragging in people from the nearby villages. If time had taught something to the ancient vampire, it was that rushing thing always spelled disaster. He hated brash tactics. He loved savoring every minute—every second. Running was never his style. And he sensed that Dante had lost his way. Siegfried's loss left Dante blind—and a blind demon is crazier and wreckless.

"Penny for your thoughts," Neil heard a female voice ask from behind.

"Nothing that concerns you, child," Neil responded, not bothering to turn his head and acknowledge Lucinda. She had intruded into his private quarters, and there would be hell to pay.

"You forget that I can see in your mind," Lucinda said, standing beside the ancient vampire. "You try to hide behind this facade of elderhood and wisdom. But I sense fear in you."

"I don't waste my time on fruitless human emotion." He turned toward Lucinda. His eyes were enough to frighten the living and the dead. "You may read emotion among the darkness… but it takes more than parlor tricks to fathom my true intentions in all of this."

"You think we're doing something wrong," Lucinda concluded as she saw the army of vampires grow before her.

"You expect a different result by doing exactly what numerous vampires and demons have done in the past. I've seen ascended demons rise and fall; artificial demons laid to waste. Even Hell's first general failed. What makes you think this time you'll succeed?"

"We changed the rules of the game," Lucinda replied. "Dante changed everything. Vampires are stronger and faster, thanks to him."

"Dante's like a child who just found his father's gun," Neil smirked.

"What do you suggest? Wait it out?"

"We have nothing but time," Neil said, shrugging a bit. "We're immortal. I have outlived demon hunters and master vampires alike—powerful demons and monsters that would make your skin crawl."

"And this gives you an advantage?" Lucinda asked incredulously.

"The ego on you young ones continues to amaze me. But as I said before, I am curious about Dante's plan."

"You saw the demon hunters we brought in. You saw how scared they were. Fear overwhelms their hearts; the stench reaches the pits of hell. Soon our army will be ready to strike at the core of that wretched institution."

But Neil's mind wandered; for a moment, his mental defenses were down—but only for a moment. But it was enough for

Lucinda to grasp an image from his mind. "You know one of them," Lucinda whispered as a cruel smile curved on her lips.

Neil's hand shot out and grasped Lucinda's throat. The female vampire grunted as the old one lifted her off her feet. She could feel Neil squeezing hard, cracking the bones in her neck. "You dare peer into my mind, child?" Neil hissed in anger. Nearby vampires stopped what they were doing as they saw the elder one unleash his fury. His growling voice made even the bravest vampires in the cursed town buckle a bit at their knees. They watched as Lucinda dangled from Neil's hand.

"Neil!" Dante exclaimed. "Let her go!"

Neil turned and saw the long-haired demon, accompanied by his two hell gargoyles. "Don't make me put you down," Dante said.

"You think you can?" He flung Lucinda to the ground; she landed on her back and screamed in pain as the impact cracked the concrete floor; her bones splintered in response to the brutal punishment. Lucinda whimpered in pain as Neil straightened his suit. Dante did not dare move, nor did he order the Gargoyles to attack. He just stood in silence.

"Children should be taught some manners when disrespecting your elders. I congratulate you, Dante. I was powerful before your little magic show. Now it seems I'm unstoppable. You think your hell demons and vampires can succeed where more powerful warriors have failed?"

Dante gritted his teeth in rage but controlled his anger. He knew what Neil was capable of. "You're an honored guest in my home. Please tell me what causes you such displeasure."

"Intrusion," Neil said, glancing at Lucinda's broken body. "Don't let her try to pry my mind again. That is all I ask."

Dante nodded as he tended to Lucinda. Neil waved off the gargoyles, signaling they were no longer needed. Four vampires entered Neil's room and helped Lucinda off the destroyed floor. "She's healing quickly. It does seem that your spell does wonders."

"There was no need for this," Dante said, gritting his teeth. Lucinda was a vital part of his plan; he needed her healthy. This event, although minor, was a setback for his grander scheme.

"Indeed." Neil repeated, "There was no need for this. Why send her to pry my mind when you can simply ask me yourself?" Dante didn't even try to hide his surprise at Neil's words. "Are you trying to impress me with all that you've accomplished? Are you trying to rub it in my face that you have a great plan that no one has ever thought of in a lifetime of battles against the forces of light?" Dante remained silent. "You don't need to impress me, Dante. All you have to understand is that I'm on a different playing field than you. I observe from the shadows and remain silent."

Neil walked back to the balcony and looked at the vampire army Dante had raised. There were hundreds, accompanied by Hillions and other creatures of the night. "You have power. And unearned power lusts for more power. You have enough to destroy the Guardians and all the demon hunters, but that's not enough for you. You crave something bigger—something greater."

"Apocalyps," Dante whispered.

"I'm older than you," Neil said. "I was there when the legend was written. What makes you think you're a worthy warrior to wield Apocalyps?" Dante remained silent. "What do you plan to do with all that power? The Guardians and demon hunters destroyed, and you alone as king of the vampires? With Apocalyps in one hand and the broken assembly in the other?"

"A memorable image," Dante said.

"As I told your lover," Neil said, "You children amuse me with your thirst for power. I enjoy simple things. You get your army ready—one that can travel great distances if it weren't for the sun above us."

Dante smiled. "Lucinda has a solution for the sun. And she will put it in effect as soon as she recovers."

"Then proceed," Neil said. "Your course is set. Don't let the grumblings of an old fart like myself stand in the way."

Dante nodded and walked out of Neil's room. He was angry, but he didn't show it. Not there. He would wait. Once Apocalyps was in his hands, not even an old fart like Neil would stop him.

Guardians' Castle, Ireland; August 9, 7:00 a.m.

John Simmons rubbed his eyes, exhausted from looking at the nine screens in front of him. He was on the relieving team while Alex took a few minutes to rest. But no one was sleeping, not today, and not in these conditions. The entire staff was on high alert. The young Guardian had been working with the organization for just a few days, and it seemed like an eternity. His sole motivation came from the looks of helplessness he had seen on the young demon hunters. The young man had seen that look before, under a different set of conditions and circumstances—much more intimate, but no less grave. He would not fail. Not this time.

He shook past the memories and continued looking at the screens in front of him. He coded quickly and efficiently as he looked at the two video feeds. One was from Ammarra's previous Guardian, a small video which showed an incident when she had dispatched several vampires. *This demon hunter from Indonesia was outstanding in her fighting style.* He then saw the video of Athena in Ammarra's body, from the small training exercises they had held the day before.

The door behind John opened, and in came Brent and Clara,

each carrying a few folders and fresh coffee. "Any luck?" Brent asked as he handed a mug of coffee to John while looking at the monitor. The young Guardian looked at Clara and was glad to see the color back in her face.

"Feeling better?" John asked the young brunette.

"A bit," Clara said. "Still managing those dizzy spells, and the strength comes and goes. What have you got?"

"This Dark Shadow is something else," John muttered as he pointed at the video. "She replicates Ammarra's style to the letter. It's like she has access to the dead person's essence."

"You mean she has access to everything Ammarra knew from us?" Clara asked.

"Looks like it," John said. "Not only that—Athena seems to bring in all the past memories with her."

"Which means that she harbors the knowledge of every warrior she's killed," Brent concluded.

"It's far more grave than that," John said. "Not only can she replicate the skill, but also the mindset—the mannerisms of the victims. This is another type of possession, on a neurological level."

"You know what the others are going to ask," Clara said. "How can she be killed?"

John smiled a little. "Valid question. But I wouldn't ask it just yet. She is the head of the assassin's order for a reason. It's next to impossible to kill her."

"But there is a way?" Brent asked.

John looked at both Guardians. "Dark shadow is a replicant demon. She has over a hundred iterations, based on how many she has murdered so far. From some reading I've been doing, she can summon five replicants within her body at a time. That gives her the strength to fight. If one of the five replicants is outside of her body, which I assume is a backup measure, she can regenerate into one of the others and start the process again."

"So the only way to kill her is to make sure all the replicants are within her, so she doesn't generate again," Clara said.

"Okay," Brent asked, "how do we do that?"

John looked back desperately at the monitors. "We can generate a spell to bind that ability, making sure that our demon hunters are only facing one opponent. But that would mean that body would be fueled by the powers of more than one warrior."

"Athena would have the strength of five demons and not only one," Brent concluded.

"Or four, if she has a backup outside the current iteration," John said. "Like the one that is blocking the hell spot in St. Helena."

"This Dante hired a powerful demon," Clara said.

"If we managed to isolate Athena," Brent started saying, "even if she has harnessed the power of multiple demons, how would we kill her?"

"Based on all the evidence I've read," John said. "I would stick with ripping her heart out."

"Stabbing a demon in the heart is not enough for you?" Brent said. "You have to take it out of the chest cavity?"

"I think that the essence of every demon she has killed resides there," John said. "Ripping it out would finally take away her power."

"And it would kill her in the process," Clara said. "I'll inform the demon hunters."

"That is only half of it," John said. "There is another issue that requires attention."

"What is it?" Clara asked, fearing the answer.

"What else have you found out?" Brent asked, just wanting an ounce of good news to come from the newcomer.

"I hacked into the email account linked to Ammarra's Guardian," John said, popping up a program he was running. "I also hacked into Ammarra's."

"I don't like where this is going," Brent said, looking at the truth John presented in the monitors.

"It seems Athena has gotten inside our system," John said grimly. "Accounts have been active way after the presumed deaths of both Ammarra and her Guardian."

"What info is compromised?" Clara asked.

John turned toward both Guardians. "All of it." He then turned toward the monitors while Brent and Clara looked at each other. The idea that their records and files were out in the open brought about a new sense of doom. "I am looking into what Athena downloaded. I am also trying to crack info on what has been shared."

"And?" Brent asked.

"The master list is out," John said. Clara gasped. The master list had the location of every single demon hunter and Guardian on the globe. If that information was exposed, it meant the entire organization was compromised. "The list being downloaded means it's encrypted," John continued. "And according to the records, it was downloaded last week."

"But Athena has been on our system for more than a year," Brent said. "What other information was she after?"

"The information Dante paid for her to obtain," Clara concluded. "The list is a bonus for her."

"The first information she accessed was the profile of the main guard," John said. "Information on Williams, Elizabeth, and the rest of the main Guardians. Also information on perimeter security and castle layout."

"Dante is planning to breach the castle?" Brent asked.

"It would seem like that," John responded as he pulled up and pointed to a picture of a beautiful sword on the main screen. "Most of the documents downloaded are related to that." Clara and Brent looked at each other and then at the picture of the sword. John sighed. "The demon hunters and the Guardians are the protectors of Apocalyps," he said as he turned toward his fellow Guardians. "Dante has weakened the warriors who keep the weapon safe for him to take it."

"Do you have a date?" Lewis asked from behind them.

Lewis's voice startled the younger team. John gulped a bit before he responded. "Soon, I guess. The sooner, the better. The more time they take to assault the castle, the more time we have to find a cure for the poison and prepare for a possible attack. They won't allow us that."

Lewis sighed and cleaned his glasses. "Brent and Clara," Lewis ordered as he looked at the screens. "Wake Alex up. Fortify our defenses. Better be prepared. Take Joy to the outside perimeter and check the four mausoleums. If they go, then the magic that protects the castle will go with them."

Brent and Clara left the control room with gloomy looks on their faces. Lewis looked at John and asked, "Any idea on how to cure the demon hunters?"

"I can't think of any sane one," John said, turning back to the computers. "The poison is something pulled from deep within the dark arts. It would need something of pure light to wipe it out."

"What about your Apocalyps theory?" Lewis asked.

John hastily turned back toward him. "These are not the conditions to try that out," John spat out. "We could put the entire line in greater danger."

"Is this the Guardian in you that is concluding that," Lewis asked, "or is it Angie's boyfriend?" John tensed up as the name left the older man's lips. He felt the color leave his face. "We know what happened to Angela," Lewis continued. "Did you honestly think you could keep that relationship a secret?" John remained silent. "As Guardians, I am against the emotional involvement of one of the members of the assembly with one of the demon hunters. It jeopardizes what we do; it puts too many lives at risk. But I am overruled on that. So we follow the new standard, even if I disagree with it." John gulped as Lewis proceeded. "So, which is it?" Lewis asked again. "Is it the Guardian in you, or Angie's boyfriend?"

John gritted his teeth in anger. He knew Lewis was pushing his buttons. *Was this a test?* the young man thought to himself. "The demon hunters can't withstand the blinding power of Apocalyps."

"Elizabeth could," Lewis said. "She's held Apocalyps in her hands."

"Apocalyps was forged to strike down evil. What we want from it this time is completely different."

Lewis sighed. "The demon hunters will die. If you are correct and we are about to suffer an assault on the castle, they will all die, and us with them."

"This is bullshit," John exclaimed, standing up. "Are you saying we're out of ideas? And since we're out of ideas, we are resorting to insanity?"

"I am just stating the facts," Lewis said calmly. "That is what I do, unfortunately. We all have to die at one point, John. It is what you do until you get to that point that defines you. As much as the Guardians try to extend the lives of the demon hunters, we are all fighting a war. And death takes no prisoners."

John remained silent as Lewis walked toward the exit. "If Angela were here..." Lewis pondered with curiosity, "...what would she tell you?"

John looked at Lewis and took a breath. "She would risk it all. She would make the hard choice that would save the innocent."

"A true Demon Hunter," Lewis said.

"My heroine to the end," John replied.

"We're Guardians," Lewis said. "You're a Guardian. Our job is to pass the information to the right people—no matter how difficult it is to hear."

"I understand," John said.

"Do you?" Lewis asked.

"I gave Angie the information she needed to save lives," John said. "At the cost of her own."

Lewis nodded. "Williams and I will pass on the information to Sean and Elizabeth. They may not process the information well. I trust you will do your job and pass the information to the correct people as well." With those final words, the older man left John alone. The younger man returned his view to the monitor and studied the sword Apocalyps. The information once again was right there in front of him. The young man grasped his chair tightly. And again, the life of a demon hunter would be in his hands.

Guardians' Castle, Ireland; August 9, 8:30 a.m.

Elizabeth and Sean walked down to the cellar together. Elizabeth was feeling a little better after the attack of the previous night. Weakness still overwhelmed her body, though, and she felt a slight sting in her lower back. As they walked through the concrete hall, Elizabeth looked and saw Williams and Lewis waiting before the locked black door. She frowned as she viewed the faces of the senior Guardians. They had answers, and they knew she was not going to like what they had to say.

"How are you feeling?" Williams asked his demon hunter. His voice filled with genuine concern.

"Recovering," Elizabeth said. "Did you find anything?'

"Yes," Williams said, looking at Lewis for support. Lewis nodded and turned his attention toward the door.

Elizabeth looked at the door and frowned. No explanation was needed for the door and what it hid. The weapon that ended the reign of Terror in New York rested behind the door. Only true warriors could wield it. The sword did not recognize intent—only power.

"What happened today to the hunter line was something I had feared for a long time," Williams started.

"What do you mean?" Sean asked.

"When we created the spell that replicated…" Williams started haltingly, but Lewis put his hand on the older man's shoulder. He motioned for him to sit down while Lewis delivered the news. The fact that Lewis spoke put Sean on edge. The younger Guardian was blunter and more to the point. There would be no sugarcoating the news.

"Ever since the first demon hunter, the essence of a demon has been bound into a young girl," Lewis said. "A human girl with a strong will was chosen to contain the power of this demon and wield it consciously."

"Go on," Elizabeth said. She knew part of the story, but hearing it again meant the Guardians had found additional information.

"Once the girl was killed, the next one with the will to withstand the dark essence was called. This process continued until the hunter line deviated to a chosen few. You were part of that exclusive lineage—probably the strongest in generations. It was you who created the replication spell once you wielded Apocalyps," Lewis said.

"All the girls with the will to carry that demon power were called," Sean said. "Our demon hunter army was created."

"There is a consequence to all this power," Lewis flatly said. Elizabeth looked at Williams. He seemed embarrassed at the information that was being shared.

"What is it?" Elizabeth asked, fearing the worst.

"The spell that created the demon hunter army," Williams said. "Every girl strong enough was called. But the essence of the original demon itself is the same. The spell replicated the essence of this demon and put it inside each of the girls."

"The spell practically puts a demon inside each of the demon hunters," Lewis said.

"Are you saying we're all possessed?" Elizabeth said.

"No," Williams said, standing up. "The will of each girl is strong enough to control the dark essence inside. But since its origin is from darkness, it is susceptible to manipulation. It can be tampered with. Just like all demonic essence, it can be controlled using powerful magic."

"That is why the poison replicated so quickly in the demon hunter line," Lewis said. "It's attacking the demon within each hunter." Lewis stopped and looked at Williams, who did not return the stare. "As soon as we created this assembly of Guardians, Williams and I started our research. We both knew that this was an Achilles' heel, a dent in the demon hunter's armor. If the enemy found out, it wouldn't take long for someone to take advantage of this weakness in the hunter line."

Sean looked at Williams and Lewis. "You did this?" Sean asked, already knowing the answer. Elizabeth's eyes widened. A mixture of emotions was going through her. She hadn't added everything up, but Sean obviously had.

"You created this poison?" Elizabeth asked, not wanting to believe what she was asking.

"We feared that a powerful force could turn the demon hunters against each other," Williams said, not wanting to look at Elizabeth. "We created this poison to incapacitate the entire hunter line without…"

"Without putting you down," Lewis finished the sentence.

"What!?" Elizabeth exclaimed. "We would never turn on you! We would never turn on ourselves!" She then looked at her Guardian—her father since she was sixteen. "Did you think I would turn on you?"

"No," Williams said. "You and the demon hunters would never harm us."

"It was the demon inside you we feared," Lewis said.

Elizabeth wanted to take Lewis apart. "You knew all this," Elizabeth hissed. "And you let me send three of my demon hunters out there, knowing something like this would happen? My daughter was out there!"

"We didn't know this was the case," Williams said. "It was not until Andreia started feeling sick and Izzy confirmed Dark Shadow's breach of our information."

Sean's temper flared, but he grabbed Elizabeth's shoulder to calm her and himself down. He trusted both Williams and Lewis enough to know that even if it was stupid, they had their best intentions at heart. They were good men. Flawed, but good at heart. "Okay. You created this poison. Athena found it when she hacked out systems and used it against us. Is there a cure?"

"The poison will clear," Lewis said, "but the main issue remains. The weakness of the demon hunter line will continue, even after this. A more powerful demon can harm the hunter line, and the Guardians in the process."

Elizabeth calmed down a bit. "And you have a plan for this?"

"Redemption," Lewis said.

"Redemption?" Elizabeth asked. "As if what I've done alone doesn't count for all that. And that's not mentioning Joy and Clara's contribution in saving this world."

"It's not saving the world," Williams said. "When you created the new demon hunter line, I told you that we would write history. Nothing of what we've done is documented. We are always walking in new territory."

"A new way to redeem ourselves?" Sean asked.

"A way to redeem the darkness inside the demon hunter line is to cleanse it," Lewis said. "Apocalyps must be brought forth again."

Elizabeth thought for a moment, recalling the battle of New York. She recalled facing the end of the world on a grander scale. She lost an excellent demon hunter that day; she also lost her best friend. It all started with the search for Apocalyps itself. As a small squad, they entered a hellish dimension and reclaimed the weapon to end the darkness.

"We already used the sword once," Elizabeth said, pointing at the closed door. "We banished it into the Nightmare Dimension for it to never be used. It was under your instruction—you sealed the door."

"I know," Williams said. He then turned toward Lewis, looking for the courage to say what he needed to say. Lewis nodded, and Elizabeth feared the worst. "The sword has divine properties. It can only be wielded by the purest warriors chosen by the higher powers."

"With Apocalyps," Lewis continued, "a single demon hunter could cleanse the line, creating a similar ripple effect, redeeming the darkness within and sealing the hunter's fate with a weapon destined for good."

Elizabeth understood. "So, you want me to go into the Nightmare Dimension and reclaim the sword?"

Lewis shook his head. "You reclaiming Apocalyps would not help the cause. Just as if Joy, Clara, or any other hunter with a demon inside would—just another warrior in the chain grabbing it."

"The person to reclaim Apocalyps must be a warrior groomed by the powers themselves," Williams said. "A hunter with a demon, but who has experienced their light."

"A hunter who has been in the presence of the beings of light," Lewis concluded.

"Out of the question!" Sean exclaimed. "I've put my daughter through one hell after the next. And now you want me to send her to a Nightmare Dimension to try something you have no idea will work."

"I know it's a lot to ask," Williams said. "That's why we came to you."

"You have no idea what is 'a lot,'" Elizabeth said, gritting her teeth. "It's not enough that for my entire life, I've given everything for this fight, and now you're asking for my daughter."

"I thought you had accepted this," Lewis said bluntly. "You know exactly what is required of every demon hunter—what you've given up. Did you honestly think that your daughter would not have shared your same fate?"

Elizabeth remained quiet. She looked at Sean and knew they were thinking the same thing. For years, they had carried out the task of reducing the time of the demon hunters' service. The idea was to have Izzy experience life in darkness, to leave it at the end of her time of service, then have an ordinary life. But circumstances had driven a point deep down into Elizabeth's heart. As often as she and her husband tried to twist or cheat fate, destiny always caught up with them. And now it seemed to be catching up to their daughter.

A ground tremor interrupted the conversation the Guardians were having. The earth shook lightly at first, then violently. Sean grabbed Elizabeth and hugged her tight against the concrete pillar. The old castle creaked and rumbled as the small earthquake shook the aged structure.

After what seemed an eternity, the tremor stopped. They did not need any additional motivation to run up to the main floor. Elizabeth's heart raced as she feared the worst. When they opened the door to the main hall, a scorched sky greeted them;

it was dark as night, due to massive black clouds blocking the sunlight. Elizabeth turned her attention toward Sean and the others. They saw the demon hunters had gathered in Hunter Hall, murmuring among themselves of the predicament they were in. The older heads walked in and eavesdropped on the conversation.

The demon hunters watched in horror through the window as a dark purple column of energy fueled the black clouds on the horizon. The dark cloud spread rapidly, covering the sky like fire. "The vampires are blocking the sunlight," Andreia said to the others. "Nothing can stop them now."

"That's powerful magic they are using," Eisha said. "Blocking the sun requires plenty of dark energy."

"And creating a new breed of vampires didn't?" Almeida asked. "We're dealing with something way over our heads. They have taken our powers. How can we deal with them?"

"That's the point, isn't it?" Andreia cried out, falling into despair. "This is not putting us on an even playing field. This is putting us on a silver platter for them. We will be the first." Most girls agreed with Andreia. "We've come here to die."

"Andreia is right," Eisha said, adding to the despair. "They will come for us."

All the girls spoke at the same time. The hopelessness was reaching their hearts. Elizabeth was about to interrupt them when she heard her daughter speak up.

"Hey!" Izzy called to the frightened demon hunters. "What's wrong with us? Are we giving up just like that?"

"What can we do?" Andreia asked. "We have no powers to fight this evil. It's all about power. They have it. We don't."

"Screw that!" Izzy exclaimed. "You've been chosen. All of you have been chosen. We are not damsels in distress. They fear us. We don't fear them."

"Don't you get it?" Almeida protested. "The vampires are stronger and faster. They will come, and they will kill us."

Izzy looked at Grace and Nikki for support. They returned the stare. For a moment, a memory flashed in her mind. There was a glimmer of hope, followed by a sense of dread. Izzy turned toward her sister demon hunters. "They won't. We faced them, and we survived. You can survive too."

Nikki and Grace looked at each other and then at Izzy, unsure if they heard right. "You barely survived," Andreia said. "What makes this situation different?"

"We know they're coming," Izzy said with a smile. The girls murmured again, unsure about what they were hearing. "You're right," Izzy said. "They're faster and stronger. But that doesn't mean they're invincible. They can still be killed."

"With what powers?" Andreia asked. "You're delusional."

"Does having power make you what you are?" Izzy confronted Andreia and then her sisters. "All of you are chosen. Not because of power but because of fate. We are chosen to do great things—overcome adversity, not be crushed by it."

The girls quieted down and started paying attention. "Times have changed," Izzy said. "Long ago, we would have been the ones who did the hiding. Long ago, no one dared to imagine young girls would be the tip of the spear to fight the forces of darkness. This is our time. This Dante vampire is scared of us. He's scared of what we can do and what we are capable of. He fears us. That is why he's done all this—out of fear. He wants us surrounded in darkness, so we're as helpless as he has been all this time. He thinks we will cower as he has in the past. But he's dead wrong. He messed with the wrong group of girls. He will come and hit us with everything he's got, but that is all. When he sees us standing together as a united front, we will remind him why he's feared us all this time." The other demon hunters started nodding in agreement as Izzy finished her speech. "We're the best in the world. And tonight, we will show the world of darkness why they don't mess with a demon hunter."

"Yeah!" Nikki exclaimed, rallying the troops. "Let's get ready for war. We have stopped the end of the world in the past. These demons have never faced two dozen of us before." Somehow the speech worked. The mood changed radically as the girls started getting pumped up. "Head to the gym, and let's weapon up!"

Elizabeth and Sean caught up to Izzy as every single demon hunter headed toward the gym. "What are you doing?" Sean asked, noting that only Lewis, Williams, and John were there.

"What's expected of us," Izzy replied, noticing that John was present for the first time.

"If this is a full assault…" Sean started.

"Then you better start feeling better," Izzy said to Elizabeth. "We're going to need you when they come. Unless you have a better idea."

"We escape," Elizabeth said, not believing she was saying that. She had never fled in her life. "We get out of the castle and leave everything."

"Who're you trying to convince?" Izzy asked defiantly. "Me or you?"

Lewis interrupted the tense conversation. "Sorry to interrupt. Brent and Joy are fortifying the outer perimeter. Alex is on the security feed. He will be our eyes and ears."

Elizabeth was visibly tense. She had never felt as powerless as she did at that moment. The Blonde demon hunter had lost control, which was unlike her. She then looked at Izzy, who suddenly seemed so grown up. Elizabeth looked into Izzy's eyes, which showed a determination that had not been present before. "We'll take Izzy's lead on this." Sean was about to explode when Elizabeth grabbed his arm. "Walk with me," she said as she pulled him away from the conversation. "Izzy—get the girls in position."

Izzy saw her parents walk away, followed by Williams and Lewis. She stood alone in the hallway with only the new Guardian, John, looking at her. "You have something to say, don't you?" she asked. "You're John, right?"

John sighed and looked around, making sure they were alone. "And you're Isabella. Nice to finally meet you."

"Say what you have to say," Izzy said. "As you can see, we're about to be walloped, and I have places to be."

"We can't win," John said. "Not like this. Not with these odds."

"It's not about winning," Izzy said. "It's about doing what's right. If this place falls, then darkness will have a fair shot at the world. Vampires and demons will be unleashed, knowing full well that nothing will stop them."

"I know," John said. "You feel your powers are back?"

"Yes," Izzy said, looking down at her body. "My mom is getting better."

"She will get worse," John said. "The poison is cycling until Elizabeth's put down."

"Are you saying there is no cure?" Izzy asked, her voice trembling.

John sighed as he gathered the strength to give out the information. "I'm just the guy who provides the information to the right people."

Izzy looked at the young man for the first time. He seemed vulnerable with his green eyes hiding a deep sadness behind his glasses. "This information that you have has already been given to my parents."

John slowly nodded. "As I said, I am the one who gives the right people the information needed."

Izzy understood. Her parents were protecting her from making the call. "Walk with me. What is it that my parents don't want me to know?"

"That you can cure the demon hunters," John said. "That you can bring light to the darkness. Since you have been in the presence of light, you are the only demon hunter who can cleanse your fellow sisters, here and around the world."

As they reached the entrance of the main gym, Izzy stopped and looked at John. "What do you mean?"

John sighed. "Demon hunters are rooted in evil. All the demon hunters in the line have the spirit of a demon that gives them the strength to fight the forces of darkness. This demon is not a possessive type, but it's corruptible. The only way to cleanse the line is for a warrior that was in the presence of light to wield a weapon forged in the light."

"And that warrior is me?" Izzy asked, somewhat incredulous. "If it were me, how am I supposed to pull this off?"

John took a deep breath. "You must reclaim Apocalyps."

Izzie laughed at John's statement. "You're kidding, right?"

"Apocalyps was a weapon forged in light," John said as he watched as all the demon hunters gear up. "Besides… it's better for you to get your hands on it than Dante. Dante will come to kill you all and take the weapon." Izzy thought for a moment as she looked at the girls. Nikki and Grace distributed crossbows and short swords while they paid close attention to what they were discussing. "So, what's it going to be?"

Izzy had all the information she needed to make the call: the past tales of her mother, Clara, and Joy as mighty demon hunters; the legend of Apocalyps and its current nightmarish location, as well as the recent stories of her sister demon hunters. She also had a bit of input about Dante and his deeds. Soon, the vampires would strike and come for them and the forbidden weapon. They also had the information on Athena and her weakness. Izzy's eyes lit up as the pieces of the puzzle came together in her mind. John frowned at the girl as he saw in her face that a plan was forming. "John," Izzy said as she looked at the outer wall. "Get everybody in here. I have a plan."

Outside the Underground Town of York, Ireland; August 9, 9:30 a.m.

Dante looked at the scorched sky and smiled, then turned his attention toward the cave entrance as his army of vampires and demons came out and experienced a day without sunlight. Three large Hillions came out, as well as three large demon gargoyles. Both types of monsters were impressive in height as well as build. The Hillions were eight-foot-five inches tall, with wide frames and hideous faces. Brown skin covered their large muscles, making them the juggernauts of the demon world. In contrast to the Hillions, the black gargoyles were smaller, but still towered over average creatures of the night at seven feet. They looked even more massive than the Hillions, with extended wings that had an impressive fifteen-foot reach from end to end.

Behind the small army, the heads of the vampire clan appreciated what he had done. Neil looked amazed.

"Finally, it seems I have impressed you," Dante said to Neil as the elder one experienced the dark magic. "In this darkness, your power is now immeasurable. You can thank Lucinda for her efforts to pull this off in her weakened state."

Neil did indeed feel stronger but impressed he was not. He turned toward the younger vampire as well as the heads of the clans. "It is not all about power. It is not how strong you are or how many vampires follow you. It is all in the will."

"Are you saying that my army lacks the will to destroy a bunch of teenagers?" Dante said. It was his turn to be amused as he looked at the hundreds of demons who had decided to join them out in the open. "I think that our little army can manage."

"The same way Siegfried managed?" Neil asked ironically. "How is his back after one weak little girl broke it?"

Dante scowled at the comment made at his friend's expense. "A minor setback," Dante said, controlling his anger as Athena stepped up beside him. Athena looked at Neil and measured him with her eyes.

"Do you have an open contract on me, little girl?" Neil asked the assassin.

Athena looked at him intensely, then turned her attention toward Dante. "No need to get flustered," Dante said, composing himself. "This is a moment for triumph." He turned toward his little army. "When was the last time you walked this cursed earth at this time? It's our time! It is our world for the taking!"

The army growled in approval. Nemo climbed a small boulder and looked on the hundreds of demons, thirsty for blood. "We march for blood! I want that castle for my clan. Kill all humans in sight."

"Can we penetrate their magical defense?" Dragnor asked.

A loud explosion was heard in the distance, followed by a second and a third. Dante smiled evilly at Athena, and then at Dragnor. "We can now," Dante said.

CHAPTER XIX

Guardians' Castle, Ireland; August 9, 9:30 a.m.

ISABELLA LOOKED AT THE horizon from the castle's outer perimeter wall. Three fireballs illuminated the dark surroundings of her property. "The mausoleums are gone," Izzy said to her earpiece, knowing full well that this meant the magic protecting the castle was down. "Get Brent and Joy back to the castle now. They cover the main HQ."

"Inbound," she heard Alex reply. She looked at the rest of the wall, where ten other demon hunters were spread out, fully equipped with compound bows and arrows to spare. Small fire-lamp bowls were at their feet, ready to be used. Izzy covered one end while Grace covered the other side. "No fear, ladies," Izzy said. "Whatever is coming beyond the woods is nothing we haven't faced before."

"Wait for your targets to be in range," Grace ordered. "Don't waste wood when you don't have to."

"A witch or a warlock is blocking the sun," Alex said through the intercom. "According to John, and based on how the sun is covered, they are using a tenebris sphere. Find the one that wields its power and destroy it. That will bring back the sun."

Izzy looked down to see Nikki near the front gate, the only way into the perimeter. Along with the redhead, there were four of the strongest demon hunters guarding the closed entrance: Sophia, Anna, Angelina, and Selene. The girls had longswords for weapons, ready for anything that crashed through the front. Demon-hunter steel would greet the monsters of the night. "Got it," Izzy replied to Alex. "Demon hunters, be on the lookout for this witch or warlock. Take them out, and the sun will shine again."

Izzy then turned toward the front entrance of the castle. She saw the European Demon hunter Andreia with the three demon hunters from Russia. They were the last stand and in charge of protecting the Guardians. "You okay, Andreia?" Izzy asked through her earpiece.

"I'm fine," Andreia responded in her Romanian accent. "Just get us through this."

Isabella turned toward the horizon. From the woods, dozens of vampires started emerging. Those numbers grew as demons joined the army that desired to breach the castle. "Do you see them, Alex? How many?"

There was a small pause as the horde approached the perimeter. "A couple of hundred," Alex said. "Vampires are the tip of the spear."

Izzy looked at her fellow sisters, who tensed up as the horde approached. "No fear, girls," Grace instructed on the other side of the wall. "We got this."

"Let them come," Izzy spoke to her intercom. "Be steady on the trigger, Alex."

Suddenly, from the back of the horde, two demons sprouted their wings and launched from the ground. Three Hillions started running toward the front gates. "Gargoyles are airborne!" Izzy exclaimed. She turned toward Nikki. "Hillions are approaching, Nikki!"

Nikki smiled as the adrenaline started pumping. "Decent demons," Nikki said to her fellow demon hunters. "They are sending their best to give us hell."

The gargoyles flew over the castle and focused their attention on the demon hunters on the wall. The flying demons flung themselves at the girls just as the Hillions hit the front gates hard. "Mind the horde!" Grace ordered. "The gargoyles are mine!"

Izzy nodded as she and the girls ducked, just as one of the gargoyles made the first pass. When the second one flew by with the same intentions, Grace jumped high, landing on the demon's back. The demon shrieked as Grace plunged two daggers on each side of its spine. The beast flew out of control while Grace hung on, anchored to the blades. She turned her attention to the other flying demon that flew toward her. The demon hunter let go of one of the knives to pull a small crossbow from her side. She fired one shot at the second gargoyle flying around. The small projectile hit the beast in the eye, making it screech in agony.

The first gargoyle sensed the demon hunter on its back and started flying erratically, trying to throw off the girl. Grace breathed hard but controlled her emotions as the beast went on a dead spin, spiraling toward the ground. Grace knew if the monster detected an ounce of fear from her, it would be all over. Just as the beast was feet from the ground, it pulled up and growled, frustrated at the girl. Grace had enough of the beast's antics. She slowly grabbed the demon's wings, trying to direct the wild animal. "You go where I tell you!" Grace yelled as she snapped a wing bone from the right side. The beast growled in pain as it went down toward the concrete, head first, and out of control. Grace braced for impact as she held firm to the wings of the wild demon and stood on its back. Just as the beast neared the hard ground, she pulled hard on the extremities, using her feet and legs for leverage. The tearing of flesh and breaking of bones echoed in her ears as its wings detached from the demon's body. The beast howled in pain as Grace jumped back and flipped in the air, then landed elegantly while the gargoyle crashed headfirst into the pavement, cracking the hard floor.

Grace did not have time to rejoice, as a violent shriek from the skies alerted her of a second gargoyle. Grace jumped out of the way just as the beast flew toward her.

The flying demon changed direction, flying straight toward Andreia's group of demon hunters.

"Incoming!" Andreia warned as she jumped up, slashing down and aiming at the demon's neck with her sword. The blade connected hard, severing the head from the spine. The other demon hunters somersaulted sideways with their swords extended. The sharp steel plucked the wings right out of the gargoyle's frame, making the lifeless demon fly out of control, slamming onto the sidewall of the castle.

The Hillions broke down the main gate. "The main gate has been breached!" Nikki exclaimed as the three Hillions towered over her small squad led by Nikki. The redhead could see the mob of vampires running toward the broken entrance. "You're up, O'Brien!" She swung the sword toward the demon, causing minimal damage.

Izzy looked over the wall and saw the flood of vampires running toward the breached entrance and moving swiftly across the field. She had never seen vampires run so fast. "Now, Alex!"

"Perimeter defense activated," Alex responded. The demon hunters on the wall saw several small pipes spurt out from the ground. Water sprayed the field, with the vampires inside the mist. The vampires howled in pain as holy water burned their skin. They tried to move onward, but the pain was too much for them as they crumpled and turned to ash. It was a momentary victory for the demon hunters; the holy water had cut the horde in half.

"It worked!" Izzy said, looking back at Andreia, who still covered the main entrance. Nikki, along with Grace and four other demon hunters, battled the three Hillions that had breached the front gate.

"Izzy!" Eisha called out. Izzy turned toward the demon hunter from Africa, and then toward the field. She could see Dante smiling at her from a distance. He didn't seem fazed by the fact that the holy water had taken out a good portion of his army; he just started to bark orders at his remaining vampires. She saw several vampires take a running start and saw them jump over the holy water impact area. "Fire!" Izzy shouted at her demon hunters. They did not need to be told twice and fired arrows from their compound bows. The arrows pierced the vampires, bringing them down right in front of the wall. "Light 'em up!"

The demon hunters lit up their arrows and fired at the demons that had almost reached the breached gate. They howled in pain as the flames started to engulf their bodies. "Fire at will," Izzy ordered, as she fired her fire-lit arrow at the second batch of vampires that decided to jump the holy water trap.

A cry of pain brought Izzy to reality. She turned in time to see Almeida's body being flung toward the group that Andreia was leading. The Hillions were not going down without a fight. "Eisha! You're in command! Cover this wall!" Izzy dropped down toward the biggest Hillion. She pulled two small knives just as she landed on the creature's shoulders; the fifteen-year-old thrust the blades into the creature's eyes. The beast growled in agony as it tried to grasp Izzy with its arms. She evaded the muscular limbs by doing a backflip and landing beside the sword Almeida had dropped. She rolled to grab it just as one of the Hillions tried to smack her but missed. Izzy clutched the weapon and flung herself between the demons and the main castle door.

Izzy felt a wave of nausea hit her, followed by a dizzy spell. *Not now*, she thought to herself as one of her knees buckled due to the weight of the sword. One of the Hillions shrieked a battle cry before steamrolling toward the front entrance. Grace somersaulted out of the way. Nikki dodged to the side, only to catch a giant fist ramming her upper body. Nikki screamed in pain, feeling she had just been hit by a truck as her body flew a few feet before tumbling to the ground. "That definitely hurt," Nikki gasped as she stood up. The redhead stumbled a bit, feeling a wave of dizziness hit her. She then saw Izzy get punched equally hard, making her body fly toward the wall where the gargoyle had landed. Her friend smashed back-first into the stone wall. Nikki turned toward her team and saw that they had put down one of the Hillions, while the blind one stumbled in the darkness, looking for a target.

Nikki tried to shake the dizziness from her as she saw Grace tending to Izzy. She turned her eyes toward the wall, and Eisha pointed at the breached gate. A dozen vampires had managed to make their way through.

"Pull back!" Nikki managed to order as she saw a Hillion reach Andreia's team. The eight demon hunters posted at the wall grabbed their weapons and ran toward the entrance of the castle. Nikki could see half of them were stumbling. Andreia's team had just managed to put the Hillion down when the demon hunters from the wall got to them. They blocked the entrance as Grace helped Izzy inside. As Nikki turned toward the door—three dozen vampires had come in, followed by Dante and what seemed to be his posse. Athena, still in possession of Ammarra's body, smiled evilly.

Nikki was surprised to see that the demon hunters had taken a chunk out of Dante's army. Nikki looked down at the ground and pulled up a massive long sword, then walked toward the entrance of the castle to stand next to her sisters.

"Well done, girls," Dante said, taking a step forward while what was left of his demon army assembled behind him. "You're truly the best the Guardians have to offer."

Nikki could hear Izzy whispering instructions in her ear through the intercom. But the orders were not directed at her. "Vampires have breached the wall," Izzy whispered for all the Guardians and demon hunters to hear. "First-line ineffective. Starting to pull back. John—how are you doing?"

"Excuse me?" Dante asked the group of demon hunters. "I am sorry to spoil your plans, but who is whispering those orders? After my little experiment with the dark arts today, our hearing is a little bit more enhanced. Is that you, Isabella?"

Izzy took a step forward, looking a little bruised from the battle. Dante smiled as he admired the group of demon hunters. He could smell their weakness; he could still not sense their fear, though, but that would soon change. "My children," Dante said, referring to his small horde of vampires. "Have I not driven the Guardians and their demon hunters to their knees?" The vampires cheered in approval as they prepared to attack again. "Now," Dante said, stepping forward and turning back to Izzy. "Before I burn this cursed place to the ground, may I see your parents?"

"They're busy at the moment," Izzy said, smiling a bit. "They left us home alone."

"I refuse to believe they would leave in my moment of glory," Dante said, turning toward Athena. "Get in there and kill them for me, won't you?"

"My pleasure," Athena answered as she started to turn into the purple mist. She flickered for a moment as the purple smoke formed, then turned back to her solid-state. Athena looked at her body, surprised at what was happening to her. She then looked at the demon hunters.

"Having trouble?" Nikki asked, snickering a bit.

"Feeling poisoned?" Grace asked defiantly. "Not feeling yourself?"

"What are they talking about?" Dante asked his top enforcer.

"They cursed me," Athena concluded as she pulled out two black daggers. "I'll have to do this hard way."

"Good luck with that," Izzy said as she pointed up. Dante turned his attention to the upper windows located above the entrance. He could see Sean and Elizabeth, along with other senior Guardians, pointing down at them with crossbows. Dante did not have time to react when the first flaming arrow was shot down to his horde. The master vampire put his arm up and grunted in pain as a flaming arrow pierced his flesh. Screams of agony came from some of his vampires as flames engulfed their bodies. Dante turned toward the entrance and saw the demon hunters run inside, closing the door behind them.

"Breach the door!" Dante ordered. "Take the shooters out!" A third gargoyle popped up beyond the wall and flew directly into the windows above the entrance. Two more Hillions came through the breached gate and made their way toward the castle entrance. "Apocalyps will be mine," Dante whispered to himself as Dragnor and Nemo aligned along the wall with him. "Breach the castle!" Dante ordered his army. "Leave no one alive!"

Izzy turned back and saw the front door begin to give. "Hurry up, John!" Izzy exclaimed on the intercom.

The demon hunters ran toward the garden while Izzy called on the intercom. "Vulnerable Guardians, lock yourself down!

Head to HQ with Alex! Lockdown effective immediately."

The door cracked as the vampires and demons tried to smash their way through. "Let's take the battle to the garden!" Izzy instructed the other girls. "Don't stand close to the center!"

Izzy watched as the demon hunters blocked the main entrance to the castle. Some demons and vampires were jumping to the breached second floor. She could hear roars and screams from just beyond. The young teen turned toward some of the other girls. "Valerie, Fei, and Tansey," she called out. The girls from Colombia, China, and South Africa gave her their attention. "We have a breach on the second floor," Izzy informed them. "Provide support and get the vulnerable Guardians to safety."

Guardians' Castle Basement, Ireland; August 9, 9:45 a.m.

John's hand trembled as he heard the commotion from above. Izzy and Alex were barking orders on the intercom. Vampires were breaching the castle, while a gargoyle had broken through the second-floor defense. The urgency of the demon hunters and the Guardians was overwhelming. The young Guardian turned the page on the small brown journal Lewis had handed him as he whispered the last phrases in Latin when a shiver went down his spine. Izzy's voice on his earpiece spoke to his soul. "We're at the center garden, John. Vampires and demons have breached us. It's on you now."

A soft wind blew by his side as he reached for the padlock that locked the forbidden black door. He inserted the key and unlocked the ancient chain. "*Why?*" John heard a soft female whisper in his ear. The syllable was elongated and put him on edge. "Because I have to," John replied to the rhetorical question. He opened the black door and revealed a six-foot-tall static black vortex in front of a three-foot-tall white pillar.

The energy whirlwind and column seemed to be floating on a stone platform. John looked up inside the room and saw the trap door that led to the commotion taking place in the center garden. That commotion would soon have another variable added. But he had to deal with his personal nightmare fast.

The young Guardian stepped on the stone platform. A strong wind blew as he felt a soft, delicate hand touch his shoulder that made the hairs on his back stand. He did not dare turn to see whom it belonged to; he knew very well who it was. *"You failed me, John,"* her voice seemed sweet yet low. *"You failed me, and now you will fail her."*

"You lie," John said as he turned back to the journal. He needed to lift the platform so that it reached the central garden.

"Why are you afraid to look at me, John?" she asked. *"Afraid of seeing what you lost?"*

John closed his eyes and stammered as he tried to recite the Latin spell. He shook his head and opened his eyes, looking at the journal. All he could see was a female hand covering the page he needed to read. "Stop it," John whispered, as tears started flooding his eyes. "Please stop it."

"Look at me, then."

John's eyes slowly looked up. The love of his life stood before him, just as beautiful as he remembered her. Long, dark hair, and light brown skin. He looked into the brown eyes hidden by her spectacles. Almost as tall as him. Her appearance was the same as the last day he saw her: dark jeans and a soft plaid dress shirt with black Converse sneakers. *"Your knowledge failed me,"* Angie said. *"It will fail the Guardians and all the demon hunters."*

John looked back at the journal as the words dug deep into his heart. His mind tried to reason through what he was seeing. The Nightmare Dimension's energy was bleeding through to his reality. "You're not real," John said as he murmured the spell in Latin. He had known full well this would happen. The moment the door opened, the Nightmare Dimension would slip into anyone near it, and he was the first.

"*Are you sure about that?*" the specter of Angie asked. "*I am as real as the thought in your mind. You make me real. Don't you want to be with me?*"

John looked at the illusion in front of him—those dark eyes, that sweet smile. He reached out, trying to stroke her cheek, trying to feel her soft skin in his hands. Deep down, the young man knew the truth. But he relished the idea of being with her one more time—to hold her close and to smell her dark hair—just to feel her heartbeat one more time. "My mind can't do you justice," John said, wiping the tears from his eyes. "You are not my Angie. You are an imperfect version of what she used to be. Nothing more." He continued reading the spell. He knew that the demon hunters and the rest of the Guardians did not have any more time.

"*How do you know I am not the one you love?*" Angie's projection continued to ask as her arms wrapped around his waist from behind him.

"Angie always put her calling before me," John said, closing the journal as the trap door above him opened. "That is what made me fall in love with her."

There was a small tremor as the sound he heard from the battle above reached the opening. Dark energy flowed from the portal. "The gate will join you shortly, Isabella," John said through the intercom. "The nightmares will soon invade the minds of all who are in the central garden. The demon hunters must remain strong."

Izzy wiped the blood from the side of her face and looked at the center of the garden. A black vortex was rising as red mist flew out of it. John was near the white pillar, just looking at the sky. Izzy picked up a sword from the ground and looked at her surroundings. Vampires were crawling all over the garden, and the demon hunters fought valiantly, but they were losing. The vampires were just too strong. Athena faced Nikki and Grace. The assassin had the weakened demon hunters down. "Izzy!" a voice called her. She turned and saw her father cradling her mom by one arm, trying to move the older warrior out of the way. Sean pointed at Dante as he made a move to the open portal.

"Dante!" Izzy exclaimed as she twirled the sword in her hand and threw it at the demon. The vampire turned and caught the blade with his right hand as Izzy ran toward him. The vampire dropped the sword as Izzy swung, trying to connect. The vampire just dodged and parried with his hands behind his back. Izzy moved like a blur, but the vampire was faster. He lashed out with a backhand slap that struck Izzy down. She gasped in pain as she felt the stinging sensation on her cheek.

"Stop wasting my time," Dante said as he calmly walked toward the portal. John stood up, maintaining his position as the last line of defense. The blond vampire towered over him, but he was not letting the vampire pass. Out of the corner of his eye, he noticed the dark energy from the portal start to engulf the castle. Soon all living and undead would suffer the effects of the dimension. Dante looked down at John and sneered. "Pathetic human. Step aside and let me claim what is mine."

John looked behind Dante, seeing Izzy stand up and run toward the portal. John could hear Sean's screams of terror as he saw everything in slow motion. It seemed as if time had frozen. She was moving; she had steel determination written all over her face.

Dante noticed John's attention fixated on the commotion behind him. As he turned, he saw the young demon hunter tackle him at the waist. John jumped out of the way as the dark vortex's purple electricity engulfed both Izzy and Dante in an instant.

"No!" Sean screamed as the body of his daughter collapsed in front of him. Her green eyes were lifeless. Sean looked around as his heart seemed to get stuck in his throat. He tried to reason with what he was seeing as he touched his daughter's lifeless hand. She was gone. He tried to grab his wife's palm, only to see the body of Elizabeth slowly turn to ash. "Liz…" Sean whispered as he saw the bodies of his loved ones taken from him. He looked at his surroundings in horror, seeing the corpses of all the demon hunters and Guardians. The portal's dark energy engulfed the castle bringing a sense of doom to Sean's stomach. The vampires and demons tore the building down brick by brick as the building was set ablaze. "This is not happening," Sean whispered to himself. In the distance, he heard a voice call his name.

He turned around, and John was in front of him, screaming his name. It wasn't until John shook him that he finally heard John's voice. "Sean! Wake up!"

Sean blinked and looked around. He saw demon hunters, Guardians, demons, and vampires screaming at nothing. Some had faces full of sorrow, while others had fear and anguish written all over them. "What's happening?"

"The Nightmare Dimension!" John stated. "As long as the portal remains open, our minds will replay the nightmares paralyzing us!"

"It's not real?" Sean asked, partially realizing the truth. He looked down and saw Elizabeth lying on the ground with a blank stare. "Liz! Wake up!"

"The nightmares will keep on coming in our minds," John said, as he watched his projection of Angie being devoured by demons. He closed his eyes and shook his head. "You must help Elizabeth recognize the nightmare in her head to pull her out while the portal is open."

Sean realized something as he looked at John and the portal. "Where's Izzy?"

John looked at the black vortex. "She went into the nightmare itself with Dante. She has to reclaim Apocalyps before he does."

CHAPTER XX

The Infinite Plain–Date Unknown, Time Unknown.

IZZY LOOKED AROUND THE white void. Her body ached as she tried to get a handle on her surroundings. There was nothing, just empty white space. She closed her eyes and opened them again to adjust to this new environment. *Where is Dante?* She asked herself as she walked in the white void. She looked down at her feet. Beyond her boots, there was a white plain. It was a strange sensation, but above all, she felt peace. She did not understand why this was a Nightmare Dimension.

The young demon hunter continued walking, seeing something far from her. As she reached her destination, she saw several French windows hanging from the white void itself. As she peered through them, she could see different scenes which seemed to reflect moments in her life, apparently taken from her subconscious. In one window, Izzy could see her mom and dad crying and looking at a distorted teenage girl. The girl had ash and burn marks all over her body. The dark curls of her hair covered her pale face. Izzy shivered as the girl looked beyond her parents and looked at her. Her eyes were red and yellow.

The look was terrifying but familiar to her in some way. Izzy felt something missing from her heart. The mysterious girl had been for some time present in her nightmares. That is when she realized what she was looking at. It was her dreams.

Izzy looked at the next window. She saw both her parents turned into vampires, chasing her down a backstreet. Their growls echoed through the window. There was no humanity in them; only the demon side and the alley seemed to have no end. Izzy could feel her heart beating faster as she witnessed the endless chase. She could feel helplessness and despair, the powerlessness of being unable to do her duty since the demons had the faces of those she loved.

Izzy tried to look to the next window, only to see a hoard of demons slaughter her new friends and sisters. Izzy closed her eyes. "This is not real," she said out loud.

"Why?" a voice echoed. Izzy turned and saw a tall, blonde-haired woman dressed in a blue robe. Her build looked impressive—strong and powerful, like a warrior of ancient times as if she were a Greek goddess. "What makes this not real?"

"Those are my dreams," Izzy said, referring to the scenes displayed beyond the windows. "I recognize them. It's this dimension that is projecting them from my mind."

"Is this dimension real?" the woman asked, strolling toward her. "It does seem real, doesn't it?"

"Who are you?" Izzy asked, noting she was wasting time. Dante had entered the dimension and was on the same quest as she.

"You seem rushed," the woman said, ignoring the question. "As if time is flying by. Time is merely a concept here. Time as you know it stands still. Fear not. You have nothing but time."

"What do you mean? Who are you? Where am I?"

"You're home," the woman said, pointing at her side.

Izzy looked toward where the woman was pointing. She

could see a small pink bed with white wooden furnishing. Izzy's mind clicked while approaching the bed. She could see a little white dresser and a medium bookshelf filled with ancient books. Izzy's mind was transported for an instant. She saw her four-year-old self, sitting on the white floor with an old book in her hand. "This is my room."

"This is Limbo," the woman said. "A personal, vast nothingness filled only with what is in your mind."

"Why would we put Apocalyps here?" Izzy asked. "I assumed that the Nightmare Dimension was the protective barrier."

"It is. Limbo is full of things, creatures, and monsters. It is filled by those who inhabit this dimension. Some are here of their free will, as your friend. Others are here with no say in the matter."

"Who are you talking about?" Izzy asked.

The woman smiled and lifted her hands. The white surroundings disappeared. Izzy gasped in awe as she saw what seemed to be millions of creatures on rocky red terrain. They were fighting and screaming in agony. They seemed to fight an invisible force that had them trapped—an endless struggle for survival.

"They all came in here," the woman said. "All of them are searching for me—searching for power without understanding it." She moved her hands slowly, and the beings disappeared. Only one remained—Dante. The ancient vampire tried to crawl away from an invisible vision that was plaguing his mind, but he was unsuccessful. "Like your friend there."

"He's not my friend," Izzy whispered as she saw fear in the vampire's eyes. It is evident that whatever gripped his mind had his full attention.

"I was attempting humor," the woman said with a soft smile. "My apologies. You want to see what this demon fears?" Izzy nodded as the woman revealed the image Dante saw. Izzy was a little shocked. She could see Dante cowering away from Nikki, Grace, and herself. Izzy's mom, Joy, and behind them, an entire army of demon hunters. All young teenage girls from all over the world. All with the will to fight the forces of darkness. "Fear what you hate and hate what you fear," the woman said as she brought Izzy back to the white plain.

"Who are you?" Izzy asked the woman again, even though deep down, she knew the answer.

"I am whom you seek," the woman said. "If it makes you feel better, you can call me by the name you seem to have baptized me with. You can call me Apocalyps."

"But you're human," Izzy said. "You're supposed to be a weapon."

"Yes, I know," the woman said. "A weapon forged to banish eternal darkness."

"I don't understand," Izzy said.

"Let me explain, then," Apocalyps said as she drew in the sky. Izzy looked up and saw blue heavens. "When all of this was created, everything was good, pure, and magnificent. All creation in space and time reflected glory and power, born out of love." Izzy took in the sight as the planets, stars, and beautiful creatures reflected on the heavens. It was indeed, beautiful. Apocalyps continued as the skies turned red. "A creature of light turned against us all, purely out of envy. Everything had a purpose, but this creature of light corrupted others, and the first battle between darkness and light began."

Izzy looked on and saw beings of light in conflict with creatures of darkness. The battle of the heavens was ancient lore. But she saw it drawn in the sky. "You were a warrior of light," Izzy concluded. "You were there."

Apocalyps smiled. "I fought alongside the greatest warriors time has ever contemplated. My general decided that it was all to end that day. Alongside another warrior like myself, he forged a single blade to end it all, using our essence to fuel it. A powerful sword to banish darkness and cast it down to oblivion."

Izzy looked at the sky as two beings of light merged as one single blade made of white light. A third being grasped the sword and pierced the darkness in two. "Light prevailed," Apocalyps continued. "But banishing darkness came with a cost. My sister forged in arms with me was corrupted with the blow. She fell from the heavens, separating from the weapon, and was cast out." Izzy could see a being made of light itself, separate from the sword in the heavens. The being fell upon the earth and wandered aimlessly across the terrestrial plain. Her essence was corrupted into darkness. The light diminished as the creature transformed into an earthly demon. Izzy's eyes widened as the image was no longer formed in the sky but her mind. Apocalyps was feeding knowledge directly to her.

Izzy looked at Apocalyps with sadness in her heart. She could feel Apocalyps' sense of loss. She could feel profound sorrow as the story unfolded—the loss of her sister.

Demons walked in the shadows as humans took pleasure in the world that was designed for them. And Apocalyps' sister walked among them—a being of darkness, cursed to battle on a different plane as a demon outcast. The war between good and evil transpired on earth. Humans were terrified of the cursed monsters that walked their plain. The fear fed on the hatred. Men battled the monsters but failed to contain their strength. Hope faded as people feared the demons would reclaim the earth. That is when Izzy gasped at what she saw. Men captured Apocalyps' sister and bound the demon by strong magic. The humans dragged the essence of the monster to a young girl. Izzy cried in agony as something inside her pierced her chest, feeling the dark magic ancient men used. She screamed, sensing the demon within herself. The young demon hunter fell to her knees right before Apocalyps. "Do you understand now?"

"We were linked long before time was created," Izzy gasped. *What's happening to me?* She asked herself. She couldn't contain it anymore. She screamed as she crumpled to the floor in pain while images poured into her mind. She could see vampires burning the Guardians' castle down. She could see vampires killing the Guardians and the demon hunters while Athena killed both Nikki and Grace. She could see Dante breaking her dad's neck as a storm raged on in a castle engulfed in flame. "Stop! No more!"

"Will you crumble in fear and be like the rest?" Apocalyps asked as she walked around her. "Unworthy."

Izzy opened her eyes; her mom was there. She could see her, larger than life itself—invincible and unstoppable, with fierceness and determination in her eyes. The blonde demon hunter was neither a mother nor a leader but a living legend. She was also alone. Izzy could see bodies of men, women, and demons at her mother's feet. She was the last line—the one who made the final call. No remorse. Just duty.

"No!" Izzy exclaimed as she slowly stood up, fighting the pain inside. "This is not the way it is." She struggled with her own mind as she tried to form a new idea. She could feel a familiar, motherly warmth. She could feel love. Elizabeth's face turned and looked down. Isabella could see what she longed in those green eyes—the love of a mother. Elizabeth's fierceness melted away. All that was left was the loving face of her mom. Izzy reached out and hugged her mom. Izzy's physical pain was replaced with a swelling of her heart. She could feel kindness and love.

Izzy turned and looked at the devastation the hatred had caused to the Guardians' castle. Hate was not what fueled the

Guardians and demon hunters to fulfill their duties. It was love for those in need, for those who could not fight for themselves. That was the reason for everything. Izzy could feel as the images paused and melted away. Soon the white plane was back.

Izzy looked around as a splitting headache pierced her mind, and more knowledge poured in—images of past and present. She could feel the poison circulate throughout her body. The brown-haired girl could feel the entire demon hunter line ailing because of it. She could see the first demon; Apocalyps' sister screamed in agony because of the poison, dying, and calling for help. Izzy could see the image of Apocalyps reaching down to her sister. As their hands touched, their bodies became one single being of pure light.

Izzy closed her eyes and then opened them. The mystical sword that she had only read about in books was in front of her. It was even more beautiful than she could ever imagine. The blade was forty-five inches in length and three inches in width. The cross-guard was a thick, silver plate with golden horses encrusted in it as if they galloped to the center. Where the hilt and the blade met at the silver plate, a silver heart merged with a cross, both made of solid gold. The metal and bronze grip had the form of two angelic creatures that fused as one being. A round ruby pommel at its end finished the superb blade.

It was a weapon bound for glory, forged to eradicate darkness. The sword floated before Izzy with the point aiming downward, waiting to be taken. She could hear the whisper from Apocalyps calling out to her to reclaim the light.

A crack of lightning and the booming sound of thunder caught her attention. She turned to her side and saw an external force pierce the white plane. Blue bolts of electricity shot out of the opening. Izzy watched in horror as she saw a small blade pierce through the reality, ripping right through.

The dimensions bled together as Dante emerged from his nightmarish ordeal. He looked at Izzy and then at the sword. He smiled as he put his mystical knife away. Izzy could not figure out whether this was her nightmare speaking, or harsh reality. She stood up and ran toward the sword; Dante did the same. Both beings reached the sword at the same time with their hands grasping the metal grip of the blade. There was a pause in time as both demon hunter and vampire touched the angelic weapon. An explosion of energy followed. Izzy felt her body straining as the power of Apocalyps was unleashed.

On Dante's face, an evil and sadistic smile spread from ear to ear as he felt the power of the blade. Both demon hunter and vampire held tight as the invisible force of Apocalyps strained their bodies to the limit.

"Apocalyps is mine!" Dante yelled over the thundering noise, trying to rip the sword away from Izzy.

"You're not worthy!" Izzy screamed back, using the sword as a pole to support her body. She flipped to her side and connected a solid kick to Dante's face. He grunted in pain, releasing the blade. Izzy landed gracefully on her feet and pulled hard on Apocalyps, retrieving it from its resting place. The sword followed the demon hunter's command. She felt its power run across her body.

CHAPTER XXI

Guardians' Castle, Main Courtyard, Ireland; August 9–9:46 a.m.

Grace strained in pain as she tried to crawl away from Athena, who towered over her in Ammarra's body. The Hawaiian demon hunter had tears running down her eyes as she tried to process the ache her entire body suffered, as well as her heart. The girl crawled past her parents' dead bodies lying on the ground. Her heart beat faster as she turned to see behind Athena, the vampire who haunted her dreams. The fear in her was overwhelming; it had gripped her soul, and petrified her yet again. The pain and the images were too much to handle.

Athena relished the thought of killing another demon hunter. She looked around and saw all the demon hunters either crying or screaming as the Nightmare Dimension bled over them. "The end of the demon hunters," she exclaimed as she twirled two small knives in her hands. "Why kill one when I can kill hundreds?" She plunged toward Grace, only to be stopped by a kick to the side. Athena screamed in pain when she saw Nikki standing, ready to fight.

"What do you say?" Nikki asked, taunting Athena. "Want a shot at the title?"

Athena growled as she stood up and faced Nikki. "Time to die, little girl." The demon screamed as she launched herself to attack. Nikki dodged a roundhouse kick while flipping away from a haymaker. She blocked high and then low as Athena attacked viciously, trying to connect. Nikki did a backflip, trying to gain distance herself from the demon. She picked up a sword and threw it at the beast. Athena dodged to the side and kept on coming for the young demon hunter.

"Grace!" Nikki called, seeing that Athena was not stopping. "Get your butt up and help me!" Athena attacked with lightning-fast strikes. Nikki managed to block the blows coming toward her face. Athena changed her strategy into something Nikki had not seen before—the demon shifted her attention from Nikki's face to her upper chest, connecting with five straight hooks, treating Nikki's body like a punching bag. Nikki just took the blows, feeling the air escape her lungs. Her knees buckled, but Athena jumped and struck Nikki's temple brutally with a knee. Nikki didn't have time to react, as Athena pivoted in place and fired a spinning kick toward Nikki's head. The redhead fell hard on the ground while the world spun. She tried to crawl away, but Athena stomped hard on Nikki's back, causing her to scream in agony.

The demon flipped Nikki, so the demon hunter faced her. "I will kill all of you. No matter in what order."

Nikki smiled despite the pain her body was experiencing. "No, you won't," Nikki managed to gasp out.

Athena sneered at the young demon hunter until she felt cold, hard steel pierce her in the middle of the chest. Athena gasped and saw Grace twisting the short sword Nikki had thrown earlier. Athena fell to her knees as Grace pulled the blade from the demon's body. Grace swung horizontally, connecting the sword with Athena's neck. The beast did not have a chance to scream before the head detached from its body. Grace panted hard and fell next to Nikki as the rest of Athena's body collapse. "Sorry I took so long," Grace said to Nikki, trying to ignore the image of her parents, still present in her line of sight.

Nikki nodded as she sat up. She could see vampires and demons crawling all over the castle, and while all the demon hunters were down, none had died—but they were definitely beaten. Nikki felt her last bit of strength vanish, then watched as a black liquid emerged from Athena's decapitated body. "Come on," Nikki complained as the liquid formed another version of Athena. "How many times do we have to kill you?"

Athena's purple body formed before the girls—completely unharmed and in one piece. "You can't kill me," the demon said, as she picked up her knives and stood tall before the demon hunters. "But I can kill you."

A flash of lightning, followed by the crackling of thunder, interrupted the demon. Athena turned toward the origin of the light and saw Isabella O'Brien holding a blade made of light. Izzy screamed as she swung her sword, releasing a wave of light. Athena's eyes widened in horror as the ray came toward her. She threw her body on the ground and saw the light slice over her, then turned and watched as the beam covered one side of the castle. Demon hunters covered themselves as the light passed over them and hit the demons. The demons screamed as they were struck by the beam and burst into ash. The Hillions tried to block the light wave with their massive arms, but the force sliced the demons in half.

Izzy felt powerful as she swung the sword a second time with even more force in the opposite direction. The horizontal ray of light emitted from Apocalyps covered the center garden, killing every demon that dared touch the beam of energy, by turning to dust or being sliced in half.

Izzy's heart tugged a bit as she felt the sword speak to her. Izzy looked around at her fellow sisters. Looking weak and defeated, they looked at her with fear in their eyes. "Stand up!" Izzy ordered her sisters. "The darkness that has plagued us ends tonight!" The demon hunters slowly stood up; the few that remained of the demon horde looked shocked at what was happening. Izzy turned toward her parents. She could see her dad cradling her mom, helping her to sit up. Her mother looked weak, and for once, her true age could be seen. Streaks of gray hair now adorned her head. Isabella screamed and plunged the sword into the ground. A flash of light created a ripple effect through the air. Izzy looked up and saw her sisters being flooded with restorative energy; she felt her strength return. She could see in her mind as Apocalyps became one with her body and in the body of every single demon hunter on the planet.

Dante looked around as fear gripped his undead heart for the first time. The master vampire stood up as he realized what was happening. "You will not take this from me!" Dante growled as he approached Isabella, who was still trapped in Apocalyps' trance. The master vampire fired a sidekick that connected with the teenager's ribs. Izzy grunted in pain as she released the sword and crumpled to the side, gasping for air as she saw the tall vampire remove the blade from the ground and swing at her. Izzy moved to the side, kicking up into a fighting stance to face Dante. He gripped the sword hard as he looked at Athena, who was still in shock. "Kill them all!"

Athena looked at her employer and rapidly evaluated the conditions that surrounded her. She saw the demon hunters standing tall and proud, with fire and determination in their eyes. The fear that gripped them just moments ago was gone. The assassin looked for what remained of the undead army—they had been decimated by Apocalyps' power. The demon did the only thing reasonable and ran. Grace and Nikki looked at Izzy. Isabella just nodded, and both Nikki and Grace started running after the rogue assassin. Isabella turned toward all the other demon hunters. "Clear the castle," Izzy ordered. "Kill any undead that still lingers on the property. Help our wounded." The girls followed the command and dispersed toward the inside of the building.

Izzy turned toward Dante. "You're alone now. Drop Apocalyps, and I will destroy you quickly."

Dante laughed as he looked around. Only Sean and Elizabeth remained in the courtyard, along with John, who stood beside the now closed portal to the Nightmare Dimension. "Little girl," Dante said as he gripped the sword tightly, "You are in no position to dictate orders."

"Are you?" Izzy retorted.

"I have Apocalyps in my grasp," Dante said as he looked at the sword. It was more beautiful than he could ever imagine. "It is all that matters."

"The sword is not meant for you," Izzy said with a sly smile. "Nor will it bend to your will."

"The first blood I take will be that of your parents," Dante said. "Right before I play with your own." The master vampire swung the blade horizontally and pointed toward Sean and Elizabeth. Nothing happened. The master vampire looked at the sword in his hand. He felt nothing—only emptiness and fear.

"Run out of batteries?" Izzie mocked.

Dante turned toward the demon hunter. His anger flared, as for the first time, he felt out of control. "You did this," Dante hissed as he walked menacingly toward the teenager. Izzy could see her dad trying to make a move, but Elizabeth held him back gently and nodded at her daughter. They both knew who was in control. The tall vampire swung the sharp blade in deadly arcs. "You have no idea who you're messing with."

"I have a clear idea," Izzy said confidently. "A demon with a little too much hair bleach on his head."

Dante screamed as he swung the sword at her. Izzy stepped to the side. The master vampire was fast—faster than her. Izzy had to stay on her toes in this battle if she wanted to come out of it alive. She cartwheeled out of the path of a sideswipe of the weapon and then back-cartwheeled as the demon slashed horizontally. "You can't dodge me all day."

"You're right," Izzy replied as she blocked a front strike with both her hands. "I can also kick you in the face." She front-kicked the vampire hard in the gut. The vampire grunted. Izzy was airborne and spinning; the sole of her heeled boot connected hard with the side of his face.

Dante grunted again, feeling the blow. This girl was strong. "Well done, child," the vampire said, wiping blood from his lips. "But that is all you will do today." The vampire attacked again, even faster than before. Izzy was surprised; he was beyond supernatural. Izzy dodged his slashes by mere millimeters. Dante slashed horizontally, aware as to where the fifteen-year-old would be likely to move. He turned and lashed out with a kick, connecting with Izzy's face. She grunted in pain and was dizzy for a moment, then stumbled a bit, only for Dante to stabilize her with the hand he held the sword with so he could deliver three consecutive punches to Izzy's stomach.

Izzy felt like she wanted to throw up as the tall demon struck her mercilessly. With each blow, he pushed the young teenager back toward a sidewall. The monster delivered a right hook that connected with Izzy's cheek. Izzy felt her face explode with pain as the momentum of the blow caused her to spin in place. Dante smiled as he saw his chance. He sliced downward across Izzy's turned back. She felt a burning sensation, unlike anything she had ever felt before as a long gash opened across her back. Izzy's eyes widened, seeing everything in slow motion. She saw Dante thrust the sword toward her chest. With what little energy she had, she moved downward and slightly to the right. She was not fast enough—Dante pierced the young demon hunter right where her left clavicle and the scapula met. Izzy screamed in pain as the sword impaled her and was embedded in the stone wall behind her.

Sean and Elizabeth were up and moving the moment Dante sliced their daughter across the back. Dante noticed their movement. "Stick around," he whispered into the demon hunter's ears as he let go of the sword and met Elizabeth and Sean head-on. Izzy's parents tried to reach her, but Dante was too much for them.

Izzy looked past the tears in her eyes—she could see Dante pummeling her parents. Izzy grimaced as she grabbed Apocalyps by the blade. She grunted in pain as she pulled the sword out and through her shoulder. Dante grabbed both of her parents by the throat and slammed both of them hard on the ground. "I've got you now," Dante said as he flipped his wrists; two stakes came out from his sleeves. "I get to kill Sean and Elizabeth with their own weapons."

Izzy said a small, silent prayer before flipping the sword, catching it by the grip, and swinging horizontally. Dante turned around and saw the flash of energy slice the air. The master vampire ducked and recovered; the young teen was already airborne. The demon's eyes widened as he felt something hit his throat when the demon hunter landed at his side. Dante could not move. He looked to the side, only to see Isabella one last time.

"This is where you turn to dust," Izzy said. She fell to her knees as Dante's head detached from his body. The master vampire then crumbled to dust in the courtyard. Izzy's bracelets, which had somehow been left intact, were visible among the ashes. The teenage girl winced a bit as her parents wrapped their arms around her. It all seemed so distant to her. She could feel her parents' tears as they hugged her as they would never let go, and she just wanted to collapse in their arms. She looked to the center of the courtyard and saw John stand up. He looked at her and gave her a soft smile as he walked back to the castle, where Lewis Powell and Arthur Williams waited. The older Guardians shook John's hand while they smiled back at Izzy. The young demon hunter tried to get up, but it seemed the energy was abandoning her body. She laid her head on her father's chest and rested. Just for a moment. Just for an instant.

Nikki and Grace ran after Athena, across the open field and away from the castle. Half a dozen demon hunters followed right behind. A few others stayed back, clearing the rest of the property and helping the wounded. Nikki and Grace separated from the pack just before Athena entered the forest surrounding the castle grounds. "She's heading back to the underground town," Grace noted as she halted, motioning everyone else to stop. Grace looked at the demon hunters that accompanied them—the trio from Russia, plus Anna, Chhavi, and Katia. "Surround the forest," Grace ordered the Russian trio. "The demons must have an exit that leads them outside the forest. Clear any undead on sight."

The girls nodded as they separated and started to run along the forest perimeter. Grace looked at Nikki, who inspected the entrance. She then turned toward the remaining demon hunters. "Let's go," she said. The five demon hunters half-jogged, half-ran, following Grace's lead. They soon reached the entrance, where the Izzy, Grace, and Nikki had escaped a few hours prior. Grace was about to say something when she heard a soft growl from above the entrance. The girls looked up and saw a white and black wolf snarling at them. Nikki froze for a moment upon seeing the beast. The animal seemed to have an open wound on its side. "Aidan," Grace called out. The wolf snarled softly and climbed down right before the Hawaiian demon hunter. Grace slowly extended her hand to touch the wolf's head. The wolf looked right back at her with its piercing blue eyes. "It's okay," Grace said with a soothing voice. "We're friends of Izzy."

As if the wolf understood, the animal moved to the side of the entrance and sat down, waiting. Grace looked at Katia and Anna. "You two," she ordered. "Split up here and sweep the forest. There may be another exit within the woods, from the underground. Clear the area around it, but don't enter. The cave formation will disorient you, and you may never find a way out."

The girls nodded and darted in separate ways. She turned toward Chhavi next. "Remain here with Aidan," Grace said. "Anything comes out other than us, kill it. Nikki and I will finish this."

Nikki looked at Aidan, then at Grace. She took a deep breath as she braced herself into going back inside. She pulled out a short sword and her favorite stake, signaling her sister demon hunter that she was ready. Grace led while Nikki followed, going back into the cave system. Grace's demon hunter instinct was at its peak. She could feel the dark energy being emitted from the cursed town, and could almost sense how many demons were down there. Nikki's voice distracted her a bit. "Nice seeing you take charge of the girls like that," the redhead said.

Grace could feel when Nikki's breath shortened a bit as a part of the cave system narrowed. The brunette turned back toward her friend. "You okay?"

"Yeah," Nikki said, taking a breath. "I can deal." She then stopped for a second. "Do you feel that?"

Grace nodded as she understood what Nikki was referring to. The dark energy was guiding them to the center of town. "Our instinct is sharper. Whatever Izzy did has affected us all."

A few more twists and turns, and both demon hunters reached the cursed underground town. It was utterly deserted. But there was a dark presence that could not be denied. "Look over there," Nikki pointed out. Grace turned toward where Nikki pointed. They both saw Athena leading a small group of vampires and demons toward what appeared to be a second exit from the town. The group carried what seemed to be a stretcher, with a dark-haired vampire lying on his back. They were about to move toward the group when a crackle of purple power emerged from a third-floor room located in the largest building of the square. Both girls could see a dark-haired female vampire holding a black and orange ball of energy standing on the terrace. Two gargoyles stood beside her. "That vampire looks like she is yours," Nikki said with a smile, pointing at the female vampire.

"How do you figure?" Grace asked.

"Duh," Nikki said. "You're the magic expert."

"Fine," Grace said. "Can you take Dark Shadow on your own?"

"Fully powered now," Nikki said, rubbing her hands. "Piece of cake."

"Meet you here in five," Grace said as she made her way toward the underground mansion. She could see Nikki out of the corner of her eye, jumping over several obstacles to reach Athena. Grace stepped down the stairs and entered the run-down building, feeling her power grow as she entered—it felt ancient and powerful, yet familiar and intimate as well. Grace's heart started beating faster as her mind and soul immediately recognized a dark essence—it was not the female vampire on the upper floor balcony. The dark-haired demon hunter could feel her blood freeze as a deadly shiver ran down her spine. The silhouette of the vampire that haunted her nightmares rounded the corner near the stairs. Grace froze as she admired the demon, linked forever to her past. Dressed resplendently in a tailored gray suit with a white dress shirt, he looked like a giant in her eyes.

"Welcome, darling," Neil said dryly. "I knew you'd come."

Grace was unable to move; thoughts were bombarding her head. *Why can't I move?* She asked herself.

Neil slowly walked toward Grace, seeming so relaxed and in control. "You've grown strong since we met last time," Neil said, almost paternally. "Your father would be so proud of you."

Grace could feel a tear run down her cheek. The way Neil spoke of her father was uniquely sorrowful. Always in control, yet there was no menace in his tone—only something that could be confused with profound guilt and regret.

"I always knew you would become a powerful demon hunter," Neil said as he softly wiped Grace's tear from her cheek. "The most powerful I would ever meet. So powerful—and so frightened," Neil marveled a bit. "So paradoxical in your line of work."

Grace tried again to move but still felt powerless to do so. She could feel time stop as she tried to control her emotions. She tried to breathe and calm her heart by pushing the sadness and fear away so she could channelize her hate and anger. Neil just shook his head in disapproval. "You haven't learned what you need to learn. You are trying to work the problem the wrong way. That is all I needed to see." He crouched a bit so he could see directly into her dark eyes. "Don't push the fear and sadness away. It's when you are at your weakest that you're at your strongest."

Grace blinked as she felt her body start to cooperate. She fired a punch, trying to connect with the vampire's face. Neil simply blocked the strike and held Grace's fist with his hand. "You're stronger," Neil said. Grace kicked forward, but the vampire danced to the side, dodging the attack. Grace fired a spin kick, trying to connect with his head, but Neil just arched back, weaving with his hands behind his back. "You're faster," Neil admired. "You have the skill, and you're at your peak. But the fire in you needs to be harnessed. It needs to be controlled."

Grace looked at the vampire, trying to understand what he was saying. *Why is he giving me advice?* She thought to herself. She was about to attack when she saw a purple light drop down the staircase. Grace knew the female vampire was doing something that needed to be stopped.

"She's blocking the sun," Neil said. Grace turned toward the master vampire as he was already at the doorway. "Killing her will shatter the darkness and bring the sunlight back," Neil explained from the entrance of the building. "You have a choice now. You either continue your futile attempt to attack me or bring the sunlight back to your side of the battle." He paused for a moment and smiled at the girl. "Will you sacrifice the wellbeing of the innocent, as long as you avenge your parents?"

"You bastard," Grace seethed through her teeth as her fists tightened.

"There's the anger," Neil pointed out. "There's the rage we're talking about. There's the hate. What are you going to do?"

Grace stepped back a bit. "The next time I see you, I'll kill you."

Neil genuinely smiled as he saw Grace walk up the stairs.

"Well done, little girl," Neil whispered to himself as he fixed his suit and walked out of the cave.

Grace needed to focus—a job needed to be done. She could feel her rage boil inside her heart and mind. The girl got to the top of the stairs and saw the female vampire floating on the balcony with a purple aura surrounding her. Seeing her closely, Grace noted the vampire had a ball of energy she was trying to contain. *Kill the vampire, and the sun will come back*, Grace thought to herself. *Simple.*

As she stepped closer toward the vampire, the two gargoyles that guarded the vampire emerged from the side. They looked at Grace, and each howled a cry of war. Grace was ready for them as they launched at her. The low ceiling of the room meant the demons would need to remain on the ground. The tall beasts fired heavy haymakers at her. Grace danced and dodged out of the way, not daring to block the massive fists. She ducked and flipped to the side, making a run toward the far side wall feeling the demons trying to grab her. Grace jumped and used the wall as a platform, then twirled and extended her leg, connecting with the side of one demon's face. A sickening crack was heard as the creature screeched in pain. Grace used her other foot to jump over the gargoyle, using its shoulder to jump from. She flipped over the second demon as it tried to sink its claws into her. Grace grabbed the wings of the second gargoyle; she planted her feet on its back and yanked hard. The familiar ripping sound of flesh and bone caused the beast to wail in agony as its wings were separated violently from its shoulders. Grace flipped back and landed on her two feet, then dropped the wings as the first beast recovered and fired a haymaker aimed at her face. Grace somersaulted, using the demon's arm as a platform. As she flew upside down in the air, she grabbed the demon's head by the jaw and top of the skull.

A crack was heard as she landed gracefully to the side, and the gargoyle fell dead. Grace turned toward the other beast, who was still flip-flopping in pain on the floor. She walked to the head of the demon and crouched down, just to snap its neck.

Grace turned her attention toward the vampire that still floated on the balcony. The young girl admired the black-haired vampire, noting the purple energy that engulfed her leather-clad body. The ball of energy in her hands seemed to have a life of its own. Grace could feel the vampire was in a complete trance holding all the power together. Grace's mind raced as she could hear a commotion on the outside. It was possibly Nikki starting a fight with Dark Shadow. She pulled a long silver dagger from the small of her back. She slowly approached the vampire.

Lucinda's eyes opened up. Grace gasped when she saw a soft purple light emerge from them. "You killed him!" the vampire screamed. Grace did not have time to process the information as purple lightning emerged from the ball. The bolts hit Grace in the chest, catapulting the young girl off her feet and launching her back to the opposite wall. The force was so strong that the stone cracked as she crashed into it. Grace screamed in pain as she fell face first. Her body shook—that same sensation was crippling her again. She looked up, only to see the energy come at her one more time. As if it were an invisible force, the purple lightning tangled around her like chains of pure voltage. Grace screamed in agony as the electricity shot through her entire body. The vampire threw the lightning to one side, causing Grace's body to be flung to a sidewall. This stone, too, cracked as her body smashed against it. The vampire then threw her against the ceiling and released the energy; Grace crumbled down to the floor awkwardly. The young girl coughed up blood and strained to look at the vampire who had floated up to her. As if the vampire had used her mind,

Grace felt her body being picked up. The Hawaiian demon hunter seemed to have run out of ideas. She felt her body go limp as the vampire admired the defeated warrior.

"You killed him," the vampire said, with the purple energy flashing in her hands. "Now, you will be forced to live in eternal darkness. I can live forever and hold the spell a thousand lifetimes over."

"Wait," Grace managed to say weakly, as her mind processed the scenarios in her head. The vampire looked at her in confusion, not understanding the request. "In claritate solis ortum!" Grace shouted. The vampire gasped as a flash of blinding white light engulfed the room. As the light faded away, the vampire looked and saw Grace was gone. The vampire turned and watched as Grace struggled to walk outside to the balcony.

"I'm not done with you yet," the female vampire said.

"But I'm done with you," Grace said, leaning back against the handrail of the balcony. She could see out of the corner of her eyes that Nikki was battling Athena. Grace turned her attention back to the confused vampire until she noticed the demon hunter had stuck a silver dagger into the ball of energy. The vampire gasped as the ball cracked, releasing energy from its weakest points. "You'll soon be joining your friends," Grace said as she flung her body back first off the balcony. As she fell, she heard a high-pitched scream, followed by a thunderous explosion. Grace smiled as she fell, seeing a purple beam of light pierce the cave. Then everything went black.

Underground, Town of York, Ireland; August 9, Ten Minutes Earlier.

Nikki jumped several obstacles as she saw Grace enter the worn-down mansion. She could feel a substantial amount of dark power emerging from the place. *Don't let me down, Ice Princess,* Grace thought to herself as the girl jumped the final obstacle before reaching the second set of stone steps. She looked up and saw Athena, still in Ammarra's body, leading a group of vampires. The vampire they carried on the stretcher was almost out of the second exit. "You're leaving without going to round three?" Nikki yelled up at Athena with a mischievous smile.

Athena looked down and smiled a bit herself. She whispered a few orders to the vampires to carry on without her as she slowly walked down the stairs. "I've killed a lot of demon hunters in my time; It never gets old."

Nikki rolled her eyes. "You said that already. Be more creative, will you?"

Athena walked down the steps and tried to generate another replicant figure, but she was unable to do so. "This curse you place on my body is very creative."

"Pretty neat, huh?" Nikki said, stretching a bit as she faced off with the taller demon. "With all these ideas of unbalanced power, we just needed to involve you some way or form."

"Limiting my power won't stop me," Athena said. "My replicant is out there, unstoppable and unforgiving."

"Yes," Nikki said as both demon and demon hunter circled. "And all alone with a target on her back. How does it feel to be hunted?"

"I don't know," Athena said. "I will ask your father and brother when I play with their insides." The comment wiped the smile off Nikki's face in an instant and made her blood freeze. "Where is your confident smile now, little girl?" Athena asked, seeing the power had shifted. "Nicole Rogers. Age sixteen. Daughter of Colonel Hank Rogers and Laura Rogers. Mother deceased. Older brother is Ryan Rogers. Both father and son have been deployed to a classified location." Athena just tapped the side of her temple. "All the information is here—your information, and the information about ten thousand girls who don't know that my order will hunt them down and kill them. But I won't start with them. I'll start with their families and friends, then their Guardians, and when they are all alone, I will extinguish their pathetic and miserable existence from the face of the earth."

Nikki's teeth gritted in rage. Her heart pounded at the idea this demon had the personal information of every single demon hunter on the field. "We will stop you," Grace said flatly.

"You may," Athena replied. "But not before I hurt you all so much, you will prefer death. Should I start with your brother or your dad?"

Nikki screamed and attacked, firing a haymaker at the side of Athena's face. Athena arched back, then dodged to the side as Nikki followed up with a sidekick. Athena fired a blow of her own, aiming at her face. Nikki blocked and kicked Athena behind her right knee. Athena crumbled down, but sensed Nikki's next attack and crouched down, connecting with a one-two combination on Nikki's thighs. She staggered, only to receive a ferocious uppercut right under the chin. Nikki saw stars as her head and body arched up and backward. Athena recuperated and fired a spin kick that connected with Nikki's midsection. All Athena heard was an "Oof" as the wind was knocked out of Nikki's lungs. She landed against a stone, face-down.

Nikki tried to get up awkwardly, only to receive a shoulder in the midsection. Her back collided with the stone again, and she went tumbling down. Athena walked over to the demon hunter and lifted her by the scruff of her neck. Nikki screamed in pain and attacked as she was pulled, against her will, to her feet, firing a one-two punch combination at Athena's chest. Athena gasped in pain at Nikki's speed and force. The demon tried to block, but Nikki was too fast in her counterattack. Athena tried to raise her leg to kick, but Nikki saw the attempt and crouched down, punching the demon's stomach and thigh. Athena had finally had enough. She jumped and hammer-punched Nikki on the back. Nikki screamed in pain as she was struck on her already-sore back. Before she could recover, she felt Athena grab her by the scruff of the neck again, sinking her knee into her unprotected belly. Before she knew what was happening, Athena guided her forward and pushed her upward, only to receive a final hammer fist right on the chest.

Nikki grimaced in pain as her back hit the floor—Athena was unleashing her full power on her now. She fired a kick that connected with Athena's head and pushed her back; Nikki flipped her legs around and stood back up. She jumped and vertically spun a kick, approaching Athena. Athena just waited for the opportunity and landed a kick of her own, connecting with Nikki's unprotected chest. Nikki landed hard on her back. The demon grabbed the demon hunter by her neck and right leg and flung her to the side. Nikki rolled on the stone until she finally came to a full stop, experiencing pain like never before. She smiled a bit at her predicament. "Had enough?" Nikki asked Athena as she tried to stand up.

"You are no match for me," Athena said. "Even though I can't replicate, the soul of every single warrior I have taken fuels my strength. You are not fighting one, but thousands of warriors, with different variants and styles."

"A thousand to one," Nikki smiled as she cleaned the blood from her lips. "My kind of odds." She fired an attack, with right and left jabs. The attacks were quick and precise, aimed at the face. Athena blocked the blows, straining as Nikki unleashed her formidable power. The teenager kicked Athena's right knee, causing it to buckle under her. As Athena went down, Nikki hammered her with an elbow at the back of the head.

As Athena's head dropped, Nikki delivered a stiff knee to the jaw. Athena staggered back, while Nikki twirled in the air and landed a spinning kick to the top of Athena's skull. Athena crumbled down as Nikki stood back. "You felt the power behind that, right?"

Athena spat out blood and growled at her opponent. The demon stood up fast and started running toward Nikki, tackling her by the waist and pushing her back. Nikki held Athena back but felt the demon arch her body to deliver a scorpion kick. Nikki blocked with one hand and struck Athena right on the ear with her other elbow. Athena screamed and fired a roundhouse kick, connecting with Nikki's side. Athena then delivered an elbow of her own, connecting with Nikki's temple. Her vision blurred as tears filled her eyes. Athena pulled the young girl by her hair and fired consecutive punches to Nikki's unprotected chest. Nikki tried to block the attacks, but as she raised her hands, Athena changed combinations and fired strikes to her liver and kidney. Nikki just took in the blows as blood spurted from her mouth.

Athena stopped the assault and looked at her defeated foe. "You're done, little girl." An explosion then distracted Athena. She turned toward the noise and saw purple light emerging from Dante's room—a vertical beam of light erupted from the structure, hitting the cave ceiling with destructive force. The cave started to crumble as the energy released began to tear down the ancient buildings around the mansion.

Athena gasped as pain registered in her brain. She looked down and saw Nikki's arm deep inside her chest cavity. Athena looked at Nikki in fear, knowing what had happened.

"Got your heart," Nikki said, pulling the organ out from Athena's body. Athena gasped as she saw her own beating heart in the young girl's hand. Athena fell to her knees as the will to live abandoned her. She looked at the redhead and tried to say something, but the demon hunter had crushed the demon's heart. The last thing Athena saw was her essence flowing from Nikki's hand.

Nikki fell to her knees as well, processing the pain she was feeling throughout her entire body until a brief tremor brought Nikki back to reality. Her body complained as she stood up and moved toward where Grace was supposed to be. Her heart panicked, not seeing her friend there. She turned toward the crumbled mansion to see the purple light reaching the darkened sky above. As the light from the ruins faded, large boulders fell from above, and the tremors were getting more intense—the underground town was about to be buried by tons of earth. Nikki stumbled as she headed toward the mansion. She then saw her fallen sister on the ground. Nikki fell as the tremors were increasing exponentially. She half-walked and half-crawled toward Grace. "Grace!" Nikki called. "Wake up! We have to go!"

Grace opened her eyes and grimaced at the intense headache she was feeling. She looked at Nikki and was about to say something when a tremor finally woke her up. The ground broke apart right where they stood. Grace and Nikki scrambled back where they had come from, just as part of the old town began to sink. Stone boulders were coming down; neither of the girls needed any more motivation as they climbed and crawled toward the entrance. The tremors were no longer tremors. The ground was violently shaking as the earth was swallowing the cursed town. Grace and Nikki made it to the cave exit just as the stone steps gave out. "Move!" Grace screamed as she pushed Nikki out. The walls were closing in as the cave system was collapsing on itself. Nikki's heart was pounding—she was demanding her body to perform above and beyond its limits, but her survival instinct was greater. She pushed up and crawled onwards.

The ground behind them gave way. Grace's heart dropped as she felt her body being pulled down. Nikki looked back and grabbed her sister's hand and pulled. "We're getting out of here!" Nikki exclaimed as she pulled on her sister and continued upward. There was light coming from above, but the light was fading. Nikki could feel a cool breeze; the cave was collapsing. Nikki thought in horror as her nightmare of being buried alive was coming true. "Hurry up!" Grace urged as she pushed Nikki onward. There was still hope as both girls struggled through the constricted space.

"Hold my hand!" Nikki heard a voice from above. She extended her hand just as rubble surrounded both her and Grace. Nikki's heart was about to explode, but she felt someone grab her hand and pull hard. Nikki was not letting go of salvation on the one hand and Grace on the other. Soon she was being pulled out of the rubble. Nikki coughed up dust, seeing Katia and Anna pulling her out. The red-headed girl crumpled on the ground as she took big gulps of air and felt as another body falling beside her. She looked and saw Grace smile softly at her. Nikki returned the smile before being embraced by Katia, Anna, and Chhavi. The five girls laughed and cried at the same time. Grace looked and saw that a vast crater of dirt, trees, and bushes had all been pulled down by the vampires' energy. She turned her attention to the sky and saw that it was again a light blue. The clouds that had hidden the sun were gone.

"You did it!" Anna said excitedly.

Grace looked at Nikki and then back at her other sisters. "We all did it." Chhavi and Katia nodded as they turned their attention toward something happening behind them. Two large Jeeps roared toward them. The demon hunters could see Williams and Brent at the wheel, with Lewis and Clara accompanying them.

Clara got out first with a first aid kit, followed by Lewis. Nikki and Grace smiled as Clara started tending to their wounds while Lewis bombarded them with questions.

CHAPTER XXII

Guardians' Castle, Ireland; August 10, 2:00 p.m.

IZZY'S EYES FLUTTERED OPEN. As she looked around, she realized she was in her bedroom. She tried to move but winced as her body did not want to respond. She ached all over. She looked down at her shoulder and saw her left arm in a fresh sling. Izzy tried to move her fingers, finding it was painful to do so. She tried to stand up, but her body was not cooperating, feeling weak all over. She turned her head and saw both her mom and dad hunched together in a small barrel chair. Izzy tried to say something, but nothing came out. She closed her eyes, trying to regroup and find her strength, then felt the surge of power deep inside of her. The demon hunter clenched her fists and felt as if electricity was running through every cell of her being. She felt different—she could feel the healing power flow down from the top of her head to the tips of her toes. It was a different sort of energy, something she hadn't felt before.

Elizabeth stirred next to her husband and saw her daughter sitting upright in her bed. It seemed this golden aura of energy was surrounding her body while Izzy's dark brown hair floated around her head. "Izzy!" Elizabeth called as she jumped from her resting place and hugged her daughter.

Izzy took in her mom's embrace; soon, she felt her father's muscular arms around both of them. The teenager's mind was a blur for a moment. Suppressed emotions started to surface as tears began streaming from her eyes. "I'm sorry," she managed to say.

"It's okay," Sean said. "You're safe now. Everything is over."

"You did it," Elizabeth said. "You pulled it off."

"We pulled it off," Izzy corrected her mother softly. "I couldn't have done it without you."

"How do you feel?" Sean asked.

Izzy was about to answer when a knock on the door interrupted them. "Come in," Elizabeth called out as she inspected her daughter's body. The superficial scratches were all healed. Not a bruise on her body. Except for the sling on her arm, the girl looked extremely healthy. Elizabeth turned toward the doorway, and in came John, with a stethoscope around his neck.

"Sorry to interrupt," John said. "I can come later if you want."

"It's okay," Sean said, holding Elizabeth's hand and taking a step back. "Do your thing."

John walked over to Izzy and placed the icy medical instrument on her chest. He listened as he counted in his head. He then pulled out a small penlight and looked in Izzy's green eyes. "Feeling okay?"

"Just a bit hungry," Izzy replied. "How are the girls? Did we lose anyone?"

John smiled a bit, marveled by Izzy's mind going out toward her sisters. One-of-a-kind demon hunter. "They're all fine," John responded as he inspected Izzy's shoulder. "Can you move it?"

"I think I can," Izzy said. "I can close my fist now. I couldn't when I first woke up."

John gently removed the bandage that protected Izzy's shoulder. He looked at Sean and Elizabeth, signaling them to come closer. As the cloth came off, John's gaze targeted where the wound should have been. It was completely healed up, leaving only an ugly scar in its place. John stood up and signaled for Elizabeth and Sean to look at Izzy's back. "We can't do anything about those scars," John said. "Can you stand up?"

Izzy stood up slowly, fearing a wave of dizziness would hit her. The wave never came. The young demon hunter turned around, looking at her parents. They smiled, seeing their daughter was okay as John continued rotating and testing her arm. If it weren't for the ugly scar, Izzy didn't look damaged one bit. She felt a bit rejuvenated.

"Everything looks okay," John said. "You should take it easy for a couple of days, though. Try to rest."

"I'm hungry," Izzy said, again looking at her parents.

Sean and Elizabeth smiled. "Let's have something to eat, then." the blonde demon hunter said.

A few minutes later, Sean and Elizabeth were at one of the kitchen tables, watching their daughter have a late brunch. It was as if she hadn't had a bite for days. Izzy felt good, finally being able to have some food. The scrambled eggs and toast seemed to have such a rich and savory taste—something she had never felt before. The young girl looked at her parents. "You're not eating?" she asked.

"I just had lunch," Sean said. "Just happy to see you eating."

"It seems Izzy is okay now," Elizabeth said to her husband. "Maybe you should go and check how Alex and Brent are dealing with the collapsed castle defenses."

Sean smiled, catching the hint from his wife. He stood up, kissed his daughter on her forehead, and walked out. Izzy stopped eating and looked at her mother, focusing on her eyes, filled with love and admiration. "I am proud of you," Elizabeth said.

The words coming from her mother's lips tugged at Izzy's heart. "I just did what you would have done," Izzy said, looking at her half-eaten food.

Elizabeth scooted closer to her daughter, sitting right next to her. "Do you remember the story of the first big demon I had to face?"

Izzy nodded. "Yeah. You kicked its butt and saved half your school in the process."

Elizabeth smiled as she looked down. "That's what the journal says. Williams always tried to make me look good."

"That's not what happened?" Izzy asked, looking at her mom.

"It did," her mom said. "The day before that fight, Williams was with your father, discussing what was going to go down. They were arguing, and they didn't know I was listening."

"They didn't involve you?" Izzy asked.

"They were trying to figure things out," Elizabeth said, looking at the closed door of the kitchen. "I remember my heart pounding in my ears. Arthur's words stung in my heart, saying I was going to die, that nothing could stop it." Izzy remained silent as her mom carried on. "That moment was so surreal. Williams was telling a sixteen-year-old she was going to die. I screamed at him. I screamed at your father. I threw books at him, accusing him of being completely useless behind all his papers and books. Their life was not on the line—it was mine. Looking back at it, I was a scared little girl, not sure what my purpose was."

"But you regrouped," Izzy said. "You beat that demon."

Elizabeth turned toward her daughter. "I quit that day, Izzy. I grabbed the crucifix around my neck and threw it to the ground. I ran home, away from everything. I cried into my pillow for hours. I was terrified." Izzy gulped at the comment. She never imagined her mom being that scared about anything.

"When I saw you take the initiative yesterday," Elizabeth said, "I couldn't believe it. Not even sixteen, and you were already pulling rank and leading and guiding others. I was shopping for a prom dress at your age. You were guiding twenty demon hunters into battle."

"I learned from the best," Izzy said.

"That's the point, isn't it?" Elizabeth said. "You're not me, honey. You're you. You've always been you. The story is not about my past glory days. The story is about you and your path. It has always been about you."

Elizabeth hugged her daughter tightly. Izzy let the warm embrace of her mother lower her emotional defenses. "When I saw you take the lead. I pulled your father away. It was so clear to me, but not to your dad. He needed a little convincing. He wanted to fight for you. But it wasn't his or my place. It was yours. And you pulled it off." Izzy felt warm inside as the words reached her heart. For the first time, she realized the truth—that this was her story. "While you do what you do best," Elizabeth said, kissing her daughter on her forehead, "Your father and I will always be behind you. Supporting and guiding you."

"You promise?" Izzy asked.

Elizabeth nodded. "What you've gone through will have repercussions. Nightmares, fits of rage, panic attacks, etc. When these episodes occur, you can count on me and your dad. We will be there for you." Izzy nodded, not fully understanding what her mother meant. "Have you heard the whisper?" Elizabeth asked, changing the path of the conversation.

Izzy looked at her, somewhat confused. She felt a cold shiver run down her spine. "Apocalyps," she whispered.

Elizabeth nodded, knowing well what her daughter felt after she grasped the sword. "Apocalyps is part of you now."

"Where is it?" Izzy asked.

"It's in the gym," Elizabeth said, standing up, knowing her daughter's intentions.

Izzy stood up and walked out toward the gym. As she approached the door, she could hear the commotion of her fellow sisters performing fighting drills. Izzy stepped inside the gym and saw Grace surrounded by Clara and the Russian trio, armed with short staffs in their hands, while Joy, Nikki, and the rest of the demon hunters sat around them. The Russian trio moved fast, striking Grace hard. The black-haired girl grunted in pain as the wood hit her forearms and shins. She deflected the strikes, using only her extremities. All the demon hunters focused as Grace allowed the punishment to continue.

"Enough!" Clara exclaimed.

"No," Grace protested, wincing in pain. "I can handle more."

"Rest," Clara said as she looked at Izzy. Grace noticed Clara's attention shift and looked back, seeing Izzy by the gym entrance. Both she and Nikki started running toward their brown-haired friend. The trio embraced in a hug, while the rest of the demon hunters surrounded them. Izzy felt her heart settle a bit more, seeing her fellow demon hunters alive and well.

"It seems O'Brien pulled it off," Joy said out loud, looking at Elizabeth, who just smiled. "She could still use some pointers on saving the world, though."

Some of the demon hunters giggled as they caught the joke. Izzy smiled at Nikki and Grace. "Where is it?" Izzy asked.

Nikki and Grace looked at each other and then turned toward the weapon rack, where Apocalyps hung peacefully with the rest of the earth-forged weapons. Izzy strolled toward the beautiful sword, hearing the whispers in her mind. She wanted to think the voices she heard were in her imagination, but they were real. Izzy's hand caressed the hilt of the weapon, feeling the coolness of the sword. Her hand took hold of the grip and pulled the blade from its resting place, sensing an immeasurable power running through it. She looked at her fellow sisters and the senior warriors. "What do we do with it now?" Izzy asked.

Clara and Joy looked at Elizabeth, who shook her head and shrugged. "Last time, we followed the instructions of the Guardians and sealed it inside the Nightmare Dimension. What do you think we should do now?"

Izzy looked at the sword, then at Grace, while she twirled the blade, feeling it out. She then handed it to Grace, who reluctantly grabbed the sword and swung the blade. "Do you feel that?" Izzy asked.

"Power," Grace said as she twirled it a few more times before handing the sword to Nikki.

Nikki took hold of the sword and felt a surge of energy run through her veins. "It belongs to us," she said, twirling the blade as she looked at Izzy. Then she handed the weapon to Anna.

The demon hunter from Mexico reluctantly grabbed the weapon; her eyes widened as she felt something within. "It calls my name," she said, then handed the sword to Andrea.

Izzy looked at the senior demon hunters. "The weapon was forged to be wielded by warriors of light. The sword is there for us, being the last line of defense against the forces of darkness. It is ours to use it when we need it most."

"When will that be?" Joy asked.

"I don't know," Izzy said, shrugging her shoulders. "Apocalyps will not respond to evil—only pure intentions. While our intentions remain noble, we will use it to strike down whatever comes, whenever that is."

"The sword must be ready to use for all of us," Nikki said. "We need a Demon hunter to keep it safe and move it to the location where it is needed the most."

"Apocalyps will let us know," Grace said as the sword reached Clara. Clara looked at the sword, then at Joy and Elizabeth. The guardian and demon hunter grabbed the weapon. As soon as the sword was in her grasp, the blade glowed with a soft white light.

"What does she say?" Elizabeth asked Clara.

Clara looked at her older sister, and then at the demon hunters. "I will guard it. When a demon hunter needs it, I will bring it to them using our portal systems."

All the girls nodded in agreement as John watched from the front door of the gym. Silently, he agreed. Apocalyps was bound to the demon hunters. It was only right that they decide what to do with it.

"What do you think?" Lewis asked behind him.

John turned around and looked at the older Guardian. He then looked at the group of female warriors in front of him. "It's their choice. They know what is best." He took a step back and walked back toward his room with the older man.

Once they were alone in the halls of the castle, Lewis asked him, "Have you considered our proposal?"

John looked at the artistic details of the walls as he pondered the question for a few seconds. "I don't know, sir," John finally responded with a little shrug of his shoulders. Both Guardians continued walking to the second level, seeing only a few butlers doing maintenance inside the castle. As the two men walked the halls back to John's room, John looked at the central garden. Thanks to the castle staff, the place looked restored, as if nothing had happened. But the events were hard to erase from everybody's mind.

"You don't trust us, do you?" Lewis asked as they reached John's room.

"I don't trust what we do," John said as he opened the door and laid his glasses on top of his night table. "We're an organization that constantly puts young girls in harm's way for a purpose that is barely known to us. We give out the excuse that it's for some mysterious greater good. Something doesn't seem right."

Lewis removed his glasses and sighed for a moment. "You're right," he said as he walked out of the room. John followed the older guardian and stared in the same direction. He pondered for a moment, looking at the central garden. John wondered if they were thinking the same thing. "You're a good man, John. Your character has proven itself in these couple of days we've had you here." Lewis paused for a moment. "As the new generation of demon hunters come, we need good men like you. We don't know when this war against the forces of darkness will end. What we do know is that as time goes by, we become more susceptible to deceit and corruption. Our eyes are old and weary. Our time comes to an end. We need good people to keep us in check and help guide the new warriors through the coming storms."

"Your fear put all the girls at risk," John said, as the truth sank into his mind and heart. "You were thinking of your hide before anyone else. And the demon hunters almost paid with their lives."

"Fear makes us act stupidly," Lewis said. "Were you afraid when you provided the information to Angela?"

John took a sharp breath as he admired the loneliness of the castle. He thought for what seemed ages before responding. "I was afraid of the decision Angie would make."

"Because deep down, you knew the choice she would make," Lewis concluded. "I admire the women in this castle. They are strong and brilliant. Above all else, they are full of love for those who tremble in darkness. These women are always there, willing to go on the front line by their own choice. Not by ours. They stay vigilant, and tell the weak nothing from the dark will hurt us. Not on their watch." Lewis turned toward him. "We forget that they do not work for us. We work for them, and that's why we need you. You live and breathe that truth. Even if it's painful to bear."

John looked blankly as his mind and heart tried to reconcile with the notion of his task. "It's always their choice."

"And we must never allow ourselves to forget that," Lewis said as he walked away.

"Do I get dental?" John asked with a smile on his face.

"And vision," Lewis called back, pointing at his own set of spectacles. "Brent will help you with the paperwork."

Anna, Balish, and Raymond, LLP; Los Angeles; August 20, 8:30 a.m.

Daniel Anderson rolled his eyes as the voice on the phone rambled on. He had long stopped listening, but his position obliged him to be there for the clients assigned to him. "You can't give up on us now," the voice on the other line pleaded.

Daniel just stood up and looked out the window of his corner office. The view was spectacular. "I am not giving up on you," he said to the speakerphone. "The firm is not giving up on you. However, your clans and families played your hand and lost big. My superiors were disappointed with the colossal failure of what transpired in Ireland but were not surprised. Our recommendation, for now, is for you to lay low and rebuild. Once that happens, come back to us with a plan, and we will gladly assist with what you need."

"I have your word on this?" the voice asked.

"You are a client of ours," Daniel said. "We never leave our clients out to dry, no matter how bad you screw up. However, with the death of most of your friends, our standard fees have doubled."

There was a brief silence after that statement. "We're good for it," the voice said, somewhat defeated.

"Excellent," Daniel said, pushing the button on the phone and dropping the call. As soon as he hung up, the door opened, and a young man in his twenties entered the room. Daniel looked at his assistant and shook his head. "When they call back, you pass that call to someone other than me. I don't deal with losers."

"Understood, Mr. Anderson," his assistant said as he jotted things down on his tablet.

"What's next?" Daniel asked.

"You have an appointment with Dr. Pearson down at the lab," his assistant said. "She wanted to show you her findings on the specimens provided by Hela Corp."

"Walk with me," Daniel said as he exited his corner office and headed toward the elevator. As the elevator doors opened and he entered, the man fixed his tailored suit and tie. "Anything else?"

"Yes," the assistant said, as the elevator traveled to the lower level of the building. "Hela Corp. wants to book a meeting with you. There are also remnants of vampire clans from Europe that are now seeking asylum. I moved that to a lower-level grunt. Also, Mr. Balish wanted to invite you and a guest this Friday for dinner at his place."

"Excellent," Daniel said, as the elevator doors opened at the lowest level of the building. "Book time with Hela Corp. tomorrow, and please thank Mr. Balish for the invitation. I will see him this Friday." Upon saying that, the elevator doors closed, taking Daniel's assistant back to the upper levels of the firm.

Daniel walked the white halls of the basement. He could hear growls and screams echoing throughout the lower level. Soon he reached a large lobby; men and women walked about in lab coats. They all talked among themselves as Daniel passed around them. He could see, on the far side of the lobby, crystal cells where vampires and demons were being held captive. As he reached the far end of the hall, he opened a door, and a black-haired female doctor greeted him. "Mr. Anderson," she said with a smile on her face.

"Doctor Pearson," he acknowledged her as he looked behind the scientist. Only a crystal screen separated the humans from a vicious red-eyed vampire. The demon crashed against the hardened glass, but the barrier remained intact. "How is our gift from Hela?"

"Unprecedented," Dr. Pearson said. "Vampire strength and agility have increased exponentially."

"Compared to the demon hunters?" Daniel asked.

"It's hard to say," Dr. Pearson said. "Based on information received and data gathered from Hela Corp. as of yesterday, it would appear that vampires are now stronger than the average demon hunter."

"But?" Daniel asked.

"The demon hunters are unpredictable," Dr. Pearson said. "Even with the ones we've managed to study, our notes are still inconclusive."

"Can you give me a best guess?" Daniel asked. "I have a meeting with Hela Corp., as well as my superiors, and I want to give them something to digest."

Dr. Pearson smiled and opened a trap door inside the vampire cell. Two young men and a young teenage girl were thrown in with the vampire. The vampire didn't need any additional motivation; it growled and attacked its human prey. Dr. Pearson gleefully smiled as the demon tore into the human bodies like they were butter. Human blood splattered across the crystal screen while Daniel watched the destruction. Soon there was nothing.

Daniel seemed unfazed by the carnage. "Were they normal humans?" the man asked.

Dr. Pearson shook her head with a smile. "Those were two trained guardians and a young demon hunter. She was put into service in Arizona a couple of days ago."

Daniel nodded his head in acknowledgment. "She was called into service a couple of days ago," he repeated, as he watched the vampire feast on the lifeless body of the teenage girl.

"You want a note for your meetings?" Dr. Pearson said. "Tell them vampires have evolved exponentially, while demon hunters are in the fight of their lives now. The scale slightly tips in the vampires' favor. That's my professional observation."

Daniel smiled at the conclusion. "Excellent. The clans in Ireland didn't die in vain. That is good to hear. Thank you, doctor."

EPILOGUE

Guardians' Castle, Ireland; August 20, 3:30 p.m.

GRACE RUBBED THE BRUISES on her arms. For the entire gathering, she had asked for specialized training, for her to learn to deal with pain. The Guardians and the senior demon hunters had kindly obliged. Her body hadn't stopped complaining since then.

"Feeling down?" Nikki asked as she touched Grace's arm.

Grace winced in agony and glared at her fellow sister as they hiked the grassy hill with their fellow demon hunters. "You guys aren't going to stop bickering, are you?" Izzy asked, now right beside them.

"Never," Nikki said, relishing the chance to torment Grace.

"You better control your friend," Grace said to Izzy. "I can find other ways to cause serious damage."

"Scary," Nikki said with a giggle.

Izzy smiled as she continued with the hike, led by her mom and Joy.

The days had passed quickly during the gathering. After the events that had transpired, activities were re-oriented, testing the newfound strength of the demon hunters. They had also done small skirmishes to measure the vampires' new power. The demons were stronger and more agile, with some girls struggling with the increase in risk and difficulty in hunting them down. But Elizabeth and Joy, along with John and the rest of the Guardians, gave inspiring speeches and lectures. The Demon Hunters had new powers as well, although most of it remained undiscovered. All of them were in a new playing field, and they were to discover new abilities as time progressed.

Izzy could see smiles and laughter from all the girls. The teen had gotten to know all of them personally—their dreams and aspirations matched their passion and will to pursue them. All nineteen girls, plus Clara, Elizabeth, and Joy, had formed an unbreakable bond—a newly found sisterhood. There was an emotional and physical dependence on each other. They would be there for each other, from most reliable to their weakest link, all moving toward the same goal. They had all chosen to walk this path and protect the innocent from the darkness.

Isabella was thankful for the terrible experience they all had gone through—it kept all of them grounded. They all knew full well that death would always accompany them. It would nip at their heels, no matter their age or location. She touched her left clavicle; she could still feel the scar that would accompany her for the rest of her life. She was amazed by how her body had healed so fast, as well as her fellow sisters.

The entire group reached a vast green prairie. Elizabeth and Joy turned toward the girls at their command. "We made it. We're here." The girls looked around and saw nothing but green grass and green hills all around. It was a beautiful landscape, where the earth met the sky and the sea. "When Joy and I were called," Elizabeth started, "we believed that we fought alone against the darkness. It felt like walking on burning sand in an endless desert. Nothing but dust and dunes, with the blistering sun weighing us down until we could no longer continue."

"That was then," Joy said as she walked among all the girls. "We're not alone anymore. We have each other to count on in the time of most need. It's no longer a desert, but a green field, full of life—a world worthy of protection from those who desire to cause anarchy and chaos."

"You will go out into the world of darkness," Elizabeth said. "You will each be the beacon in your region. Other demon hunters will look up to you."

"Age will not matter," Joy said. "Each of you will now be the tip of a spear. We'll all follow your lead. You are our points of reference."

"It's a new beginning for us," Elizabeth said as she pulled out her phone. "You are now ready to embark on a new journey." She paused for a moment and looked at her cell phone. She then turned toward the long-haired brunette from Australia. "Sophia," Elizabeth called out. "You will watch over the city of Newcastle." The rest of the demon hunters congratulated Sophia on the city she would protect. Elizabeth hushed the team. "I know this is exciting, but please restrain the congratulatory pats on the back until I finish giving out the assignments." All the girls quieted down as Elizabeth continued reading from her list. "Chhavi and Fei," Elizabeth called on the demon hunters from Eastern Asia. "You will cover Luang Prabang in Laos."

Izzy took note of each of the locations the Guardians had assigned these demon hunters to watch over. Congratulations were still being given, just with looks of recognition. She felt proud to be part of this group. Angelina from Russia would be stationed in the city of Krasnoyarsk, while Arinka and Kristina would be in Moscow. Katia would cover the city of Abuja in Nigeria, while Eisha and Tansey would protect Lubumbashi in the Congo.

The European demon hunters, Sofia, Louise, and Andreia, would watch over Budapest, while the South American demon hunters, Almeida, Selene, and Valerie, would be in Porto Alegre, Brazil. Finally, Anna would cover Mexico City. Elizabeth looked up from her phone, and for the first time, she stared back at Izzy. All the demon hunters noticed the attention she was being given. Izzy swallowed hard as she knew exactly where this was going. "Izzy, Nikki, and Grace," the veteran said, "You get St. Helena."

There was a brief silence after that. The weight that two demon hunters died in action in the previous weeks still lingered on the group. They all knew what was implied, going to a hell spot where a demon hunter had fallen—let alone two.

"When we return to the castle," Joy said, breaking the silence as Elizabeth took a step back. "The Guardians have prepped small packages detailing all that you will need on the specific hell spot you have each been assigned. It contains information for your respective Guardian, who will be going along with you. You will also receive contact information on how to get in touch with Clara in case Apocalyps needs to be taken to your respective area. If you have any questions, please let us know." Joy now stood next to Elizabeth. They nodded at each other. Izzy took note of this, as this was something she had never seen happen before.

"The events of these past weeks have been interesting," Elizabeth said, taking a step forward. Her voice trembled a bit as she spoke. "Never have demon hunters been tested as you have these past days. Our senior Guardians experience new challenges. All the things we went through were against our will, and we prevailed. Not because of the senior Guardians here in Ireland, but because of all of you. We're venturing on new ground in our fight against darkness." Elizabeth paused for a moment as she looked at the ground. Izzy had never seen her mom like this. She was searching for words to say. "As of today," Elizabeth continued. "I'm resigning as the Head of the Demon Hunters Division."

Several demon hunters gasped, and their mouths dropped as she said those last words. Izzy's eyes teared up as she saw her mom's green eyes. The demon hunter general that was Elizabeth was gone, and now before them stood just a normal girl like them. All that Izzy could see was her mother. "For years now," Elizabeth said, "I've tried to perform as best as I can as a guide to the upcoming generations. As time progresses, we meet new challenges, and with all that has happened these past weeks, I don't trust myself in the role any longer to guide you to the next chapter." The girls could not believe what they were hearing. They murmured amongst themselves.

"The Guardians will send word on who my replacement will be," Elizabeth said. "But for now, all I can say is that it's been my pleasure meeting you in these past weeks. You are all an inspiration to me. I wish I were half the demon hunter you all are."

Joy took a step forward and nodded at Elizabeth. "Your petition has been noted and received by the Guardians," Joy said. "At the closing of this demon hunters gathering, the first line of warriors being witness, you're now relieved from your position." She then looked at the girls before her. "You have your assignments. May this newly found bond strengthen your sisterhood. You do not fight the darkness alone. You're never alone. Now you must go and fulfill your duty."

Guardians' Castle–Ireland August-20–4:30 p.m.

Nikki finished packing her military duffle pack and looked at her friend and newly found sister sitting across the bed. Izzy's mind seemed to be in another world. Grace entered their room, all ready to go to the airport. All the other demon hunters had gone back home. They were the only ones left. Nikki looked at Grace and then at Izzy, trying to figure out what was going on. It seemed both were searching for the words to say. "It's okay," Izzy said finally. "Mom is just retiring from being the head of the demon hunter division. I am just surprised, that's all."

Grace sat next to Izzy, with Nikki on the other side. Both of them hugged their sister, letting her know they were there for her. "Do the Guardians have a good retirement plan for their demon hunters and their staff?" Nikki asked.

Izzy giggled at the question, and Grace smiled. "Yes, we do. Not all of us have the millions that Grace has."

"Hey," Grace protested. "Not my fault my family had great investments."

"How much does your family have?" Nikki asked.

"Enough," Grace said, standing up.

"That is what rich people say," Izzy said.

All three laughed a bit. "Hey," Grace interrupted. "We will be working together in St. Helena. Has anyone talked to you about when our service begins?"

Nikki and Grace shook their heads. "I assume that when you go out, you will get the details," Izzy said.

Elizabeth popped up into their room and looked at the trio. "You girls are still here?"

"We were saying goodbye, " Nikki said, standing up. "Wanted to clarify when we would meet in St. Helena, though."

"Well," Elizabeth dragged a bit. "I spoke to your dad. He says that he can hook you up to stay with a friend at the Edwards Airforce Base."

"Oh," Nikki said, a little disappointed. "Just an eight-hour drive from the action. That's great."

"You can stay with your new Guardian if you'd like," Elizabeth said. "Well, your two new Guardians. They will be stationed right in the middle of St. Helena. If your dad approves, you can be as close to the action as you want."

"Are we sharing the same Guardians?" Grace asked. "I am not too keen on moving from Hawaii, but if it's needed."

"Your Guardian has approved," Elizabeth said with a smile. "You will be on your regular budget, though."

"You're our Guardian, aren't you?" Izzy asked as she stood from her bed.

"Well," Elizabeth said. "Not only me. Your dad as well."

"And we have to move fast," Sean said as he entered the room. "Need to do some heavy construction at our vineyard to set up the new gear."

Izzy felt somewhat overwhelmed. She looked at both Grace and Nikki, who didn't know what to say. Izzy looked at her mom, who drew a knowing smile. "Since when did you plan this?" Izzy asked her mother.

Elizabeth took a deep breath as she sat down. "For a few years now," she said. "Seeing how St. Helena is probably the most dangerous hell spot to take care of, I've never felt comfortable staying that far from it. It wasn't fair. And the death of the Smith twins just drove the point home. That place needs our undivided attention and our best demon hunters. I never imagined I would be sending my daughter, though."

The comment stung Izzy's heart, and Elizabeth saw it in her eyes. "Not because I didn't believe in you," her mother said. "I thought I could cheat the system. I contemplated that I would find a solution before your time came. But it wasn't fair. What I saw these past weeks is that I can't cheat destiny, no matter how hard I try." The girls looked at each other, realizing what she meant. "You girls are now linked in this journey. You will meet it head-on. Sean and I will guide you in the best way we can. But this will be your battle."

There was a brief silence after the older demon hunter finished speaking. "Okay," Nikki said. "So Sean and Elizabeth are our new Guardians. I see this as a complete win. Demon Hunter of Legend with her former demon lover with a tortured past. What more can one ask?"

Grace giggled, and Izzy just made a face. She was bored with her parents' dumb story, no matter how many times she heard it. Sean caught his daughter's eyes. "Maybe if we start the celebration early, you will feel better," Sean said as he stepped outside and brought in a birthday cake with the number 16 written on it. "Happy Birthday!" he said as he presented the cake to his daughter.

Izzy's face turned from bored to embarrassed. She'd forgotten her birthday was just a couple of days away. She smiled at her newfound sisters, as well as her parents. She looked at her cake and then frowned at her dad. "What about my party?"

"Your birthday party," Sean repeated as he sat next to his wife and hugged her. "We can discuss that after you explain that pet wolf that is strolling around the property."

Izzy looked at her mom and then at her friends. "What wolf?" Izzy asked, knowing full well her dad hated canine animals.

"Wait," Grace said. "Your dad is scared of dogs?"

"Now I don't feel that bad," Nikki said, sitting on her bed.

"Who said I was scared?" Sean defended himself.

"I will remain silent," Elizabeth said with a smile.

Sean's eyes widened at his wife's betrayal while the girls giggled.

Izzy felt at peace with the interaction. The challenges she and her fellow demon hunters would encounter would be daunting, but not impossible to conquer. And with her newfound sisters and her parents, there was nothing they could not face.